DESPERATE PURSUIT
IN VENICE

KARYNNE SUMMARS

Desperate Pursuit in Venice/Karynne Summars—1st Edition
ISBN 978-0-9893910-1-6

ACKNOWLEDGEMENTS

I would like to thank my close friends and family for their encouragement, support and understanding while I was writing this novel.

A special thank you goes to Jane and Shuj for taking the time to proofread my work before it was published and to my sister for her valuable input in the food and wine area.

I also would like to express my gratitude to my friend, fashion designer, Chabella Gomez who provided the descriptions for various dress designs for the main character Kataryna Taylor. Chabella is off to an exciting start with her design company Chabella, and I wish her all the success in the world.

In memory of my mother with gratitude
for her unconditional love and support

"You know that you are in love when you can't fall asleep because reality is finally better than your dreams."
Dr. Seuss

"Love that we cannot have is the one that lasts the longest, hurts the deepest, and feels the strongest."
Unknown

ONE

Kataryna Taylor was doing a final walk-through in her luxurious high-rise New York City apartment while waiting for the car service to take her to JFK. She was looking forward to her business trip to Milan, Italy, where she was meeting with the shareholder and senior management of the company her private equity firm was pursuing to acquire. The fact that she was about to meet and spend some time with the very attractive Luca Romano, who together with his family, owned the target company, was definitely a plus she was looking forward to. During their video conference calls over the past three months, she had become attracted to his captivating personality. Because of her long working hours Kataryna's love life was presently non-existent. She did have several interesting opportunities and suitors, but she was very selective. Falling in love did not come easy to her, but if the right person came along she would be able to fall in love deeply.

She had been very successful in the past five years that she and her partner Stephen Wagner had established their private equity firm. Both of them had worked for private equity divisions in major financial institutions before they established their own firm. Their 50/50 partnership had worked out well. They were mostly on the same page with the deals they wanted to pursue and were good friends in their personal lives. Both of them had accumulated a considerable amount of wealth and they enjoyed the finer things in life. Kataryna and Stephen had worked very hard over the years, putting in 80-plus work hours per week and therefore did not feel guilty of being able to afford their luxurious lifestyles.

Kataryna had bought her 3-bedroom, 3.5-bathroom New York City apartment during the financial crisis, when many wealthy investors had lost a lot of money and couldn't afford their luxurious lifestyles anymore. She was able to get this fabulous apartment for a steal from one of the Madoff Ponzi scheme victims who needed money fast because the mortgage-holding bank was breathing down the seller's neck. Kataryna had always been financially responsible and was a prudent investor. Her personal investment portfolio was relatively safe when the market crashed in 2008. Although she had an aggressive equity allocation, she remained calm and didn't sell any of the positions during that time. When she looked at the apartment, she saw an opportunity and grabbed it. She loved this apartment the minute she stepped into it to view it, and she was able to push the initial purchase price further down by offering cash instead of having to go through a long mortgage approval process. This place had everything she wanted, including a fireplace in the large grand room that opened up to a wall of windows overlooking the Manhattan skyline, which was especially fabulous at night to look at. The apartment had three well-proportioned bedrooms, one of which she also equipped to be used as her home office, where she could spend late hours to work on her deals without being interrupted. This proved to be very productive. Her large master bedroom suite also had a wall of windows with a spectacular view. She had furnished the apartment contemporary and tastefully with some pointers from one of her interior designer friends. Her home was her castle and sanctuary and she took excellent care of it. But Kataryna was not the typical city person. During her free time she would often leave the city and either travel or visit friends in their country homes. She loved to be near water. The ocean, a lake, or whatever body of water she could be around. She only lived in the city to be close to her office; otherwise, she would have moved somewhere near water, which she vowed to do in the future.

It was an ugly mid-November day, the kind of day that would always remind her of her childhood and teenage years in Germany. The fall days in Germany were usually grey and gloomy and the moods of people accordingly. An uneasy feeling came over her as she was reliving her childhood and young adult life in the Old World in her mind.

She grew up as the daughter of lower middle-class parents Greta and Klaus Wolff. They lived in a small apartment in a nice suburban district in the city of Berlin, which at that time was still separated between East and West Berlin. She had grown up in the West Berlin area, but the wall between the East and West was a constant reminder that the people on the other side were kept like prisoners, which became even more apparent when the East Berlin residents tried to escape to the West and were killed in that attempt by the East Berlin border guards.

Her mother was a beautiful, loving and optimistic woman, caring deeply for her and her sister Aleksandra and trying to make every wish come true for them. She showered them with love and affection. Her father took a more nonchalant attitude to fatherhood. He did not spend much time with the children. He was a ruggedly handsome man with sarcastic tendencies, often teasing the girls and emphasizing their weaknesses or what he perceived to be weaknesses. Kataryna was able to put it away more easily than her sister, who was instantly hurt by his words and actions. Worse than the teasing and insensitive remarks, however, were the times of aggression against their mother. These events would typically occur when he was in a bad mood or when their mother defended them after he scolded the girls and screamed at them. Kataryna, Aleksandra and their mother usually tried to plan an escape from this hell. But the girls were too young and Greta was emotionally too weak to really take that next step, which resulted in them having to endure this for most of their childhood and teenage years. Her mother had only worked briefly before she got married, and had learned no real trade. She was afraid to leave her unhappy marriage after the girls were born. Even Klaus' infidelities would not give her the determination, strength and courage to leave with the two children and try to make a living on her own.

Kataryna's thoughts went back to the times when her father was in a mellow mood around Christmas. Sometimes she caught him in deep thought around this time and maybe a little melancholic. At other times he seemed to enjoy certain pieces of music being played either on TV or the radio, especially the song "Kalinka" seemed to get him in a different kind of mood. It filled him with joy one moment as he was singing along with it and even doing some dance steps and then at other times he seemed to get sentimental. Kataryna was wondering why this song and similar ones would stir up feelings in him. What was it about this type of music that put him into this mood? Whatever it was she didn't care as long as her father was in a good mood and they all had a beautiful day. Kataryna began to have some strange attraction to this song herself. When she was a little older she felt the same about the movie "Anna Karenina." Later on in life she learned of her father's Ukrainian ancestry.

Kataryna remembered that she was a serious and intuitive child with deep thoughts about life and death at an early age. One night, when she couldn't sleep and her mother was sitting next to her on the bed to help her fall asleep, Kataryna asked her mother, "what happens when we die, Mom? We will never be here again and won't see each other again?" Her mother comforted her and after the usual bedtime prayer she finally fell asleep. She figured that Kataryna asked this question after the children had been told that the child their mother was carrying was born prematurely and had not survived. Kataryna was especially sad when she learned that the child was a boy. She always wanted to have a brother.

As time went on the girls grew up to become young women and started their careers. Their mother moved in with them and finally divorced their father. He was devastated by the divorce, but the girls explained to him that it was for the best because the way he had treated their mother was very depressing for her and for them. He didn't understand it because he thought he had provided whatever he could for the family. What he didn't realize was that it was love that had been missing in the family. Kataryna sometimes felt sorry for him after she analyzed his childhood, which was not talked about much at home. But she knew that he had gone through tough times and had left home at an early age. She therefore concluded that a man, who himself had not experienced much love growing up and being on his own at such an early age, would not know how to give love and be patient himself. Deep down he was a good person, but he was always so stressed building up his businesses that he needed a release somehow. He could not handle the slightest situations not going his way at home. Having this deep insight, however, made it easier for her to forgive and understand him. As Kataryna became successful in her career she realized that her strength and ambitions were a result of her childhood experiences, which would allow her never to be dependent on any man. But these experiences also had an influence on how she would relate to the men in her life.

The intercom rang with the doorman announcing the arrival of her car service, tearing her away from her childhood memories. Her luggage was stowed and off she was to the airport. One step closer to her destination in Milan, Italy, and to the important acquisition deal she was hoping to complete. Except for the due diligence still to be done, she vowed that nothing would stand in her way to make it happen. While waiting for the flight to board, she calls her partner Stephen to update him on a phone call she had with Luca Romano earlier.

"What did you two discuss?" Stephen asks.

"I reiterated that I really want this," she responds.

Stephen laughs wickedly. "And by 'this' you mean him or the company?"

"Stephen," Kataryna yells into the phone laughing. "Get your mind out of the gutter."

"Well, it hasn't escaped me that you two were quite flirtatious during our last video call with him. I think he is really into you."

"You think?" she responds giggling. "He is kind of cute."

"Yeah, take it from me. He may try to sell himself to you along with the company. And then there is Roberto, the CEO of our acquisition target. He also seems to be a bit of a flirt. Those two are like moths around a light bulb with you. Any idea how you would react if they both came after you?"

"I'll cross that bridge when I get there," she says determined. "First of all I want to make sure that we get to acquire NatMedica. Anything else will have to wait until after we close the acquisition."

"As usual, you are cool like a cucumber," Stephen says amused. "But really, try to have some fun, too. You have been working very hard the last few months. Who knows your flirting with him may have a positive effect on who wins the bid for this company. Have a safe flight and good luck."

"I can't believe you just said that," Kataryna responds. "If I flirt with Luca it will be because I want to do so on a personal level not because of the deal."

Kataryna boards her plane traveling first-class to Malpensa, Milan. She settles in comfortably, enjoying a glass of Champagne, and after dinner puts her seat into the flat bed position to get some much-needed sleep in preparation for the next few days of stress but hopefully also some fun to come.

Luca Romano was still in his office at 22:30h European time, preparing for his meeting with Kataryna Taylor the next day. He had thought long and hard before offering one of the family's profitable holdings for sale. The Romano family, in turn, was interested in acquiring another company. They needed the necessary capital to avoid a huge capital market financing and the subsequent interest expense. Cash is king in these situations and the amount expected from the sale of one of their holdings would most likely cover the acquisition costs of their target.

Luca went through the financial statements and other relevant material of NatMedica, the company to be sold, again. He was sure he could get a very good price, which was set at about eight times current earnings. Several private equity companies in Europe and multinational companies in the United States had shown a strong interest in this biomedical company. Initially, NatMedica's Senior Management had planned a management buy-out, however, that did not materialize for various reasons, one of them being the steep purchase price.

Kataryna is the last of the interested parties Luca would meet with. The three others on the short list had already met with the Romano family and had indicated that they were working on their letter of intent. All three of them were impressive parties and Luca was relieved that this deal might close faster than he thought, which was important so he could focus on the acquisition of his new target

Luca and Kataryna had spoken on the phone, emailed and had several video conference calls regarding the NatMedica acquisition over the past three months. Luca was acutely aware that Kataryna, and her partner Stephen, were extremely interested in the company provided that the due diligence reports were favorable. He was not concerned about that. He knew that these reports would show the high value of the company. Everything was clean, including corporate governance and compliance. After putting the final touches on the Executive Summary he called it a day.

He arrived at his home close to Cernobbio, a small town located at Lake Como, just after midnight. He poured himself a glass of Prosecco, opened the French doors and stepped out on his large terrace overlooking Lake Como, reflecting on the last few days. He loved this view from his elegant villa and the tranquility around it. He was grateful that his ex-wife had not fought him for the villa in their recent divorce. This villa had a sentimental value, which money could not buy. He thought about his failed marriage. Yes, he generally worked late hours and had to travel a lot, but he never neglected her and was always ready to take her with him on business trips when possible. She usually declined to join him, stating that it was too stressful for her. One day when he returned early from one of his business trips, he found his then-wife in a compromising position with one of his business partners. That moment was painful, but he got himself together and started divorce proceedings the next day. As attractive as he was, in addition to his wealth, he had many women throwing themselves at him over the years but he had never cheated on his wife, although he was tempted a few times by extremely beautiful and alluring women.

A new chapter of his life would begin now. At soon to be 42, he was longing to fall in love again with the right woman and enjoy his life. During the various video conference calls with Kataryna Taylor, Luca had become quite attracted to her. He was looking forward to finally meeting her in person and spending some time with her getting to know her better. Things are looking up he thought, as he finished his Prosecco. Tomorrow would be the first day of the rest of his life. He closed the terrace doors and fell into bed, tired and exhausted.

TWO

"Ciao bella," Luca greets Kataryna, kissing her on both cheeks in typical European fashion as she enters his office.

"Buongiorno Luca," Kataryna replies with a big smile. "It is a pleasure to finally meet you in person."

"Likewise," he says. "I have been looking forward to this day. May I offer you some refreshments?"

"Café decaffeinato per favore," she says, trying out the few Italian words she knows. He smiles and calls his executive assistant to bring decaf coffee for both of them.

"I trust you had a pleasant trip over and are well rested," he says in perfect English with an Italian accent. He had studied in the United States and was completely fluent in English.

"I did indeed," Kataryna answers. "I was so much looking forward to coming to Italy, one of my favorite places in the world."

"I am glad to hear you like our country so much," he says with a huge smile. "I hope you have some time after our meetings so I can show you around a bit," he inquires.

"Absolutely," Kataryna responds, "we will paint the town red."

He laughs out loud at that thought.

"I like that idea. Why didn't I come up with that first?"

"Does it matter who came up with it first?" she questions him, somewhat flirtatious.

"Actually no," he replies with an equally flirtatious tone, "it seems we both have the same idea of how to kick off our alliance. It's been too long since I had some real fun. I have been working pretty long hours over the last six months."

Kataryna smirks at him as the executive assistant enters with the coffee and some sparkling water.

"So have I. I guess we deserve to have some fun."

"What would you like to do this evening, any special request?" he quickly asks after the assistant left his office.

"Well, since you are the Milan expert, I will leave that plan in your capable hands," Kataryna responds, "just make sure we start out with a fabulous Italian dinner in a somewhat relaxed setting, but nothing boring."

"I know just the place to take you to," he responds, "it is breath-taking."

"I can't wait. Now that that is out of the way, shall we talk some business before we get too carried away with the night activities?"

"Very well, Principessa, your wish is my command," he responds with a cute smile.

"P r i n c i p e s s a?" Kataryna asks laughing.

Luca pauses for a moment and then answers.

"It means princess in Italian. I will treat you like royalty tonight."

Kataryna is flattered. *Wow, this man can put on the charm*, she thinks, *together with his great looks, this could get dangerous fast. Stephen was right, he might want to sell himself to me together with the company.*

She takes a sip of her decaf coffee and grins at him. "Time to go over the most recent financials."

Luca gets up to get a folder from his desk and hands it to her. "Here you go. Let me know if anything is missing. I am certain you will be impressed with the financial condition and the forecasts. I would never sell this company if it weren't for the other target our family always wanted to acquire, but so far the present shareholders were unwilling to sell. This is our chance to finally get what we wanted for a very long time."

Kataryna opens the folder and looks at the first page. She smiles and shakes her head. The first page of the folder holds an elegant invitation card made out for her from Luca, inviting her to join him for dinner that evening.

The card reads:

"May I request the pleasure of your company for dinner tonight?"

"You may," she accepts giggling. "That actually means that you thought about painting the town red before me, I guess?"

"I believe it does but I am glad you said it first," he responds.

Back to business fast, Kataryna thinks, as she continues on to the executive summary, key investment considerations and risk sections. The facts still need a deeper analysis, but on first glance she is impressed. No debt, highly profitable and very good free cash flow. Her firm would not have a problem finding investors for this company in the future, if they were to decide to do an initial public offering, but for the moment they are looking at a buy and hold investment and to expand the business. She will send the facts over to New York immediately for the usual due diligence analysis. After inspecting their already signed non-disclosure and confidentiality agreement, she closes the folder and looks up at Luca who had watched her reviewing the material to observe her reaction.

"Almost too good to be true," she remarks

"I agree," he sighs. "I wish we could keep this jewel, but we can't do both and I do want that other target. It is a perfect fit for our holdings and provides a great deal of synergies. So, whoever gets to acquire this jewel here," he points at the presentation folder, "will be very lucky."

"What do you mean by whoever?" she looks at him smiling, "I thought we already established that I will be the one who gets this jewel."

"How quick-witted you are, Principessa," he responds, "but the jury is still out on that. As you know we have a few interested parties."

"Well, Luca, you may have just ruined my evening," she says with a playful frown. "Are you trying to hike up the purchase price?"

"Not at all," he grins, "why don't we wait and see how things develop."

His iPhone rings before she can respond. He excuses himself and picks up the call. His mood turns somewhat subdued as he tells the caller that he will call back when he is free. He turns back to Kataryna.

"Forgive me for the interruption, my ex-wife never had good timing."

Kataryna decides not to touch that statement as she expects that there is more to that story and nothing good at that. She gets up collecting the presentation folder.

"I am looking forward to tonight, Luca. See you at 8 p.m. By the way, what is the dress code for tonight?"

He ponders his response for a moment.

"Let's say spectacular."

"Spectacular it is," she concurs grinning, extending her hand to say good-bye.

"So formal, Principessa," he says, coming closer. Instead of shaking her hand he kisses her lightly on each cheek again.

"We will have a memorable evening," he promises.

"I am counting on that," Kataryna responds, "especially the part when you agree to sell NatMedica to me."

Back at her luxurious Milan hotel, Kataryna decides to go to the spa for a relaxing massage and a facial. She also has her makeup done professionally, which she usually does herself and she masters it well. Since the theme of the evening seems to be spectacular, she wants to feel and look special tonight and may even pick up some pointers from the Italian makeup professional for future use. She has been through a lot emotionally and work-wise the past six months, so she is in the mood for a special and fun evening. Her mood is further enhanced by the thought that she will be in the company of a very attractive and alluring man. She recalls her first face-to-face meeting with Luca earlier. A stimulating feeling comes over her. She takes a deep breath realizing that he entices her like no one has in a long time; but she doesn't want to give in to that feeling, at least not right now.

On her way back to the hotel she had picked up a stunning dress at one of the Milan boutiques whose upscale apparel she was immediately attracted to when she passed by. *Leave it up to the Italians*, she thinks, *to make a dress, which fits me perfectly*. The dress is electric blue in a shiny material and weave pattern, which is a great contrast to her blonde hair and blue eyes. It has a plunge neckline and is tightly fitted, ending above her knees. The sales staff offered matching shoes, which she also bought.

Standing in front of the full-length mirror in her hotel suite, she contemplates how to wear her hair. She decides on elegant with her hair in a modern up-do and some loose strands on the sides. Luckily she brought her favorite diamond drop earrings, which go with almost anything. The makeup professional did a spectacular job. Happy with the outcome, she smiles and turns on her iPhone to listen to some relaxing lounge music while waiting for Luca to pick her up.

The hotel phone rings and the reception staff announces that Luca has arrived. She grabs her room card and coat and steps into the lobby heading for the elevator. A strange feeling comes over her almost like a teenager going on a first date. She shakes her head at herself wondering what brought that on. I am going to a business dinner with a business partner. Relax and stay cool Kataryna, she tells herself. She boards the elevator. Seeing her reflection in the mirror an uneasy feeling pops up again, this time wondering if the neckline of her dress is too low. *Shut up*, she tells herself. *You know how to wear and handle a dress like this*. The elevator finally arrives in the lobby. As soon as the door opens Luca stands in front of her with his enigmatic smile. She is startled as he meets her right at the entrance, almost pushing her back into the elevator, in an element of surprise.

"Buonanotte, Principessa," he greets her, kissing her on both cheeks again.

He is dressed in a black perfectly fitted Italian suit, probably Armani, white shirt and electric blue tie. His dark brown hair shines and is meticulously styled. His deep dark eyes are smiling and appearing somewhat mischievous. *What an attractive man*, she thinks. He looks like a model out of a fashion magazine and on top of it has such a captivating personality. Kataryna feels her heart racing. Attractive men usually do not throw her off balance but there is something different about this one, which almost makes her feel a little vulnerable. It is a feeling that is strange to her. She starts giggling as she discovers that the color of his tie matches her dress exactly. After regaining composure she greets him in a casual tone.

"Hello there, Prince Charming."

At last, she is back at being herself, she thinks.

"You just set the tone for the evening," Luca says, "the Princess and Prince out for the evening. Your coach awaits you, Principessa."

Kataryna becomes slightly flustered again wanting to kick herself for the Prince Charming remark, but decides to play along and enjoy the impending adventure. She really needs a drink, she figures, to relax herself a bit. This is getting way too exciting this early on.

The valet attendant arrives with Luca's car, a silver Maserati Quarttroporte. Luca opens the door for her. She steps into the expensive car. Once he is seated in the driver's seat, he gives her an intense look.

"May I pay you a compliment?" he asks, gazing deep into her eyes.

Kataryna needs to cut the tension she is feeling. "Bring it on," she manages to say casually, smiling at him.

"You look stunning Principessa. I am so looking forward to this evening."

"Well, let's get going then," she says laughing slightly, trying to appear witty, "off to the palace we go. I hope I can trust you without a chaperone."

Deep inside she pats herself on the back, well done Kataryna, back on track. *I am not going to let this man rattle me. I am in control.*

"Don't worry, I will take good care of you, Principessa," Luca counters, "you are precious cargo."

He drives off speeding up the car as they enter the autostrada heading towards Lago di Como.

"Where are we going?" Kataryna enquires. "It looks like we are heading out of town."

"We are," he answers. "We have less than an hour's drive, but it will be well worth it."

"I wasn't prepared for that," she says surprised.

"Why, do you have to be somewhere early tomorrow in town?" he asks casually with a wicked smile.

"Nothing special. Just meeting with you and the Senior Management of NatMedica tomorrow morning," she responds in a slightly sarcastic tone.

"I found something more fitting for you, in a more tranquil setting out of town. You said you wanted to start out with a relaxing fabulous Italian meal. I hope it is all right with you? I will not hold it against you if you are late tomorrow morning. The senior management will be standing by for you the entire day."

"I wasn't planning on staying out that late," she utters somewhat irked that he didn't ask her before if she would mind having dinner that far out of town.

"Just go with the flow and enjoy the beautiful evening I have planned for us," he pleads.

She leans back into her seat and relaxes, smiling at him sweetly.

"Okay, this is me, going with the flow."

And with that she makes peace with the idea of having dinner somewhere out of town.

"Will you at least tell me where you are taking me?" she probes a few moments later.

"Patience, Principessa," he replies. "I am sure you will like it. It is one of the most beautiful spots in the world, at least in my opinion."

"Of course," she whispers. "I wouldn't expect anything less."

After a 45-minute drive the Maserati pulls into Villa D'Este in Cernobbio, Lake Como. A majestic castle-like building right on Lake Como appears in front of them. Kataryna can't believe the beautiful sight.

"I am impressed," she says, "this is breathtaking."

"I knew this would be the right place to take you to."

The valet attendant approaches the car. Luca hands him the key and some money and then turns to Kataryna with a bow.

"Please join me in the castle, Principessa."

He offers her his arm to lead her to the entrance. The inside is beautiful and elegant with Old World charm. After recovering from the amazing view out to Lake Como with lights of lakeside villas and hotels twinkling all around, they are entering the restaurant. A host appears and Luca and he have a brief conversation in Italian. Kataryna regrets that she had not been more diligent in keeping up with learning Italian. Such a beautiful and fun language, she thinks, as she listens to the two men. Note to self: pick up an Italian language course ASAP. Or better yet, have Luca give me private lessons. She smiles imagining that. Her thoughts are interrupted when Luca turns back to her and a handsome host leads them to their table. As soon as they sit down a waiter appears out of nowhere, greeting Luca by name and offering an aperitif. Luca looks at Kataryna and then orders a bottle of Roederer Cristal Champagne asking her, however, if she would prefer something else. She does not, the Champagne sounds just fine. Within a few minutes the Champagne is at their table along with delicious starters, compliments of the house.

"So," Luca starts the conversation, "what do you think? Did I make the right choice of restaurant?"

"I love it," she says softly, "thank you for making the effort of driving out here and introducing me to this magical spot. It is definitely worth the drive and even if it gets late until we get back to Milano, I won't mind."

He picks up his Champagne glass for a toast, and as their glasses clink he gives her a mischievous smile. "Who said we are going back to Milano tonight?"

Although startled by that remark, Kataryna stays calm and relaxed.

"It's way too early for that kind of joke," she counters. "I won't even grace that idea with another thought."

She takes a sip of the expensive Champagne and raises the glass as if she just made a toast and then sets it down on the table.

"And by the way," she continues, "we haven't even talked about the company yet. When are we getting to that part?"

"As far as I am concerned, Principessa, we are already there. I am about to offer you my company on a silver platter."

"Oh really?" she says pleased, "so you have decided to sell your company to me if I come up with an offer?"

"Not so fast, Principessa," he responds, "as you know in the English language company can either mean the enterprise I am about to sell or it can mean me being your company tonight."

Okay, Kataryna thinks, before she opens her mouth again, *he wants to play cat and mouse. I will play along for a while.*

"Oh, how ignorant of me not to realize that you were offering yourself to me on a silver platter. I probably can't accept such a precious gift right at this moment. Any chance we can exchange you for the actual company/enterprise on that platter?"

"Well played," he praises her. "I didn't expect such a formidable come-back. I like the challenge, it never gets boring this way."

"Thank you for the compliment," she responds, pleased with herself.

"Credit where credit is due. So let's talk about that before our dinner arrives. What I didn't tell you yet, is, that I have moved our meeting with the senior management tomorrow to Bellagio and later in the day. In case you don't know where Bellagio is, it is farther up Lago di Como from here. Another beautiful spot for you to see before we head back to Milano tomorrow evening."

Kataryna is taken by surprise. How in the world can she meet with the management in Bellagio tomorrow when she has no change of clothes, etc., with her? She is definitely not showing up in this dress.

"Okay Luca," she sighs, "let's get serious now. How do you expect me to meet with the executives tomorrow when I don't have any business apparel here?"

"Not a problem, Principessa, we have a lot of shops along the lake and any of the boutique owners would be more than pleased to come with a selection to Villa D'Este."

"Nice try," she replies, "what about my notes and notepad, etc., stuff that one usually brings to a business meeting?"

"We also have notepads and pens in Italy," he answers laughing, "and the meeting material will be delivered to you by the executives tomorrow in Bellagio."

Kataryna lifts her second glass of Champagne and almost empties the entire glass at once. Leaning back in a comfortable position in her chair she stares at him.

"I am so glad you thought of almost everything."

"Almost?" he asks curiously, "what didn't I think of?"

"My willingness to go along with that plan," she says with a broad grin.

"I have no doubt that you will rise to the occasion," he says. "I would be surprised if anything would throw you off balance."

"Aha, assuming that I am on board with that plan where do I sleep tonight?"

"You have two options," he starts out, "either you can sleep in a suite here at Villa D'Este, which I arranged for, or I can offer you a guest room in my villa not far from here."

He looks at her amused, anticipating her reply. Kataryna starts laughing out loud attracting the attention of some of the other restaurant guests who briefly look over to their table.

"Well, PC," she declares in an intriguing voice, "you just thought of everything, didn't you?"

"PC?" he asks, raising his eyebrows.

"Stands for Prince Charming."

He smiles, shaking his head at her. "Are you ready to let me know your choice of accommodation?" he inquires somewhat anxious.

"Sure," she fires back at him, "this is a no-brainer. I will accept your generous invitation for the guest room in your villa provided I can lock the door so I don't have to worry about intruders."

Wow, she thinks, *did I just say this? Well, I can't back out now.*

"Excellent," he replies giving her a reassuring smile, "and yes, there is a key so no worries about intruders and other suspects. You will be completely safe."

Kataryna feels at ease, looking forward to the exquisite meal they ordered. The antipasto arrives and Luca speaks to one of the waiters about his wine selection with their main course. Kataryna had mentioned that she would prefer either a Barolo or Amarone. The waiter leaves their table with the wine order, quickly returns with a bottle of 2007 Barolo and presents it to Luca for approval.

Luca tastes the wine and then gives his permission for the waiter to fill the two glasses. When the main course arrives, Kataryna gets her homemade pasta with seafood and Luca his Saltimbocca. After dinner they have a fancy dessert, a combination of chocolate tart with a hazelnut mousse followed by after-dinner drinks, compliments of the house.

They leave the Villa D'Este restaurant at 12:30 a.m. The valet arrives with the Maserati. Luca drives off heading to his close-by villa. The private gate to the villa entrance opens leading them towards the magnificent house overlooking Lake Como where another spectacular view awaits Kataryna. She is swept into a different world. *There are so many beautiful places in the world*, she thinks, *but unfortunately we are only a short time on this earth, not enough time to see and experience them all.*

Luca's staff waits at the entrance of the villa to park the car in one of the garages adjacent to the villa. Inside the villa Kataryna steps into an elegant foyer with an Italian marble floor. She can feel the warmth from the floor heating at her feet. The foyer leads into a large living room with huge windows and French doors looking out over Lake Como. The terrace behind the French doors is spectacular. Kataryna imagines what it would be like lounging on it during warm-weather months, looking at the beautiful lake, watching boats come by while sipping some delicious summer drink. The room is furnished with contemporary Italian furniture and has a huge modern fireplace. Kataryna walks over to stare at the flames.

Luca joins her at the fireplace.

"I think you like fire," he murmurs.

"I like fire and water. You are lucky to have both right here."

They sit down by the fireplace. Both are silent for a moment watching the flames grow bigger.

"What may I offer you to drink?" he breaks the silence.

"Something hot would be appropriate," she replies with a dreamy smile.

"Hot as in temperature or spicy?"

"Hot as in temperature, please."

He walks out of the room speaking to a female staff member in Italian. Sitting between the water, which is the majestic and beautiful Lake Como, and the warm crackling fire inside this spectacular room has Kataryna mesmerized. She leans back and closes her eyes feeling totally relaxed. Her female intuition, which never fails her, tells her that she is totally safe here.

Luca returns followed by the female staff member carrying a tray with two glasses of hot red wine with spices of cinnamon, cloves and orange peel. The aroma of the spices fills the room and reminds her of winter in Germany when she used to drink this beverage called 'Gluehwein' in German. Although she feels a bit of jet lag coming on, the magic of this moment prevails and she finishes her drink slowly.

"Thank you for the beautiful evening," Kataryna says. "You have an excellent taste in restaurants. I couldn't have imagined anything more suitable."

"You are most welcome, Principessa. It was my pleasure," he responds. "I couldn't have imagined a more beautiful and entertaining guest. This was the best evening I had in a long time. I hope I can show you more beautiful places in the future and in turn be rewarded with your company."

Kataryna gives him a mysterious smile. "To say it in your words, Luca, the jury is still out on that."

"I will do anything in my power, so that the verdict turns in my favor," he says as he comes over and sits next to her on the couch. He takes her hand and places a key in it.

"This is the key for the guest area of the villa," he says softly. "You will find everything you need in there, I believe. I also took the liberty to have some of the boutiques in the area deliver a few business outfits tomorrow after breakfast, so we can get you properly dressed for the meeting in Bellagio. So, if you are ready to go to sleep, I will show you the way to the guest area. If you need anything just pick up the phone, and call the number on the directory, and one of my house staff will assist you. My number is on there, too, if you would like to speak with me."

"Thank you," Kataryna responds, "everything will be perfect, I am sure, just like this evening."

"I have to thank you for playing along so nicely with me in the restaurant. It was so much fun because neither one of us knew how it would turn out at that moment. I am quite impressed how you handled this situation and, of course, I am very happy that you chose to be my guest here. It is a gift that keeps on giving because the memory of you in my villa will stay with me until the next time you come back here."

"The evening couldn't have been more perfect," Kataryna admits. "You are so lucky to call such a beautiful place your home."

"I would consider myself very lucky to have you back here very soon," Luca says. "You just complete this villa like no one ever has been able to do before."

Kataryna is pleased and relieved that this man turned out to be a gentleman instead of a Casanova as it appeared for some moments earlier this evening. But then her female intuition had already told her that she had nothing to worry about.

They leave the living room and walk towards the guest area. Luca takes the key and opens the double doors leading to the guest rooms. He hands the key back to Kataryna.

"Good night and sweet dreams." He kisses her lightly on both cheeks. "Call me when you are ready for breakfast or if you need anything before."

"Good night Luca, you are a very gracious host."

Kataryna closes the door behind her and turns the key. *This is unbelievable*, she says to herself, *a totally secluded guest area with three individual bedroom suites and en suite bathrooms*. Beautifully decorated with modern Italian art and huge beds with luxurious linens and down comforters. She walks into the first bedroom. A large TV is hanging on the wall with a welcome screen displaying a message for her:

Good Evening Kataryna,

It is a great pleasure to have you here as my guest. I hope you will sleep well and feel completely safe. I am looking forward to having breakfast with you tomorrow morning. Please call me if you need anything. If you press the video button on the TV one of my staff members will be with you instantly.
Ciao,
Luca

Wow, wow and wow, Kataryna thinks, *how cool is this? One can call a staff member on a TV via video. I wonder if I should try it out.* She decides against it and then walks to the window, which opens with French doors to a smaller terrace overlooking Lake Como. What do you know; even the guest rooms have this magnificent view. She closes the window, kicks off her shoes and steps into the large luxurious bathroom. Heated floors in the bathroom, how absolutely comfortable this feels. A large fancy bathtub adjacent to a window, again with lake views and a separate shower large enough for four people with showerheads coming from both sides as well as a handheld shower. All are electronically operated. She presses one of the buttons and music comes on. Oh no, better turn that off again. She will deal with this shower set up tomorrow when she is awake and alert. A beautiful robe hangs on a luxurious hanger. Underneath is an elegant nightdress. How convenient. The vanity has everything a woman needs, but she is glad that she has at least small sizes of her own makeup articles in her bag. *Thank God that I always come prepared*, she thinks. After her usual evening bathroom routine, she falls into the luxurious bed and drifts off into a deep sleep.

Kataryna opens her eyes and looks around. For a moment she doesn't know where exactly she is but then it comes to her: Luca's villa. She sits up to get her bearings. The clock shows 8 a.m. She gets out of bed and opens the shades. Whoa, that view again, this time in broad daylight and the sun is shining. What a beautiful sight. She would venture onto the terrace but it is November after all and probably chilly outside.

She steps into the bathroom, takes a long hot shower and then applies her makeup. *Oh, oh* she thinks, *what am I going to wear for breakfast? Not that dress from last night, but what else?* She decides to check the closet in the room to see if there is anything suitable in there. Relief, there are a couple of items that look like they might fit. She inspects the apparel closer and settles on a turquoise two-piece lounge suit, which happens to fit her. After fixing her hair in a high ponytail, she walks over to the TV and presses the video call button. A female staff member called Mariya comes on the screen.

"Buongiorno Signora, what can I do for you?" Mariya asks in English with a heavy Italian accent.
"Buongiorno, I am wondering where breakfast will be served?" Kataryna asks.
"I will meet you in the guest area and escort you to the breakfast room," Mariya responds.

Kataryna walks out of her room to the entrance door of the guest area, which leads to the villa's foyer. She opens the door. Mariya is standing in front of her asking to please follow her. They walk down a couple of steps and pass by the phenomenal kitchen. Kataryna immediately thinks about her sister Aleksandra, who loves to cook, and is crazy about large and modern kitchens like this one. Adjacent to the huge kitchen is the spacious breakfast room with views to Lake Como and a terrace behind another set of French doors. On the other side of the room is an open fireplace, which separates the kitchen from the breakfast room.

Luca is standing by the fire. He greets her as she comes around the corner. "Good morning, Principessa. That color suits you well."
"Good morning, Luca. I was glad to find some comfortable clothes to wear."

She looks around. "Wow, another room with a beautiful view."

Luca pulls out one of the chairs for her from the table and motions her to have a seat. Mariya and another younger staff member come over to inquire what Kataryna and Luca would like for breakfast.

"Surprise me," Kataryna suggests.

Luca makes a request in Italian and the two women take off to the kitchen.

"How did you sleep?" he asks, "I hope you were comfortable."

"Very comfortable," Kataryna replies, "I just had to figure out that fancy shower this morning. I could have stayed in there for hours."

"I am so glad you had some fun this morning already," he says with a charming smile, "while I was studying the financial newspapers." He points to the Financial Times and Wall Street Journal sitting on a coffee table by the fireplace.

"I don't feel even a bit guilty," she says, smiling back at him. "So, what is the agenda for the day?"

"First, we will have a nice breakfast. Then we will look at some business apparel for you, which will be brought over; thereafter, I would like to show you the company's manufacturing facility. We should be back at the villa around 1 p.m., have a light lunch and then go via private boat to Bellagio, where we will meet the senior management of NatMedica. The meeting should take about two hours. Around 6:30 p.m., we will have an early dinner at the hotel and take the private boat back to Cernobbio thereafter."

"Okay, and what happens after we are back in Cernobbio?" she asks curiously.

"I hope that you will accept my invitation to be my guest for another night. Tomorrow morning we will drive to Milano and I will bring you to your hotel or my office, if there is anything else we need to go over in connection with the deal," he says.

"Sounds like a good plan," she responds. "Although, I could have saved a couple of nights in hotel bills in Milano if you had revealed that plan before."

"I am sorry I surprised you like that. Don't worry, I will handle that part with the hotel," he says. "They won't charge you for these two nights. Tell me a little about yourself and what you like to do in your free time," he starts a new conversation. "Do you like to travel?"

"Yes, I love to travel," Kataryna responds. "I prefer warm weather so I try to leave New York when it gets cold and ugly. I like to spend time in Hawaii in the winter. Apart from that I usually attend the premieres at the Bregenzer Festspiele in Austria at Lake Constance, which take place every other year in July."

"I have been there once," he says. "I liked it a lot. So you like opera? Have you been to the Arena di Verona to their outside opera performances yet?" he asks.

"Yes, once. Aida was playing then. It was a great experience. I want to do that again one day."

He smiles leaning into her. "Maybe you will allow me to take you to the Arena di Verona one day? However, we will have to wait for the summer months and unfortunately it is only November now. So, I would like to extend an invitation to a spectacular event in the beginning of February, the Carnevale in Venezia. Would you entertain that idea?" he asks.

"Tell me more," she responds, "it sounds intriguing. Do we have to wear a costume?"

"But, of course," he replies quickly, "that is one of the major parts of that event. The costumes and matching masks can be rented for that time, but I would have one designed especially for you."

"Do I have a say on how that costume would look?" Kataryna asks with great interest.

"Sure. I think we could come up with something enthralling together."

"Sounds promising," she says. "I already have an idea of what costume I would want to wear for that event."

"I have tickets for 'Il Ballo del Doge'. This is a spectacular event and in 2013 the theme is all about Amore."

"All about love," she exclaims, raising her glass of orange juice in a toast. "I'll drink to that."

Mariya enters the breakfast area. "Scusi Signor Romano, the apparel has arrived."

"Shall we have a look to see if you can find something suitable for the occasion?" he asks, taking Kataryna's arm and leading her to the lounge area.

Kataryna is amused by the spectacle. She walks over to inspect the suits a little closer. Beautiful Italian-made suits, she loves all of them. How convenient to shop like this. *I could get used to this,* she thinks. She chooses three suits. One in charcoal grey with a pencil skirt and tailored jacket, one in royal blue with straight leg pants and one in black with grey pin stripes and silver buttons. She also picks three tops to go with the suits and decides to wear the charcoal-colored suit with a lavender-colored blouse for this afternoon's business meeting in Bellagio.

"Oh, no," she shouts out, "I don't have any shoes to wear with this suit."

"Not a problem, Signora," the boutique owner exclaims in a strong Italian accent, "we brought matching shoes for all suits."

Relieved, Kataryna tries on the charcoal grey suede shoes. Perfect. She also takes a pair of blue pumps for the royal blue suit.

"You really thought of everything," she says to Luca with a big smile.

"Oh, Principessa, I grew up with two sisters and I had a very fashion-conscious wife. I know a thing or two about putting an outfit together and so do the staff at the boutiques. This was easy and I really enjoyed doing this, especially when I saw your face light up when you inspected the suits. So now that you know that I can be trusted with good taste will you let me design your costume for the Carnevale in Venezia?" he asks.

"I have some ideas of my own, which I am sure you would approve of," she answers in a flirtatious tone.

With the suits, blouses and shoes in hand, Kataryna moves towards the guest area to get dressed. "I made out like a bandit," she says giggling.

Mariya takes the apparel from Kataryna and follows her.

"Signora, I have taken the liberty to wash your undergarments and put new ones out for you, too" she says, "you will find everything on your bed."

First-class establishment, Kataryna thinks. She turns to Mariya and thanks her with a "Grazie".

"It is my pleasure," Mariya responds.

"And mine," Luca calls out after them grinning.

Kataryna turns around and bows in Luca's direction.

"Thank you so much, Luca. I am totally impressed how smoothly everything went and what beautiful suits I am going home with. By the way, I need to know how to pay the boutique."

"It's already taken care of. I have an account at the local boutiques," he explains. "I guess you will just be in my debt for now."

Kataryna turns to him embarrassed. "I can't accept that. Please let me transfer the funds to you. After all, I just chose three suits with the intention to pay for them."

"Let's discuss it later," he says casually.

"You bet we will," she states with determination.

Kataryna gets dressed in her guest suite and then fixes her hair. She walks to the large window and looks out to Lake Como. It's a breathtaking view and a breathtaking man. Who wants to go back to New York? *Get a grip Kataryna*, she tells herself after that thought. But deep down inside she knows that she is already in too deep to think that she can escape the charm of this man. She looks into the mirror, smiles and shakes her head. *Life is short and then you die,* she tells herself; *so enjoy it while you can.*

Luca is waiting for her in the lounge area dressed in a grey suit, white shirt and purple tie. He smiles at her admiringly as she walks towards him.

"You look fantastic," he compliments her. "No one would ever guess that you arrived here in evening wear only".

Kataryna looks at him, noticing that he matched her color combination.

"So do you, Prince Charming," she says. "Let's get this show on the road."

Mariya arrives with their coats. They drive towards Milano to visit the manufacturing facility where Kataryna is introduced to the Chief Operating Officer Umberto, the plant manager and a few other key employees. It is a state-of-the art facility. Kataryna is impressed. When they return to the villa at 1:30 p.m., they are served a delicious pasta dish with a light red wine followed by a homemade dessert.

At 3 p.m., Kataryna and Luca walk out to the landing where an impressive boat waits for them. The captain comes to meet them and escorts them onto the boat. Luca shakes his hand and pats him on the shoulder. They have a brief jovial conversation in Italian. A staff member enters from the galley and asks what he may bring for them. Kataryna looks around the luxurious boat, which is furnished with contemporary off-white Italian leather seating. The large windows show off the beauty of Lake Como. Soft music is playing in the background.

"Is this your boat?" Kataryna asks.

"Yes, of course," he answers. "When you live at the lake, a boat is a must."

"I guess so, but this is a little fancier than a regular boat."

"That it is. Would you like a tour?" Luca asks Kataryna.

They walk past a couple of doors. He opens one of them. "This is the master bedroom," he explains, "and behind the other two doors are guest bedrooms."

He opens the doors to the other rooms. Kataryna walks into each bedroom with ensuite bathrooms and let's out a sigh.

Luca looks at her. "Do you like it?" he asks softly.

"What's not to like?" she responds. "I am at a loss for words."

He takes her to the deck, which has a Jacuzzi and a sunbathing area.

She nods approvingly. "I could see myself sunbathing here in the summer."

Luca puts his arm around her shoulders and pulls her closer to him. "Now you are talking."

For a moment they are very close to each other with intense eye contact. *Oh, no,* she thinks, *do not get weak Kataryna.* It takes a lot for her to stay cool. She steps back slightly and turns around. They return to the lounge area where they have a coffee and some biscuits. Looking out of the window, Kataryna marvels at the area and the villas to the left and right of Lake Como. It looks like in a travel magazine, so beautiful and so surreal.

Her mind wanders off again. She imagines herself on this boat in the summer with a glass of Champagne while she and Luca are in the hot tub listening to romantic lounge music playing over the surround system.

Luca steps behind her. "What are you thinking about, Principessa?"

"Nothing in particular," she quickly answers, startled, "I was just admiring the beautiful view."

"I bet we were thinking the same thing," he says seductively.

"Are you a mind reader now, too?" she asks him grinning, trying to regain composure.

He just smiles and shakes his head. "You are a challenge, Principessa, but I like challenges, especially when they are as beautiful and alluring as you are."

Kataryna is slightly flustered again by Luca's vivid compliments. She tries to hide it desperately. The sexual tension between them is almost getting too much for her and there is no escape. *If this was a movie,* she thinks, *they would be in each other's arms already giving in to the passion.* But this is real life and she wants to keep it professional, at least for now.

The staff member re-enters the lounge area interrupting their intense moment, allowing Kataryna to catch her breath.

"Signor Romano we are about to arrive in Bellagio," he announces.

"Already?" Kataryna asks kind of surprised.

"Yes, it is only a 45-minute ride with a private boat from my villa. But when you come back in the summer, we will take a much longer ride than this one," he continues amused.

Kataryna looks down and smiles to herself, then looks up and glances at Luca. They have another intense eye contact moment, staring silently into each other's eyes. My fate is sealed, she decides, as the boat arrives at the landing dock with a bump, which almost knocks her over. Luca rushes to hold her and takes the opportunity to embrace her with both arms, holding her a moment longer than necessary.

"I bet you asked the captain to do that," she says smiling as she frees herself gently from his embrace.

"It was fate this time, Principessa, but I will remember to ask him to do it on the way back," he responds laughing.

"Looks like you are a man on a mission."

"Yes, on an urgent mission," he replies, leading her towards the exit.

He offers her his arm to escort her off the boat and she takes it. *Darn,* she thinks, *this is getting harder by the minute. He really knows how to get to me.* She is afraid she won't be able to resist him much longer. At least she will be safe for the next few hours, when they are meeting with the NatMedica Senior Management team.

When they arrive at the Bellagio hotel, they meet Roberto Silvestri, the CEO of NatMedica, and Francesco Barone, the Chief Financial Officer.

Roberto greets Kataryna with a light kiss on her hand.

"I am pleased to finally meet you," he says, staring at her, "you are even more beautiful in person."

Kataryna doesn't know how to interpret the look Roberto had just given her, but she is distracted when Francesco moves towards her to greet her. After some small talk and the usual pleasantries over drinks, they start discussing the company's history, financials, outlook, and marketing plans and then move on to each of their backgrounds and tenure with the company. Roberto, the CEO, has an impressive background. Under his management the company became the success it is today. Kataryna guesses that he is in his mid forties. She wonders what would happen if Roberto either left or if something bad happened to him.

"Roberto, what kind of succession plan do you have in place for a worst-case scenario?" she addresses the subject.

Roberto clears his throat. He turns to Francesco and then again to Kataryna to respond.

"Francesco would rise up to become CEO. He has been around for the last five years and has filled in for me at times. He has my full trust. I couldn't imagine a better successor."

Kataryna is glad to hear that they have a succession plan in place, which could be acted upon immediately since this is crucial for the continued success of any company. Francesco, she figures, is probably in his early thirties.

"Francesco is also engaged to my sister Patrizia. So we are extremely happy and fortunate that he would qualify to fill the CEO position from day one in a worst-case scenario." Luca elaborates.

"Excellent," she says, "we've got that covered, too."

"Shall we start with dinner?" Luca asks politely, "Kataryna and I have to be back on the boat by 9:30 p.m."

They sit down at the dinner table. Roberto sits next to Kataryna on one side and Luca on the other side. The waiter rushes to the table with a wine list and menu and proceeds to announce the specials for the evening. Luca orders a bottle of Amarone and sparkling water while everyone reviews the menu. The waiter returns with the wine and fills the glasses after Luca has tasted and approved the selection.

Roberto raises his glass.

"Here is to a mutually rewarding relationship," he says, gazing deep into Kataryna's eyes.

She looks away quickly and clinks glasses with the others. Roberto puts his hand on her shoulder to get her attention. She turns to him with a somewhat puzzled look.

"So, tell us about yourself," he prompts her.

Kataryna starts running down her professional background when he cuts in after the third sentence.

"I have read your bio. I was hoping for a little more personal information. Are you married?" he asks, giving her a challenging smile.

Luca immediately becomes annoyed and raises an eyebrow at Roberto hoping to get his attention. Roberto ignores him.

After initially being caught off-guard, Kataryna recovers. "Is that a prerequisite for the deal?" she hurls at him.

Roberto laughs and weighs his response, taking a sip of his wine. Before he can utter another word, Francesco decides to extinguish the fire developing between Luca and Roberto by asking Kataryna a multi-part question regarding her private equity firm, which she gladly answers.

Luca gives Roberto a stern look, but Roberto just grins and shrugs his shoulders at him as if to say, "What's the problem?"

After Kataryna has finished answering Francesco's questions, Luca takes over the conversation to keep it professional. They discuss the company's outlook and the financial assumptions presented in the offering memorandum. Roberto is very well prepared and has plausible answers for all questions. She is impressed with the management.

Roberto takes the word again. "Kataryna," he starts, "initially the senior management was thinking about a management buy-out, but the price is a little too steep for us and we didn't want to load up the company with a huge amount of debt. We were hoping that we could negotiate a five to ten percent equity share for the senior management. How do you feel about that?"

"I can't make that kind of decision right now," she replies, "first, I have an equal partner in the firm who would have to be on board with that idea; and second, we still need to do some major due diligence work. So let me get back to you on that."

"If you decide that this is not an option for your firm, it would not be a deal breaker," Luca adds quickly.

Kataryna turns to Roberto. "Would you still stay on as CEO if we don't agree to that structure or is that something you need to think about?"

"I would stay on especially if you get to acquire the company. It would be a great pleasure working with such a beautiful woman."

Kataryna laughs. "You have no idea how tough this beautiful woman can get."

"I like tough," he counters with a suggestive smile. "I promise I won't resist you. You can count on me day and night."

Kataryna is slightly amused by his ambiguous answer and word play with her. *Another flirt,* she thinks. *I can't catch a break tonight. Stephen was right again.*

"Don't make any promises you can't keep," she warns him jokingly.

Roberto smiles at her broadly. He likes her playful banter. He puts his arm around her shoulders, pulling her closer to him.

"I can deliver what I promise. We would make a great team on many levels. Don't you think?"

Kataryna decides to ignore his question. She turns to Francesco.

"What about you, Francesco, will you stay on as Chief Financial Officer if you don't get an equity share right away?"

"Absolutely," he replies. "I have no intention of leaving. What is important to me, and I believe also to Roberto, is that the new shareholders are on the same wavelength as us from a business point of view. As you can see from the financials, we have run a very profitable operation and have solid expansion plans worldwide. We would expect the new shareholders to share our vision and mission."

"I fully understand and respect that. As far as I can see we would not anticipate making major changes. We may have some additional expansion and new product ideas, which, however, would be complementary to the existing business and your expansion plans. We believe that the United States would be a major market for your products, but we also have to consider that any future new products may need FDA approval depending on the claim they are making in the product description."

"Sure, we are aware of that. So far most of our natural products did not require such approvals but needless to say our R&D department may come up with something in the future, which would require FDA approval should we want to sell in the U.S."

"I will get back to you regarding an equity share for the management after we have reviewed everything," Kataryna responds, looking at Roberto and Francesco.

Luca, who has been listening quietly to the conversation, is slightly irked at Roberto's word play with Kataryna. He got concerned for a moment when Roberto put his arm around Kataryna's shoulders. The image of the incident involving Roberto and a female employee at the last company Christmas party flashed in front of his eyes briefly and he was holding his breath. Thank God nothing of that nature happened tonight.

"I think we had a good meeting," Luca ends this conversation.
He motions the waiter to bring the check when his phone rings. Picking up the call, he excuses himself and leaves the table to focus on his phone conversation.

Kataryna gets up, too. "Well gentlemen, I will take this opportunity to visit the powder room."
She heads towards the ladies room. When she exits, Roberto is standing by the door waiting for her.
"I hope you don't mind, but I wanted a moment alone with you, Kataryna. Could I talk you into having a drink with me? I know a nice bar in the area, which I think you would enjoy."
"Sorry Roberto," Kataryna responds, "but I am a guest at Luca's house and I can't just leave with you now."
"How about tomorrow? When are you going back to Milano? I could meet you at your hotel," he replies.
"I am leaving tomorrow. Luca will take me to the hotel to pick up my luggage and then we will go to the airport from there."
"I am so disappointed," he says. "I really would like to spend some time with my potential future boss."
"I am sorry," she says starting to walk towards the restaurant and their table, "but as you can see it is just not in the cards this time."

Luca watches them coming back to the table together. He is slightly worried about Roberto's intentions vis-à-vis Kataryna. He recalls that after one of their joint video conference calls, Roberto had remarked how much he liked her and how thrilled he would be if she became the new shareholder.

Luca gets up to meet Kataryna halfway and ushers her towards the exit. Roberto moves towards Kataryna and kisses her on both cheeks to say good-bye.

"I hope to see you soon," he says holding both of her hands as he steps back to let her go. "Please call me if you have any additional questions. As I already said, I am here for you day and night."

"Thank you, I will," she responds smiling, still amused at his choice of words. "My due diligence team may also come over to meet with you and Francesco and take a tour of the company's facilities."

"It will be our pleasure to show them around and go over anything they wish to discuss further," Roberto offers. "What a shame that you can't stay longer so I could show you around the area a bit."

"I have done that already," Luca says smirking at Roberto.

"Well, next time when you come over, I will show you some other sights," Roberto says, focusing on Kataryna. "I understand you are staying at Luca's villa tonight."

He turns to Luca. "How come you didn't invite us to stay with you tonight? We could have had a little party at your villa."

Luca shakes his head at Roberto. "I think Kataryna needs some peace and quiet tonight after her short and busy trip to Italy."

He takes Kataryna's arm to lead her quickly out of the hotel before Roberto gets any other ideas. Roberto stares after them. Kataryna turns around and waves at him. He waves back at her and blows her a kiss.

"Wow, Roberto," Francesco says when they are alone, "that was borderline daring."

"Why?" Roberto asks. "I really like her. I didn't see her getting upset. On the contrary, I think she enjoyed our little banter."

"Yeah, but this is not just some woman. She could be our boss soon. And in addition, did you see Luca's face?"

"I don't know what the big deal is?" Roberto sneers. "Luca is way too uptight sometimes."

"I know Luca pretty well and I think he tried to tell you that he wanted you to behave more professionally around Kataryna. After all, this is the first time we all met her in person."

"Or maybe he was jealous that she played along with me. Anyway, let's get out of here. Have a good night. See you tomorrow."

The captain greets Kataryna and Luca when they return to the boat.

Luca turns to Kataryna. "I would like to apologize for Roberto's personal questions this evening. That was not very professional. I have no idea what's gotten into him to get so personal and touchy feely. I will have a word with him tomorrow. But I have to say you handled it quite well."

"Luca, please don't worry about it," she responds, "it was kind of amusing. I am a big girl. I know how to handle these situations. Trust me, if it had gotten out of control I would have put an end to it."

"You are very gracious, but that doesn't mean that I have to like it."

"Relax," she says laughing, touching his arm, "and may I remind you, Signor Romano, that you pulled a pretty good stunt yourself with the out-of-town dinner last night and invitation to stay overnight at your villa."

He grins and sighs. "You really are a tough one, Principessa. I thought you liked our evening and your stay at the villa or did you feel pressured in any way?"

"I did like our evening but you have to admit it was kind of risky. We had just met for the first time in person. That could have easily backfired."

"I never thought about it that way," he says, "but I guess you are right. I just wanted to show you a good time. The idea to drive out to Villa D'Este came to me when you said you were looking forward to a relaxing but not boring dinner, and I gave you a choice to either stay at Villa D'Este or my villa overnight. May I assume that you have forgiven me for putting you in this position?"

"I have to think about it," she says grinning. "Just don't be so judgmental about Roberto's little word play tonight."

"That's because I know him better than you do, but let's not talk about it anymore. I get the point."

Kataryna and Luca arrive back at the villa shortly after 10 p.m. A fire is burning again in the fireplace. Kataryna moves closer to it as a chill comes over her. Luca sits next to her and puts his jacket and arms around her.

"So, have you forgiven me?" he asks her softly.

"I have," she responds, watching the fire.

He draws her closer to him. Kataryna is in agony. One side of her wants to get up to put some space between them but the other side just wants to give in to this feeling. Before she can decide he gently touches her chin and pulls her face towards him. Staring deeply into her eyes he softly kisses her on the cheek and then continues on to her lips. She struggles with herself at first but the intensity of his kiss is too strong to resist. They start kissing more passionately. An extreme heat is rushing through her body and it is not from the fire. *Oh boy*, she thinks, *what am I doing? This was not supposed to happen tonight.*

"You are so beautiful, Principessa. I am so happy you came into my life," he whispers in her ear as he kisses her neck continuing further down to her shoulders underneath her blouse.

Her blouse button pops open revealing her bra. Luca moans as his lips move further down to her cleavage. His tongue moves into the bra cups and swirls around as the bra cup gives way and exposes her breast. His mouth is hovering over her nipple, sending electrifying sensations all over her body. His lips move to the other side repeating the stimulating caress.

Luca is getting more and more aroused. He groans and passionately kisses her all over while his hand is moving under her skirt and up her thighs. He touches her very softly right in the G-spot. She moans and moves her hips towards his hand as he continues inside her underwear, stroking her gently and breathing heavily into her ear. He caresses her, moving up and down as she gives in to the inevitable orgasm clutching him tightly. She opens his pants and touches him only a few seconds making him explode into an orgasm. They lay on the couch holding each other for a while enjoying the release of the sexual tension, which had been building the whole day and which they had managed to hide from each other until now.

"That was pretty intense," she says, "and we didn't even get to do it all the way."

"Hmm, that's what happens when you try to suppress it the whole day. Or as in my case since yesterday," he adds while kissing the inside of her hand. "I couldn't fall asleep for quite some time last night knowing you were so near and yet so far," he confesses.

"Good thing I had that key; otherwise you may have come to my guest room and attacked me in the middle of the night," she jokes.

"It took all my strength of will and self-control not to come over there. It was brutal," he admits.

She laughs out loud. "Come on. Now you are exaggerating."

"I swear. I finally had to take a cold shower."

Kataryna cracks up laughing. "Well, I had made a deal with myself to keep it professional, so I didn't allow myself to go there. But that deal almost fell apart on the boat today. If your boat attendant hadn't interrupted that intense moment we had, all my good intentions would have been out of the window."

"I am glad that is behind us. Shall we get ready for bed?" he asks.

"Meaning what?" she questions him, sitting down in his lap, "going to sleep in separate rooms or getting ready for the second round?"

He kisses her cleavage looking at her passionately.

"No more separate rooms for us. I won't be able to keep my hands off you anymore. I hope the feeling is mutual."

She kisses him softly. "I am ready whenever you are. Lead the way Prince Charming."

Wow, this is another beautiful room, she thinks, as they walk into the large master bedroom suite. The king-size bed has an upholstered headboard and inviting luxurious sheets and duvet, all in taupe nuances. The lighting is soft and seductive. She can't wait to lie on this bed with Luca next to her. But a shower would be good first.

She steps into the ensuite bathroom, which reminds her of early Roman times. It's a large sunken bathtub, with Jacuzzi feature and an extra large separate shower with showerheads on both sides, just like the one in the guest bathroom.

Luca, already in his underwear, follows her into the bathroom holding a bottle of Champagne and two glasses.

"I like the way you think," she says, taking off her clothes.

Luca moves toward the bathtub to turn on the faucets.

"So, we are taking a bath?" she asks flirtatiously.

"Not just a bath, a sensuous bath with the Jacuzzi jets on," he answers. "I love that feeling and tonight it will be even more special with you in there with me."

He opens the bottle of Champagne and pours it into the two glasses.

"Let me make a toast. To a beautiful erotic night with an even more beautiful lady and many more nights like this."

"I'll drink to that," Kataryna adds, taking a sip of the chilled Champagne.

Luca gets a bottle with bath gel and pours it into the streaming warm water. It smells so good, a combination of lavender and lemon. The tub is filled and the bath gel has formed a light foam on top of the water. Luca dims the lights, turns on the jets and some seductive Italian lounge music. They both get into the tub and sit facing each other, legs to the side of each other.

Kataryna leans back and closes her eyes. What a great feeling, this room, this music, this man, she is in seventh heaven now. This can only get better. She feels a certain tingle down there already, anticipating what is coming next. Luca gently strokes her legs while slowly sipping his Champagne. He leans back against the tub giving her his enigmatic smile.

Kataryna decides to up the ante. She parts her legs so both of his are in between hers now. The light foam on top of the water, in addition to the bubbles from the jets, only lets him see her body slightly under the water, but he becomes immediately aroused and moans. "Here we go again."

Kataryna moves her hips up and down and sideways to the rhythm of the music. He attempts to grab her but she quickly moves and crosses her legs.

"You are killing me, Principessa," he murmurs in a seductive voice with his deep dark eyes staring at her.

He relaxes somewhat and lifts the glass to drink when Kataryna opens her legs again and moves deeper into the tub with her upper body.

"Please," he begs, "let me touch you."

"Do not even attempt to move," she commands him seductively moving her knees together and apart again in rhythm.

"This is painful," he murmurs, running his hands through his hair.

"I know but also very exciting."

"I am dying here," he responds, moaning loudly at the same time.

So am I, she thinks, but she is not ready to end this seductive game yet and relieve him and herself of this sweet pain. They stare into each other's eyes. She puts her hand under water and touches him lightly almost causing her to climax again from all the excitement. Luca moans and squirms attempting to touch her. She puts her foot against his chest to make him stay in place. His squirming in the tub makes the foam move so that he now has a direct view of her under water with her legs slightly parted. He explodes into an orgasm, which doesn't seem to end. Kataryna is on the edge of an orgasm when Luca lunges at her legs moving her up over the water and kissing her passionately running his tongue over her and inside of her. She screams out in pleasure and climaxes immediately clutching her hands over her eyes. Luca continues his passionate kissing and probing, until it becomes too intense and she withdraws quickly closing her legs and succumbing to the feeling and the soothing water. He moves over to her side holding her in his arms and kissing her softly.

"I have never experienced anything like this in my entire life, who are you and what are you doing to me?" he whispers in her ear. "This is unreal. I don't know if I am coming or going."

"I prefer you coming," she whispers, and they both start laughing.

After some relaxing moments holding and kissing each other and finishing the Champagne, they get out of the tub. Kataryna dries herself with the bath towel, which has been hanging on a towel warmer. Luca puts a luxurious body lotion on her and she does the same for him. Completely relaxed and exhausted they fall into the comfortable bed and are soon fast asleep.

Kataryna wakes up in the morning reliving last night's events. She is surprised at how she came up with the tantalizing sexual interlude last night in the bathtub. She doesn't quite know where all this came from, but she is intrigued now to continue this exciting adventure. She thinks of her next coup and how to escalate it. Luca has inspired her to go all out and she is ready to please and be pleased.

She looks at Luca who is fast asleep next to her. He seems to have a smile on his face. She kisses him lightly and then gets up making sure not to make any noise. She decides to shower and get ready in the guest suite. In one of the closets she finds a sexy, rather low-cut one-piece lounge suit in red and some extra underwear, which wasn't there yesterday. She gets dressed and looks in the mirror. She likes the red one-piece suit on her. *This girl is on fire*, she thinks, as the song by Alicia Keyes comes to mind. She starts walking towards the breakfast area. A female staff member greets her when she arrives there.

"Buongiorno Signora, what can I do for you?"
"Buongiorno, where is Mariya?" Kataryna asks her.
"Mariya has a day off today. I am Isabella."

"Hi Isabella, I would like to get some tea please. Do you have Rooibos tea by any chance?" Kataryna asks.

"Si Signora, I can offer you a Rooibos tea or lemon verbena," Isabella responds.

"Rooibos is excellent," Kataryna says. "Does Signor Romano like that tea, too?"

"Yes, Signora, it is his favorite, although he usually has coffee in the morning."

Kataryna smiles at her. "He will have the Rooibos tea this morning," she says. "Please also let me have a couple of rolls and a little honey on the side."

Isabella prepares a tray with the tea, rolls and honey on the side.

"Would you like me to serve the tea in the bedroom when it is ready?" she asks.

"No, thank you Isabella, I will take it myself," Kataryna replies sweetly touching Isabella's arm.

"As you wish Signora."

When Kataryna returns to the master bedroom, Luca is sitting up leaning against the headboard.

"Buongiorno, Signor Romano," she greets him smiling seductively, setting the tray on the nightstand next to him.

"Buongiorno, Mariya," he replies facetiously, "you changed quite a bit since yesterday. Why didn't you wake me?"

She laughs and kisses him softly on the mouth. "I figured you needed that sleep. You have been working rather long hours over the past months and you hardly got any sleep the night before because of me."

"Yeah, but I wanted to wake up with you in my bed and give you the proper greeting."

"Did you?" she asks provocatively, "but maybe I have something else in mind."

"You are scaring me, Principessa. Are you planning another hands-off torture?"

"Good things come to those who wait," she counters, slowly pulling the duvet cover downwards.

He grabs the cover quickly to stop her.

"My, my," she murmurs, "aren't we shy this morning."

"Shy I am not," he replies, "but apprehensive of what you have in mind."

"Just relax and enjoy the ride," she whispers in his ear, "or to say it in your words, just go with the flow."

She walks into the bathroom and returns with one of the luxurious bath towels and a hot, wet hand towel. She puts the bath towel on the bed and then makes him lie on it on his stomach. Placing the hot, wet hand towel on his shoulders she starts massaging him.

"I am going to give you an invigorating massage."

Luca, who was already aroused by the sight of her when she walked in, is groaning. "I am ready. Be gentle with me." He tightens his muscles.

"Don't do that," she whispers softly, "try to relax."

"I will do my best," he sighs, "but it is not easy. If I had a choice I would tear off your clothes and make love to you passionately now."

Kataryna kisses his shoulders as she moves her hands to the back of his thighs parting them.

"Yeah, but we are going to do it my way now," she murmurs, enjoying his excitement.

She massages his thighs and then dips her finger into the honey putting it in between his thighs. She softly licks the honey from the inside of his thighs. He becomes agitated and moans. Letting him turn over she faces his erection and applies some honey on it. She slowly takes it off with her lips. He climaxes immediately moving his hips excitedly towards her. *Mission accomplished,* Kataryna thinks, smirking impishly as he pulls her up to him and kisses her passionately.

"Another mind-blowing sexual encounter with you," he says. "The morning started like the evening ended. Now what can I do for you?"

"You are in no position to do much at this very moment," she teases him.

"Oh, I wouldn't say that. I can be very creative. Let me show you."

"Yeah, yeah, yeah," she says laughing, trying to keep his hands away from her. "Mission impossible."

"Where there's a will there's a way," he counters, tearing at the top portion of the suit, trying to get it off her.

Kataryna laughs out loud, kissing his neck and wrapping her legs around him.

Luca looks at her helplessly. "Are you going to help me remove this suit or do I have to cut it off you?"

"You wouldn't dare come close to me with scissors," she says in a warning tone while stopping his hands from tearing the suit off her.

She thoroughly enjoys this sexy game, which arouses her tremendously. He grabs her and puts his head between her legs. Kataryna can't hold back and lets out a scream of pleasure. A knock at the bedroom suite door interrupts their sexy playful moment. Luca grabs his robe and goes to open the door while Kataryna tidies herself up trying to regain control.

"Scusi, scusi, Signor Romano," Isabella says with her hands folded in a prayer-like fashion in front of her. She continues to talk to him in Italian and Kataryna is lost in translation.

"My mother tried to reach me," he explains as he returns to the bed. "She called Isabella for assistance. Must be urgent. I better call her and then get ready for our drive back to Milano."

He kisses her and then picks up the phone to call his mother. He generally puts his phones on silent during the night but due to this morning's seductive events forgot to turn them back on.

"Mamma," he talks into the phone and then continues again in Italian.

Kataryna decides meanwhile to go to the guest suite to get dressed and ready for departure. She still has an all over tingling feeling from their sexual encounter and wishes they had time to stay in bed a little longer. The fact that she is leaving today makes her sad for a moment. Better not think about that now. Admiring the beautiful suits again, she puts them in the garment bag, which came with them. She takes a last look around the room and at the beautiful view of Lake Como. *I really don't want to leave*, she thinks, *this is so difficult*. Her emotions are all over the place.

Luca and Kataryna meet back in the lounge area of the villa.

"I wasn't done with you yet," he says taking her in his arms and kissing her down her neck. "As always you look spectacular. These suits were made for you, I think. No one could wear them better than you."

She looks at him, caressing his upper arms. "Right back at you. And by the way, I wasn't done with you yet, either."

"How about you change your flight and stay another night so we can finish what we started?" he looks at her hopefully.

"I wish I could but another man is waiting for me in Berlin."

Luca stares at her in horror and clutches his chest. "What?"

"Oh no," she quickly continues, laughing, "not that kind of man. I am talking about my father."

"You almost killed me," Luca whispers in her ear holding her tightly. "Please tell me there is no other man anywhere I have to compete with."

"There is no other man and I would have a hard time imagining that there is anyone out there who could compete with you," she whispers back.

"Good answer," he exhales relieved, "let's have something to eat before we leave for Milano."

They sit down to a sumptuous brunch. Luca opens a bottle of Champagne.

"It will be some time until we can be together like this again, so let's enjoy our last few hours," he says. "I am already dreading the farewell at the airport."

"So am I," she admits, "it's going to be really tough."

After their brunch they sit in front of the fireplace finishing their Champagne and kissing passionately, making plans for their reunion in the not too distant future. Neither one of them wants to get up and leave, but they know the time to depart is just a few moments away.

Isabella appears with Kataryna's garment bags. Luca takes them from her. He lets out a deep sigh.

"I am getting into the car with a heavy heart. I hate to see you go."

"I will be back," she says reassuringly, but his face remains serious. He knows it will be quite some time until he sees her again, but he is already planning where and when. Any amount of time will be too long, though.

She nudges him playfully in the side.

"Remember, absence makes the heart grow fonder. I will meanwhile have some time to cook up more intriguing erotic encounters with you. The rewards will be endless."

"Kataryna," he says in a more serious tone now, "for me this is not just some sexual adventure or affair. I am scared of the long distance between us and what is waiting for you in New York."

"A lot of work awaits me in New York," she tries to reassure him. "And in case you are wondering, I will miss you, too. I am just trying to not make it more difficult for us."

He embraces her and she leans into him. When he releases her, he takes her hand and leads her to the car. They drive silently for a while, both in a somber mood. Kataryna takes his hand and holds it in both of hers.

"Do you have any plans for Christmas yet?" he finally asks her.

"That depends on what you want to do," she answers smiling, her mood lightening somewhat at the thought of spending Christmas with Luca.

"Anything that involves you," he says smiling back at her, kissing her hand.

"In that case I suggest you come to New York and spend Christmas with me and my sister and her family."

"I will be there," he answers joyfully.

When they arrive at the hotel in Milan, Kataryna packs her bags and then proceeds to check out. As promised Luca had the two nights they spent at his villa removed from her hotel bill. *Well,* she thinks, *he is a man of his word.* They get back into the car and head towards Malpensa airport.

"Are you sure you can't stay a few more days?" he pleads with her.

"You have no idea how much I would love to stay here with you, but I promised my father that I would stop by for a few days before returning to New York. I hope you understand because I don't get to see him that often."

"Of course, I understand but I hope you don't blame me for trying to keep you here for a few more days. I can't recall ever feeling this strongly about any woman before, but I don't quite know how to deal with you being so far away."

"Luca, I am not jumping for joy either leaving today," she says, "as long as we trust each other we will make it work."

After Kataryna is checked in, they decide to have a quick drink at the airport bar. They sit tightly embraced and kick around some ideas for Christmas. Luca then walks her to the security area where they share a passionate good-bye kiss and long embrace. Before proceeding to the boarding gate, Kataryna turns around to Luca who stands motionless staring after her. She manages a smile, throws him a kiss and then moves on towards the gate. *That was a tough one,* she thinks, breathing in and out deeply, fighting tears. She really doesn't want to leave. This man has rocked her world, but she made a prior commitment to visit her father in Berlin.

THREE

Kataryna's plane arrives on time in Berlin. She picks up her luggage and proceeds to the exit where her father awaits her anxiously. As usual, he hands her a bouquet of red roses as a welcome token.

"Hello Papa," she says, kissing him on both cheeks. "How are you?"

"I am okay. How about you?"

"Pretty good. I am glad you are doing well."

He takes her luggage and they head towards his car. After stowing her luggage in the trunk they get into the Mercedes. He shivers, "this damned cold weather, I can't stand it."

"Neither can I," she says, "I hope the heat is on high in the house."

"You better believe it."

After a 30-minute drive they arrive at her father's home, which is located in one of Berlin's wealthier suburbs. Kataryna unpacks a few of her clothes and toiletries and then meets her father in the living room.

"What would you like to do for dinner?" he asks her.

She shrugs her shoulders. "I don't know. Shall we cook something or go out?"

They decide to eat in and catch up that evening, talking about Kataryna's trip and work.

"Let's have an after-dinner drink," her father suggests. "I need to discuss something with you if you are not too tired."

"I am fine," she responds. "What would you like to discuss?"

He opens a bottle of red wine and pours a glass for each of them. Kataryna senses some nervousness in him.

"I am not getting any younger and life is uncertain," he starts. "I think it is time I tell you that you have a brother."

"What?" Kataryna screams out. "Are you serious or is this one of your bad jokes you like to make? Does this mean you have an illegitimate child, which Mom and us never knew about?"

"Oh no, this is a child your mother delivered and it is your real brother," he confesses. "Remember when you were kids and Mom was pregnant? We told you girls at that time that Mom had lost the baby. Well, actually she didn't lose the baby. It was born prematurely but survived. Due to our financial situation at that time we had decided that the child would be given up for adoption. I was in the middle of building up a new business when your mother got pregnant. It was more your mother's decision than mine. I would have liked to keep the child, especially when I found out it was a boy because I always wanted a son."

"I am in shock," Kataryna states. "How did you manage to keep this from us for so long?"

"We didn't want you to know at the time. You were too young to understand this kind of decision and later on we decided it would be best if we didn't bring this up with you and your sister."

"Well, Papa," Kataryna starts talking again after the initial shock. "I don't think it was just the financial situation which made Mom decide to give up the child. Your marriage wasn't the happiest one and Mom was glad that Aleksandra and I were old enough to take care of ourselves somewhat. She couldn't have handled the stress of raising another child with you."

"What stress?" he asks. "I worked very hard to take care of our family and to provide what you needed while building up my business."

"That may be the case," Kataryna says sternly, "but Mom's stress was emotional in nature because you were very tough and intolerant at that time. I recall many times when Mom and us girls were sitting in the kitchen crying, because you had one of your temper tantrums. We were witness to your frequent heavy arguments with Mom and we always felt sorry for her and us when you got this way. I recall vividly that we were glad when we moved out and took Mom with us. We couldn't bear to leave her alone with you in that situation. You were sheer terror at times and she was such a loving, patient and beautiful woman. She did not deserve this kind of treatment ever."

Kataryna's voice cracks and tears shoot to her eyes as she continues. "I am just glad that she moved in with us then and lived the rest of her life the way she wanted to."

"I had a tough life then," he tries to justify his past behavior. "I tried to build up several businesses so that you kids and your mother would have a good life."

"I don't doubt that and we are grateful for everything you did for us," Kataryna gives back, "but there was no reason to terrorize us the way you did sometimes. Anyway, the past is the past. We have forgiven you so let's just not rehash this because it is getting to me just thinking about it. I want to go back to our lost brother. What else can you tell me about the adoption? Did you know or meet the adoptive parents?"

"I don't know much just that he was adopted by a nice, well-off couple," he answers. "After all, this is over 30 years ago."

"Didn't you ever want to know what your son looked like and what became of him?"

"Yes, of course, there were times when I could hardly think of anything else. However, the couple that adopted him wanted to stay anonymous. I hope that he is well, happy and successful."

Kataryna jumps out of her seat and takes her father by the shoulders. "Papa, we have to find him," she says with tears in her eyes. "I want to meet and have a relationship with my brother. I can't let this go now that you have told me about him."

Her father is also in tears now. He can't believe that she wants to take on such a huge task, especially since they don't have that much information to go by. Kataryna gets her notepad and writes down all the facts she can get from her father. Tomorrow she will call the family lawyer to help her with the legal matters. She is totally excited about her new mission and can't wait to tell her sister the astonishing news. She pours herself another glass of red wine, wipes the tears off her face and picks up the phone. It is 6:30 p.m., in New York and Aleksandra should be home.

After the third ring, Aleksandra answers the call.

"Aleksandra," Kataryna yells into the phone, "how are you?"

"I am fine," her sister responds, sensing something is up, "you sound excited, your acquisition deal must be going very well."

"It's not the deal," Kataryna responds, "although that is quite exciting, too. You have no idea what I just found out. Please sit down before I tell you what our father just came out with."

"Oh, God, this must be bad news when you are calling this late. It is 12:30 a.m. in Germany. I thought you might be sleeping by now, preparing for the onslaught of work coming your way. This deal has consumed you the last few weeks," Aleksandra says with anticipation of what's to come.

"Are you sitting down" Kataryna asks her sister.

"Yes, yes, I am sitting, now spill the beans already before I die of curiosity," Aleksandra yells.

"I honestly don't know where to begin, so here it goes. Aleksa, we have a brother, a real brother," Kataryna screams into the phone while she glances at her father whose eyes are still wet.

"What? How much have you two been drinking?" Aleksandra shouts back at her. "What is going on over there?"

Kataryna's voice mellows as she softly responds, trying to hold back tears.

"No, we are not drunk. Our father just told me that we have a brother. Remember when we were kids and Mom was pregnant? Well, Papa just admitted that the baby was born prematurely but did not die, as they told us at the time. He was adopted by an affluent couple."

Aleksandra is as stunned as Kataryna was when she first heard that out of her father's mouth.

"Hey, are you still there?" Kataryna yells into the phone.

"Yes, I am here but I can't believe it. I will have to process this first. Is he sure that the boy survived? You have to press him for more information."

"Of course, you are right," Kataryna agrees, "but it looks like this is true, based on the information I got from him so far. However, it won't be easy to find this man. This was over 30 years ago and God knows what kind of paperwork they kept here at that time for adoptions. But we have to try. In any event, I will talk to a lawyer tomorrow to help us with the search and legal requirements. I hope you are on board with this since we don't know what we will find or what kind of hornets' nest we are stirring up. This could turn out to be really good or even bad. But I can't imagine not trying. We will be careful and let the lawyer handle it before we reveal our identities."

"OK," Aleksandra agrees, "but let's be really careful. It's a crazy world out there and we don't know how he grew up and what his situation is today. What do we do if we find him and he is some drug addict, criminal or even a serial killer?"

"Oh, come on now Aleksa," Kataryna throws back at her. "Let's not start out with negative feelings, otherwise we may as well forget about it immediately. Think positive. I wonder what he looks like," she continues. "I hope he is handsome. I always knew there was something missing in my life. I just couldn't put my finger on it so far. I guess the mystery has been solved now."

"Keep me posted after your meeting with the lawyer," Aleksandra says, "I am also getting excited now. Hopefully he will be as excited as we are when we find him. What if he turns us away? Oh God, have you thought about that?"

"Stop it Aleksa," Kataryna yells back, "you are entering the negative zone again. You are usually so adventurous and now you are acting this way. Life is short; we must hurry up and find this guy. Anyway, have a good evening. I am exhausted and have to go to sleep now. Papa wants to talk to you before we hang up."

She hands the phone to her father and starts getting ready for bed. Tomorrow will be a long day and she has to be rested for that. In addition, she still needs to do major work on the acquisition deal with the Italian company. Her Italian business partner turned into her lover and has captured her in a huge way. She hates to admit it, but can't deny it any longer after the night they had.

What happened to my belief never to mix business with pleasure, she thinks? Hopefully this doesn't turn into a disaster. This acquisition deal is important and she has to focus on that now to get it closed. There are other interested parties out there. Luca told her so far he was impressed with the other parties, but said he didn't have the same rapport with the other principals. Well, maybe that's because the other three are men? She needs to make sure that it stays this way. Oh wow, so many things to juggle tomorrow and the next months to come.

Kataryna wakes up around 7 a.m. She tries to go back to sleep but finds herself rather restless. Her first thought is Luca. She relives the dinner at Villa D'Este and the nights in his villa. All kinds of feelings come over her. She doesn't know how to deal with these feelings yet.

She thinks about her past marriage, a subsequent relationship and the engagement she broke up about six months ago. All three relationships had started out well, but didn't last. Was it her fault? Was she too demanding, impatient or expecting too much? Well, after the childhood she had, witnessing her parents' unhappy marriage, she had vowed to never stay with a man if she felt he was not the right one. Her mother had endured her unhappy marriage for a long time because she had been afraid to leave her father with two children. Kataryna swore she would never put herself in this position. She wanted to have a good career and become financially independent, so she would never be forced to stay with a man if she didn't want to. Thank God she never experienced any trauma in her marriage like her mother, but there were certain situations she didn't care for and one day the romance was gone somehow. She was bored and was well aware that she was looking at other men and enjoying flirtatious encounters here and there without committing adultery. After her divorce, she met a man she fell in love with head over heels. They had a hot and passionate relationship and eventually moved in together. Yes, it was perfect in the beginning and she enjoyed that life immensely. It was an immediate and strong mutual attraction. They always joked that if their feelings and attraction for each other could be bottled and sold, they would be very wealthy. Unfortunately this didn't last, either. Although they loved each other and fitted perfectly together, he gradually developed jealous tendencies. They got worse over time, even though he had absolutely no reason to be jealous. Kataryna was in love and devoted to him. She didn't look at other men and didn't flirt with anyone, although she had plenty of opportunities. He tried to control her and became possessive. They would argue over her wanting to go out and have a drink or two with colleagues after work occasionally, or if she attended the annual office holiday parties, which spouses and significant others were not invited to. During the final stages she sensed danger. One night after she told him that she would leave him if this jealousy didn't stop, he had warned her: "If I can't have you no one will." Soon after, his jealousy and actions escalated. That was the end of that turbulent relationship.

A few years ago, she had met a nice man and they almost became engaged after a year of dating. However, she never felt the fire she had felt in her prior relationship. As time went on she realized that there was no passion and never would be, so she ended the relationship. He was devastated and struggling with depression, but she convinced him that they were not meant for each other and helped him through it. And now Luca has ignited her passion like no one before, she has to admit. She hadn't felt that kind of excitement for anyone before. It actually had become apparent to her already, during the phone and video conferences with him, over the past three months that he was special. She likes everything about him, his voice, his choice of words and the way he says them with that sexy Italian accent; and last but not least, his looks, elegance and charismatic personality. All this in the middle of a huge business transaction. Ideally she had wanted to close the acquisition transaction first before embarking on a romantic adventure with Luca. *The best-laid plans don't always work out that way*, she reminds herself. And what about the long distance between them? Love via Face Time? Ha-ha, she has to laugh at that thought, but the idea is intriguing.

Her iPhone rings. She picks it up immediately.

"Buongiorno, Principessa, I miss you. I hope you miss me, too," she hears Luca saying.

"Guten Morgen, Prince Charming, how nice of you to call. Of course, I miss you. What can I do for you?"

"Oh, I'd rather not answer this question right now," he replies with a sexy undertone.

"Okay," she says, "good answer. What's up?"

He starts laughing out loud, and so does she, realizing that this might be equally hard for him to answer. When they compose themselves she rephrases her question.

"Let me try this again. Are you just calling to say hello or do you have any news regarding the deal?"

"I really just wanted to hear your voice and confirm that I will come to New York for Christmas."

"I can't wait to see you again. I am really looking forward to your visit," she responds softly. "We should make some plans before you get to New York."

"As long as I am in your company I am interested in whatever you choose. Have you made any plans for us for Christmas Eve and Christmas Day yet?"

"Other than Christmas Eve at my sister's, I have not made any further plans for us yet."

"That sounds very nice. Please tell your sister I will be there."

"I shall do so right away. We will have the traditional German Christmas goose with all the trimmings. My sister is an excellent cook."

"Sounds amazing, I can't wait. Have a beautiful day. I wish I could be in Berlin with you. Your departure yesterday was tough. I was in a depressed mood for the rest of the day and night."

"You seem to have recovered," she softly speaks into the phone.

"Only in this moment because I am talking to you," he explains. "Enjoy the visit with your father. Hey, how about a Face Time call later on so I can see you?" he asks excitedly.

Kataryna laughs out loud. "Believe it or not, the same thought came to me earlier this morning, but with a twist."

"What's the twist?"

"I will tell you later, otherwise we may have an X-rated conversation this early in the morning."

"Uh, sounds promising. I can't wait to hear more. Ciao bella."

"Ciao bello," she ends the call.

Kataryna is in a daze, clutching her phone to her chest. She leans back against the pillows and closes her eyes getting all excited and wishing Luca were here with her now. Her feelings are going overboard so she quickly rises to take a shower in an attempt to keep her sexual attraction for him at bay for now. She has to keep busy and Christmas is not that far away. There are so many things for her to deal with, including finding her brother and hopefully completing the acquisition deal. But most important is spending more time with Luca. How typical of her life, everything is usually coming at her at the same time.

Kataryna has prepared breakfast and is waiting for her father to join her. Luca enters her mind again and she becomes all hot and bothered. *Damn,* she thinks, this is *just what I wanted to avoid but it's too late now. He is just too irresistible.*

"Guten Morgen," Kataryna's father says as he walks towards the breakfast table, interrupting her intimate thoughts.
"Guten Morgen, Papa," she responds, "did you sleep well?"
"Yes, I did," he answers. "What do you want to do first today?"
"I am going to call our lawyer to see if he can help us find your son, my brother or if he can recommend someone. After lunch I would like to go visit Mom's grave. We can leave when I come back from lunch with my girlfriend Nadia."
"OK. I have to run an errand myself around noon. We can meet back here again then."

After breakfast Kataryna picks up the phone to call Norbert Bergmann, the family lawyer. She explains the situation to him.
"I will do some initial research," he says "but I am afraid I am going to have to involve another legal specialist. This will take some time and there are no guarantees that we will find your brother. It could be quite costly depending on how much time we will have to spend and we may hit a dead-end at some point. Please tell your father we need as much information as he can remember. I will check to see if we can locate a birth certificate for this boy and we'll go from there. I will be in touch with your father in the next few days with some questions. How long will you be in Berlin?"

"I am planning to leave on Saturday," Kataryna replies. "Let's speak when I am back in New York to see if you have come up with anything you can work with. Why don't I email you my contact details, so you can get in touch with me for periodic updates?"

As she hangs up the phone, her cell phone rings. She looks at the screen but doesn't recognize the number. It is an Italian phone number. Kataryna accepts the call.

"Hello, Kataryna Taylor speaking."

At first there is a moment of silence, and then a male voice comes on.

"Hello beautiful, how are you doing? How is New York?"

"Who is this?" Kataryna asks.

"You don't recognize my voice? I am crushed," the man says in a joking tone.

"I am sorry. Should I?"

"This is Roberto Silvestri."

"Oh, hello, Roberto. You sound different. To answer your question, I am not in New York, so I wouldn't know what's going on over there right now."

She has a strange feeling and doesn't know what else to say.

"If you are not in New York," he says, "where are you hiding?"

"I am in Berlin, visiting family."

"When are you going back to New York?" he wants to know.

"Why are you asking?"

"Believe it or not, I am on my way to Berlin on a business matter. I have some additional material regarding NatMedica, which I would like to go over with you. Can we meet for dinner?"

"Well, it is kind of tight but if it is important we can meet for a quick dinner. I just can't stay out too long," she explains.

"Excellent. I will call you with the details after I arrive. Would 7:30 p.m. be good to meet for dinner?"

"Yes, that should work," she answers. "Talk to you later."

Looks like my days here will be even busier after that phone call, she thinks, *but as a potential future shareholder I have to have open communication lines with the management.*

Kataryna decides to call Luca to ask him if he knew what new material Roberto might have to present.

"Ciao Principessa," Luca greets her. "What a pleasant surprise. I really miss you and it is getting worse by the minute."

"I miss you, too. I am actually calling to see if you can shed some light on something. Roberto just called me and arranged a dinner meeting with me here in Berlin. He said he had some new material to go over with me regarding the acquisition deal. I am sure you must know what the new material is about."

"What?" she hears him yell into the phone. "Roberto is going to Berlin to meet you for dinner? I am speechless. There is no new material that I know of and if there was I should see and review it first before it is made public. What the heck is he up to?"

Kataryna is stunned for a moment.

"He didn't run it by you?" she asks totally surprised.

"No, he didn't say a word to me," Luca responds somewhat calmer. "I am going to call him to see what this is all about."

"That is kind of strange. Let me know what he has to say."

"I have to make one other important call first, but afterwards I will try to get him on the phone and straighten this out."

"OK, thank you darling. I guess we will speak a little later then?"

"I will call you as soon as I have spoken to him. I will probably not tell him that you called me to enquire about the so-called new material. Let's see what he has to say."

F O U R

Luca can't believe that Roberto had the audacity to call Kataryna and arrange to meet her in Berlin. And what about the new material he wants to discuss with Kataryna? He should run that by the existing shareholders first. Luca is not pleased with Roberto's actions. He has to calm down first before he calls him and lays down the law, so to speak. Fortunately Kataryna didn't notice how much it disturbed him. He hid it well, he believes. He is pretty sure that Roberto's motivation to meet her in Berlin is more personal than business. Deep down inside he can't blame Roberto. Kataryna is a very attractive, smart and intriguing woman, a winning combination. She attracts men without even trying and doesn't seem to realize how alluring she is. It all comes naturally to her. Since their night together in his villa, Luca is head over heels in love. He hasn't felt this strongly about anyone before and can't wait to be with Kataryna again to deepen his relationship with her. And now he has to deal with this unfortunate situation involving Roberto. Kataryna did the right thing calling him and telling him about Roberto's plan to meet her in Berlin.

Luca has known Roberto for a long time and has always respected him professionally. He never got involved in his personal life very much, but had heard a couple of stories involving women. One incident involved one of Roberto's female colleagues a couple of years ago. She had reported him to the board because of unwanted sexual advances he apparently had made towards her, which didn't stop even after she had asked him to refrain from asking her out and constantly commenting on how sexy she looked. It got pretty ugly because Roberto allegedly even touched her inappropriately during a company Christmas party. According to the employee, Roberto had put his arm around her shoulders and then put his hand deep down inside her low-cut dress squeezing her breasts and whispering something into her ear. Everyone had blamed too much alcohol for this misstep at that time. Eventually the employee left the company but not without making a big deal out of it. Luca was convinced at that time that all she wanted was money. They made an agreement with her for a certain amount. The agreement contained a gag order stating that neither party could talk about the contents of the agreement. Roberto's explanation for the incident was that she had trapped him into this behavior and that it was actually she who had pursued him for some time. When he refused to have a relationship with her she had turned the tables and accused him of unwanted sexual advances. Roberto insisted that before the Christmas party had started, she had walked into his office and tried to seduce him by exposing her breasts. He tried to let her down easy and was saved when his assistant came into his office to bring him his messages. Later on during the party, after he had had a couple of drinks, she gave him a sexy look. That is when he put his arm around her shoulders and his hand on her breasts whispering in her ear, "make sure you keep these covered."

Luca had accepted Roberto's explanation at the time. He had heard from other men that this particular female employee was a loose cannon and had told other employees that she was totally in love with Roberto. She was determined to have a relationship with him despite the fact that he was married. Luca and Roberto both agreed that Roberto could have handled this situation more professionally in order not to put him and the company at risk.

After the meeting with Kataryna in Bellagio, Luca has to face the fact that Roberto can be quite aggressive when he goes after a woman he wants. The way he behaved around Kataryna at the dinner in Bellagio was an indication that he has no qualms about pursuing what he wants, even at the risk of appearing unprofessional. Kataryna had stood her ground that evening, which should have given Roberto a signal that she is not interested in getting to know him on a more personal basis. How could he have missed that, unless his pride wouldn't allow him to give up that easily? Regardless, Luca is aware he has to step in now to make sure that Roberto understands that he cannot pursue Kataryna any further. In addition, Kataryna's private equity company could end up being the new shareholder of NatMedica where Roberto holds the position of CEO.

Luca recalls that the female employee incident involving Roberto was not mentioned in the company's dossier mainly because it was several years ago; and it had been settled without any public knowledge and no further repercussions were expected at this stage. It would also have put a flaw on the CEO and there were no further incidents like this since then. He is weighing the idea of communicating it to Kataryna when he calls her back just to be on the safe side, but he quickly dismisses the idea because they signed an agreement with the employee so neither one of them can talk about it.

Luca gets ready to make the call to Roberto. He picks up the phone and dials his number.

"Pronto," he hears Roberto say at the other end.

"Ciao Roberto," Luca greets him in a friendly tone. "I would like to discuss something with you over lunch or dinner today. Are you available?"

"Can you give me a hint about what it is you want to discuss?" Roberto asks equally friendly.

"I would prefer to wait until we meet," Luca responds.

"I am afraid it will have to wait until I am back from my trip," Roberto says.

"What trip?" Luca asks anxiously.

"I am on my way to Germany," Roberto responds casually.

"I see. Is this business or pleasure?" Luca enquires.

"A little bit of both," Roberto replies.

"Anything I should know about?" Luca probes further, impatiently.

"I will fill you in when I am back. So when do you want to get together?"

"Call me when you are back from Germany," Luca instructs him.

"Will do."

Luca decided not to confront Roberto on the phone. However, he is more than concerned that Roberto didn't mention his meeting with Kataryna and suspects a personal agenda. He sends Kataryna an email to her business address since this is the only email address he has for her. He will get her private email address later so they can communicate more freely in the future.

From: Luca Romano
  To: Kataryna Taylor
Subject: Meeting in Berlin

Kataryna,
I spoke to Roberto. He told me that he is on his way to Germany, but did not mention that he would meet with you for dinner. I will have a chat with him when he is back in Milan.
Looking forward to speaking with you later.
Luca Romano
Member of the Managing Board
RVLCP, S.p.A.
Milan, Italy

Kataryna's phone pings alerting her that she has received an email message. She reads the message and then hits the reply button to respond:

From: Kataryna Taylor
  To: Luca Romano
Subject: Meeting in Berlin

Luca,

Thank you for keeping me updated on this. I will let you know how the dinner went and what additional material he presented. Also, in the spirit of full disclosure, I will have to tell Stephen about our "situation". I hope you are OK with that?

Ciao,
Kataryna

Kataryna Taylor
Managing Partner
Adryana Investments, LLP
New York, New York

A few minutes later she gets an email reply from Luca.

From: Luca Romano
  To: Kataryna Taylor
Subject: Disclosure

Yes, of course. Feel free to disclose all. Call you later.
Ciao,
Luca

Kataryna dials Stephen's number. He picks up the call.

"Hi there, Missy how goes it? How is Berlin? I was wondering when you would call me. I received the UPS package with the latest info memorandum."

"I am well, Stephen," Kataryna answers a little anxiously. "I have a lot to discuss with you. But why don't you go first."

"Well, I think the company looks real good so far. I spoke briefly with our analyst Clarissa and the due diligence guys last night. While Clarissa didn't find any negative facts yet on the company itself, she voiced some concern over the fact that it is an Italian company and Italy is one of the European Union countries, which are weak and may get weaker, etc. She said she couldn't foresee what would happen if anything went wrong with the Euro over there. So she is not willing to put her approval on it at the moment without doing further due diligence. She will speak to some economists and other qualified people to see what they have to say about the European situation. Can we can stall this a bit?"

"I understand her concern and have thought about it myself," Kataryna responds "but as a mitigant I would offer the fact that the company is not dependent on sales in Italy, since it exports its biomedical products all over the world. I don't know how fast the other interested parties will move, but I believe that the two European companies interested in this opportunity are thinking about this fact, too. One is German and the other one is Swiss. I wish I knew their thoughts on this. So, what do you want to do?"

"Don't know yet," he says, "but you make a good point. Let's see what Clarissa comes up with. We will sit down and discuss it again when you are back in New York. You are leaving Berlin on Saturday, right?"

"Yes, that's the plan" she responds.

"So, what did you want to discuss with me or was that it?" Stephen asks.

"For starters, the CEO and CFO of NatMedica asked if we would consider an equity portion of about five to ten percent for them. The rest can wait. Let's see what Clarissa has to say. We can sit down with her when I am back in the office on Monday, unless there are further developments before Monday in which case we can meet over the weekend."

"Sounds like a good plan. Have a safe flight back and get some rest, you deserve it."

Kataryna ends the call. "OK, thanks Stephen, so long."

Time to get out of the house and have lunch, she thinks, as she dials her girlfriend's number.

"Hallo," she hears her girlfriend Nadia answering the phone.

"Hallo Nadia, when and where are we meeting for lunch? Can't wait to see you. I have a lot to tell you."

"Super," Nadia responds. "I am happy to get out and hear about your interesting life, mine is soooo boring. I found a great new restaurant not too far from us. It is called Trattoria Romano. Let's meet there in half an hour."

Kataryna bursts out laughing.

"What did I say that was so funny?" Nadia asks, "fill me in. I also want to have a good laugh."

"You are going to have to wait for another half hour or so," Kataryna says, "this I have to tell you when I see you. We can crack up together then."

"OK, then let's hurry up and meet fast. I can sense this is going to be really good. Actually, why don't I pick you up?"

"That would be great. See you in a few."

Kataryna looks at her watch. It is shortly before 1 p.m. She wonders if Roberto is in Berlin already. He hasn't called or emailed yet with the restaurant details. She is somewhat anxious about this ad hoc meeting. Hopefully the lunch with Nadia will distract her from that for a while. She grabs her bag and coat before heading towards the door, waving good-bye to her father. Nadia arrives as she exits the house. They run towards each other and hug tightly.

"So good to see you again. I missed you," Nadia cheers, "when you are here it is always like a breath of fresh air."

"Yes, it's been way too long," Kataryna responds.

They get into Nadia's Audi and start driving to the restaurant. Nadia looks at Kataryna as they stop at a traffic light.

"Wow, you look great," she says in an admiring tone, "how do you do that with all the long working hours you keep?"

"Well, I might work long hours, but I also take time out to relax and sleep when I can. I go to the spa regularly to have a relaxing massage and some other treatments and I try to eat healthy food, but I don't think that is it," Kataryna continues smiling mysteriously. "I think I am crazy in love."

"Really? This must be something brand new," Nadia asks curiously. "Tell me more. You know my life is so boring. I always live vicariously through you."

"Nice restaurant," Kataryna says, looking around, when they arrive and are seated at their table.

"Oh, yeah, it is. We have been here a couple of times. Each time the food was fabulous and we also like the ambience here. The bar is hopping in the evening and full of interesting people," Nadia explains excitedly.

"Who do you mean by we?" Kataryna asks, "you and your husband?"

"No, me and a couple of girlfriends. My husband is getting more boring each year and just wants to stay home. He acts as if he is an old man sometimes, but he is only 45 years old. I don't know what is going on with him but I am tired of it. I am contemplating moving out and divorcing him."

"Oh dear," Kataryna cuts in, "he is such a nice man. Maybe he needs a boost of testosterone. You know that there are bio-identical hormone creams available now. Actually the company my firm is bidding for is involved in these types of natural products. Why don't you send him to the doctor to have his testosterone levels checked? It may do the trick."

"Thanks for the advice. I will mention it to him. Let's see what he does with that. Anyway, I met a charming man here the other evening. We have a date Friday night."

Kataryna is stunned. "Wow, you are moving on. Are you sure about this?"

"Yes, absolutely, there are no ifs or buts about it. I have warned my husband many times that I would end our marriage if things don't change, but he doesn't seem to care. He made some lame attempts but nothing really effective, which would change my mind. Enough of me now, let's hear your love story. You said you might be crazy in love. Who is the guy that can excite you like this? I know you are soo picky when it comes to men."

"He is a managing board member of a privately held Italian holding company, which is divesting one of its companies. Stephen and I are interested in this target. His name is Luca. He owns the holding company together with his family--father, mother and two sisters. I have known him for about three months. We had several video conferences and phone calls in connection with the deal I am working on. A couple of days ago I went to Milan to meet with him and the company executives for further due diligence meetings. We went out for dinner the first night I was over there and I ended up staying overnight in his villa located at Lake Como. I stayed in one of the guest rooms, of course, and other than some suggestive banter nothing happened that night. The moment we met we had a strong attraction for each other, but suppressed it at least for the first 24 hours or so. On the second night, when we came back from the business meeting, we had a nightcap in his villa by the fireplace. I had fully intended to sleep in the guest suite again, but then he started kissing me and I went right with it. He is too irresistible. He is so good-looking and has this captivating personality. But listen to this. We had a hot sexual interlude, but didn't actually have intercourse. I guess both of us were so excited that we exploded by merely touching and kissing. After that we went to his master bedroom suite and before going to bed decided on a Jacuzzi bath together. You have to see that bathroom, Nadia. It is out of this world. Sitting in that tub, sipping Champagne and listening to the erotic lounge music alone can get you going, but having this man in there with you was the ultimate experience in sexual excitement. I came up with moves that I never thought of before. I created a very sexy scenario in the water. He just didn't have a chance. Well, you can imagine what happened next. Again, we did not make it to have actual intercourse, but it was the most exhilarating experience and I can't wait to play more exciting sensual games with him. Just telling you about it is almost getting me going again. Oh, I am really into this man."

Nadia is staring at Kataryna with wide eyes and is totally speechless for a moment. She takes a large sip of the red wine they had ordered.

"I am jealous. I want this, too," she finally murmurs. "You have no idea how lucky you are to have had such an experience. I don't think I ever was turned on like that by anyone in my entire life, but now that I have heard this and can vividly imagine it, I want to rip off the clothes of the next good-looking man who walks in here."

Kataryna giggles. "And here is why I was laughing so hard on the phone earlier. His last name is Romano. So when you said we are going to this great restaurant called Trattoria Romano, I lost it."

They both start laughing uncontrollably with tears running down their cheeks when the waiter comes to the table to take their order. He looks at them with a raised eyebrow.

"Ladies," he says, "are you crying because we ran out of the salmon on the menu?"

Now all three of them are cracking up laughing.

"Are you ready to order?" he asks, still chuckling.

"Yes, yes," they answer quickly, "let's order before we drink the entire bottle of wine on an empty stomach."

They order the homemade pasta with shrimps and a seafood salad as an appetizer.

"Salute," Kataryna toasts as she raises her glass and Nadia follows her.

"There is something else I have to tell you," Kataryna continues.

"What? There is more of that?" Nadia shrieks.

"As if all this wasn't enough for me to digest, the CEO of the company we are pursuing to acquire kind of made a pass at me right in front of Luca, which didn't go over well with Luca, although at that point we weren't intimate yet. There were some tense moments between those two. I ignored it and managed to prevent a potential blow-up. However, this morning this CEO named Roberto called me to arrange a meeting with me in Berlin for dinner. He said he had additional material he wanted to discuss with me in connection with the acquisition deal. I am going to meet him for dinner tonight. I am not sure what to make of it because he didn't tell Luca about it. So I called Luca to tell him about Roberto's dinner invitation and that he apparently has new material to present. Luca had never heard about any new material and was not happy about these developments. He will be meeting with Roberto after he returns from Berlin to tell him that we have started an intimate relationship."

"Oh my goodness," Nadia says. "I can't believe it. There is a lot going on in your life. What kind of person is this Roberto? He is probably unattractive because these are the bold ones. They think they have nothing to lose anyway."

"Oh no, au contraire," Kataryna responds quickly. "He is quite attractive, about 45 years old, great hair, deep dark brown, almost black, big brown eyes, athletic build, well-dressed and very successful. He's a brilliant CEO and directly responsible for the success of this company. I am not sure about his personality. He was a little too bold, too in-your-face right away when we met for the first time in Bellagio, which usually translates into womanizer. I definitely prefer Luca to him but they are both smoking hot. I can imagine a lot of women throwing themselves at Roberto. So he hopefully won't be too bummed out that he cannot pursue me."

"I guess we will see, but in my experience men always want to chase what they can't have," Nadia murmurs. "Hey, I would like to meet this smoking hot man. Maybe you could introduce him to me?" Nadia asks with a huge smile.

"Are you serious?" Kataryna asks.

"Why not, I always wanted to have a smoking hot man, and this may just be the cure for my boredom."

"Yeah, but I don't really know him that well and he might be a Casanova type, so to speak. Let's see how things develop," Kataryna closes the subject.

Kataryna looks at her watch. Wow, it is 3 p.m., time flies. She decides to call her father and have him pick her up from the restaurant to save time. Nadia calls the waiter to get the check and hands him her credit card.

"Oh no," Kataryna yells out, "this is on me." She quickly pulls out her credit card.

"Thank you, sweetie," Nadia says, "but I really wanted to treat you today because you always pay when we get together."

"Let's just do it my way," Kataryna insists, "and by the way, when are you coming to New York to visit me?"

"I don't have definite plans yet, so let's play it by ear. Maybe I'll visit when Roberto comes to New York. Ha-ha."

Kataryna shakes her head and smirks as they leave the restaurant. *Oh boy,* she thinks, *Nadia is going off the deep end here.* They hug and say their good-byes, vowing not to let so much time pass before they see each other again.

Kataryna stands at her mother's grave and puts down the flower arrangement she bought.

"Mom, I miss you so much," she whispers, her voice cracking and tears in her eyes. "If you only knew all the things that are happening here. I would give anything just to be able to hug you again and tell you how much I love you. Your sudden death has taught me how precious and unpredictable life can be and to enjoy every moment as if it were your last."

What a day, Kataryna is thinking, as she leaves the cemetery. First the fun lunch with Nadia; then the somber and sad moment at her mother's grave; and tonight the ambiguous dinner with Roberto. *What is this guy up to,* she wonders? These are moments when she wants to go into a deep trance to prepare her for whatever is still to come in her life.

It is 4:30 p.m. when she gets into her father's car. She checks her phone to see if Roberto called with the meeting place. There are two missed calls. One is from Roberto. Kataryna calls him back.

"Ciao bella," he greets her. "I just sent you an email with the restaurant details. I am looking forward to seeing you there at 7:30 p.m."

"Thank you Roberto, I will see you then."

FIVE

Kataryna arrives at the chic Italian restaurant located on Friedrichstrasse at 7:35 p.m. Roberto, who had been waiting at the bar already, rushes towards her with open arms.

"You look absolutely fantastic," he says, hugging and kissing her on both cheeks. "Would you like to have a drink at the bar before dinner?
"No, thanks. I can't stay that long."

The hostess shows them to their table, which is pretty secluded.

"Beautiful restaurant," Kataryna states, "how did you find this one? Do you come here often?"
"No, I haven't been to Berlin in a while," he answers. "But I have a list of the latest 'in' restaurants in Berlin, and a good friend of mine highly recommended this one. I thought you would like it."
"Great choice," Kataryna says, "I am sure the food here is fabulous, too."

Roberto orders a bottle of red wine and a selection of appetizers for the table. The waiter fills the glasses after Roberto tasted and approved his choice.
He raises his glass and makes a toast. "Here is to a nice evening."
They clink their glasses and take a sip of the excellent wine.

"You said you would bring some additional material," Kataryna starts the conversation. "I am curious, what else you have to present."
"All in good time," Roberto responds," let's have some wine and food first. I am so happy you made time to have dinner with me."

He starts talking about his daughter Verena and how much she likes New York and shows her a photo of Verena on his cell phone.

"What a beautiful young woman," Kataryna says. "Is she still studying or does she have a job already?"

"She wants to study business and finance," he replies. "I was thinking of asking you if you might have a trainee/internship position for her in New York in the near future, so she can see how the financial service industry works. I want her to stay focused on that."

"I guess we can talk about that in the future," Kataryna responds. He takes her hand in his and kisses it.

"Thank you, for considering that. Do you have any children?" he asks her, still holding her hand.

"No, I don't." She gently pulls her hand out of his. "I never took time out from my career for that."

"You were never married?" he goes further into that subject.

"Yes, I was, but I didn't want to bring a child into this situation and my career was taking off at that time, too. The marriage didn't last anyhow."

He looks at her intensely. "You didn't want to get married again after your divorce?"

"It's not that I consciously decided never to get married again. I just never met the right man to want to do it again and I don't settle," she replies.

"Kataryna," he starts out, taking her hand in his again, "since ever we met in Bellagio, I couldn't stop thinking about you. I have never felt so strongly about any woman. So, if the situation was right, would you marry me?"

"What?" Kataryna yells out, laughing, "you can't be serious. You don't even know me or what I am like in my personal life. I could be a total witch."

"I would love to be bewitched by you," he says, staring deep into her blue eyes. "And to answer your question, yes, I am completely serious. I have never been more serious in my life. I would marry you tonight if it was possible." He touches her face and gently caresses her cheek.

Kataryna starts laughing nervously.

"Whoa, Roberto, let's take this down a couple of notches. I am flattered that you think of me in that regard, but this is not appropriate. I met you here for business reasons and not to start a romantic relationship. You really caught me off guard here and I am pretty uncomfortable right about now."

"I am sorry," he offers "but I wanted you to know how I feel about you. You don't have to give me an answer tonight. I understand that you need to get to know me a little better before you can answer that question. So, I have an idea. How about if I come to New York for a few weeks, we can spend some time together and get to know each other better?"

Kataryna is speechless. She has no idea how to respond to this. She is contemplating telling him about her intimate relationship with Luca, but decides against it. It would only put more salt into his wounds. She wants to let him down gently. This can't be easy for him.

"Roberto," she says, "I am seeing someone. I can't have this kind of conversation with you."

"Is it serious?"

"It appears to be quite serious," she replies, "time will tell. I know that I am serious about this relationship."

"Appears? You don't seem to be too sure about this relationship. I am not prepared to give this idea up yet. I know that one day one can be in love and the next it is all over. So until you are really taken, meaning either seriously engaged or married, I believe we would have a chance. You are worth waiting for."

Kataryna realizes she won't get through to him tonight. He seems determined. She decides to change the subject and then excuse herself and go home.

"How about looking at the new company material now you wanted to show me?" she suggests in a more serious tone. "As I mentioned, I have a busy day tomorrow and an early flight back to New York the day after tomorrow."

"There is a little snag. I didn't get a chance to run it by Luca so I can't make it public yet," he explains. "But to be completely honest that wasn't my priority. I wanted the opportunity to express my feelings for you in person. I am totally under your spell. I can't think of anything else."

Kataryna is stunned to hear all this. She wishes Luca was here with her so that they could tell Roberto about their relationship together. But she has to master this storm on her own now.

"As I said earlier, Roberto, I am seeing someone and can't entertain these kind of thoughts and feelings. So we better change the subject now."

They finish their dinner, both with less of an appetite for different reasons. When they leave the restaurant Kataryna walks up to one of the cabs waiting in line for passengers. She turns to Roberto to say good-bye.

"Thank you for dinner, Roberto," she starts out, "I am sorry that the evening turned out differently than what you had hoped or imagined.

I appreciate your candor, but at the same time I have to say that it would be best if you put the idea of you and me out of your head and move on."

"That is easier said than done," he responds, "I don't know if I can do that. These are emotions that you can't just wish away, if you know what I mean. Just put yourself in my place for a moment. I guess you have never been in love with a person who was not available. Neither was I, before I met you. This is a totally new situation for me and I don't know how to deal with it."

"In love?" she questions him, "Roberto, we only met once in a video conference call and once in person at a business dinner with two other men around us. We didn't even have a private moment. How can you be in love with me?"

"It was love at first sight," he replies, "which I never experienced before. I may have been interested in women for various reasons, but in love that I would go through great length I can't recall. I would give up my entire life in Italy and move to New York immediately if you asked me to."

"This is very difficult to accept, Roberto," Kataryna declares. "I have no idea how we can work together this way if my firm becomes the shareholder of NatMedica."

"I don't know. You tell me," he says shrugging his shoulders. "I haven't even thought about that."

"Well, I have to think about this some more," Kataryna goes on. "I have no idea how my business partner would feel about this delicate situation. Anyway, we are not going to solve this problem tonight and I really have to get some sleep."

"I don't even know if I can sleep tonight or any night thereafter," he says visibly disappointed, looking almost sad.

"I understand, but other than friendship, there is nothing I can offer to make you feel better. You will have to get over this and move on."

"Let me ask you one more question," Roberto probes further, "if you would not be in this relationship you mentioned, would there be a chance of us having a romantic relationship?"

"I am not a big fan of answering hypothetical questions, Roberto, because it doesn't change the situation. In addition, it would only be more painful if I told you we would have a chance if I was not in that relationship," Kataryna says softly.

Roberto embraces Kataryna to say good-bye and kisses her on the cheek. He holds her longer than he should, but she doesn't have the heart to abruptly break away from him. She really feels sorry for him having these strong feelings for her, which she can't reciprocate. If things were different and she wasn't in love, and in a relationship with Luca, she may have entertained a relationship with Roberto. *Why did this have to happen now*, she thinks, *two attractive eligible men coming into my life at the same time?* She kisses him good-bye on the cheek. He lets go of her knowing that there is nothing he can do tonight to change her mind but he senses that she would not be opposed to a relationship with him if the other man didn't exist. He respects her strong conviction for her relationship, but it hurts really badly and he knows that he can't just give up the idea of a possible future with her.

Kataryna gets into the cab and closes the door. She waves at Roberto, who is staring at her attempting to smile, as he waves back at her. She lets out a deep sigh as the cab takes off. This was emotionally draining. Unrequited love is never easy for anyone and especially not for the person deeply in love. Kataryna is sad and fighting tears. She has no idea what to tell Luca about her dinner meeting with Roberto. She really doesn't want to mention Roberto's proposal and declaration of love for her to Luca. He would probably go crazy and rake Roberto over the coals; and he doesn't deserve that when he is already feeling so much emotional pain. However, Luca and Roberto will meet once he is back in Milan. The idea that Luca will tell Roberto then that Kataryna and him are in an intimate relationship almost brings on an anxiety attack. *Oh my God*, she thinks, *how will Roberto handle this piece of news?* Should she have told Roberto that Luca is the man she is in a relationship with?

It is 11 p.m., when the cab arrives at her father's house. Her cell phone rings as she approaches the front door and she picks it up without looking at the screen first.

"I just want to make sure that you got home safe," she hears Roberto say. "I would have offered to take you home, but I sensed you needed some space after our conversation."
"Thank you for calling," Kataryna says quietly. "Yes, I definitely needed to be alone to let everything sink in. After thinking about it a little deeper I believe I owe you another explanation. This may be difficult for you to hear, but I want to be completely honest with you."
"After what you told me tonight I don't think there is anything that would be more difficult to hear," Roberto says, exhaling heavily.

Kataryna has a full-blown anxiety attack now. Her chest is heavy and aching. Her head is pounding and her heart is beating faster.

"I don't know where to start, so I'll come right out with it to get it over with."

She takes a deep breath. "The man who I am in a relationship with is Luca."

There is silence at the other end. She closes her eyes and exhales. *He must be in agony*, she thinks.

"Roberto," she calls out, "are you still there?"

"Yes. I am in shock. When did this start?"

"The actual consummation of our intimate relationship took place after we all met in Bellagio," she explains.

"That is even more painful," he murmurs, his voice wavering. "Just knowing that you were available when we met in Bellagio makes me sick. All I had to do was not let you leave with Luca that evening. I would probably be a very happy man now."

"As I said earlier, Roberto, let's not engage in hypothetical situations. We don't know what would have happened that evening if I hadn't stayed at Luca's villa. It doesn't matter anymore at this point. I am in love with Luca and have no intention to end it and as far as I know the feeling is mutual."

"I hope that your being in love with Luca is not because you want to acquire NatMedica, hoping you can increase the chances of winning the bid."

"No, Roberto, I can guarantee you that is not how I operate. I don't fall in love for money or lucrative deals. As a matter of fact, I haven't really fallen in love for a long time, so Luca is very special to me. I think we are perfect together on many levels except, of course, for the long distance between us which is something we will have to work on."

"Thank you for telling me, Karyna, even if it hurts like hell, but it would have been much worse if you had not said anything and Luca would have told me when I meet him in the next few days. I think I need a drink now and reflect on my life ahead. But I want you to know that the little time I spent with you was magical and I am a different person because of it. Only time can heal my wounds. I don't know where to go from here yet."

"I am so sorry that I am causing you so much pain, Roberto," Karyna murmurs. "If there is anything I can do to make it easier for you, other than the obvious, please let me know. I also would recommend that you don't tell Luca about your feelings for me or about your proposal tonight for that matter. It wouldn't be good for either one of you. Nothing will be gained by that."

"I have no idea how I will handle that when I meet with Luca," Roberto says.

"Please think about it carefully. A lot may be at stake for you and I really don't want to be the reason for a meltdown between you two. Some feelings should stay private. Have a safe trip back to Milan. Ciao Roberto."

"Ciao bella, I will always be here for you if things don't work out with Luca," he says as they hang up.

Kataryna is really sad now. Why, why, why did she have to become the object of attraction for these two men who are friends and business partners on top of it, she is asking herself? There is no easy way to deal with this. *I will just have to put it out to the universe and hope for the best*, she decides.

Her father meets her at the door as she enters the house.

"How was your business meeting?"

"It turned out differently than I thought," she responds.

"It didn't go well?"

"I don't know yet. I have to analyze this situation a little more, but not tonight. I am exhausted and we have a pretty busy day tomorrow before I go back to New York on Saturday."

"I wish you could stay a little longer," he says with sadness in his voice.

"I have been hearing that a couple of times on this trip," she says laughing lightly.

"When do you think you will be back in Berlin again?"

"Don't know," she responds, "if something promising develops in connection with the search for my brother, I may come over then and bring Aleksandra, of course. But other than that I don't see myself back here really soon. I have a close friend coming to New York for Christmas. We will have Christmas Eve dinner at Aleksandra's and then I am going to Hawaii with him," she replies.

She can see the disappointment in his face.

"Papa," she starts explaining, "I have been working very hard the whole year and didn't have much time for my private life. This is the first vacation I am taking in a long time and I am really looking forward to spending some quality time with this friend."

"I understand," he says, "I am happy that you are getting a chance to do that."

"Yes, so am I. He means a lot to me. Good night, see you tomorrow morning.

Friday night after a busy day visiting relatives and friends, Kataryna packs a few more things in her suitcase and then falls into bed, physically and emotionally exhausted from the experiences of the last few days.

At 6 a.m., Kataryna wakes up. The events of the last few days enter her mind, especially the look on Roberto's face when she took off in the cab. She recalls their phone conversation when she told him about her relationship with Luca. Thank God she couldn't see his face in that moment. It was painful enough to hear his strained voice and the words he said. He will meet with Luca in the next few days. *Luca-oh my God- I never called him back last night*, she remembers. Well, he was on a business trip so they didn't get a chance to talk about her dinner with Roberto yet. She ponders what exactly she should she tell him. Maybe she should call Roberto to find out what he intends to tell Luca?

Kataryna gets dressed and then prepares a light breakfast for herself. Her father is still sleeping. As usual the breakfast doesn't go down that easy before the early flight, but Thursday night's events are also hanging over her heavily and almost make her sad. Right about now she is glad that she is going back to New York, far away from this situation.

"Good morning," her father greets her as he enters the kitchen.

Kataryna's deep thoughts are interrupted as she turns around to hug her father.

"Good morning, Papa."

She hands him a cup of tea. "Do you want to eat something?"

"No, thank you. I am not hungry yet. I will eat when I come back from the airport."

Her luggage is already standing in the hallway ready to go. He takes it to the car and stows it in the trunk. Kataryna finishes her tea, gets her coat and heads for the car when her phone rings. She sees Luca's number on the screen and answers the call.

"I got really worried, Principessa. How did the dinner go and what kind of material did Roberto come up with?" he asks tensely.

"I am sorry," she explains, "it took longer than I thought and when I left the restaurant I got a call and had to extinguish some fires, so to speak. And yesterday it got very late spending the evening with friends and relatives. Please forgive me for letting you wait that long."

"So, tell me, what did he have to say?" Luca probes further.

"Actually, he told me that he could not make the new material public yet because you had not reviewed and approved it," she explains.

"At least that is a positive," he says casually, "but why did he want to meet you then?"

"He said he was in Berlin on a business appointment and wanted to take the opportunity to meet with me again. He told me about his daughter Verena who is planning on taking business and finance courses and asked if it would be possible to get a trainee / internship position for her in my firm in New York so she can see how the financial industry works. She apparently has been talking about wanting to take a trip to New York for some time. He wants to surprise her with something like that to keep her interested in that field."

"Interesting," Luca mutters. "I didn't know that Verena was interested in finance. Must be something relatively new. But he is right she does need some focus. What did you tell him?"

"I said that I would have to discuss it with my partner. Do you know her well?"

"Yes, she generally is a nice young lady, but she needs some direction. I recall not too long ago she was all over the place with her career plans. I am glad to hear that she is interested in something solid. I am certain you would be a good mentor for her if you were to offer her an internship."

"It's something to consider after I have spoken to Stephen about it," Kataryna says.

"What else was Roberto up to? Did he flirt with you again or try something more?"

Kataryna takes a deep breath. "Well, you know, men will be men," she responds as casually as she can manage.

"What does that mean?" he asks somewhat alarmed.

"Let me call you back when I am checked in at the airport. I am in the car with my father and would like to spend the last 30 minutes with him, if you don't mind."

"Of course, I am sorry. Please call me when you have a minute before take off."

"Okay, speak to you later. Ciao," she ends the call.

Kataryna and her father arrive at the Berlin-Tegel airport. He parks the car, gets her luggage out of the trunk and takes her to the check-in counter.

"I will call you when I am back home," Kataryna says as she hugs him to say good-bye. "Please try to remember some more details about the adoption."

"I will do my best, but don't get your hopes up too high."

"I won't, but I am not giving up either. There has to be a record somewhere."

"Say hello to Aleksandra, Brian and the twins for me," he says.

"When is your girlfriend coming back from her trip?" Kataryna asks.

"Probably the day after tomorrow, unless her mother takes a turn for the worse," he answers.

"Good, she can show you how to do a Skype call on her computer so we can see you more often. I know you are not so technology savvy."

He smiles at her. "That sounds good. Maybe I have to learn doing that on my own."

Kataryna laughs. "That'll be the day when you can manage that kind of technology. I guess we'll see. I told you many times you should take some computer classes."

"I may surprise you one day," he says grinning.

"That would be great. Take care of yourself and stay well."

She starts walking towards the passport control booth. The usual sadness is in his face. She has seen it many times when her and Aleksandra leave again after their visits. After the security check Kataryna calls Luca back.

"I am all checked in. I think they will let us board soon, so we won't have much time to talk," she informs him.

"So, did Roberto behave himself?" he starts up again.

"Yes, he did," she answers "but I think we also know that he likes me. He was pretty stunned when I told him that you and I are in an intimate relationship. I wouldn't put any more salt into that wound."

"What do you mean?" Luca asks.

"Well, don't rub it in. You know what I mean," she insists.

"I understand. I am not sure how I would react if the tables were turned. I am just glad that I am not in his position. If he has the same feelings for you like I do, I can understand how he would be very disappointed now."

"This is an unfortunate situation also from a business point of view," Kataryna declares. "If Stephen and I acquire NatMedica, we would practically be Roberto's bosses and there would be a lot of interaction with him at some level. Needless to say, we would not be the day-to-day managers; but as a 50 percent shareholder, I can't remove myself from important business decisions to be made. This would mean a close business relationship with Roberto."

"You are right. There is a lot to think about," Luca sounds concerned.

The ground personnel announce that they are starting the boarding process.

"Okay, here we go, they are ready for boarding. Let me go. We can continue this when I call you from New York, if there is anything further to talk about."

"Have a safe flight, Principessa," Luca says. "Please call me when you have arrived in New York."

Once boarded and settled in her seat Kataryna closes her eyes hoping to relax and get some sleep. But her mind is racing and flashbacks of Roberto's face after their dinner appear in front of her. She quickly opens her eyes to escape the repeat of the sad moment playing in front of her. She is fighting tears realizing that her and Luca's happiness is the cause for Roberto's anguish.

S I X

Roberto Silvestri is not happy after the dinner he had with Kataryna yesterday. When he met her in Bellagio, together with Luca and Francesco, he immediately fell in love with her. Luca had given him a dirty look when he asked Kataryna a personal question about her marital status. It is very clear to him now that Luca wanted to make sure that he had the first chance with Kataryna. So it wasn't really a professional thing as he thought at first. Luca had his own agenda. They have only been in an intimate relationship for a couple of days; that doesn't mean anything. This could be over tomorrow.

He hadn't expected such a downer day. He sits back, closing his eyes imagining Kataryna and Luca together. This is painful. If *it was anyone else than Luca I would press on*, he thinks, *but Luca is like family and that would not be cool.* He downs his drink. What happened after Luca and Kataryna left Bellagio together? According to Luca, Kataryna stayed at his villa that night and the night before. Roberto wonders if Kataryna seduced Luca that night. Luca is so vulnerable after his divorce. He might also be on a rebound. So he probably fell for it, hook, line and sinker, not realizing that the she may actually be more interested in the acquisition target than him personally. The alluring Kataryna was probably the right thing to happen to him to cure his bruised ego after he found his ex-wife with her lover in their villa. Well, all is not lost yet. Let's see how this develops. He may have a chance with Kataryna yet. *I will back off for the moment, but I am not done with this subject by a long shot*, he vows.

He picks up his phone and calls his friend Sergio de Angelis.

"Hey, how about meeting for dinner? I had a tough day and need to let out some steam."

"Sounds good to me," Sergio answers, "my wife is visiting her sister for a couple of days and I am ready for a night out. Shall we meet in an hour at our usual place?"

"See you there."

Roberto steps out of the shower and looks at himself in the mirror. He doesn't look his age at all. His athletic build is a result of his working out whenever he gets a chance. His face is firm and he has fabulous hair with only very few silver hairs on the sides. When Luca and Roberto went out after Luca got divorced, both men turned heads when they walked into a restaurant or bar. They actually could be brothers. Those nights were fun, he remembers, two attractive, well-dressed men with luxury cars and enough money to throw around if they wanted to. They were the desire of many women and were envied by many men. And now these two men seemed to have fallen for one and the same woman, when there are so many women out there who would kill for being with either one of them.

After his divorce Roberto was looking for a woman of substance, who is interesting and alluring. Kataryna fits that description perfectly. The failed marriage was his fault because he had committed adultery. His ex-wife had forgiven him for his trespassing but then came the incident with the female employee at the Christmas party, which she found out about from someone working at the company. That was the straw that broke the camel's back. She left him the day after she found out.

Roberto had been dating several beautiful women since then; but they were mostly airheads who couldn't keep an interesting or meaningful conversation, except for fashion topics or senseless gossip. He got easily bored with that. He knows he needs a challenge to remain interested. He can't recall ever having had the kind of attraction for a woman like he has for Kataryna. *What is it about her that intrigues me that much*, he asks himself? Sure, she is stunning, but that is not all that has this hold on him. *She is also quick on her feet*, Roberto thinks, smiling to himself. He recalls her response to his question if she was married at their meeting in Bellagio. She asked if that was a prerequisite for the acquisition. A clever way not to have to answer that question, he admits. Her unfaltering confidence in the wake of that moment was something he had not expected. She commands a room when she walks in and can keep it up when it gets hairy. He admires that. She could straighten him out for life. So far he was always in control when it came to his women, but the tables would be turned if Kataryna would just give in to him. He sits down and fantasizes about her putting him into his place sexually and otherwise. He feels his arousal, immediately imagining her in control over him and tantalizing him in every way possible. Yes, that is what he needs, a challenge called Kataryna. *Damn you, Luca,* he thinks, *you are so in the way of my happiness.*

Roberto arrives at the restaurant where Sergio already waits for him with a drink in his hand.

"Direttore," he greets him laughing with a pat on the shoulder, "have you been behaving yourself with your wife out of town?"

Sergio laughs out loud. "You know me. I am not such a ladies man like you are, Roberto."

Roberto comes up with a sad smile. "If you only knew the latest."

He summons the bartender to bring him his usual drink and gulps it down, immediately gesturing for a refill.

"Whoa," Sergio exclaims, "that must have been a hell of a day. I have never seen you pour down a drink like that. Can you talk about it?"

Roberto throws up his hands, closes his eyes and lets out a deep sigh. The bartender puts the second drink in front of Roberto. He downs it again.

"Take it easy, Roberto, whatever happened it can't be that bad," Sergio implores his friend.

Roberto signals for another refill and the bartender rushes the drink to him. Sergio takes the drink and holds it.

"Sit down and talk to me, Roberto," he says in a more serious tone. "I am really getting worried now. What the heck is going on?"

Roberto sits down reaching to take his drink back from Sergio, who is not sure if he should let him have it.

"I am in love," Roberto blurts out, looking at his friend, waiting for a reaction.

"Tell me something new," Sergio laughs. "This is why you are downing the drinks like there is no tomorrow? You are always in love."

"No, this is different," Roberto responds determined.

"What is so different this time? Is she married or has the impossible happened and she doesn't feel the same way about you?" Sergio asks with great interest.

"Suffice it to say I have met my match. She is insanely beautiful and she has a very intriguing personality. I think she would have the ability to destroy me."

"Jeez, Roberto. Is this the alcohol talking or have you gone out of your mind?"

Roberto takes a sip from his drink, which Sergio has finally handed to him.

"I met her through our deal. You know that the Romano family is selling the company I work for. So we had a 'get-to-know-the senior management' meeting in Bellagio. She wants to buy the company. She and her partner own a private equity company in New York and she came over for the preliminary due diligence meeting."

Sergio lets out a whistle. "She is Americano? Wow, New York, that is a bit far for a romantic relationship."

"No, she is actually German, but has lived in the United States for many years."

"Tedesca," Sergio repeats astonished, which means German in Italian.

"Go on," Sergio rushes him, "what is the problem, the long distance?"

"I wish it was as simple as long distance," Roberto explains softly. "My boss and good friend, Luca Romano, got to her first and I am totally crushed. She is something I have been looking for all my life. Guess why I fooled around so much? It's because I was never happy and fully satisfied with the women in my life. And now the one woman I would adore and be faithful to has been snapped away from me in a matter of seconds, basically right in front of my eyes. I don't know how to handle this."

"Don't look at me for advice. I have no clue how something like this can be handled," Sergio says patting Roberto's shoulder. "Help me understand this a little better," Sergio continues, "why does she have such a hold on you? You only met her once and nothing happened between you two, right?"

"I can't explain it exactly," Roberto says, "all I know is that she has some kind of spell on me. When she walked into the room, the way she looked at me, the way she talks. You name it. She is a combination of beautiful, smart and totally in command, which disarmed me within seconds. I could hardly concentrate on the deal. I have been fantasizing about her since that evening, imagining us together and how she would be in complete charge over me. I can actually feel how she would tear off my clothes and slowly caress me, driving me to the point of going insane under her touch and then exploding into the deepest orgasm I ever had. And now I want her for real in my house, on my couch, on my bed and wherever else she wants to go. I would let her be in total control over me."

"Please stop," Sergio says laughing, "you are getting me excited now. I don't want to walk around with a bulge here."

They both laugh out loud and clink their glasses in a toast.

"Good luck, Roberto," Sergio says, "let's have dinner now and cool off. My wife is out of town so I will have to take a cold shower later on if we don't change the subject."

"You and me both," Roberto adds. "Who knows, I may call her later. Just hearing her voice could bring on an orgasm," Roberto continues, smirking.

"I would advise against that," Sergio says, "phoning a love interest under the influence of too much alcohol could be a recipe for disaster. And didn't you just tell me that she is romantically involved with Luca Romano? She may react badly and that could kill your long-standing relationship with the Romano family, and may even cost you your job in the worst-case scenario. I think you would be better off finding another appealing woman to play with."

"You may be right. I seem to be on a mission to destroy myself, but I can't let it go," Roberto murmurs.

They sit down for dinner. "How is your daughter doing?" Sergio asks, trying to change the subject.

"Oh, she is doing fine. She is still upset over the divorce but seems to have forgiven me. I am planning to take her on a trip for her 21st birthday."

"Where are you taking her?" Sergio asks.

"Hmm, let's see," Roberto starts out, "how about New York. She has been talking about wanting to go there."

Sergio is shaking his head, smiling. "You must be kidding, you don't want to bring Verena into this international web. What are her plans for the future?" he asks.

"I think she wants to take Finance and Business Management courses, but with her I really don't know because a few months ago she wanted to do something in the fashion area. So let's see what she finally decides on."

They talk about a few other general things over dinner.

"So are we going home or are we going to hit a bar for a nightcap?" Sergio asks.

"Let's have an after-dinner drink here. I am getting a little tired."

"I am not surprised," Sergio responds, "the way you downed the three drinks at the bar earlier and then we had a bottle of wine for dinner. Are you sure you are up for an after-dinner drink?"

"Yes, I am. I want to make sure I sleep well later."

The waiter brings the after-dinner drinks. Roberto asks him for the check.

"Thank you for coming out to dinner with me. I really needed to talk to someone about this," Roberto says to his friend.

"I am always here for you," Sergio responds, "just don't do anything stupid. Let it go."

"Easier said than done," Roberto comes back with. "What I didn't tell you earlier is that I met her in Berlin yesterday and proposed marriage to her."

"Are you serious, Roberto?" What in the world prompted you to do that?"

"As I said, she is it for me. I felt it the first time I met her. You just know when it is right."

"How did she react to that?" Sergio inquires.

"She said she couldn't have that kind of conversation with me because she is in a relationship. To make a long story short she told me later that it was Luca. That hit me hard. I could have dealt with some stranger in New York, but Luca? I asked her when this relationship started and she told me after our meeting in Bellagio. So, you see, Sergio, if things had turned out differently, I might have been the lucky one."

"Sorry you are going through something like this," Sergio comforts his distressed friend.

"This could play out like an Italian opera. Two men fighting for the same woman." Roberto shrugs his shoulders.

"Yeah, but usually at the end of an Italian opera someone is dying. So let's make sure that is not the case here," Sergio lectures him.

Roberto arrives back home around midnight. He pours himself a drink and sits down, closing his eyes in an attempt to put this day behind him. He thinks about Kataryna. What might she be doing now? She should be back in New York, which means she is not with Luca. He really wants to talk to her. He goes to his home office and gets a cell phone, which is not traceable to him. His heart starts beating faster as he dials Kataryna's number. She picks up her phone at the second ring.

"Hello." She doesn't hear anyone on the line. "Hello, can you hear me?" she asks. There is no response, but she hears a muffled sound like someone breathing or moaning.

Roberto breathes heavily when he hears Kataryna's voice. He tries to hold his breath, but a slight moan escapes from his lips as his arousal becomes more intense. Then he hears the click as she is hanging up. He wants to hear her voice again and redials her number.

"Hello, hello" she yells into the phone, "who is this?" She wonders if someone is trying to call her specifically or if some kid is playing with his parents' phone.

Roberto listens to her answering the phone when his music player comes on. He hangs up immediately. His arousal is painful now. He decides to call her office number in New York. Her voice mail message comes on. "You have reached the voice mail of Kataryna Taylor. I am currently not available. Please leave a detailed message and I will get back to you as soon as I can. If you need immediate assistance, please call my assistant Melanie Williams."

He hangs up. *Oh, yes, I need immediate assistance,* he thinks. *I need you here with me making love to me.* He gets his laptop computer and goes to her private equity firm's website, searching for the bio of the partners. After downloading the photo to his desktop he starts talking to it as if she were in front of him.

"I know we could be good together. I really need you in my life. Give me a sign if you feel the same."

He leans back and imagines her in his arms and in his bed wanting him as much as he wants her. The image of her in his arms touching him sexually makes him climax instantly. He stretches out on the couch and drifts off.

He wakes up when his cell phone rings. His head hurts and he is in his clothes on the lounger.

"Ciao Roberto?" he hears Luca greet him when he answers his phone. "Is everything alright?"

"Yeah, yeah," he says, trying to pull himself together wondering what happened.

"I was concerned because I didn't hear from you yet after your trip to Berlin," Luca explains.

Roberto looks at his watch. Dio mio, it is 10 a.m., already.

"I was just going to call you," he offers as an explanation. "I have a personal situation, which I have to deal with first."

"OK, " Luca responds, "take care of your personal situation and then call me to set up a lunch or dinner meeting."

"Sure, thank you. I will call you as soon as I can," Roberto says, ending the call. He has an idea why Luca wants to get together with him.

He takes off his clothes and goes to the bathroom to take a shower. "Oh God, I look like hell," he says as he looks in the mirror. What happened? He slowly recalls the last events. Dinner with Kataryna in Berlin, Kataryna and Luca in a romantic relationship, heavy drinking and dinner with Sergio, more drinking at home and his anonymous calls to Kataryna. He steps out of the shower and gets dressed. After a light breakfast he calls Luca back.

"Ciao Luca, how about meeting for lunch on Tuesday?"
"OK, let's meet for lunch then," Luca says, "my assistant will call you with the restaurant details."

As soon as Roberto hangs up the phone he goes to the bathroom and throws up. He is not sure if it was yesterday's heavy alcohol consumption, which made him sick, or his telephone conversation with Luca. Either way, he is facing a tough day ahead.

Luca stares at this phone. Roberto sounded strange and distant. He has to wonder if it has anything to do with his dinner meeting with Kataryna where she revealed their romantic relationship.

S E V E N

The flight to New York was uneventful and arrives on time at JFK. Her car service driver meets her in the international arrival area.

"Hello, Ms. Taylor," he greets her, taking her bags. "I hope you had a nice trip and the flight was not too bumpy."

"Hello Tony. The flight was calm and I actually got a little sleep."

"Traffic is decent," he says. "I should have you home within the hour."

Kataryna gets comfortable while Tony is loading her bags. She is thinking about calling Luca, but then changes her mind and sends him a quick email. She rather wants to talk to him in the privacy of her home.

> *Ciao darling,*
> *Just arrived at JFK, I am in the car on my way home. Will call*
> *you when I get there.*
> *Miss you.*
> *K*

Her iPhone pings with an email from Luca.

> *Can't wait to talk to you, Principessa. I am glad you arrived*
> *safely. Call me whatever time. Miss you terribly.*
> *Luca*

Traffic is moving smoothly. Kataryna arrives home at 5 p.m. The doorman rushes to the car to retrieve her bags and welcomes her home. He gives her luggage to a porter who takes it to the elevator while the Concierge hands Kataryna a spectacular flower arrangement. It is from Luca, of course, the card reads: "Welcome home. Wish I was there with you".

The porter puts Kataryna's luggage in her apartment. She tips him and closes the door. Ah, home, sweet home. Only one thing is missing--Luca. After a refreshing shower she puts some sexy loungewear on and hot red lipstick. She pours herself a glass of red wine, sits down on the couch and dials Luca's number. He picks up immediately.

"Principessa," he says. "I have to see you. How about a video call?"

"You took the words right out of my mouth," she responds, "I want to see you, too and thank you for the beautiful flowers."

When she turns on her laptop, Luca is already ringing her. She accepts the video call, looking at him on the screen.

"Hi darling," she says smiling broadly, "it's great to see you, but you are so far away. She holds her arms out towards the screen.

"I wish I could touch you."

"I want to kiss you all over," he sighs.

"Careful," she teases him, "you are entering the danger zone. I am all flustered already just seeing you."

"I am more than flustered," he says. "Do you want me to prove it?"

Kataryna laughs and puts her hands in front of her eyes.

"No, no don't you dare."

She looks at him with smoldering eyes and lets one of her spaghetti straps drop down her shoulder. Leaning forward revealing her cleavage, she kisses the screen and then gets up and starts moving her hips slowly and seductively to the song: "Flowmotion from the Album Exotica," which is playing on her laptop. Raising her already short lounge dress up, she reveals her sexy panties. She puts her thumbs into her panties as if she wants to remove them. Luca stares at the screen and bites his lip in agony. The temptress is at it again and he is so ready for her. He wants to touch her, moving his hand towards the screen. She sits down and faces him now with both straps down, her crossed arms holding the satin dress up and her hands cupped over her breasts. She starts moving in a slow dance again as the dress slides down her body. She puts one of her feet on the couch and moves in rhythm, with the music moving her hips from side to side. Luca starts moaning, leaning back, and closing his eyes.

"There you go, Prince Charming," she says seductively, "do you feel better now? You were saying you wanted to show me something," she laughs.

When he opens his eyes her slinky lounge dress is back on. He looks at her dreamily and rubs his temples.

"Too late. Whatever I wanted to show you, before you interrupted me with your seductive dance, is gone," he murmurs. "You are quite the temptress. How is it that you always manage to turn the tables on me?"

"Relax, Prince Charming, we made it happen again and I still have a similar situation to deal with."

"Good," he says laughing, "I would hate to be the only one in this position. How are we going to make it that far apart until Christmas? Although this was a sexy experience I really want to be able to touch you and do this together."

"For now we just have to live with the thought that absence makes the heart grow fonder," she responds softly.

"Yeah, and it makes other body parts grow harder," he says with a smirk.

She smiles at him sweetly and nods.

"Don't forget we are both in the same position. I feel whatever you feel, but it makes me feel alive. I am living for the day when we can be back together. I think we better end this now before we work ourselves up again and pick it back up tomorrow when I am more rested."

"Mamma mia," he sighs. "God knows what you come up with when you are rested. Should I get worried?"

"Yes, yes, of course," she says laughing, "be afraid, be very afraid. Good night my darling, sleep tight and no wet dreams please."

"I am not making any promises," he says, "when I think of our first night in my bathtub, I have no control over what happens to my body; and your dance a few minutes ago isn't helping, either."

She grins broadly. "I will make a note to repeat that bathtub experience, it was so sexy. Oh, oh, here we go again. I am getting all tingly at the thought of that, but I don't want to go down that road with you right now so let's close this down fast."

"A domani," he ends the video call.

"See you tomorrow," she says waving good-bye and blowing him a kiss.

Kataryna shuts down the laptop. She leans back and closes her eyes, listening to the soft music and imagining Luca with her. *Soon,* she thinks, *less than four weeks and he will be right here with me.* She is getting very tired now. It's only 8 p.m., but her body is still on European time. Time to go to sleep.

The clock shows 4 a.m. Kataryna is awake and can't get back to sleep. Jet lag is setting in. It is 10a.m. in Europe and over there she would have been up for hours already. She goes to the kitchen to make a cup of tea, which she takes back to bed with her. She props up her pillows and leans back. Her eyes are tired, but her body wants to be up. She slowly sips her tea thinking about the delicious Rooibos tea she had in Luca's villa the morning after their sensual night. She recalls the fun morning they had when he couldn't get the lounge suit off her, which makes her smile.

Since I can't sleep anymore, I might as well give Luca a call, she thinks. She dials his cell phone number from her home phone. He picks up after the second ring.

"Pronto," Luca answers his phone.

Kataryna's home phone number is unlisted so he can't see the number calling him.

"Buongiorno," she greets him with a deeper voice than usual.

Luca doesn't recognize her voice immediately and asks who is calling.

"You have forgotten me already?" she yells into the phone giggling.

"Principessa," he calls out surprised. "I didn't recognize your voice and honestly I thought you would still be sleeping. It is the middle of the night in New York."

"Well, it is 4:30 a.m., and the jet lag got to me. Are you in Milan or at the Lake Como villa?"

"I am at the villa, but it is lonely here without you. I don't even dare to go into the bathroom and look at that Jacuzzi tub."

Kataryna giggles. "I think we created a special bond with that tub."

"We better change the subject. Anyway, I am going to visit my parents in a little while. We are having a Sunday family lunch at their house. I wish you would be here for that. My mother said she can't wait to meet you."

"Your mother knows about me?" she asks.

"Naturalmente," he answers in Italian. "My mother noticed that something was going on with me. You know, mothers have a sixth sense, especially when it comes to their children. She asked me why I was so happy and energized lately and I told her. I showed her the photo I took of you with my phone. She thinks you are very beautiful."

"Oh, my God," Kataryna screams out, "I am going to send you a better photo of me right now if you are starting to show photos around.

Actually, you could have taken one of me last night during the video call," she laughs.

"That would be too X-rated to show to my family. I should be the only one seeing you like this," he advises her.

"Here you go, please use this one from now on."

She uploads one of her favorite photos into an email and sends it to him. The photo is a half shot of her in a beautiful, sexy but sophisticated dress.

"This is an amazing photo of you. If I weren't in love already this would do it. I will make this my wallpaper on the phone and on my computer."

"Oh dear," Kataryna responds, "my face will be plastered all over Italy now. Scary."

"No, not all over, only on my phone and my computer. But now I can take you with me wherever I go. Can't wait to show it to my family."

"Where do your parents live?"

"In the Bellagio area."

"Oh, beautiful Bellagio," she sighs, "I wish I could go with you."

"So do I, but you chose to go to New York instead," he responds jokingly.

"Maybe we can do a video call from there so you can meet my parents and sisters at least via video. Francesco will also be there, of course."

"That is a great idea. Let's do it. Call me when you are ready for the video call. I will make sure I will be dressed appropriately. I promise not to perform any seductive dances, either."

"Only for me, Principessa."

"When are you going to be back at your villa?" she asks.

"Probably late afternoon, early evening."

"I guess it is going to be an interesting afternoon for you," she says. "I will just rest and catch up on some business emails later on, so I am prepared for my day at the office tomorrow. I will probably go to bed early tonight. We could try to have a more private video call later on. Let's say about 9 p.m., your time when you are back at your villa."

"I was hoping you would suggest that," he says. "I will ring you around that time. Meanwhile, try to get some sleep, ciao Principessa."

Kataryna hangs up the phone and looks at the clock. It is 5:15 a.m., New York time. She yawns and soon is back asleep. She wakes up again at 7:45 a.m., has some tea and a light breakfast and then gets ready for the video call scheduled in about an hour with Luca and his family. She is wearing a beige silk, scoop-neck top and a navy blue skirt paired with some nice, but low-key, gold earrings. Casually elegant is the theme for this video call, she decides. Her makeup is light and in earth tones. Her hair is swept up in a loose French twist. She looks in the mirror for a last check and nods approvingly-- ready to meet the family. Ten minutes later her phone rings.

"Are you ready for us, Principessa?" she hears Luca asking.

"I am indeed," she responds.

Her heart is beating faster as the video call comes in. She is excited to meet the Romano family. Luca is sitting in the front row flanked by his two beautiful sisters. Behind them are Luca's mother Valentina, his father Riccardo and Francesco Barone, Patrizia's fiancé. All are holding a glass of Champagne. As they see her coming on the screen they raise their glasses and greet her.

"Buongiorno, Kataryna, we are delighted to see you."

Kataryna smiles at them happily. "Buongiorno, I am so excited to meet you all. I wish I could be there with you."

Valentina Romano, a beautiful woman in her mid-sixties, hugs her son from behind and whispers something in his ear as she looks at Kataryna.

"My mother says you look just like in the beautiful photo I showed them earlier. You should have seen the excitement when I came up with the photo you sent me this morning."

Kataryna smiles at Luca and then looks at his mother.

"Grazie, Signora Romano. You look beautiful."

"Grazie, please call me Valentina," she says in a heavy Italian accent. "My English is not as good as my husband's and children's. Forgive me if what I am saying doesn't make sense."

"Your English is better than my Italian," Kataryna communicates apologetically, "but I promise to learn more in the future."

"Kataryna," Luca's father starts, "it is a great pleasure to see you. I am Riccardo, Luca's father. I am sorry that I was out of town when you were over here. Luca has been talking non-stop about you and now I can see why."

Luca nods his head in agreement.

Kataryna flushes lightly. "Thank you for saying that," she says shyly to Riccardo Romano.

"Hello Kataryna," Luca's sister comes into the conversation. "Patrizia and I are so glad to meet you. I think we will have a lot of fun together. We hope you are coming back to Italy soon. Otherwise, Patrizia and I will have to come to New York and explore the city with you."

"Whoa," Luca chimes in, "if anyone is going to New York exploring the city with Kataryna, it will be me."

Everyone starts laughing. The two sisters are rolling their eyes at him. "You will have to share her with us a little bit, Luca, or we might just kidnap her," they tease him.

"I see I am already overruled here," he says laughing.

Kataryna looks at him, smiling sweetly.

"You will always come first, of course."

Luca throws her a kiss. "Grazie, Principessa, and you will always come first in my life."

Kataryna looks at everyone.

"This is so overwhelming, having all of you in front of me at the same time and for the first time, except for Luca and Francesco, of course."

Francesco, who has been quiet so far, takes the word and waves his hand at her.

"Great to see you again, Kataryna. I can imagine how you feel, but don't be overwhelmed. I can say from personal experience that this is a very welcoming family and they obviously have already embraced you."

Kataryna exhales. "The feeling is mutual. I am so looking forward to meeting you all in person really soon."

"And I am really, really looking forward to seeing you soon and spending Christmas with you in New York," Luca quickly throws in.

Patrizia looks at her fiancé. "Actually, we could go to New York for Christmas, too."

Francesco smiles and nods in agreement. "Yes, we could."

"Well, let's discuss it later," Luca says, "as long as you give Kataryna and me some much-needed privacy I'll consider it."

"Oh, great," Kataryna says joyfully, clapping her hands. "If you do come over, we all will have Christmas Eve dinner together at my sister's. She would be thrilled. She loves to entertain."

"Sounds like a plan," Francesco responds excitedly. "I can also take the opportunity to visit a good friend of mine in Greenwich, Connecticut. He has been after me for some time to come see him."

Patrizia gets up and kisses him. "It is decided then, we are going to New York for Christmas, bellissimo."

"Buon Natale," Luca says. "This is my Christmas gift to you two."

Carlotta looks at them enviously. "I wish I could go, too, but my son has plans over here, so I have to stay in Italy."

"Dio grazie," Luca's father comes out with, hugging his wife. "At least we will have one of our children here for Christmas."

"Carlotta," Kataryna addresses her, "you and your son are welcome to come any other time to visit me. I have plenty of room for you two. How old is your son?"

"Thank you, Kataryna," Carlotta says smiling, "I will definitely take you up on that offer in the near future. Enrico is 16. He will turn 17 on March 25. He will be so excited when I tell him. Actually that will be his birthday present. Perfect. I don't have to look for anything big anymore."

Luca comes back on. "I think we will let Kataryna rest a little now. The Romano family can be quite exhausting," he laughs.

They all wave good-bye. Luca tells her he will check in with her again when he is back at his villa.

Kataryna gets comfortable on her couch and relives the video call. What a beautiful family. *I am so lucky to have them in my life. I should have gone back to Italy for the weekend before coming back New York.* Meeting the family brings up the thought of her mother. She picks up her mother's photo, which is standing on a console table.

"Oh Mom," she says out loud, tears in her eyes, "I miss you so. I wish you were alive and could meet this wonderful man and his family. I know how much you always loved Italy and the Italians. If you were here now, you could also shed some more light on my brother who is out there somewhere. Knowing you, it couldn't have been easy for you to give him up, but I promise you I won't stop trying to find him and explain to him why you had to give him up. Now more than ever I want him in my life and so does Aleksandra." *I'll better get busy with some work,* she thinks, *Mom would not want me to be that sad.* She walks to the window and looks to the sky. "Love you forever, Mom."

It is only 9 a.m. She feels tired and lies down on the couch to rest her eyes a little. When she opens her eyes again it is noon. Feeling more rested and hungry, she goes to the kitchen to fix a light lunch wondering what time Luca would be back at his villa. He is the first thing she thinks of when she wakes up and the last thing before she goes to sleep. *I guess it's official,* she thinks, *I am in love and it feels great. How did this happen so fast, she wonders?* It definitely is true that life can be unpredictable--you can lose a loved one at a moment's notice but also find love when you least expect it.

She picks up her phone and calls her father first and then her sister. "Hello, what are you doing?" she asks Aleksandra.

"Nothing really important," Aleksandra answers, "and you?"

"I am fighting some mild jet lag."

"Did you find out more about our lost brother?" her sister asks.

"No, unfortunately not. I have a feeling this is going to be a long and exhausting task, but I am determined to go all the way with this. However, I have some other interesting news."

"Oh?" Aleksandra questions her, "what might that be?"

"I am in love," she responds quietly.

For a moment there is silence, then Kataryna hears her sister breathe deeply.

"Really, who is the lucky guy?" Aleksandra asks. "You haven't mentioned any man you are interested in lately."

Kataryna exhales. "He is a member of the managing board of the Italian holding company, which is selling one of their subsidiaries that Stephen and I want to acquire."

"I can't believe it," Aleksandra yells into the phone. "Didn't you always tell me that mixing business with pleasure is not a good idea? What do you know about him? He might be one of those Casanova-types with a wife at home."

"Relax, Aleksandra, you are so wrong," Kataryna responds sharply to her sister's remarks. "First of all, he is divorced. Secondly, he is not a Casanova-type Italian and I didn't plan on falling in love with a business partner. It just happened and we both are in love. I invited him for Christmas Eve dinner at your place. His sister and her fiancé, who is the CFO of the company I want to acquire, are joining him. I invited them, too, of course. You know that I don't just fall in love with anybody and how selective I am when it comes to men. So when I tell you I am in love you can believe that this is real and that the feeling is totally mutual. We had two fantastic nights at his villa at Lake Como. Other than some playful banter, nothing happened the first night. I stayed in one of his guest rooms and he did not attempt anything. He was a total gentleman. I was immediately very attracted to him, not only to his looks but also his personality. I will tell you everything in more detail when I see you and you will understand. We had a video call this morning together with his entire family. What a great family. I can't wait to meet them in person. I am sure you will love them, too."

"OK," Aleksandra responds calmly. "I believe you and I know that you don't fall in love easily. So, wow, I have to digest this first. Anyway, I am very happy for you and hope it works out. I am looking forward to meeting him, his sister and her fiancé for Christmas at my house."

Kataryna is relieved that her sister is on board with the invitation she extended without asking her first.

"I am totally blown away by the turn of these events. If there is anything negative at all it is the long distance between us," Kataryna explains.

"Yeah, how are you going to deal with that in the long run?" Aleksandra asks.

"This is all very new. I haven't even thought about that at this point. Let's see where this is going. All I know I am deeply in love and I want to enjoy this feeling without putting anything negative or heavy in the equation. I am going to take it one day at a time."

"I can't wait to meet the man who enchanted you this much," Aleksandra says when Kataryna's home phone rings.

"I got to go, Aleksa. Luca is calling me on the other phone."

"OK, let's talk later or tomorrow again."

"Maybe we can do a video call soon with him and you together," Kataryna says before she hangs up and picks up her landline.

"Pronto," she says laughing into the phone.

"Ciao bella," she hears Luca saying, "I like how you answer the phone in Italian already. My entire family is completely in love with you, as am I, of course."

"That's good to know," Kataryna says, "you can tell them I feel the same way about them and you, of course."

"Thank you. I am glad you said that, you made my night."

"I wish I could make your night in another way, but unfortunately that will have to wait until Christmas."

"Very painful," he sighs, "just hearing you say these words is driving me crazy already."

"Okay, okay," she responds, "I will try not to drive you crazy anymore unless I have you right in front of me."

"And now that you put that image in my mind, it is getting even worse," he says softly.

"Sorry," she murmurs, "that wasn't intentional. I was attempting to get you off the subject, but I guess it backfired."

"Si, Principessa, it did. I really, really miss you. I wish there was a pill for that which I could take until Christmas."

"I can't offer you any pills, but would you like to meet via video in a few minutes?" she asks.

"You have the best ideas, Principessa."

"Give me about 10 minutes."

Kataryna dresses in seductive underwear with a super sexy push-up bra in a leopard print and puts on a cat mask and cat ears, which she had bought for Halloween. She puts the laptop on the entertainment console facing her bed and rings Luca. Seductive music plays from her iPod as she walks out of the room, deciding to make a big entrance when he comes on the screen. Luca accepts the video call and stares at the screen. *Where is she*, he wonders? All he can see is the room with the bed and an open door. Kataryna comes into the room walking up to the screen dancing slowly and seductively to the music.

"Oh, my God," he moans, "what are you trying to do to me?"

She kisses the screen and then lies on the bed and moves around seductively moaning softly as she becomes aroused by the action and imagination of Luca's arousal. He is groaning and breathing heavily as the sexy scene develops in front of him. She goes under the covers, removes her panties putting it in his sight and wraps the sheet around her, covering her body, except for her legs. For a split second the sheet falls to the side as she moves her legs slightly. She quickly puts it back in place. Luca is groaning loudly as he has this view of her for just seconds and he comes in ecstasy; and so does Kataryna, still with her cat mask and cat ears in place. She sits up and looks into the screen.

"Meow," she whispers, forming her lips into a kiss, "how did you like that wild cat in heat and all because of you? You should be here to tame it."

Luca is still in awe when he finally catches his breath.

"Other than our night in my bathtub, this must have been the most erotic experience I ever had. You never cease to amaze me. And thank you for making me feel so much better now."

"Darling," she says, taking off the cat mask and looking at him with smoldering eyes, "you bring it out in me. I have never done this for anyone before."

He smiles shyly. "I am glad you feel this way. And, by the way, I have never felt this much for anyone before either, nor has anyone ever excited me like you can. Not being able to be with you in the same room is a feeling I don't wish on my worst enemy."

"I have to admit, this is pretty surreal for me, too," Kataryna agrees.

"Well, on a lighter note," he says, "with your mask tonight you already got some practice for our events in February at the Carnevale in Venezia."

"Yeah, I did," she responds, "but I won't be dressed up as a wild cat for that event. I have something more regal in mind for the Venetian Carnevale. It will be a surprise and I am absolutely sure you will love it."

"So am I. Whatever you come up with will be spectacular."

"Okay, it is sleepy time for you now," she teases him. "Have a good night my handsome prince and dream of me."

"That won't be hard to do. Buonanotte, gatta selvatica."

"Translation, please," Kataryna demands, "what does gatta selvatica mean?"

"It means wild cat."

"Of course," Kataryna giggles, "I should have figured that out on my own. By the way, please send me a photo of you, so I can take you with me wherever I go."

"Coming up," he promises as they end the video call.

Kataryna lies back onto her bed recalling Luca's reaction. *That was so much fun, the next best thing to having him here with me*, she thinks. *Let's see what else I can come up with for future video calls. I have to keep it exciting.* A few minutes later her phone alerts her that she has a message. An email from Luca with his photo and the words:

> *Ciao Gatta Selvatica,*
> *I wish I could send myself over there as easy as I can send this photo.*
> *All my love,*
> *Luca*

She looks at the photo, smiles and types a response:

> *Hot-looking guy. You have to introduce me to him one day.*
> *XOXO*
> *Gatta Selvatica ready to devour you.*

Luca opens the email message and starts laughing. He hits Reply:

> *Watch out gatta selvatica, I will tame you before you can devour me and have you eating out of my hand.*

She reads his email and types her response:

> *You might just be the one to do it. Now sleep on that.*
> *Good Night.*
> *GS (can't wait to be tamed by you)*

EIGHT

Carlotta Romano Moretti arrives back in her penthouse apartment in Milan on Monday afternoon. She and her son Enrico had stayed with her parents' over the weekend at the Bellagio villa and enjoyed it thoroughly. It is so relaxing and beautiful at her parents' villa-- a stark contrast to her life in Milano. Her position at the family's holding company is keeping her extremely busy and is taking a lot of time away from her son; but she needs that now that her love life is rather unexciting, except for that secret obsession, how she calls it, with a certain man. Her feelings for him are getting stronger constantly and she fantasizes about him when she is lonely at night.

Carlotta, a strikingly attractive woman with dark brown hair and mahogany highlights and dark eyes, just turned 40, but she looks about 10 years younger. She has always taken good care of herself, a result of working as a model when she was in her early 20s. She stopped modeling after she had Enrico when she was 23. Her ex-husband had insisted that she stay at home with their newborn, and she never forgave him for it. There was so much resentment that the marriage eventually fell apart. They finally divorced a year ago when she moved back to her parents' villa for a while. After she recovered from the ordeal, she moved to the Milan penthouse she is living in now. Her position as public relations director at the family's holding company, as well as motherhood, have kept her pretty much out of trouble when it comes to matters of the heart, but she often feels lonely when she has time to relax, especially on those weekends when Enrico stays with his father. She dated a few men she met through her business connections or her friends who were trying to set her up with suitable men, but she has not found the proverbial Mr. Right. After a few weeks of dating she came to the realization that they were not what she was hoping to spend the rest of her life with. Or was it the strong attraction she has for this man, which she has not dared to reveal to anyone, that was keeping her subconsciously from falling in love with anyone else?

She recalls the video call the family had with Luca's new girlfriend Kataryna on Sunday and envied her brother as she watched him interact with his new love interest. They make a great couple and seem to be so much in love. Luca couldn't stop talking about her the whole afternoon. Kataryna appeared equally smitten with her brother. She is happy for her brother. He deserves a great woman like Kataryna after the train wreck of a woman he was married to. Carlotta never had a good feeling about Luca's ex-wife Traviata. The name says it all, Traviata, which means the woman who strayed. All she always wanted is being the center of attention and she loved to flirt with other men. Luca never saw it coming, Carlotta figures, because he was working so hard. Thank God that woman is out of his life and out of our family with minimal financial damage, thanks to the prenuptial agreement they had signed.

Sadness overcomes Carlotta as she thinks about the object of her attraction. This has been going on for quite some time and she really wants to tell someone. Better yet, she wants to tell the man, whom she is so in love with, how she feels. They know each other well. He is a long-time friend of her family, but up to about six months ago he was married. She doesn't really know what prompted the divorce and she doesn't want to speculate. All she is interested in is that he is free now. Probably not for long as attractive and successful as he is. *But why hasn't he made a move*, she wonders? He is not shy when it comes to women. She thought she felt a spark one day when they were talking alone for a while at one of her parents' parties, and was hoping he would ask her out on a date. Is it because he is afraid that her family would not approve of them getting together romantically or is he not interested in her in that way?

She pours herself a glass of Prosecco and contemplates calling him and inviting him over for dinner at her apartment this weekend when Enrico will be staying with his father. What if he says no? She feels uneasy about the idea, but her feelings are so much stronger than her uneasiness. She imagines him in her apartment having dinner and making love thereafter. The idea gets her all excited, but somehow she is still not sure how to go about it. Maybe there is a better way of doing this. She would prefer if he asked her out first, but she is really ready for a steamy love affair. He may not approach her out of respect for the family. She refills her glass and takes a big sip, getting a bit more relaxed, and then an idea hits her. Why not discuss it with Luca and see if he can help her in some way to speed this along. He can talk to him and somehow encourage him to ask her out. Yeah, that's a good idea. She dials Luca's number.

"Pronto," he comes on. "Ciao Carlotta. Is everything alright?"

"Not really. I think I need your assistance with something. Could you come over to my place for dinner tonight? We can talk more then."

"Sure, I would love to have dinner with you. I don't want to be alone anyway because then I have to think about Kataryna all the time and how much I miss her. What time do you want me there?"

"Whenever you are finished in the office, just come over. I need my big brother to help me with a delicate matter."

"I am a little concerned," Luca admits to his sister, "is anyone in the family sick?"

"No, nothing like that," she calms him down, "well, I might be lovesick."

He is silent for a moment and then sighs. "I will be over as soon as I can. Can't wait to hear more about this. I wasn't aware you had started seeing someone. Wouldn't it be great if we both found the love of our lives at the same time?"

"Let's discuss it later," she says.

Carlotta is not sure how Luca will react to what she has to tell him. She is too anxious to cook and orders dinner in from a nearby restaurant. Enrico is staying overnight with a school friend, so Luca and her will be undisturbed this evening. Hopefully, by the end of the night, they will have come up with a good plan on how to address this situation.

Luca arrives around 7 p.m., at his sister's penthouse. She opens the door with a glass of Champagne in her hand. He kisses her hello.

"I see you have started celebrating without me," he says laughing and hugging her.

She smiles warily. "Let's see if we have anything to celebrate." She hands him a glass of Champagne.

"Here is to love," Luca makes a toast.

Carlotta just nods smiling at her brother. "Have you spoken to Kataryna today?"

"Not yet, she is at work and it is only 1:30 p.m., in New York right now. I hope we will speak later on this evening if she comes home at a decent hour. But we had another video call last night after I got home, and a spicy one at that," he laughs.

"Spicy?" Carlotta asks. "What does that mean?"

"I am not going into details. Suffice it to say that we worked ourselves up quite a bit, but the end result was very satisfying. She is so sexy and knows how to push the right buttons, so to speak. But you have no idea how hard this long distance thing is. If I hadn't so much on my plate at the office right now, I would take the jet and fly over there tonight. When I think of her my body is going in all kind of directions. It is a matter of love and lust like I have never experienced before. Can you imagine what it feels like to really love the person you are craving for so intensely?"

"Mamma mia, Luca," Carlotta says, "you really fell in love deeply with her in that short period that you have known her."

"We have really known each other for the last three months or so when we had the video conference calls regarding the acquisition. We had flirted a bit during a few private conversations we had after we were finished with the business part. I got kind of excited then already because she is naturally sexy; she doesn't have to do much to turn me on. All she has to do is look at me and I am there. So you can imagine how much I was looking forward to meeting her in person. The first night we went out I took her to Villa D'Este and invited her to be my guest in my villa. Of course, we didn't do anything that night but it was so hard for me not to take her in my arms and kiss her. At dinner we exchanged some banter, which almost caused me to have a biological reaction, if you know what I mean. I have no idea how I managed to keep it under control. I guess I wanted to show her that I respect her and not fall all over her like an animal. The sexual tension had been building up between us the next day and we had a close call on the boat before we got to Bellagio. We then met with Roberto and Francesco. I was doing okay during the business meeting, but when we got back to the villa and had an after-dinner drink by the fireplace we literally couldn't hold back anymore."

He pauses for a moment. "I am sorry, Carlotta, I am rambling on here about Kataryna and me. We really wanted to talk about your lovesick situation. So what is going on and how can I help?"

"Don't worry, Luca, I like to hear about you and Kataryna," Carlotta says. "It sounds more like a movie than a real life experience and I am very happy for you. I can see why you are totally head over heels. She is a very beautiful and interesting woman. I can't wait to meet her in person and spend time with her. Unfortunately, my situation isn't as clear. As a matter of fact, I have no idea how my love interest feels about me, but I am very attracted to him. I think I am in love, although we haven't even gone out on a date yet."

"Sounds mysterious," Luca interjects.

Carlotta looks at her brother intensely. "Before I reveal more you have to promise to have an open mind."

"Why wouldn't I?" Luca asks inquisitively.

"Because the man I am so in love with is a close friend of our family. It is Roberto Silvestri," she blurts out.

Luca is stunned, but hides it well. He runs his hands through his hair contemplating what to say.

"Wow," he finally gets out of his mouth. "I wasn't prepared for that one. How long did you have these feelings for him already?"

"For quite some time, but it became even stronger after his divorce was final about six months ago. While he was still married, I didn't want to allow myself to have these feelings for him and I suppressed it. After his divorce the feelings came back with a vengeance, and I gave into it. But I don't know how to move this forward. Do I call him and invite him to dinner at my place, or just have a drink with him somewhere to see what is going on in his life? What do you think?"

"Let me ask you this first," Luca responds, "what do you know about Roberto and the reason for his divorce?"

"Not much. I believe his wife wanted the divorce, but I don't know what happened between them. Do you know exactly what was going on there?" she asks.

Luca is uncomfortable with the subject and stalls, shrugging his shoulders. He knows he can't talk about the incident with the employee at the Christmas party and he definitely doesn't want to tell her about Roberto's attempt to pursue Kataryna. But what shall he tell his sister?"

"Let me see what I can find out," he responds. "Please don't rush into anything."

"I don't know if you can call it rushing into. After all, we have known Roberto and his family since we were children. He is not a stranger to me."

"I know, nevertheless, we have not been so close to him recently that we are aware of what has been going on in his life in detail. I think it would be best to proceed with caution. The last thing I want to see is you heartbroken," Luca says.

"I appreciate that you are so protective of me, but I am a mature woman, Luca, and I am really in love. If anyone should understand how I feel, it should be you since you are also so much in love now," Carlotta says laughing.

"Let's eat, I am starving," Luca says, moving on to change the subject. He really needs to think about this situation later on and hopefully come up with something good. On the other side, if Roberto were also interested in Carlotta, it would take his mind off Kataryna. It might be a win-win situation, but he does not want to err at the expense of his sister's happiness.

Carlotta serves the dinner. For the rest of the evening they talk about her son Enrico and work-related situations.

Luca leaves his sister's apartment around 10:30 p.m., promising to get back to her as soon as possible. When he gets home to his penthouse apartment in Milan around 11 p.m., he fixes himself a drink and thinks about how to deal with this situation. He is not happy about Carlotta's interest in Roberto, but he knows when these kind of feelings are involved it would be very difficult to talk her out of it; unless, of course, he can make a good case but that would mean discrediting Roberto without revealing details. Would she accept it and forget about him without trying to find out more details? *Unlikely,* he thinks, *I wouldn't if I were in that situation.*

Around 11:45 p.m., he dials Kataryna's cell phone number. She picks up the call seeing his photo pop up.

"Buonasera Signore," she says laughing, "how are you?"

Luca's mood improves immediately hearing her voice and happy laughter.

"Ciao bella, I am so-so."

Kataryna senses some distress in his voice.

"You don't sound like yourself. What is going on?" she asks somewhat concerned.

"Oh, I had a tough day and evening," he sighs. "First of all, I miss you and then my sister Carlotta approached me with a bombshell situation and asked for my assistance."

"A bombshell situation? What does that mean?"

"Can you speak freely?" he asks.

"Yes, I just got home a few minutes ago. I had several meetings, one with our due diligence team regarding the proposed acquisition of NatMedica and then Stephen and I were sitting together for a while talking about various related matters. I put some finishing touches on another smaller deal and then called it a day. Tomorrow, when I meet with Stephen for dinner, I will tell him about us and the situation with Roberto, which I believe is under control, right?"

"I guess it is if he hasn't contacted you anymore," Luca responds.

"So, what's going on with Carlotta?" Kataryna asks impatiently.

"Carlotta, who by the way is divorced and unattached, told me tonight that she has very strong feelings for Roberto for quite some time already, but he has no clue she feels that way about him. You know that we have been close friends with Roberto and his family since our childhood. I spent some time with Roberto after my and his divorces. We went out together occasionally, but Carlotta was never part of that and she never mentioned an interest in Roberto before. So I was quite stunned to hear that tonight. She asked me to help her to move this forward. I am torn about it, knowing that he just recently tried to pursue you. I have no idea how he feels about Carlotta. In addition, he was not too happy when I had that talk with him about you and me. So he might still be stuck on you deep down inside, although he knows that we are involved."

Kataryna listens to Luca's explanations.

"Wow, what are you going to do about it?"

"I have no idea," Luca replies. "What do you think I should do?"

"Do you know what is going on in his love life?"

"Only that he has dated a few women after his divorce, but he wasn't seriously interested in them. He told me he had nothing in common with them and he was hoping to meet a woman of substance who was able to keep him interested not only sexually," Luca explains.

"Maybe Carlotta could be that woman," Kataryna says. "She is beautiful, successful and has substance."

"I would prefer if she fell in love with somebody else," Luca murmurs.

"But it is not up to you. How would you react if she told you that she would prefer if you would fall in love with somebody else than me?"

"That's different."

"How is that different?"

"You are not a woman I knew for a long time and all of a sudden fell in love with."

"I have a feeling there is more to your reluctance to accept your sister's feelings for Roberto," Kataryna comes back with.

"Maybe there is something deep down that tells me this is not a good idea. Let me ask you this. What if they were to have a relationship and we all would meet at the usual family get-togethers. Would you have a problem with seeing him knowing that he tried to pursue you at one time?"

"No, I wouldn't," she responds, "at the time he tried to pursue me he didn't know that you and I had started an intimate relationship. So I was fair game. If it had been the other way around, I wouldn't mind seeing you at get-togethers, either."

"Fair enough," Luca responds, "I will give it some more thought."

"You do that, my darling," she closes the subject, "and I think it's time for you to go to sleep now. It's way past midnight over there and you had a tough day."

"Are you trying to get rid of me?" he asks facetiously.

"How can you think that? I enjoy every moment with you, but I am also concerned that you are not getting enough sleep and wearing yourself thin. You have a full plate at the office; you are stressed because you miss me, and now the Carlotta-Roberto situation. You need to relax and take care of yourself. You will need your strength and energy when you come over here at Christmastime," she says laughing.

"As usual you make perfect sense," he admits also laughing. "Good night Principessa, speak to you tomorrow."

Kataryna sits quietly for a while after hanging up with Luca. *Unbelievable developments,* she thinks, *what else could come up next?* Her thoughts turn to her family issue. She will call the lawyer in Berlin in the next few days to see if he has made any progress in finding a trace of her brother. After dinner Kataryna calls her sister Aleksandra to talk some more about Luca and the plans for Christmas as well as the search for their brother.

"Hi Aleksandra, how is everything?" Kataryna asks her sister.

"Pretty good. We are quite busy now with the catering as the holidays are approaching fast," Aleksandra answers.

"Oh, I almost forgot," Kataryna says, "Thursday is Thanks-giving."

"Yes, it is, and we expect you at 3 p.m.," Aleksandra responds. "I have some new recipes, which I am sure you will like."

"I can't wait. Your Thanksgiving menu is always delicious. Make sure you have my favorite stuffing," she giggles.

"It is already on the menu," Aleksandra assures her.

"Can I help you with something?"

"No, it's all under control. All you have to do is show up here and bring a big appetite," Aleksandra says.

"No problem. I can do that. See you on Thursday." Kataryna ends the phone call.

She decides to go to bed early. Tomorrow will be a heavy day at the office, and in the evening she will have dinner with her partner Stephen and tell him about her relationship with Luca.

After her brother is gone, Carlotta has another glass of Champagne. Luca was not too thrilled about her being in love with Roberto, it appeared. Roberto and Luca have been friends and business partners for a long time. *As a matter of fact, they are quite alike in many*

ways, she thinks. *So why would her brother possibly have a problem with her and Roberto having a romantic relationship?*

Back at her office the next morning, she makes a few business-related calls and then decides to see Luca. He is on the phone. She leaves him a message. As she walks back to her office her sister Patrizia comes down the hallway. They chat for a little while and arrange to have lunch together later on. Carlotta contemplates talking to her sister about her feelings for Roberto. Maybe Francesco knows what Roberto is up to in his love life. Francesco may also be able to help her somehow, she imagines.

As she steps into her office her phone rings. The caller ID shows Luca is calling her.

"Ciao Luca, I just wanted to see if you gave our conversation some more thought?" she asks.

"I am sorry Carlotta, I really didn't get a chance yet. I called Kataryna when I got home last night and as you can imagine, I got totally side-tracked."

"Okay, lover boy," she says laughing. "I can see you are way too busy with your own love life. But don't forget about me."

Luca sighs. "I have to think about this some more. Please give me some time. I have a lot on my plate right now with the NatMedica divestiture and the acquisition we want to make."

"Sure, I understand," she states somewhat disappointed.

She starts working on some press releases her father asked her to prepare, which keeps her busy and distracted from her personal situation for now. Patrizia shows up at 1 p.m., to pick her up for their lunch.

"Shall we ask Luca to join us?" Patrizia asks.

"No, he is too busy. I spoke to him earlier. He mentioned that he has a heavy workload. It's time for some girl talk anyway," Carlotta replies, giggling.

They decide to go to one of their favorite restaurants nearby and have a leisurely lunch. The owner of the restaurant rushes over as they enter.

"Ah, the Romano sisters. What a pleasure to have you with us today," he exclaims, leading them to their table. "We have some excellent specials but, of course, we will make anything you wish for you."

"How about bringing us a nice bottle of red wine to start?" Carlotta asks.

He motions one of his waiters to bring their favorite wine. After some small talk and rattling down the specials of the day he excuses himself. The wine arrives along with a plate of antipasto. The sisters make a toast –"salute." They talk about how happy they are for their brother. Carlotta is on her second glass of wine already and in a good mood.

"Ciao bellas," they hear a man's voice saying.

Roberto stands in front of them. Carlotta's heart starts racing.

"Ciao Roberto," Patrizia says casually. "How have you been?"

"I am surviving. How about you?"

"Surviving?" Patrizia repeats. "What are you up to these days?"

"I am quite busy with the divestiture of NatMedica, as you can imagine. You know the interested parties are doing their due diligence and I have to deliver a lot of material."

"Are you meeting someone for lunch or do you want to join us?" Patrizia asks.

"I am meeting someone, but my guest is running late."

"Have a seat while you are waiting and have a glass of wine with us." Carlotta offers.

"Thank you." He takes a seat next to Carlotta.

"It is our pleasure," Carlotta says touching his arm.

The waiter comes over to pour him a glass of wine. The three chat for a while when Patrizia's cell phone rings.

"I have to take this." She excuses herself and walks away from the table.

"It's good to see you, Roberto," Carlotta says smiling. "Other than work, what are you doing these days? How is your daughter?"

"She is fine, I am trying to plan a trip for her and me. I need to spend some quality time with her."

"Where will you be going?" Carlotta inquires.

"Don't know yet. I will let her pick the location."

"So, it's just you and Verena?" Carlotta probes.

"Yes, just us two."

Carlotta is happy to hear that there doesn't seem to be a special woman in his life.

"How is Enrico?"

"He is great, a really good boy and he has good grades in school, too. I couldn't be more thrilled," she says proudly.

"Fantastic," Roberto responds, "and how is your love life?"

Carlotta flushes. She didn't expect that kind of question.

"I am still waiting for Prince Charming," she finally comes up with.

"How about your love life?" she dares to ask him staring deeply into his eyes.

A heat wave goes through her body waiting for his answer. Luigi, the restaurant owner interrupts their conversation.

"Signor Silvestri, your guest has arrived."

Roberto gets up turning to Carlotta. "Let's have a drink one of these evenings. We can talk about my love life then," he says laughing, kissing her good-bye on the cheek.

Carlotta is in seventh heaven. He finally asked her out.

"Call me, when you are ready for that drink," she shouts after him smiling.

The restaurant owner ushers him to a table where his guest has been seated already. It's a woman. Carlotta looks over to his table wondering who that woman might be. She sees him kissing her on the cheek. Her heart drops to the floor. She goes from elation of Roberto asking her out to having to wonder who the woman he is meeting for lunch might be.

Patrizia returns to the table. "So sorry, Carlotta, but it was business. I had to take the call. Good that Roberto was here to keep you company. Where is he?"

"His guest arrived," Carlotta replies pointing to his table. "Do you know who the woman he is having lunch with is?"

"No, I don't. I have never seen her before. Probably a new love interest."

"Why do you think that?" Carlotta questions her sister.

"Francesco mentioned from time to time that Roberto was still looking for the right woman he can settle down with. That hasn't been easy with his long working hours. But in the last few weeks he apparently has been in a very mellow mood. So Francesco was figuring he might have met someone he likes a lot. By the way," Patrizia questions her sister, "are you seeing anyone these days?"

Carlotta swallows her food and takes a sip of her wine before answering.

"No," she utters, "I haven't met anyone interesting in the last few months. But I am planning to do something about that soon."

"Good," Patrizia responds. "I would like to see you in a nice relationship. Enrico will be grown up soon. Boys that age don't want to hang around at home. I am sure he is already looking at girls."

Carlotta starts laughing. "Patrizia, please don't rush my son into a relationship. He is only 16. I want him to do well in school first. But you are right. I am definitely ready for some romance."

"Time to get back to the office but I really enjoyed this lunch. We should do this more often," Patrizia suggests.

"Good idea," Carlotta declares, "we are working way too many hours."

As they leave their table to exit the restaurant Roberto waves at them and they wave back at him. Back at the office Carlotta goes straight to Luca's office.

"Do you have a moment for me?" she asks her brother.

"Sure, come on in and close the door."

"Patrizia and I just had lunch together and we met Roberto there by coincidence. I had the opportunity to speak alone with him for a little while when Patrizia had to take a phone call. He indicated that he would like to meet up for a drink, and as you can imagine, I said yes. I think I can handle this myself from here. So, you are off the hook for now. But if you hear anything meanwhile, just let me know."

Luca looks at his sister. "I guess I can't talk you out of this?" he asks her quietly.

"Why would you want to talk me out of this?" she queries him somewhat disappointed at his reaction.

"I am just not so comfortable with this idea of you and Roberto getting together romantically," he explains.

Carlotta shrugs her shoulders. "Relax, my darling brother. I will keep you posted on the developments. Who knows, he might tell me he is dating some sexy woman when we meet and then the whole thing is moot anyway."

"So you are prepared for him to not be interested in you romantically?" he digs a little deeper.

"I think I have to be prepared for something like this. He is a very attractive and successful man. I am sure there are plenty of women after him. All he has to do is choose which one he wants."

"Do you have a firm date yet when you are meeting him?" he asks.

"No, we kind of left it open, but as you can imagine I want it to be real soon. I will give it a few days and if I haven't heard from him by then I will take the initiative and call him."

"If I may give you some advice," Luca starts telling her, "when you do meet, don't fall all over him right away. I know that Roberto likes a challenge. So let him chase you for a while."

Carlotta smiles at her brother. "Thank you for the expert advice," she says. "I will try to control myself the first evening."

Luca grins at her running his hands through his hair, as she walks out of his office giggling like a schoolgirl. He is afraid that Roberto might open up his situation with Kataryna when he meets with Carlotta. That would not only ruin Carlotta's evening and plans but also bring up some discussions he doesn't want to have. He feels uneasy as he tries to get back to his enormous load of work.

NINE

After a long and grueling day, Luca arrives at his Milan apartment around 9 p.m. Some unexpected snags with the target, the family wants to acquire, came up, and he is uncomfortable about Carlotta and Roberto getting together soon. He really wants to clear the air with Roberto before these two have their evening out, but he is not sure how to approach it. While going over the paperwork he brought home from the office, he has a bite to eat and a glass of red wine, which relaxes him a bit. It is 10:30 p.m., in Milano. He dials Kataryna's office number. Her assistant Melanie answers the phone.

"Hello Melanie, this is Luca Romano, is Kataryna available?"

"Hi Luca," Melanie greets him, "Kataryna is in the office, but stepped out for a moment. Do you want me to find her for you?"

"No, thank you," Luca answers, "it is not urgent. Please ask her to call me at her earliest convenience."

"Will do," Melanie responds cheerfully. "Have a nice evening."

"Thank you. Have a great afternoon, Melanie."

Luca leans back reflecting on the day. He is stressed, lonely and unsure how to proceed with Roberto. He pours himself another glass of red wine and looks at his phone's screen with the beautiful photo of Kataryna as wallpaper. It's too late to call Roberto tonight, he decides.

At 11 p.m., Kataryna calls him back.

"Hello my dear. I just returned to my office from a longer meeting with the due diligence team regarding the acquisition. It looks really good. The guys didn't seem to have any major concerns. I was able to answer most of their questions. The other open issues are regulatory and accounting related, which they will handle on their own. Once all that is done the analysts will prepare their write-ups and then it will go to our acquisition committee. How was your day?"

"Pretty stressful for various reasons, one of them being that I miss you. It's great to hear, though, that the deal is coming along. At least I got some good news today."

"I miss you, too. I am having dinner with Stephen tonight. I will tell him about our relationship then."

"Good," Luca says. "I had some snags with my new acquisition today. Carlotta went to lunch with Patrizia and they ran into Roberto. Apparently Roberto wants to have a drink with Carlotta one of these evenings, she told me. Of course, she is on cloud nine. I am not so excited about that piece of news because I am not sure yet if he has resolved his feelings for you. I don't want to tell her that he tried to pursue you for various reasons, but I am a little afraid that he might have asked her out for a drink so he can vent his frustration over the situation regarding our relationship. Needless to say, that would be a disaster because, first of all she would be crushed, and then it puts a shadow over our relationship which is still so new."

"Darling," Kataryna reacts, "don't let it bother you that much. Everybody has to deal with the situation at hand. Even if he tells her, so what? She knows that you and I are together and that I am no threat. If he continues to sulk over the matter and make a big deal out of it, he will have to live with that. As for Carlotta, I would feel bad for her, but unfortunately that is out of our control. The most important thing is that you and I are on the same page."

"You make me feel so much better now," Luca exhales. "The only negative about this would be that she would question why I didn't tell her about it before he did."

"Yeah, that could happen. But then you tell her you didn't want to put a damper on her feelings for him, especially since it is a moot point because you and I are in a relationship and that I have no interest in Roberto whatsoever."

"Thank you, my angel, you just solved my biggest problem," he says in a much lighter mood now.

Kataryna laughs. "See how easy that was? I wish I could take your mind totally off anything that bothers you tonight with one of our famous video calls, but unfortunately that won't be possible because I am having dinner with Stephen tonight and won't be home until later when you will hopefully be sound asleep."

"By the time you come home tonight it might be time for me to get up."

"I am not planning on a late night out unless Stephen has a problem with our relationship and we end up having a long discussion about it. That is unlikely, however. As far as the situation with Roberto is concerned that could be a point of concern for him because we will have to work so closely together with him if we get to acquire this company. I suppose Stephen would want to have a one-on-one discussion with

Roberto to straighten it out, so that going forward we would not have any surprises in that area."

"Yeah, we have to make sure that this aspect is settled before the acquisition closes," Luca explains. "I also don't want any surprises for business and personal reasons as you can imagine."

"We will go over all that tomorrow. I may send you an email tonight after my dinner with Stephen so you will have some idea how the conversation went first thing in the morning."

"Thank you, Principessa, great doing business with you," Luca says jokingly.

"And with you," Kataryna responds. "Talk to you tomorrow."

Kataryna and Stephen arrive at the restaurant at 7 p.m., and are seated at their table immediately. The waiter brings the menu and takes their drink order. They engage in some small talk about the news, the weather and the new mini iPad coming out.

"This mini iPad is coming out just in time," Kataryna says enthusiastically.

"I am going to get several right away. One is for me, of course, and I am getting two more for my sister's twin daughters for Christmas."

"Yeah," Stephen responds, "my kids have hinted at that already, too. So I guess my Christmas shopping will be done soon."

The waiter arrives with the drink order. Stephen and Kataryna make a toast.

"To a successful transaction."

"If we can complete this deal, I will be a happy man," Stephen says. "This would be the largest deal we have ever done and I think it would be an excellent prospect for an IPO down the road. You have done a great job with this deal. We could end up making a lot of money, Kataryna. Having said that, I have something to discuss with you concerning future deals."

"There are a couple of things from my side we need to discuss, though, before we start celebrating," Kataryna reveals.

"I guess you mean the other interested parties could snatch the deal away from us. I have been thinking about that, too. Do you have any idea which way the Romano family is leaning?" Stephen asks.

"Well, the other interested parties is one thing, but I have to disclose something else," she says.

"Are you about to ruin my evening, Kat?" He calls her Kat whenever Kataryna is too long for him to say.

"I certainly hope not," she says, "this could be a positive for our deal."

"Jeez, thank God, you got me worried for a moment," he murmurs.

"Let me finish," she interrupts him quickly, "because I have two situations to disclose.

"OK, now I am officially worried," he declares.

"Relax Stephen. Just let me get to it so you can decide if there is any reason for concern."

He takes a sip of his Champagne. "Go on," he says somewhat anxious, "I will be quiet now."

The waiter appears at the table to take their food order. Both of them know exactly what they will be having for dinner. Stephen orders their usual bottle of red wine, a California Cabernet Sauvignon Trefethen.

"Luca Romano and I have started a romantic relationship." She pauses, looking at him to see his reaction.

Stephen looks at her with wide eyes.

"Is this something real or a casual affair?"

"I don't engage in casual affairs, Stephen. This is very real and we are in love. It is totally mutual."

"Well, that is actually good news," he says relieved. "This could mean that he will consider our offer first before the other interested parties."

"Luca will sell this company to the most suitable buyer with the best offer on the table," Kataryna explains. "If our offer is the best, we will be successful. I do not want to use my relationship with him as a negotiation point, nor do I want any perception in that direction."

"I am sorry, Kat," Stephen apologizes quickly, "I didn't mean it that way. I was just trying to convey that I think that this is not a deal breaker and, in fact, could be a positive point also for Luca unless you two break up before the family decides who to sell to."

"I think you have a point there," she says. "I don't think breaking up is a concern. We are actually trying very hard to deepen our relationship, which due to the long distance between us, is not that easy. But Luca is coming over for Christmas and we are going to Hawaii together on December 26. He is also bringing his sister Patrizia along with her fiancé Francesco Barone, who, as you know, is the CFO of our acquisition target. Francesco asked me to arrange a meeting for him with you, if at all possible."

"Uh, this is getting interesting," Stephen says smiling.

"Of course, I will meet with him when he is here. I wouldn't miss that opportunity for the world. As a matter of fact, I will have him over for dinner to our house. This is much more private than any restaurant. Your sister can cater the event so Rebecca doesn't have to cook. What about Roberto Silvestri, is he also coming over for the holidays? I really would like to meet him. This guy is brilliant."

"No, and that is the next subject I want to go in to. Are you ready for this? Roberto has also taken an interest in me."

"Get out of here," Stephen is laughing. "Didn't I already predict that? Gee, I should have known better letting a woman like you do a deal with Italian men. Well, I don't blame them. You are a good catch on many levels. So how did that one come out?"

"Roberto followed me to Berlin under the pretense that he had new material for the deal to go over with me. We met for dinner where he revealed that he couldn't make it public because Luca had not reviewed it yet. During the course of the evening he told me he fell in love with me the first time he saw me and he, get this, proceeded to propose marriage to me."

"Oh my God," Stephen shouts out. "This is ridiculous. What did Luca have to say about that?"

"I didn't tell Luca about the proposal because I didn't want to embarrass Roberto and ruin their friendship. To be honest, I felt a little sorry for Roberto when I told him about my relationship with Luca. He was not prepared for that one. In addition, Luca will meet with him to discuss his trip to Berlin, etc. I am sure that will be another sore moment for Roberto. I just hope it doesn't get ugly, but then I trust Luca to be very diplomatic. After all they and their families have been close friends for a very long time. They are like family."

Stephen lets out a deep breath. "Wow, this could be a problem if the CEO of the company we want to acquire has some type of fantasy about you. Do you think that he will get over this so we all can work together professionally?"

"Time will tell," Kataryna replies, shrugging her shoulders. "I will keep you posted."
"Please do. Let's hope that situation is resolved soon."

"Well, in the event it continues to be an issue, we have to come up with a solution," Kataryna goes on. "So far I haven't heard from him anymore. To top it off, Luca told me earlier today that his sister Carlotta revealed today that she is secretly in love with Roberto. So I am hoping if they get together the whole thing will blow over and we all will be a happy family."

"Whoa, this is getting really involved now," Stephen says. "How does Luca feel about that?"

"He is not a happy camper. For some reason he seems reluctant about the idea of Carlotta and Roberto together."

"Better Carlotta than you, I guess," Stephen adds.

Kataryna grins. "I guess that's one way to look at this. I also owe Roberto an answer if we would be willing to grant his daughter an internship. She apparently wants to take business and finance courses and Roberto wants her to focus on that. He thought that she might be more focused if she can be in New York at the same time. Needless to say, I don't want for this whole thing to get more messy, so I think it would be best to wait and see how he reacts going forward. What do you think?"

Stephen exhales. "Yeah, we have to see first how this situation develops. I am reluctant to grant that wish for now. The same goes for the idea of the senior management acquiring an equity stake in the company under our ownership. What I would entertain is to give shares as a bonus to them going forward, instead of cash payments, if they continue to do a great job. We can peg that to the results. But I would only entertain that if the situation with Roberto and his fantasy about you were completely resolved. The last thing I want is to have is a shareholder, even a minority shareholder, who has the hots for you and goes out of control. As a matter of fact, I wouldn't even want him as CEO if he can't let go of his infatuation with you. That would be a shame, though because he is a valuable asset."

"I totally agree," Kataryna says, "we can't have that."

"Well, listen," Stephen starts a new conversation, "as I mention-ed before I also wanted to discuss something with you."

"Yes, you did say that earlier. So what's on your mind?"

"Initially, I was anxious to have this conversation with you, but it just became a little easier since you told me about your relationship with Luca."

"Really?" Kataryna asks, looking at him puzzled, "now you piqued my curiosity."

"As I said, this deal is a really good one and I am glad we stumbled across it. So I was wondering what other great deals might be out there in Europe, which would be a great fit for us. I was thinking of asking you if you could imagine working out of Europe for a while and see if you can find some other pearls like this one."

"How would you imagine that? Where would I be working out of?"

"I hadn't thought it through in detail, Kat," he responds. "First of all, I wanted to know if you would even entertain the idea. But after what you just told me I think you could work out of Milan. We could rent a temporary office for you there and set you up with everything so you can work on your existing U.S. deals and at the same time look for new deals in Europe. It would be so much easier for you to travel to another European country if you were over there. And I think Luca would be thrilled to have you over there."

"That's for sure. Let me think about it a bit. I will get back to you on this."

"Great, now let's celebrate our new adventures." He raises his glass of wine.

"Cheers, here's to you and Luca. I am very happy that you found someone you are excited about. I think you two are a good fit."

"Well, thank you Stephen," Kataryna clinks his glass, "so do I."

She wonders if she should tell him about her lost brother but decides against it. This would be too much for him to digest after all the things she already hit him with tonight. There will be another more suitable time when she will tell him about that one.

They finish their dinner around 11 p.m., and leave the restaurant to head home.

"Please say hi to Rebecca for me," Kataryna says, "we have to get together again soon."

"Yes, I have to plan a night out for my wife," he says, "she has been very patient while I was working all these hours. I am planning on taking a few days off over the holidays."

"Too bad that Luca and I are leaving for Maui already on the 26th of December, otherwise we could all get together for a night out. But let's plan that for another time."

"Absolutely, I can't wait to meet the man who finally captured your heart. Luca should consider himself really lucky because you are so picky when it comes to men."

"Why don't we call it selective," Kataryna makes a point. "I told you many times that I don't settle for just anyone."

"You are right, that's probably a better word for it," Stephen agrees. "Looks like it was worth the wait."

"It was," Kataryna agrees, "now if we only wouldn't be so far apart."

"Well, don't we have a solution for that?" Stephen teases her.

"Well planned, Stephen," she says laughing, "I will take it under consideration. Living in Milan for a while may not be the worst thing that can happen to anyone."

"There you go, you are already warming up to the idea," he jokes.

"Thanks for dinner, Stephen. See you tomorrow."

After her long day, Kataryna gets home around 11:30 p.m. Looking at her emails before going to sleep, she sees one from Luca, which must have come in when she was getting ready for bed. It is almost 6 a.m., over in Italy and Luca seems to be up.

Hello Principessa,
I just got up and you are the first thing I am thinking of. I didn't want to call you in case you are already sleeping. What did Stephen have to say about our relationship? Can't wait to hear from you. LoL
Luca

She sits up in her bed and is energized again. Without giving it another thought she dials Luca's number.

"You are awake," he says, sounding pleased to get her call.

"I am now. I was just going to turn off the light, but when I saw your email I had to give you a quick call."

"You are so sweet. I was kind of hoping that you would be awake."

"Well, to answer your question, Stephen is very happy for us. He thinks we make a great couple."

"I already like that man," Luca says laughing. "Did you also tell him about the situation with Roberto?"

"Yes, of course. I can't keep that a secret. A lot could be at stake. He was very surprised and in a joking manner was questioning why he let me go to Italy to deal with Italian men. He said he should have known that something like that could happen. You Italian guys are known for seducing innocent women," she laughs into the phone.

"I am glad that you ended up working on this deal," Luca admits, " and as far as us Italian men seducing innocent women is concerned, I guess he doesn't know what kind of a temptress you are."

"Oh, let's not even go there," Kataryna giggles, "otherwise we have to reconstruct who tempted who in your villa that night."

"Guilty as charged," Luca admits. "I started it but you put me under your spell for two days and I couldn't hold back any longer. There were certain moments on the boat when we went to Bellagio where I felt that we had a strong connection and attraction for each other. I am glad I acted on that."

"So am I," Kataryna responds, "and I am already getting all hot thinking about it so we better change the subject. What are you up to today?"

"I am going to meet Roberto for lunch today," he says in a more serious tone.

"Oh dear," Kataryna sighs, "I don't envy you. That could be a tough lunch. Please promise me not to fuel the fire. Give him a graceful way out of this situation."

"I am planning to do that but at the same time he has to be told that he can't act like this. Announcing new material, which I haven't approved or was even aware of, is unprofessional. I have a sneaking suspicion that he wanted to meet you for personal reasons and the whole new material thing was bait to get you to meet him. He must have been unpleasantly surprised when you told him about our relationship."

"Yes, he was," she responds, "and now that the cat is out of the bag, he will have to live with that."

"OK, bella, why don't you get some sleep now and we will talk tonight again so I can tell you all about the lunch."

"Sounds good. Have a great day."

After she hangs up the phone she becomes somewhat anxious. Hopefully Roberto will not say anything about his marriage proposal. *That would be a real drama*, she thinks. Luca would probably flip out and in addition wonder why she didn't tell him about Roberto's proposal.

❖❖

As noontime approaches Roberto gets anxious about his lunch with Luca. *What will Luca say and how will I react*, he ponders? He dreads this meeting. Being in the company of the man who stands between him and Kataryna is nothing to look forward to. He leaves his office a little early to head to the restaurant. When he arrives, Luca already waits for him at the bar, reading his emails, it appears.

"Ciao Luca," Roberto greets him. "Looks like we are both a little early."
"Ciao Roberto. How is everything?"
"Fine, in general," Roberto answers, "but improvements would be possible."
"That can be said about everyone, I guess," Luca responds.
"More for some than for others," Roberto counters.

Luca motions the hostess that they are ready to be seated at their table. He had reserved a more private table, so they can talk openly.

"So tell me about your meeting with Kataryna in Berlin, and the new material you mentioned the other day," Luca addresses Roberto.
"You didn't speak to her yet?" Roberto probes.
"Yes, I spoke to her several times, but I am interested to hear what you have to report. You had mentioned some new material, which I hadn't seen yet. What was that all about?" Luca asks.
"It was about a potential new product and in my excitement I totally forgot that I hadn't discussed it with you yet. So I didn't reveal anything. I told her I would have to review it with you first."
"But you still went ahead and met with her," Luca continues.
"Yes, I also wanted to discuss a potential internship for Verena in her firm in New York with her. Verena has expressed an interest in finance, which I am very excited about and I want to help her stay focused on that. So I thought if I send her to New York, where she wants to go to anyway, that will do the trick."
"Don't you think that this was a little premature? We don't even know yet if Kataryna and her partner will come up with an offer."
"I didn't think that would be an issue," Roberto replies casually, "an internship for Verena has no relevance to the fact if her firm acquires NatMedica or not."
"Well, you could have run it by me first. You always did that in the past. I have to wonder why you seem to do things on your own these

days. I see a definite shift in behavior in this case. Can you explain that?" Luca goes on.

Roberto takes a deep breath. "I have a personal interest in Kataryna, too, so I wanted some time with her to get to know her a little better. Since you dominated all her time in Italy I decided to meet her in Berlin."

"And what did you find out?" Luca asks.

"Much to my surprise I learned that you and Kataryna have started a more personal relationship," Roberto responds with his voice almost cracking.

"We actually started an intimate relationship," Luca corrects him, "and I believe she already explained that to you when you met in Berlin."

"Yes, she did," Roberto replies.

"How do you feel about that?"

"To be completely honest, I wish I had gotten to her first. I understand that this didn't materialize until after we all met in Bellagio. So, if the situation had been different, it could be me in an intimate relationship with her now."

"We don't know what could have happened," Luca says, slightly annoyed at Roberto's imagination.

"Congratulations Luca, you beat me to it," Roberto smirks at him. Let's see how it all plays out."

"Are you doubting our feelings for each other?" Luca enquires. "If so, I can tell you that we are very much in love. As a matter of fact, I will be going to New York to spend Christmas with Kataryna and her family. Patrizia and Francesco are also joining me on this trip. I will stay for about two weeks and we will take a vacation together. This will deepen our relationship even further."

Roberto looks at Luca intensely. His stomach is turning into knots. He senses that Luca is not pleased about his interest in Kataryna.

"As I said, Luca, congratulations but you won because you dominated her company when she came to Italy. How was I to know that you had a personal interest in her when we met in Bellagio? I believe I showed my interest that evening already and you gave me a dirty look. But then after you two left, you moved in and seduced her in your villa. All I am saying is that if you had not had that opportunity that evening it could have ended differently."

Luca smiles slightly before he answers Roberto's scenario.

"Kataryna and I had several moments before we arrived in Bellagio, just for the record. Not that I have to justify my relationship with her or at what point it started, but I just want you to know that it didn't just start like that after Bellagio. I already sensed that we had a strong connection when we had video conference calls and we talked privately for a few moments after the business section was over. So the spark really started way before that night in my villa."

"Well, as I said, congratulations," Roberto replies, raising his glass with mineral water giving Luca a crooked smile. "How about we change the subject now?" he continues. "I don't think there is any point to go further into that. It is what it is."

"Does that mean we are good?" Luca asks, "or do I have to worry that this will affect our friendship and working relationship? Please be honest, Roberto. If we can't get past this, we may have a problem on a business level, too. My family is pretty much leaning towards Kataryna's firm if she comes up with a suitable offer, which means she and Stephen Wagner would be your bosses going forward. Can you handle that?"

"Yes, of course I can handle reporting to Stephen and Kataryna. My personal feelings for her aside, I am a professional. Have you asked her if she can handle it?"

"Kataryna is also a professional, so I am sure she can handle it unless you do something to make her uncomfortable. So let me ask you this and then we'll move on. Can I assume that you will not try to pursue her any further?" Luca questions him.

"What good would it do if she is in a relationship with you?" Roberto asks.

"OK," Luca says, "I just want to make sure we are on the same page as we are moving forward with this divestiture. I need to know if this kind of thing could cause you to want to leave the company if Kataryna and Stephen acquire it."

"As of this moment I have no intention to leave," Roberto responds nonchalantly.

"I can't guarantee what may happen after the acquisition if the new shareholders come up with a different business plan or some other adverse situation but short of that I plan to be on board."

"Good," Luca says somewhat relieved. "So, Verena wants to study finance?" Luca asks to change the subject.

"Yes, that is what she is interested in now. Hopefully, she will stick to it. She really needs to get serious about her career path," Roberto answers.

"Other than working what are you doing these days?" Luca asks.

"Mostly hanging out with friends and family," Roberto replies. "I am planning a trip with Verena to introduce her to some other cultures after we close the divestiture of NatMedica."

"That sounds nice, do you have any special place in mind?" Luca enquires.

"I will leave it up to her."

"I am sure she will come up with something good, "Luca says moving on to another subject.

"Carlotta and Patrizia mentioned that they saw you in a restaurant the other day when they had lunch together."

"Yeah, I had lunch with my interior designer. I am thinking of redoing my apartment. She came highly recommended by a friend of mine. That's another thing I have on my plate. She came over for a viewing the other day and had some great ideas. I am expecting her proposal next week."

"Looks like you are going to be occupied for a while," Luca supposes.

"Yes, I will be, which is good. You know what they say; an idle mind is the devil's workshop."

Luca and Roberto finish their lunch and prepare to leave the restaurant.

"Why don't you and Verena come up to my parents' place one weekend," Luca suggests, as they are ready to part. "They have been asking about you the other day."

"OK, I will talk to Verena and see when she can make it," Roberto agrees. "I can also visit my parents up there at the same time then."

"Great," Luca says. "Let me know when you can make it. I am leaving on December 22 for New York, so let's try to do it before I leave."

"I will let you know as soon as I have talked to Verena," Roberto says as the two head back to their offices. "Ciao, Luca. Thank you for lunch."

Roberto walks back to his office with his mind preoccupied by the conversation he just had with Luca. He feels tightness in his chest and throat imagining Luca and Kataryna together. He breathes in and out deeply several times attempting to relieve the anxiety.

"Roberto," he hears his assistant calling him as he walks by her desk to his office.

He turns around startled and looks at her.

"Are you alright?" his assistant asks him, "you look kind of pale."

He gives her a tired kind of smile.

"I am not feeling that great," he explains, "sorry for not stopping by your desk to get my messages."

"Is there anything I can do for you?" she asks, walking up to him with a concerned look.

"No, thank you, Sofia," he responds, taking his messages and closing his door.

He sits down at his desk burying his head in his hands. His chest is still feeling tight and his heart is racing. *I have to calm down*, he thinks, *otherwise I am going to have a heart attack over this situation.*

He dials Sergio's number. "Ciao Sergio," he greets his friend, "I need your help."

"Roberto, you don't sound like yourself," Sergio says, "what is going on with you? Is it still that woman you are in love with?"

"Yes, and it is getting worse," Roberto explains. "I just came back from a lunch with Luca. He pretty much told me to back off Kataryna because they are in a committed relationship and very much in love. It's a really long and more involved story, but I can't get into all that right now on the phone. In addition, I am having this tightness in my chest and it won't go away."

"You probably have an anxiety or panic attack," Sergio says. "I had an experience like that before and it is a horrible feeling. It almost feels like you are going to have a heart attack at any moment."

"That's exactly what I am feeling now," Roberto says, "do you think I should go to the hospital and have it checked out?"

"I don't know, why don't I call my father and ask if he can see you right away? He will probably be able to calm you down, or if he thinks it is something serious admit you to his clinic."

"That sounds good," Roberto responds. "I need a professional to take a look at me. I am really in bad shape. I think this entire Luca-Kataryna thing has done a number on me."

"Don't worry, I will handle it," Sergio says as they hang up.

Roberto leans back in his chair trying to relieve the tension in his chest. He feels a little better now that he has spoken to Sergio. He pours himself a glass of water and starts sipping on it. His assistant buzzes him to announce that Dr. de Angelis is calling him. Roberto picks up the line.

"Dr. de Angelis, how nice of you to call me," Roberto says. "I guess Sergio explained the symptoms I am having."

"Yes, he did," Dr. de Angelis starts, "I had to call right away when I heard about your situation. You are like a second son to me. I suggest you come to my clinic as soon as you can, so we can get to the bottom of this. I have no other appointments right now. As a matter of fact, I was going to spend some time with my family this afternoon but I am concerned about you and want to see you right away."

"Thank you Dottore, I am so grateful that you are making time for me. I have no idea what is going on, but I know I need someone to take a closer look at me because it is a scary feeling. I never experienced something like this in my life. I had a full physical about six months ago and everything was perfect. So I can't explain this tightness in my chest and throat."

"I don't want to make a diagnosis without seeing you, but from what Sergio just explained it appears to be an anxiety attack. These attacks can feel like a heart attack, but I need to see you to rule that out for sure."

"I will leave my office now. See you in about 30 minutes."

He heads out of his office to his assistant's desk to tell her that he is leaving for the day.

TEN

Dr. Salvatore de Angelis, a renowned physician for disorders of the nervous system, calls his wife to let her know that he will be home later than expected because he has to see a patient on short notice.

He opened up his clinic about five years ago, which has several board-approved specialists of different medical fields on staff and state-of-the-art medical equipment. Many celebrities have been treated at the clinic for conditions ranging from psychological to physical disorders, including substance abuse. The clinic is located on the outskirts of Milan in a tranquil setting; it appears more like a boutique luxury hotel than a medical facility. The patients love it because it doesn't have that sterile appearance of a hospital, and it has all amenities one would expect to have in the comfort of a luxury hotel.

Dr. de Angelis asked his cardiologist on staff to join in Roberto's examination just to be sure that there is no underlying heart condition, which might have been overlooked when Roberto had his last physical exam. Roberto arrives at the clinic somewhat calmer than he was earlier in his office, but the tightness in his chest is still lingering. He is directed to an exam area where an ECG, a heart scan and other related tests are done. To Roberto's relief the results are normal.

Dr. de Angelis enters the exam area with the test results.
"Ciao Roberto," he says smiling at him reassuringly. "I see your heart tests all came back normal. That's good news so we can rule heart disease out for now. As I mentioned, I suspect you are having an anxiety attack so why don't we go to my office and talk a bit about what has been going on in your life. Have you been under a lot of stress recently?" he asks.
"Well, I don't think it is work related, although I have been working late hours in connection with the divestiture of the company I am CEO of; but I have worked these hours before and never had anything like this happen to me."

"Are you personally affected by the divestiture in as much as your job might be in jeopardy?" Dr. de Angelis asks.

"No, not that I am aware of," Roberto responds. "That is not an issue."

When they arrive at Dr. de Angelis' office, which looks more like an elegant living room than a doctor's office, they sit down in comfortable armchairs facing each other.

"How long has this been going on?" the doctor questions Roberto.

"About a week or so."

"What about your personal life? I know you are divorced. Is there anything that could cause you a lot of stress, either consciously or subconsciously?" Dr. de Angelis probes further. He senses that Roberto is hesitant to respond.

"In order for me to help you, you will have to be completely open to disclose your feelings and talk about things you may otherwise not want to share with anyone."

Roberto stares into the room and sighs.

"Yes, there is one situation, which might trigger this kind of thing," he says quietly. "But before I go into it in more detail, I have to be sure that this stays completely confidential."

"Roberto, whatever happens in this clinic is completely confidential. My clinic's reputation would be ruined if anything leaks out of here. We have a lot of cases, which require complete confidentiality. And anyway, you know you are like a son to me. I have only the best intentions where you are concerned."

Roberto takes another deep breath. His heart starts racing as he attempts to open up to the doctor. He clutches his chest and then tells Dr. de Angelis all about his feelings for Kataryna and her relationship with Luca, which he admits is very painful for him because he believes it could have been him if he had not let Luca leave with her that evening in Bellagio. He describes today's lunch meeting with Luca and what was said, which he believes brought on this tightness in his chest, which hasn't subsided since then.

"You must have very strong feelings for this lady," Dr. de Angelis determines. "I am not surprised that you had this anxiety flaring up today."

"Yes, my feelings for her are very strong," Roberto admits, "I even asked her to marry me before I knew that she was in a relationship with Luca."

"Aside from the fact that you went overboard with that marriage proposal, are you prepared to accept that she is unattainable for you?"

"I don't know," Roberto answers quickly. "Most likely not."

The doctor looks at Roberto with raised eyebrows. "In that case we might have a problem. I don't know how to treat a man who is causing himself that kind of anxiety by not giving up pursuing a woman who obviously is not available to him."

"We don't know that for sure," Roberto objects. "Who knows if they stay together, or if she also may have feelings for me but suppresses them for now? When I met her for dinner in Berlin, I had a feeling that she was sorry that she couldn't show her true feelings for me because she had started a relationship with Luca already. So if I would have had that opportunity to be with her she might have preferred to be with me. When we parted after the dinner in Berlin she actually looked sad."

"I think you are reaching here, Roberto. You need to stop these thoughts and feelings immediately. Look what this is doing to you. You thought you might be having a heart attack. Thank God you don't, but long-term anxiety disorders can lead to physical damage. Here is what I can recommend to get you back to normal. You make a strong effort to forget her and stay away from any situation involving her and Luca. Go out and date other women; you never know you may meet the love of your life. I will help you along by prescribing an anti-anxiety medication for you so you get rid of that tightness in your chest and are able to lead a normal life again. Are you on board with that plan?"

"I have never taken any pills in my entire life, except for an aspirin," Roberto replies. "What are they going to do to me?"

"They will relax you and make you feel normal again, removing any anxiety you may have," the doctor explains. "I want to start you with one pill in the morning and one at night. After a week or so we will reduce the dose to half a pill in the morning and half at night, and we will monitor how you feel with that dose. Just be careful and don't take more than that without discussing it with me first. You should also avoid alcoholic drinks with that medication. At the same time you have to adjust your mindset and accept the fact that this woman is taken. If you need help with that you will have to see a therapist who will guide you in the right direction. Our psychiatrist here at the clinic is very good and therefore fully booked, but I can talk to him to take you on if you really can't do it on your own."

"Mamma mia, a psychiatrist? I am not crazy, just in love," Roberto shouts out.

"You may be unhealthy in love, Roberto, in which case you would need that kind of treatment because you are not dealing with reality. But let's not jump to conclusions. We will start you on the anti-anxiety medication and go from there. I would like to see you again in a week. You are such a handsome and successful man, Roberto. I am sure there are many beautiful women out there who would be more than happy to have a relationship with you. Just get it together."

"You are right, Dottore, there has never been a lack of beautiful women in my life, but no one has captured me like this one. And when I think about the fact that she could be my boss soon, I already feel another anxiety attack coming on."

"I understand that this woman has an influence on many aspects of your life. Let's deal with it one day at a time. I am hoping that you will be able to face her in the future without any physical or emotional repercussions for you."

Dr. de Angelis writes the prescription and asks his assistant to have it filled in the on-site pharmacy.

"Start taking one pill tonight and then one in the morning," he instructs Roberto. "You will see how much better you will feel. Call me if anything adverse happens or if you just want to talk. By the way, how are your golf skills doing?"

"Pretty lousy," Roberto answers smiling. "I haven't played in a while."

"I am lousy, too. How about you, Sergio, and me get together soon to play a round somewhere in a warmer climate? Since all three of us are lousy players we have nothing to fear."

"Sure, why not. If it gets really ugly I can take one of the anxiety pills after we are finished," Roberto says laughing out loud.

"There you go," Dr. de Angelis says also laughing now, "I see you are on the road to recovery already."

"Thank you very much for making time for me today. I was really in bad shape earlier. I thought my last hour had come," Roberto says relieved.

"Don't even mention it, you are like family to me. We have been so close with your parents for over 40 years raising you two boys and I am so glad that Sergio and you are continuing the tradition."

"Sergio is my closest friend and actually more like a brother to me," Roberto says, as he leaves the doctor's office heading to the exit with the anti-anxiety medication in his pocket.

Roberto gets into his car and dials Sergio's number as he heads back towards Milan. Sergio's caller ID shows Roberto is calling him.

"Did you see my father?"

"Yes, I did. Thank you for arranging that. It was very helpful. That is some clinic your father has built there. Doesn't feel like a hospital at all."

"Well, there is a difference between a private clinic and a regular hospital," Sergio says, "but I know that my father has done a fantastic job with this clinic. A lot of thought and money went into this place. The doctors are generally fully booked for weeks in advance, so you are really lucky that you got in there today. Was he able to determine what's going on with you?"

"It appears to be an anxiety attack," Roberto says quietly. "It is a terribly scary feeling, like a ton of bricks on your chest. In addition, I have this sensation as if something is stuck in my throat. I never imagined that stress could bring on symptoms like that."

"By stress you mean your personal situation, I guess?" Sergio enquires, "or do you have stress at work?"

"No, it must be the situation with Kataryna. I haven't been sleeping well either since my dinner with her in Berlin. Then all of a sudden I started getting this tightness in my chest. It was an on-off thing at first, but then it became a more permanent feeling. During the lunch with Luca today it became increasingly worse and hasn't gone away since. Your father prescribed some anti-anxiety medication for me. I will start tonight with that. I can't wait because I want that tightness to go away and hopefully I can get some decent sleep then, too. I also haven't been eating properly. I get very hungry but when I sit down to eat the mere sight of food makes me sick and I can hardly get anything down. I can't believe that a psychological situation can make you feel that sick although you are not really sick. It is pretty powerful how your body can react to these things."

"Go home, take the medication and get some rest. Why don't you come over for dinner to our house tomorrow night? I'll pick you up if you don't want to drive," Sergio offers.

"Good idea," Roberto responds, "I need people I trust around me during this time. I may even take off from work tomorrow."

"OK, my friend, I will see you tomorrow at 7 p.m., at our place," Sergio says, pleased that Roberto accepted his invitation. "Shall I pick you up?"

"No, thanks, that won't be necessary. Ciao Sergio, see you tomorrow."

Roberto arrives at his apartment around 6 p.m. He orders in food from a nearby restaurant and manages to eat most of it. He skips the wine he usually has with dinner. *Here comes my dessert*, he says to himself, as he opens the package with the anti-anxiety medication. He takes one of the pills with plenty of water, as instructed, wondering when it will take effect and relieve this pressure on his chest. He lies down on his couch, clutching his chest and closes his eyes. The farewell scene with Kataryna in Berlin enters his mind. She did look kind of sad, he recalls. *Could it be that she has feelings for me, too*? His chest starts pounding, reminding him not to think about her in that way. How did Dr. de Angelis call it? Unhealthy in love. The thought of that gives him chills. He gets up to get a blanket and then lies back down on his comfortable couch. Christmas is coming up soon; he wonders whom he will spend it with. His mind goes blank as he drifts off and falls asleep.

When he wakes up the tightness in his chest is gone. He looks at his watch and realizes that he was asleep for almost three hours. He remembers the beautiful dream he just had. Kataryna and he were together somewhere in a relaxing atmosphere and they were very happy enjoying their time together. He wants to go back to sleep and get back to this beautiful dream with Kataryna in his life all warm and sweet. His real life is cold and lonely. The pills seem to do the trick, though. The pressure in his chest is gone, but somehow is replaced by a general sadness. It becomes apparent to him that he shouldn't be alone during this period in his life. Tomorrow he will have dinner with Sergio and his wife, which will be just what he needs. He knows he needs to make other plans thereafter to be in the company of compassionate people whom he can trust and who only want the best for him. Hoping to have another enchanting dream about Kataryna and him, he gets ready to go to bed. His cell phone rings not revealing a caller ID.

"Pronto," he answers the phone.

"Ciao Roberto," a female voice greets him. "How are you doing?"

He doesn't immediately recognize the voice.

"Ciao," he greets the caller, "who is this?"

"It's Carlotta. Didn't you recognize my voice?" she asks.

"Carlotta," Roberto responds surprised. "Forgive me, I just woke up from a nap and I am not quite with it yet."

"A nap?" Carlotta says, "you must keep very long hours at the office these days that you are falling asleep that early. I hope you are not working yourself to death."

"No, I am just a little under the weather," Roberto responds quickly. "How are you, Carlotta?"

"I am well, thank you for asking. I wanted to give you a call to see when we can meet for a drink or so. We had discussed getting together when we met in the restaurant at lunchtime the other day," Carlotta reminds him.

"Sure, I remember. I just didn't get a chance yet to plan anything and I haven't been feeling well either," Roberto replies.

"I don't think we need major planning for that, Roberto," Carlotta says laughing. "Sometimes it is more fun to get together on the spur of the moment. I am looking forward to our get-together. I have been in some kind of rut and need a fun night out."

"I don't know how much fun I will be," Roberto says, "but when would be good for you?"

"Roberto, you are always fun to hang out with. You know how to lift my spirits."

"Well, I am also in some kind of a rut, so I need someone to lift my spirits. Can you handle that?" he asks.

"Of course, I can. You'll see I'll have you laughing the whole night."

"Just what I need," Roberto replies. "How about Friday night?"

"Friday it is," she responds cheerfully. "Can't wait to see you. Do you have any suggestions where we should go?"

"I'll call you tomorrow with some suggestions," he says, "but if you have any ideas, please don't hold back. I am pretty open when it comes to that."

"OK, see you Friday then. Ciao Roberto."

Roberto shuts off the phone and stares into the room. *Interesting developments,* he says to himself. *She probably has no idea what has been going on between Luca and me. I guess I will find out more on Friday.* He sends a text message to his assistant telling her that he will work from home tomorrow and then turns in for the night. He is calm and pleased with the results of the medication, which helps him fall asleep as soon as he puts his head on the pillow.

He wakes up at 8 a.m., trying to get back to sleep for a while, dozing off at times, but then decides to get up and make some business calls after a long hot shower and breakfast. To his surprise his chest still feels good, so he decides to skip the morning pill. *Why take the chemical stuff when you don't need it,* he tells himself. After finishing the business calls he goes to the gym for a workout, a steam bath and a massage. He returns to his apartment completely relaxed and calls his daughter.

"Ciao, papà," Verena greets him. "What are you up to?"

"I am at home today," he explains, "do you want to have lunch with me?"

"OK," she says nonchalantly, "I will be right over."

She arrives at her father's place an hour later. They have lunch at one of the restaurants nearby.

"What are you keeping yourself busy with these days?" he asks her.

"I have been studying so I can get into the finance field," she explains.

"And you?" she asks her father.

"A lot of work stuff," he tells her.

"Are you dating anyone these days," she probes.

"Why are you asking?" Roberto wonders.

"Just making conversation," she says. "I am always wondering what your love life is like since mamma and you got divorced. I imagine you going from one woman to another."

He smirks at her. "I am not. As a matter of fact, I am not dating anyone right now. How about you, are you seeing anyone?"

"Nothing serious, I haven't found the right man yet," she lets her father know.

"By the way, what about the trip we wanted to plan? I could use a change of scenery."

"So could I," he says. "So let's plan something. Where do you want to go?"

"Well," she starts, "we had talked about New York a while ago. I really, really want to go there. We can do some great shopping there, too, and see a show. You said you know someone there. It is always better to do things with a local resident rather than just as a tourist."

Roberto feels a stab in his chest. That's the last thing he wants to do at the moment. He is trying to come up with an excuse.

"New York, we can do when the weather gets warmer and then combine it with some other U.S. places," he says coolly. "Let's do a short trip first to a warmer climate."

"That makes sense," Verena agrees. "I will think about it and get back to you."

"How is your mother?' he changes the subject.

"She is fine. She is going out with a nice man. I think they are getting more serious about their relationship."

"I am glad to hear that. Please tell her I wish only the best for her."

They finish their lunch with Verena's favorite dessert and leave the restaurant. Back in his apartment Roberto makes a few more business calls, one of them to Francesco, his CFO.

"Will you be in the office tomorrow?" Francesco asks him.

"Most likely," Roberto responds. "Why, did anything unusual happen today?"

"No, not really," Francesco says, "but I would like to go over some numbers with you tomorrow before we hand them over to Luca for review and then to the accountants."

"OK, see you tomorrow," Roberto ends the call.

He turns on his laptop. The wallpaper with Kataryna's photo comes on. *Oh God,* he thinks, *I should have changed that.* His chest starts tightening up. He changes the wallpaper replacing Kataryna's photo with Verena's.

Shortly after 7 p.m., Roberto arrives at Sergio's house. Sergio's wife, Gisella, greets him as he walks into the kitchen.

"How are you Roberto? You haven't been here for quite a while," she says. She gives him a peck on both cheeks.

"I am OK, but improvements are possible." He gives her his standard response these days.

"Oh?" she asks smiling back at him, "what kind of improvements are you looking for?"

"It's a long story and I am trying to move on. So let's talk about something else."

Sergio agrees. "Yes, let's have some fun tonight. It's been too long that we all have been together like this. You should come over more often, Roberto."

The three have a pleasant dinner and talk until late at night. Sergio escorts Roberto to his car. He wants a moment alone with him.

"How are you feeling, Roberto?"

"So far OK. I took one of the pills your father prescribed for me last night and knock on wood, the chest tightness went away. I didn't even have to take a pill today."

"Good," Sergio murmurs. "I am glad you are feeling better. Are you prepared to give up the idea about you and this Kataryna?"

Roberto shrugs his shoulders. "I am not sure if I can give it up that easy. But this chest pain has me scared."

"Ciao, I will call you tomorrow and let you know how I am doing."

Roberto arrives back at his apartment around midnight. He goes to bed immediately, but can't fall asleep. All kinds of thoughts are going through his mind. Friday night out with Carlotta. What if Luca asked her to meet him to spy on him? No, he dismisses that thought instantly. She just wants to have a fun night out. At 1 a.m., he is still tossing and turning. An uncomfortable feeling in his chest seems to reappear. He sits up and turns the light on. It's 7a.m., in New York, he figures. He dials Kataryna's cell phone number. She comes on right away.

"Hello," she answers the phone.

"Hello, Kataryna, this is Roberto calling. I thought I owe you a phone call to let you know how my meeting with Luca went and what I told him."

"Hi Roberto, you are up late. If I am not mistaken, it is after 1a.m., over there."

"Yes, it is but I can't sleep. I met with Luca yesterday, which I am sure you know already."

"Yes, I do. Luca said you had a good conversation. I assume that you took my advice and did not tell him about the proposal and the other things you said to me in Berlin. I am glad that you two are still friends and that you have accepted my relationship with Luca," Kataryna says.

"Let's put it this way, I am being forced to accept it, but deep down inside I don't know if I can. I am sure you can understand that deep feelings like this cannot be turned off just like that."

"I am really sorry that you are going through this and I want to be sensitive to your feelings. Unrequited love is never easy to live with, but there is no way around it. You have to move on. As a matter of fact, I am kind of surprised at what you are telling me because the way Luca explained it you two had a heart-to-heart conversation and he was under the impression that you are moving on. He also mentioned that he invited you to come up to his parents' house with your daughter and you accepted that invitation."

"That is true. On the surface I had no choice but to accept his relationship with you, but that doesn't mean that my feelings for you are just going away. They are much too strong. I hope you won't tell Luca, but after my lunch with him I was so distressed that I had to see a doctor because I had the most terrible pain in my chest and I thought I am going to have a heart attack."

"Oh, my God, Roberto," Kataryna shouts out. "Are you OK?"

"I didn't have a heart attack or heart problem, other than a broken heart, but was told that it was an anxiety attack brought on by an extreme stress situation my body can't process. I am sitting here awake after 1 a.m., can't sleep and my chest is getting uncomfortable again. Does that sound like I am OK?"

Kataryna doesn't know what to say. She exhales searching desperately for the right words.

"I am at a loss for words, Roberto," she finally says softly. "Believe me, the last thing I want is for you to be in this kind of pain. I am very sad that this is happening."

"Not as sad as I am, I am sure, but thank you for being so compassionate," he says. "I will do my best to get over it, but please don't tell Luca that we spoke. I can't take another session with him about this subject at the moment. It would put me under extreme stress. I have to try to get well again and he is most likely the cause of my distress. So I don't know if I can be around him at the moment. When I see him, I see you with him and that triggers the chest tightness also known as anxiety attack. My doctor said that if I don't get this under control it can do actual physical damage one day."

"I won't say anything to Luca if you promise to work on getting over this and getting well again," Kataryna tries to bargain with him.

"For you, I will do my best. I hope you will continue to help me get over it."

"Sure," Kataryna says, "let me know how I can help. Good night, Roberto."

Kataryna is sad as she ends the call. *This is history repeating itself*, she thinks. She had a similar situation when she ended her last relationship and the man went into a deep depression. It took almost a year to talk him through this, she remembers. There seems to be some curse on her that men always fall so deeply for her that they end up in depression or anxiety attacks when the relationship ends or, like in this case, doesn't even start. That is why she didn't make any strong attempts to date in the recent past. However, when she met Luca that changed and she fell in love with him. Her fear had disappeared completely because she was pretty sure that Luca could be a permanent relationship, but now she is facing this situation with Roberto. She doesn't want anybody to go through something like this because of her. Unfortunately she can't talk to Luca about this.

Roberto sits wide-awake in his bed reliving the telephone conversation he just had with Kataryna. Her voice was so soothing and caring. *Does this mean that she has feelings for him, too*, he wonders? She agreed not to tell Luca, which means they have a secret together. He turns off the light and tries to go to sleep; however, the by now familiar chest tightness returns with a vengeance. He gets up to take the medication, waiting for it to take effect and make this pain go away. He decides to work another day from home and sends an email to his assistant so she will have it when she gets to the office later on.

On Friday, Roberto goes back to the office and meets with Francesco to go over the financials and a few other things. They agree on some changes, which need to be made before the material is presented to the accountants. Their meeting ends around noon.

"Is everything OK? You don't seem like yourself, Roberto." Francesco asks worried.

"Why?" Roberto asks.

"I don't know but there is something different about you. You are more serious than usual. I haven't seen you laugh in a while and working from home for two days in a row also is unusual for you," Francesco explains. "Do you have second thoughts of how you feel about this divestiture?"

"I am just tired and hadn't taken any days off for quite some time."

"OK. Are you planning to take off any more days before Christmas?"

"Don't know yet, I might. Why are you asking?"

"I am going on vacation on December 22, so let's go over whatever we need to before I leave," Francesco says. "Patrizia and I are joining Luca in New York. We will be gone until January 3."

"Are you going to be in New York the whole time?" Roberto asks.

"Patrizia and I will be in the New York area the whole time. We are also spending some time with a good friend of mine in Connecticut. Luca and Kataryna are going to Hawaii for a week," Francesco explains.

Roberto puts his hand on his chest. The thought of Luca and Kataryna together in beautiful Hawaii almost puts him over the edge again. He takes a deep breath trying to calm down to avert an anxiety attack.

"Are you alright, Roberto?" Francesco asks concerned.

"Yeah, I am OK, but I need to take care of something immediately," Roberto says.

After Francesco leaves the office Roberto decides it is time for another pill to relieve the tension he feels coming on. After 15 minutes the chest tightness is gone and he feels like himself again. *That definitely is the cause, which brings on the anxiety*, he concludes. *How can I avoid it*, he asks himself? He has to figure out something before it gets worse because he can't go on living like this.

❖ ❖

Friday evening has arrived. His cell phone calendar reminds him about his night out with Carlotta. He takes a shower and gets dressed. The change in scenery will be good for him, he feels, although Carlotta is Luca's sister and may say something, which may lead to another anxiety attack. He puts the package with the pills in his pocket, just in case.

Roberto takes a seat at the bar waiting for Carlotta. She arrives moments later walking up to him with a broad smile. *God, she looks beautiful and happy,* Roberto thinks. *Her life must be picture-perfect, like mine used to be. Well, of course, she is a Romano. Everything seems to go their way.*

"Carlotta," he gets up to meet her with open arms. "You look beautiful and so happy. What is going on, are you freshly in love?"

She starts laughing nervously. "Thank you for the compliment, Roberto. I am so glad to see you. I was looking forward to our night out."

"Believe it or not, that is just what I needed tonight," he responds, smiling at her.

"Why? Did you have a tough day at the office?"

"I had a challenging week," he responds as he leads her to the bar. "What can I get you to drink?"

"Let me start with an Aperol and Prosecco."

Roberto orders the drink for Carlotta and one for himself. He takes her coat and hands it to a staff member of the restaurant.

"Here is to a fun evening," he makes a toast.

"I'll drink to that," Carlotta says still smiling broadly. She can't help herself. She is so happy to be out with the object of her affection. *He is so good-looking,* she thinks, and his cologne smells so good. She would like to hold him in her arms. *Carlotta, stay cool,* she reminds herself. It is pretty tough for her, though, to stay cool around him.

"What are you up to these days, Roberto?" she starts a conversation. "Who was that lady you had lunch with the other day, a new love interest?"

He starts laughing out loud. "No. Why does everyone think, when they see me with a woman, that she is my lover?"

"Well, first of all you are an attractive man and you are single. Somehow, I can't imagine you without a woman in your life for a long time."

"Thank you for thinking I am attractive," he says smiling. "Even at the risk of losing my reputation, I am actually not involved with anyone at this time."

"Really?" she says pleased to hear that, "hard to believe, but I will take your word for it. Are you looking for your next victim?"

"Victim? What is that supposed to mean?"

"I heard you make these poor women fall in love with you and then you leave them."

"I haven't made anyone fall in love with me. They do that all on their own," he says a little defensive. "And as far as leaving them is concerned, if it's not right then you have to move on."

"I guess this means that you haven't found Mrs. Right yet," Carlotta says. "What would the love of your life be like?"

"A woman of substance," he says. "But enough of me. What about you? You look so happy you must be in love."

"I think I am in love but I haven't closed the deal yet," she says softly.

"Closed the deal yet," he repeats intrigued by that statement. "I never heard anyone refer to being in love as closing the deal. But I like it. Sounds mysterious. What is standing in the way of closing the deal? Is he married?"

"No, he is not. He actually doesn't know how I feel about him. What do you suggest I do about it?"

"If you hope to accomplish something you have to communicate that to him, " Roberto lectures her.

"OK, I will take it under consideration, but what if he doesn't feel the same way about me?" Carlotta asks anxiously.

Roberto takes a sip of his drink and pauses for a moment before he answers her.

"You have to take certain risks in life for something worthwhile. If you are serious about him, don't give up," he advises her, thinking about his own situation.

She nods her head. "Interesting answer. I think that men are the better risk takers when it comes to that. You guys hunt and chase down anything you want. Women are a little more subtle in that area."

"Probably true. You ladies often hide your real feelings and the men have to guess how you really feel about them," he suggests.

"What are you doing for Christmas?" she asks. "Are you going to be around or are you going away?"

"I will be here, I think. Christmas Eve I will spend with my parents and hopefully Verena. Christmas Day I don't know yet. I am hoping I will get an invitation from someone. Maybe I'll spend it with my friend Sergio and his wife. What are your plans?"

"I will be at my parents' house for Christmas Eve and Christmas Day. I am the only one around this year. Luca, Patrizia and Francesco are going to New York. Actually, Luca is also going to Maui with his new girlfriend Kataryna. I met her the other day via video call. She is great. Don't you just love her?" Carlotta says excitedly.

"Yes, I do," Roberto answers, thinking if she only knew.

"I can't wait to meet her in person," Carlotta continues. "You have met her, what is she like?"

"She is everything you can imagine," Roberto says. "Beautiful, interesting and she has a great business acumen."

"In other words, a perfect fit for Luca," Carlotta says.

"Or for any other man," Roberto responds, "I wouldn't limit it to Luca."

"Well, you know what I mean. The other day he surprised me by telling me he had a spicy video call with her, but he wouldn't tell me any details. He was totally excited, though. I tried to picture my brother in a spicy situation via video call. I even got a little bit jealous that I didn't have anything going on. Have you ever had a spicy video interaction with one of your love interests?' she asks.

"No, I have never done that but it sounds intriguing. I guess that's what you do when you are so far apart."

"Anyway," Carlotta suggests, "since you are up in the Bellagio area for Christmas, why don't you and your parents come to my parents' house for Christmas Day?"

"Good idea, I'll talk to my parents to see if they have any other plans."

After a few drinks at the bar Carlotta and Roberto are seated at their table to have dinner. They talk about Verena, Enrico, some mutual acquaintances and the divestiture of NatMedica.

"So, do you think you are going to close the deal before Christmas?" Roberto asks Carlotta amused.

"Are we still talking about the divestiture or the new acquisition?" she asks smiling.

"I have moved on to your secret love interest you mentioned earlier," he says grinning broadly at her.

"You really like that statement, don't you?" she says laughing.

"I have to admit it is an interesting way of describing that kind of situation. I may use it in the future," he says.

"I may put a copyright on that," she responds, grinning at him.

"Oh, come on, bella, let me share it with you," he tries to convince her.

"Did you just call me bella?" she asks shyly.

"Yeah, why shouldn't I? You are a beautiful woman and you called me an attractive man earlier. Why can't we compliment each other?"

"Are you flirting with me, Roberto?" she asks coquettishly.

He leans into her, looks deeply into her eyes and puts his hand on her arm. "Would you like me to flirt with you?" he asks in a seductive voice.

Carlotta feels the heat running through her body. She wasn't prepared for that and doesn't know how to respond. She quickly comes up with something.

"Are you practicing your flirting skills on me so you won't get rusty when your dream woman shows up?" she asks.

"No, I just want us to have a good time tonight. I think we deserve it. You said you were ready for a fun night out, so I don't want to disappoint you. As a matter of fact, I am going to order another bottle of wine for us."

He signals the waiter to bring another bottle of the wine they are already enjoying.

"Are you trying to get me drunk?" Carlotta teases him. "Unless you are prepared to drive me home later, I better not drink anymore."

"I'll take you home later, please have some more wine. I am having a good time. Aren't you?"

"Yes, of course I am. I just wasn't prepared to drink that much tonight," she enlightens him. "But you convinced me."

"Good, because I don't want to go home yet."

They finish the second bottle of wine. The waiter brings them their desserts and espresso.

Carlotta feels quite a buzz and her inhibitions waning. *If he only knew*, she thinks, *that he is the deal I want to close.* Roberto pays the bill and they leave the restaurant. He had ordered his car service while Carlotta was in the restroom. The car pulls up and they get in. Carlotta leans back into the seat.

"That was smart," she says, "taking a car service instead of driving yourself."

"Yes, I just didn't want to limit myself tonight," he states. "As a matter of fact, I am not tired at all. I could go for a nightcap if you are up for it."

"Let's have a nightcap at my place. I have plenty of wine and other beverages at home," she says. "And if that doesn't make you tired either, I might even make breakfast."

"Sounds good to me," Roberto responds.

When they arrive at Carlotta's place, Roberto instructs the driver that he will call him when he is ready to be picked up again. Carlotta, who is slightly wobbly from all that drinking and attempting to walk steady to the entrance, has something else in mind. She gets out her keys and drops them on the ground. Roberto picks them up and opens the door.

"No more alcohol for you," he whispers in her ear, taking her arm.

Carlotta starts laughing. "I haven't had that much to drink in a long time. But I am having so much fun."

She throws her coat and bag on a chair and takes Roberto's coat.

"Make yourself comfortable," she invites him. "What can I get you to drink?"

"I think I am going to stick with wine."

She hands him a bottle of wine. He opens it, pouring a glass for himself.

"I am going to have some water first," she says. "I am feeling quite a buzz."

She gets some sparkling water and a plate with antipasto and turns on some music. They make a toast to the nice evening they are having.

"I haven't had a relaxing evening like this in a long time," Roberto remarks as he sips the wine.

Carlotta gets comfortable on her couch, putting her feet up and leaning back while sipping her water. Roberto enjoys the view of Carlotta on her couch with her dress up high to her thighs. *She has beautiful legs and a beautiful body similar to Kataryna,* he thinks.

She smiles at him seductively.
"Are you enjoying your wine," she asks softly.
"Yes, and the view."

He wonders what it would be like if Kataryna were sitting there like this instead of Carlotta. He would be all over her by now. Just the imagination of what he would do to her gets him aroused. He closes his eyes for a moment hoping to reverse the arousal. When he opens his eyes Carlotta is standing over him leaning down revealing her cleavage. She takes his face in both of her hands and presses it against her naked skin, caressing the back of his neck. He starts kissing her cleavage imagining it is Kataryna. She takes off her underwear, puts his hand between her legs and starts panting. Roberto can't hold back anymore. He is moaning and pushes his erection against her as his arousal builds up even further.

"I want you so bad," she whispers in his ear as she works to remove his pants and underwear. She sits on him as he enters her and they move in rhythm until they climax.

"Kataryna," he calls out quietly but Carlotta doesn't realize it. She is so taken by this man and her own orgasm that the world around her disappears in that moment.

After a moment of silence and embrace, Roberto lets out a sigh. "I didn't see this one coming. I wonder what our families would say if they knew what just happened here."

Carlotta giggles as she sits down next to Roberto, smiling at him impishly. "It's none of their business," she says softly. "I do what makes me happy and I doubt you let anybody tell you what you can and cannot do."

"That's true, but this is a little different. Our families have been close friends since we were little children and we grew up together almost like brother and sister," he goes on.

"But we are not brother and sister and are free to have these feelings for each other. Anyway, I can answer your earlier question now."

"Which question?" he asks puzzled.

"You asked me if I think I will be closing the deal before Christmas. Here is my answer. I just did."

Roberto is taken aback looking at her with wide eyes. *Is she saying that I am the secret love interest she has been talking about? Oh my God*, he thinks, *we have one surprise after another tonight.* He can't come up with anything to say next.

"I have never seen you speechless," she says, "but it is kind of cute."

She kisses him on the cheek and then moves to his mouth. He kisses her back as he still doesn't know what to say.

"Listen," he starts softly after recovering from the initial shock, "I am not ready to open this up to our families. Did you tell anyone yet that you have these feelings for me?"

"Yes," she admits. "I told Luca the other day."

Roberto's eyes get even wider. He stares at her in disbelief. *Holy mother of God*, he thinks.

"You told Luca?" he yells out. "Why?"

"I asked him for advice how to go about this," she answers.

Roberto runs his hands through his tousled hair. Thoughts of Kataryna being aware of Carlotta's feeling for him are racing through his mind.

"What did he say?" Roberto probes further calmly.

"Not very much," Carlotta bends the truth a bit. She doesn't want to make him uncomfortable with Luca's initial reservations against this relationship.

"He must have said something or at least reacted to that piece of news," he continues.

"He was a bit inquisitive, wanting to know since when did I have these feelings and so on," Carlotta explains. "But never mind what Luca said or thinks; this is my life."

Roberto exhales. He wants to be alone to think about this situation and decide on his next step.

"Wow, it is 3 a.m.," he says. "I better go home and get some sleep. My interior designer is coming over at 10 a.m., and Verena will also show up to help me decide which of the options to go with."

"Interior designer?" Carlotta questions him.

"Yes, the lady you saw me with in the restaurant. I am renovating my apartment. I will call you later to see how you are doing."

Carlotta looks at him somewhat disappointed as he calls his car service. She had hoped he would stay and they would have breakfast in bed and make love again.

"Don't pout," he says embracing her, "you know that this outcome of our night out wasn't planned. As I said, I don't want to broadcast this to our families. Let's take it easy, OK?"

"Of course, I will respect your wishes," she says putting her head on his shoulder. They stand embracing each other for a few minutes both of them not knowing where this will be going after tonight.

E L E V E N

Back home in his apartment Roberto takes a shower and falls into bed. The events of the night come into his mind. Who would have thought that this would end up like this? Carlotta is a beautiful woman, but his heart is with Kataryna. He tries to imagine what Dr. de Angelis would say about last night's situation. *Carlotta really caught me off guard,* he recalls. *Was it the alcohol or is she really in love with me*? He doesn't want to hurt her but he doesn't want to lead her on either. *What is the best way to deal with this*, he wonders? At least his chest tightness is gone, that's positive. The rest he will figure out later.

Carlotta is still in heaven reliving the sexual encounter with Roberto in her mind. She remembers every detail as she is trying to go to sleep. She knows that she initiated it but as Roberto said, if you want something you have to take risks and don't give up. While she is happy how the night developed, she feels that there was something holding him back to show his feelings. Is it possible that he is not as eager being with her as she is being with him? She can't wait having him in her arms again. Hopefully he will call her later on and suggest getting together again soon. But now it is time for some beauty sleep, she reminds herself.

At 11a.m., Carlotta's phone rings. The sound tears her out of her deep sleep.

"Pronto," she answers the phone, sounding sleepy.

"Did I wake you?" Luca asks his sister.

"Yes, you did, my dear brother. I was trying to get some beauty rest."

"Did you have a late night?" he asks.

"Yes, it got kind of late and I couldn't fall asleep right away."

"I am glad you are having fun," he says. "Are you coming up to Bellagio today? If you want to we can ride together and I will take you home tomorrow."

"Of course, I wouldn't miss your birthday. I will congratulate you properly later on. What have our parents planned up there this weekend for your birthday?" she asks.

"I told them to keep it low-key. I don't want a big to do. Just some close friends and family. I was thinking of asking Roberto to come up, too. I had lunch with him the other day and asked him to come up one weekend to spend time with the family. He seemed on board with that idea. So I thought I'll call him at the spur of a moment to see if he can make it either today or tomorrow. I am sure you would like that, too, don't you?"

Carlotta hesitates trying to think about what to say next. She is torn but decides to keep her promise and not tell Luca what happened last night.

"Hmm, sure. Sounds good," she finally responds quietly.

"You don't sound very enthusiastic considering that your secret love interest might spend the weekend with us," he tells her.

"You are tearing me out of a deep sleep and expect enthusiasm?" she asks, kind of cranky. "I am not even sure yet if I am awake or dreaming. And by the way, I thought you weren't too thrilled about the idea of Roberto and me together?"

"OK, OK, why don't you get up sleeping beauty and get ready. We should leave here around 2 p.m.," Luca commands. "I think the other guests are coming around 6 p.m."

"Call me after you have spoken to Roberto. I am curious if he accepts your invitation."

"I'll call you right after I have spoken to him," Luca promises her.

Roberto sees Luca's number come up as his phone rings. *Oh no,* he thinks, *what could Luca want on a Saturday? Maybe Kataryna told Luca after all that he had called her and admitted that he is not over her yet. Or maybe Carlotta couldn't keep the secret and told her brother that they spent the night together.* He is debating whether to pick up the call or not. Verena, who is visiting, looks at her father wondering why he doesn't take the call.

"Who is it?" she asks.

"It's Luca, I don't know if I want to talk to him right now," he shrugs his shoulders.

The call goes to voice mail. Roberto listens to the message Luca left for him. "Ciao Roberto, it's Luca. Sorry for the short notice. I was wondering if you would like to come up to my parents' house today. We are having a few guests over for dinner. Your parents, Francesco, Patrizia and Carlotta will also be there. You can stay overnight if you want to and we all can have a nice day in Bellagio tomorrow. Give me a call when you get this message."

Roberto exhales, relieved after listening to the friendly message from Luca. He looks at his daughter.

"Do you want to go up to Bellagio to have dinner with Luca and his parents? Your grandparents will be there, too."

"Yes, I would love to go."

Roberto picks up the phone and calls Luca back.

"Ciao Luca," he greets him, "I just got your message. Thank you for the dinner invitation. I would like to accept, but I have Verena with me today. Can I bring her along?"

"Absolutely, I am sure your parents would love to see their granddaughter."

"Good, I will have to swing by Verena's place so we can get a change of clothes, etc., for her. We should be in Bellagio around 5 p.m."

"Excellent. I am looking forward to seeing both of you later. Just as a heads up. It is my birthday and my parents decided to have a dinner party for me. So we are supposed to dress up a bit. Is that OK with you?"

"Happy Birthday. I think we can find something festive to wear," Roberto says jovially.

The minute they hang up, Luca calls his sister.

"Are you up yet?" he teases her when she answers the call.

"I am up, showered and even had breakfast," she replies in a much lighter mood than before.

"Breakfast?" Luca laughs, "you mean lunch."

"Let's call it brunch then," she comes back with, giggling. "Did you speak to Roberto yet?"

"Yes, Verena is over at his house," Luca starts to explain.

"So he is not coming to Bellagio?" Carlotta interrupts him.

"Sure, he is coming. He is bringing Verena and they are staying overnight. And you, my dear sister, can thank me later."

"Really?" That's great. I haven't seen Verena in a while," Carlotta says elated.

Luca starts laughing. "I think your excitement is more geared towards seeing Roberto than Verena."

"One doesn't exclude the other," she says casually.

"I wish Kataryna was here to join us," Luca says in a somewhat somber tone. "This long-distance thing is getting to me. I really miss her a lot."

"Well, you'll see her soon in New York," Carlotta tries to console him, "but I can imagine how you feel. Maybe we all can do a video call with her again later on tonight on that big-screen TV in our father's study."

"I guess I will have to settle for that. Needless to say, I would much rather like her here with me. OK, enough of that. I better stop before I go insane."

"What time are you picking me up?" she changes the subject, realizing that her brother is really suffering over this and she can sympathize with that feeling. At least she will get to be with Roberto tonight and tomorrow, even if she cannot touch him affectionately in public or let on that they are much closer than anyone knows. Maybe they can find a moment to be alone somewhere, she hopes. Luca interrupts her dreamy thoughts by telling her he will pick her up at 2 p.m.

Carlotta and Luca arrive at their parents' house around 3:30 p.m., and get settled in their bedrooms. Carlotta wonders if Roberto would stay overnight in her parents' house or if he will stay at his parents' with Verena? *If he stays here*, she thinks, *she wants him to have one of the guest rooms close to her. Maybe she can sneak into his room when everyone is sleeping.* The idea excites her. She even brought some sexy nightwear, just in case.

Luca gets ready in his room. After his shower he sits on the bed to relax a bit. He hasn't even told Kataryna that he has a birthday today but if they do a video call later on she will find out. He doesn't like the idea of her finding out like that. He decides to call her to tell her and at the same time give her some prior notice about the planned video call.

"Good morning, Principessa," he greets her when she picks up the phone.

"Good morning my darling, or rather good afternoon where you are," she responds. "How are you?"

"I am OK, but I have to confess something," he continues. "I am at my parents' house. We are having a little dinner party this evening. Actually, it is for my birthday."

"Today is your birthday?" she asks astonished. "Happy Birthday my darling, you should have told me, so I could have sent you a gift. I feel terrible now."

"Please don't feel bad. Having you in my life is my gift. I purposely didn't say anything because I know how busy you are and I didn't want you to stress yourself out with that on top of everything," he offers as an excuse.

"I see," she says. "I will have to punish you for that, my love."

"Ooh, that sounds so sexy and intriguing when you say that. What kind of punishment do you have in mind?" he asks, getting slightly aroused already.

"I am not going to tell you but get ready to be punished when I see you," she says seductively.

"You have no idea what you just did to me with that statement. I can't wait to take my punishment from you. As a matter of fact, I feel I am being punished already in the present state my body is in. I better cool down quickly because I have to be dressed and proper soon, facing my parents and some family friends."

"OK," Kataryna says, "I will let you off the hook for now. So cool down and have a good time. Have a very happy birthday and say hello to everyone."

"Carlotta suggested earlier that we all might have a video call with you a little later. How about at around 1 p.m., your time?" he asks.

"I would love to do that. At least I can contribute a little bit to your birthday that way."

She starts laughing.

"I will make sure to be dressed appropriately."

"You are so sweet, Principessa. In a couple of weeks we will celebrate after the fact in New York. At least then I will have you all to myself."

"Can't wait," she responds softly. She blows him a kiss through the phone.

Luca is happy that Kataryna reacted so sweetly and in the process managed to get him excited again. He is glad he made that call and not have her find out via video call later on.

Carlotta takes a long look in the mirror. She decided to wear a rather sexy dress for the occasion hoping to entice Roberto to meet her later alone somewhere. Maybe they can tell the others they are going out for a nightcap in Bellagio. Hopefully Verena doesn't want to come along. It is 5:30 p.m., as she prepares to leave her bedroom to go to the grand room where the reception before the dinner will be held. She walks down the hallway and knocks on Luca's door.

"Whoa Carlotta, that is some dress," he laughs out loud. "You are pulling out all the stops tonight, aren't you?"

"Is it too daring?" she asks her brother grinning.

"It is daring, but it looks good on you. Well, let me escort you into the lion's den," he says laughing.

Luca and Carlotta arrive in the grand room where their parents, Patrizia and Francesco are already waiting for them. A piano player is playing light music.

"Did anyone else arrive yet?" Carlotta asks her parents.

"Yes, Roberto and his daughter just arrived. Verena is in the restroom and Roberto went to get something out of his car," Valentina Romano explains, handing everyone a glass of Champagne.

"Who else did you invite, mamma?" Luca asks.

"Francesco's parents, of course, and two other couples, close friends of ours from up here, so we will have 16 persons for dinner," Luca's mother replies.

Roberto and Verena walk into the room. Carlotta looks at him sweetly as he comes over to greet her.

"Good evening, Carlotta," he says, kissing her on both cheeks, "nice to see you. Beautiful dress."

"Thank you, Roberto," Carlotta utters, staring into his eyes. "You look very good yourself."

Carlotta's feels her knees getting weak. She wishes she could embrace and kiss him. She manages to pull herself together and takes a sip of her Champagne to ease the tension she is feeling. Luca has to smile as he watches their interaction, which seems to be laced with some undertones. Carlotta turns to Verena, who is standing next to her father.

"Ciao Verena, we haven't seen you in ages. You are getting more beautiful each time I see you."

"Thank you, I guess I was lucky to inherit the best parts of my mother and father. But look at you, you are looking very sexy tonight," Verena exclaims amused, inspecting Carlotta's dress a little closer.

Carlotta just shrugs her shoulders giving her a devious smile. Francesco's parents, Dr. Vincente Barone and his wife Sylvia Barone arrive and are greeted by everyone. Right after them the other two couples, Mr. and Mrs. Montanari and Mr. and Mrs. Cantaneo, arrive. After everyone had had their first glass of Champagne and had a chance to talk to each other, Luca's father asks for everyone's attention.

"Dear friends and family, thank you for joining us for dinner tonight to celebrate our son's birthday."

Luca rolls his eyes and smiles. He really doesn't want that kind of attention.

"Papà, can't we just have dinner without the speech," he says smiling.

"Luca," his father starts, "let me just say a few words and present you our gift."

Luca looks at his father grinning, and bows in respect to him.

"Luca, you have always made us very proud. So for your birthday we want to present you with a masterpiece to beautify your already beautiful villa and give you as much pleasure as you have given us."

Oh my God, Luca thinks, *I hope they didn't buy me the expensive painting they looked at and admired the other day in a local gallery.*

"Mr. and Mrs. Montanari were so kind to get the gift and bring it with them tonight," Luca's father continues.

He turns to his friend Paolo Montanari and gives him a signal to bring in the gift. Everyone is in suspense as Paolo Montanari leaves the grand room to get Luca's gift. When he returns he has Kataryna on his arm, escorting her into the room right into Luca's arms. Luca is beside himself and speechless. He almost drops to his knees. His heart is pounding. He embraces Kataryna tightly and then kisses her while everyone is cheering and clapping.

"Happy birthday, darling," Kataryna says, holding him tightly and kissing him softly. "I hope you like your gift."

When Luca finally recovers from the initial surprise he finds his voice.

"This is the best gift anyone could have given me. Thank you so much, mamma and papà. There are no words that can express how happy you made me with this surprise. And you, Principessa," he addresses Kataryna, "thank you for taking this long trip. You have to tell me later how you pulled that one off."

"Paolo had to go to New York on business and chartered our jet. I called Kataryna and asked her if she would come over on our jet together with Paolo for your birthday, and I swore her to secrecy because I wanted it to be a surprise. I know how much you miss her and we all wanted her over here anyway to meet her in person," Luca's father explains, beaming with pride that his surprise went that well, and seeing how happy his son is at this moment. "Except for your mother and Paolo, no one knew about this plan."

Luca is still holding on tightly to Kataryna as he hugs his mother and father. Carlotta and Patrizia who were also stunned by the surprise come over to hug Kataryna. Luca reluctantly releases Kataryna. She turns around and smiles at him reassuringly and then embraces Carlotta and Patrizia.

"We are so happy that you are here today," the sisters tell her.

"So am I," Kataryna says, "just seeing Luca's face light up when he saw me walking in was well worth it."

Kataryna looks beguiling in a short gold/green snake print dress with a plunging cowl neckline, three-quarter sleeves and slits on both sides. Luca takes Kataryna's hand again and leads her through the room introducing her to everyone formally. He can't stop smiling as they go around the room.

Roberto, who has been watching the whole spectacle from afar, is in a trance. His heart is pounding and a strange sensation is running through his body. He can't believe what is happening right in front of him. Everything becomes a blur, as he desperately tries to pull himself together when Luca and Kataryna come closer to him. He wipes his forehead with his handkerchief and takes a sip of the Champagne in his hand.

"What's the matter, papà," Verena asks her father, "are you not feeling well? Do you want some water?"

Roberto's chest starts getting tighter. He is experiencing a fully fletched anxiety attack and can barely stand up.

"Papà," Verena says a bit louder, tugging at her father's arm, trying to get his attention. "What is going on with you?"

"I am fine, Verena," he responds in a curt tone.

Verena is concerned but follows her father's request to let it go. She has never seen him like this and wonders if he may be trying to hide an illness. She will revisit this with him later when they are alone.

Luca and Kataryna are standing in front of Roberto and Verena.

"Hello Roberto," Kataryna greets him, holding out her arms to hug him realizing that he is not himself. She had no idea that he would be at this dinner tonight; otherwise she would have found a way to prepare him for it somehow.

He just stares at her but then catches himself and hugs her to say hello.

"Hello Kataryna," he manages to get out in a fairly normal tone almost business-like. "What a surprise. May I introduce my daughter Verena to you?"

Kataryna shakes hands with Verena who seems to be somewhat distracted. "Very nice to meet you," Kataryna says to Verena. "I have heard a lot about you."

"I haven't heard anything about you," Verena says bluntly. "So you are Luca's new girlfriend?"

"Yes, she his," Luca says proudly. "And she is also a partner in the private equity firm who may acquire the company your father works for."

"Yeah, I heard about that," Verena says. "That means that you would become his boss then, right?"

Kataryna nods. "Together with my partner Stephen Wagner. We each own 50 percent of the private equity firm."

"I recently decided to focus on finance and business management studies. I would like to take a trip to New York in the near future. Maybe you can give me some pointers." Verena explains.

"It's an exciting city," Kataryna responds. "I am sure you will like it."

"Excuse us, Verena, I would like to introduce Kataryna to Francesco's parents," Luca cuts in, leading Kataryna towards Dr. and Mrs. Barone.

Luca's mother announces that dinner will be served shortly and asks everyone to take their seats. Kataryna is seated between Luca and his father, who sits at the head of the table. Roberto's seat is opposite to that of Luca and Kataryna, with Carlotta and Verena to his left and right. He would prefer to leave, but that would be too obvious. Luca is still holding on to Kataryna putting his arm around her and caressing her. Attempting to ignore what is happening in front of him, Roberto starts talking to Carlotta, but it is almost impossible for him to focus on anything else but Kataryna. His chest is aching as he realizes how happy Luca and Kataryna are together. After the antipasto, he excuses himself and goes to the restroom to take one of the pills. Hopefully that will relieve his chest tightness soon and help him make it through this evening. He gets back to the dinner table in time to hear Luca's father proposing a toast.

"Please join me in a toast. We have a lot to celebrate tonight."

He raises his glass and takes Kataryna's hand.

"Welcome to the family. I am glad that Luca found a woman who makes him so happy. I also would like to drink to Patrizia and Francesco, soon to be our son-in-law."

He pauses and then continues, looking at Carlotta.

"That just leaves our beautiful Carlotta who is still single. May you find the love of your life soon," he ends the toast.

Carlotta smiles at her father. "Thank you, papà, I am working on that."

Everyone starts laughing as they raise and clink their glasses to Riccardo Romano's toast.

Roberto starts feeling more uncomfortable as Carlotta looks at him with a seductive smile and caresses him with her leg under the table. He feels his life spinning out-of-control fast. After dinner the guests mingle for a while in the grand room.

Carlotta pulls Roberto to the side.

"Are you going to stay overnight in our house?" she asks him quietly anticipating a positive response.

"No, Verena and I will of course stay with my parents," he responds. "It would be too suspicious if I part company with them."

"Suspicious?" she asks disappointed. "I was hoping we could spend some time together and continue what we started last night."

"I am sorry, Carlotta," he replies, "but I haven't been feeling so great the whole day. I really need some rest. As you may recall it got very late last night, we drank a lot, and then I had an early meeting with my interior designer. So I didn't get much sleep. I hope you understand."

"What's the matter with you?" she sounds concerned.

"I don't know. Maybe I am coming down with something. I just want to make sure that it doesn't get worse."

"Feel better," she says stroking his arm. "I hope to see you soon."

Roberto starts looking for his parents. He is more than ready to leave. He sees them talking to Kataryna and walks over to join them.

"When are we leaving?" he asks his parents.

"We are just making our rounds to say good-bye," his mother answers as she moves on.

"So, Roberto," his father adds, "this lovely lady here may soon be your new boss."

"Yes. She and her partner," he clarifies.

After his parents continue on their rounds, Roberto has a moment alone with Kataryna.

"It was great to see you," he says. "Although it was a tough night for me as you can imagine. You are even more beautiful than I remembered."

"I am really concerned about you," Kataryna says in a low voice.

"Good-bye Kataryna, have a safe trip back to New York. I will be in touch." He hugs her and kisses her on both cheeks.

Carlotta watches with an obvious sad face as Roberto leaves with Verena and his parents. Luca walks over to his sister.

"You look disappointed, but this wasn't the right night for you and him to get together. Give it some time."

"Thank you for your support," she says. "I guess I won't have a choice but to be patient. I am a little surprised, though, that you seem to be more open to the idea of him and me."

"Yeah, after what I am experiencing with Kataryna, I came to the realization that you have to grab the opportunity when love comes your way. If you think he can make you as happy as Kataryna makes me, who am I to say you two shouldn't be together. I think he also needs someone in his life and you might be the right woman. So, on that note, good luck. I hope it works out. Just be careful and don't lose your head."

"You have no idea what it means to me that my big brother is supportive of this idea. Now I can focus on pursuing this without feeling guilty. I just wonder what our parents may think when they find out," Carlotta says grinning.

"I wouldn't say anything yet," Luca replies. "Why don't you see first where this is going?"

Carlotta is tempted to tell Luca that she already spent last night with Roberto but something holds her back.

"Of course," she agrees, "first things first. Hey, I just realized that you wouldn't be able to take me back to Milano tomorrow. I suppose you and Kataryna will go to your villa instead."

"Yes, maybe Roberto can take you back to Milano with him tomorrow."

"Great idea," Carlotta says joyfully. "I will ask him to give me a ride."

Kataryna, who had been talking to Dr. and Sylvia Barone for some time, comes over to Luca and Carlotta.

"What are you two cooking up here?' she asks laughing. "It looks like some type of conspiracy."

"Just a heart-to-heart between brother and sister," Luca answers. "We don't get to do that often enough these days. Carlotta and I have always been very close since we are the oldest siblings and only two years apart. Patrizia is so much younger than us with her 27 years."

"Other than your sister, do you have any more siblings?" Carlotta asks Kataryna.

Kataryna struggles with the answer. She doesn't know how to respond to Carlotta's question truthfully. This is not the time to get into that subject with this family.

"I always wanted to have a brother," she quickly answers, "you two are so lucky to have each other and being so close."

"Yes, we are and we know it," Carlotta says. "And you can be like our sister."

"Maybe yours," Kataryna says, grinning at Carlotta, "but I don't want to be Luca's sister. I have something else in mind for him."

"You took the words right out of my mouth," Luca says, embracing Kataryna.

After all the guests leave, Luca's parents, Carlotta, Patrizia, Francesco, Luca and Kataryna sit down for a nightcap.

"What a wonderful evening we had," Luca's mother says, hugging her son.

"I can't thank you enough," Luca beams, "this was so unexpected and the best gift ever."

Carlotta starts yawning. "It's getting late. I already had a late night yesterday. I really need some sleep now."

Patrizia looks at her sister surprised. "You had a late night? Is there anything you would like to tell us about?"

"Well, let's call it a night," Luca says. "Carlotta can tell us about her late night adventure tomorrow at breakfast."

He takes Kataryna's hand and they leave heading towards Luca's bedroom, waving good night to the others. He opens the door and they walk in. Someone had already brought Kataryna's luggage to the room. She looks out of the window admiring the beautiful view of Lake Como in the distance. The villa is situated higher up overlooking the lake. Luca steps behind her and puts his arms around her waist kissing her neck.

"You like the view?"

"Yes, but its quite different than the view from your villa."

"That's because my villa is not located that high up. It is much closer to the lake than this one. But right now the best view is you here with me."

Kataryna turns around and puts her arms around Luca's neck and kisses him softly. He pulls her closer to him and she can feel his erection against her. His hands caress her back and buttocks as he kisses her cleavage.

"Let's try to do this nice and slow," he whispers in her ear as his hands move up her thighs. "No premature explosions, OK?"

They sit down on the bed. Luca takes off her shoes, puts her legs up on the bed and then lies next to her. He kisses her passionately. She starts moaning as he takes off her dress and underwear, slowly caressing her in all the right spots. She opens his pants and pulls them down taking his underwear off in the process. He sits in between her legs kissing her thighs and going higher all around her only slightly running his tongue over her vaginal area. She starts panting and moving towards him as he enters her slowly groaning in pleasure. They are lost in extreme ecstasy moving in rhythm with each other until they explode into an orgasm.

"Happy Birthday," Kataryna whispers in his ear. "This was definitely worth the long trip."

"You know how to make me happy," he says softly. "I was almost going insane without you."

"You mean you didn't enjoy our steamy video games?" she laughs.

"Oh, I did but not being able to touch you and be touched by you was extremely difficult to take."

"Well, then," Kataryna says seductively, "I shall touch you a lot for the next two days that I am here."

"I hope you do, Principessa," he says, "and I will do the same for you. I will keep you excited 24/7."

"This time around my darling, you can only keep me excited 24/2 because I have to leave on Tuesday."

"Don't even mention the word 'leave'. I am allergic to that word when it comes in connection with you."

"I won't mention it for the next two days."

"What would you like to do tomorrow after breakfast?" he asks her.

"What are my options?"

"I thought we take a little drive along the lake and then go to my villa. I can't wait to have you back there. Mariya and Isabella asked already when you would be back. You seem to have them wrapped around your finger, too."

"The villa sounds great. I have been dreaming about being back there. As for having Mariya and Isabella wrapped around my finger is concerned, who else do I have wrapped around my finger?"

"You know I was talking about me, don't you?" he replies kissing her neck and planting more kisses down her breasts.

"Good to know," she sighs, "but I rather have you wrapped around my entire body than just my finger."

He pulls her tighter and lies on top of her wrapping his legs around hers.

"Here you go, Principessa, my body wrapped around yours. I could stay like this forever. I just can't get enough of you."

They kiss passionately and are soon in ecstasy again until they climax in total bliss.

"Can you believe that we actually managed to do this all the way for the first time?" he asks.

"Yes, and it happened on your birthday," she makes her point. "So we will celebrate that anniversary along with your birthday every year."

T W E L V E

Carlotta is wide-awake sitting up in her bed leaning against the pillows. She is happy for her brother having Kataryna with him on his birthday. She can just imagine what is going on in Luca's bedroom right now and she wishes she had the same with Roberto. Roberto didn't seem like himself tonight. He appeared distracted most of the time. Did he feel guilty about last night? *Hopefully it is nothing serious*, she thinks. She is tempted to call him but then decides against it. He is probably sleeping already and needs the rest. She sends him a text message:

Roberto, can I get a ride with you tomorrow? I came here with Luca but obviously he is not going back to Milano tomorrow. Pls. let me know a.s.a.p.

Carlotta thinks about her night with Roberto. *Was she too forward coming on to him like she did last night,* she wonders? Maybe he was turned off by her bold move? *No,* she tells herself, *don't go there, he was an active participant.* No need to read anything into his cooler behavior tonight. He had already told her that he didn't want to make this public, especially not around the family. In addition, he wouldn't have wanted to steal Luca's thunder on his birthday. She recalls Luca's words "give it some time," which puts her at ease and let's her go to sleep finally.

When Roberto and Verena arrive at his parents' house, he immediately starts heading towards his bedroom. He doesn't want to be around anyone, except for Kataryna of course, but that is out of the question anyhow. The finality of this situation hits him hard and he feels the heaviness return to his chest.

"Good night," he says to his parents and his daughter with a weak smile.

"Roberto, can you stay a moment, please?" his father asks.

Roberto turns around looking at his father, trying to pull it together. "I am really tired, papà, can we talk tomorrow morning?"

"You haven't been yourself tonight. We were just wondering if anything is wrong. Usually you are the life of the party and tonight you have been unusually quiet, mostly distracted and generally out of it. You want to talk about it?"

"I just had a late night yesterday and had to be up early this morning. I am not feeling that great and everyone can have an off-night occasionally," Roberto offers as an explanation.

"OK, son," Roberto's father says, "we are glad if that is all. I thought maybe this acquisition deal is giving you sleepless nights and you are concerned what the new shareholders may decide or what plans they may have for you."

"I am very good at what I do. It would be unwise for them to replace me. I don't think I have to worry about that. Even if they had other plans for my position, I am not married to this job. I have accumulated enough wealth that I am set for life," Roberto responds.

"I know that you don't need this job, but you built up this company to what it is today," Roberto's father replies. "Well, maybe you should find yourself a nice girlfriend like Luca has. Did you see how happy he is? I think it would do you good to have someone like that in your life."

"I will take it under consideration," Roberto says smirking. "But right now, I am going to sleep. See you at breakfast. Thank you for your concern, papà."

"If there is anything you need to get off your chest just let us know," his father offers.

"Of course," Roberto says, "who else could I trust more than my own family."

Roberto finally makes it to his bedroom. He closes the door and looks at himself in the mirror. *What in the world is happening to me*, he asks himself? *I don't want to feel like this.* He takes another one of his anti-anxiety pills to get rid of the heaviness in his chest and gets ready for bed. His cell phone pings, announcing a text message. It's from Carlotta asking if she can get a ride with him back to Milano tomorrow.

Sure, he writes back. I am planning to leave at 2 p.m. I will pick you up around 2:30 p.m.

Once in bed he stares at the ceiling and relives the events of the night. It appears in front of him like a movie, a drama he really doesn't want to see. *Did this really happen*, he thinks *or was I dreaming? A dream? No, of course not, that is just wishful thinking,* he tells himself.

The aroma of Kataryna's perfume comes over him. He recalls how she came towards him to greet him with open arms and a sweet smile. He had her in his arms for seconds and wanted to hold on forever. *She said she was concerned about me. So she must care for me*, he rationalizes. Why else would she be concerned? He smiles at the thought. *Of course she can't start a love affair with me while she is with Luca,* he thinks, *she has too much integrity for that. That's the kind of woman I need,* he confirms to himself. She is probably torn inside what to do about this. It is possible that she is in love with two men at the same time, but with Luca by her side she will not be free to allow herself to think about me this way. *May the best man win,* he thinks, as he feels the heaviness disappearing from his chest. He breathes in deeply. That feels so much better. These pills are a lifesaver. He closes his eyes. Carlotta comes to his mind. He recalls their night together and how she seduced him. "Oh, Carlotta," he says out loud, "I know how you feel, but I am in love with another woman."

He is tormented by the thought that Carlotta might be as much in love with him as he is with Kataryna. That would make two very unhappy people in the same environment. He imagines how Carlotta would react if she had the chest tightness he has when he sees Kataryna and Luca together. The thought of that brings a chill to his body, but he doesn't want to deal with that right now. He is relaxed now, thanks to the pills he took, and falls asleep before he can worry about anything else.

At 10:30 a.m., on Sunday morning the Romano family starts enjoying a Champagne breakfast. After an enchanting morning in bed, Luca and Kataryna arrive at the breakfast table. Carlotta looks at them envying them for their happiness.

"God, you two look happy," she says, looking at Luca and Kataryna, "I hope it rubs off on me."

Francesco, who has his arm around Patrizia, starts laughing. "What about us, don't we look happy, too?"

"Yes, of course you do, but these two here," Carlotta points to Luca and Kataryna, "are oozing happiness this morning and who can blame them?"

Kataryna blushes lightly smiling to herself. Luca kisses her on the cheek. "Sorry, if my sister is embarrassing you. "Why don't you give us a little break here?" Luca addresses Carlotta.

"Well, let's drink to our family and what the future may bring," Riccardo Romano exclaims raising his glass. "I am very happy with what I am seeing."

The breakfast turns into a brunch and finally concludes around 1:30 p.m.

"This was delicious. I am so full now," Kataryna says as she gets up.

"Are you ready to leave?" Luca asks her. "I am going to have our luggage brought to the car in a few minutes."

"OK, I will be right behind you," Kataryna responds, walking over to Valentina and Riccardo Romano to say good-bye.

"I can't thank you enough for bringing me over here," she says as she hugs Luca's mother first and then his father. "I am looking forward to spending more time with you in the future."

"It was our pleasure," Luca's father says, "we enjoyed every minute of your visit. I wish you and Luca a great time in New York and Hawaii and come back soon."

"She will be here again at the end of January. We are going to Venice to Il Ballo del Doge in the beginning of February," Luca tells them as he returns to the room.

"Fantastic. You will love it. The Carnevale in Venezia is magical," Valentina says.

"Yes, it is a great event," Carlotta says. "I am going to have to find someone to take me there, too."

"You know what the theme is this time?" Luca asks his sister smiling. "It's all about love."

"How fitting," Carlotta replies with a wicked smile. "By the way you two, shall we have lunch together before Kataryna goes back to New York? This way Enrico can meet her, too."

Luca looks at Kataryna. "What do you think? Can we squeeze that in?"

"That is a great idea," Kataryna responds, "let's definitely plan for that. I would love to meet your son, Carlotta."

Luca is engaged in a conversation with his father as Carlotta and Kataryna start heading towards the front door to leave after everyone said their good-byes. As they enter the foyer the doorbell rings. They open the door. Roberto stands in front of them. Kataryna is startled for a moment. Carlotta smiles at him happily and hugs him.

"My chauffeur is here to take me to Milano," she laughs out loud. "You are right on time. Let me get my bags," she tells him.

She heads towards her bedroom, leaving Kataryna and Roberto staring at each other.

"Hello Kataryna," Roberto kisses her on both cheeks. "I was hoping to see you before you leave," he says in a low voice. "It will definitely make my day go easier. Although I would prefer to be able to speak to you undisturbed."

"I hope you get better soon, Roberto," Kataryna responds somewhat anxious, expecting Luca to appear soon with their coats. "You have to get this under control."

Roberto shakes his head and looks at her sadly. "You have no idea what this is doing to me. I don't know how to deal with this. I take it one day and one pill at a time."

Carlotta returns with her handbag, carry-on and coat.

"Ready when you are," she says to Roberto.

He looks at her briefly, gesturing her to move towards his car and then turns back to Kataryna embracing her to say good-bye while Carlotta steps out of the house breathing in the crisp air.

"I'll let you know how I am doing," he whispers in Kataryna's ear.

Kataryna nods silently and waves at Carlotta, hoping to end the uncomfortable moment. Somewhat relieved she closes the door behind her and starts walking to find Luca. *God, let him get over this and fall in love with Carlotta,* she silently prays. Roberto's love for her weighs heavy on her. She realizes that soon she will have to vent and talk to someone she trusts about it.

Roberto opens the car door for Carlotta and stows her carry-on in the trunk. Verena is busy with her cell phone in the back seat. She looks up briefly to greet Carlotta but then gets right back to her text messages.

"What did you do today?" Carlotta asks Roberto as he drives off.

"Not much," he starts explaining. "We all slept in. Verena had breakfast with some old friends of hers. I had a late breakfast with my parents. And you?" he asks her.

"We also had a late breakfast, which turned into a Champagne brunch."

"How long is Kataryna staying in Italy?" Roberto asks.

"Until Tuesday. I am going to have lunch with Kataryna and Luca on Monday so she can meet Enrico before she flies back to New York. He really wants to meet her because he is hoping to visit her in New York next year."

"Yeah, I can imagine," Roberto replies, "it's the dream destination for most teenagers. Verena also wants to go to New York sooner rather than later."

"I will be going along, too," Carlotta says. "I am not letting Enrico go alone yet over there. Kataryna has to work during the day. She may be able to take off a few days but not a whole week or so, I guess. Hey, I have an idea, why don't we all go to New York together, Verena, you and Enrico and me?"

"I am in," Verena yells enthusiastically from the back, all of a sudden interested in the conversation, "when are we going?"

Roberto smirks. "Now I know how to get my daughter's attention fast. When are you planning on going there?" he asks Carlotta.

"We have discussed March of next year for Enrico's birthday. We will finalize the plans in February when she is coming over here again. Luca and she are going to Il Ballo del Doge in Venice in the beginning of February. He mentioned it at breakfast this morning, emphasizing that the theme will be "Amore." It's all about love," she smiles at him, as he looks at her while they are stopping at a traffic light.

"I would also like to go to that ball," Carlotta continues. "I am hoping someone who has tickets will invite me."

"I got the hint," he says. "I will see what I can do."

Carlotta is encouraged to hear that Roberto may be willing to get tickets for them.

"That would be great," she says already imagining her and Roberto together in Venice. "I will start working on my costume design."

"If the theme is all about love, shouldn't you be going with someone you are in love with?" Verena asks casually.

"We will celebrate universal love," Carlotta responds, trying to kill the awkward moment Verena managed to create with her statement.

"Good answer," Roberto throws in. "The world needs more love."

When they arrive in Milano after the one and a half hour drive, Roberto drops Carlotta off at her apartment. He gets out of the car and walks her to the door.

"Can we have a phone call later or better yet a video call?" Carlotta asks him as he hugs her to say good-bye.

"I have to drop Verena off and then I am going to see a friend of mine. I don't know how late it will get. I'll try to call you later," he offers.

"OK," she says laughing, "I will be waiting with bated breath."

Roberto walks away fast. When he returns to the car Verena is sitting in the front seat.

"So, when are we all going to New York?" she asks her father.

"Patience, my dear," he responds, maneuvering the car into traffic. "I will let you know when the time is right."

"So Kataryna is going to be your boss in the future." Verena states.

"If her firm acquires NatMedica, then Kataryna and her partner Stephen would become my new bosses."

"Is that OK with you?" Verena questions him further.

"Yes, I think we could work well together," Roberto replies. "She has good ideas for expanding in the U.S. Why did you ask me that?"

"It seemed to me that you were somewhat stressed when she came over to say hello last night. You broke out in a sweat. I had never seen you this way. So I figured you are uncomfortable with her."

"No, contrary to what you may think, I am quite comfortable with her."

"OK, if you say so. She is very beautiful and has a strong presence. Some men are intimidated by that."

Roberto shakes his head and laughs. "Are you trying to psychoanalyze me now?"

"No, of course not. I just had this feeling that something was happening to you when she came up to us."

"Look, Verena, you don't see me that often that you would know how I react to life's influences on a daily basis. I told you already I had a late night the day before yesterday and I probably drank too much. As you can see I am perfectly fine now that I got some rest and slept late today."

"I think granddad was right that it would be good if you could find a nice girlfriend."

"I'll start searching tomorrow," he murmurs sarcastically.

"I have a feeling Carlotta might not be opposed to the idea of you and her."

"What makes you say that?" Roberto asks her somewhat panicked.

"Just a feeling, papà. Let's call it a woman's intuition."

Roberto pulls into his ex-wife's driveway to drop off Verena. She gathers her bags and opens the car door.

"You want to come in for a few minutes?"

"No, I am kind of late already. Sergio is expecting me shortly at his place."

"Maybe another time," Verena says as she exits the car. "Couldn't hurt if you would say hello to my mother occasionally. I think she misses you."

"That ship has sailed," Roberto tells his daughter as he kisses her good-bye. "And as far as I know she is in a happy relationship. I'll call you tomorrow."

"OK, papà, maybe we can talk about the New York trip then," Verena winks at him.

On the drive to Sergio's house, Roberto recalls the conversation with his father last night and with Verena on the drive home. Everybody seems to be breathing down his neck about finding a nice girlfriend. He can have a girlfriend tomorrow, but not the one he wants, at least not at this time.

Sergio opens the door. "Ciao Roberto, how are you doing?"

"I have been better," Roberto replies, "you have no idea what kind of a weekend I have behind me."

Sergio pats Roberto on the shoulder. "Come in my friend. I hope you don't mind but my father stopped by, too," Sergio alerts him.

"No, not at all," Roberto responds, "I was supposed to see him anyway this week."

Roberto enters the lounge room area.

"Dottore, good to see you. How is everything?"

"Excellent," Dr. de Angelis answers. "How about you?"

"Let's put it this way. Thank God I have the pills you prescribed; otherwise, I don't know how I would be holding up."

"Can we talk freely?" Sergio's father asks Roberto.

"Yes, Sergio knows everything about my situation," Roberto responds. "And I really need to talk to someone about it, otherwise I may experience an internal combustion."

"I assume you are still struggling with your feelings for this lady who is in a relationship with your friend Luca Romano?" Dr. de Angelis probes.

"I am afraid I am. This weekend I was invited to his parents' house for his birthday dinner and as a surprise birthday present his father had flown over his girlfriend from New York. Suddenly she walks into the room right into his arms. They fell all over each other and looked so happy to be together. I almost lost it. First of all because I didn't expect to see her there and then seeing how in love they were in that moment," Roberto explains.

"I see," Dr. de Angelis says, "what happened next?"

"I broke out in a sweat, my chest started tightening up and I couldn't focus. I was totally out of it. For a moment I thought I was going to lose consciousness. I tried to pull myself together and at the next best opportunity I went to the restroom to take one of the anti-anxiety pills, which helped with the chest tightness after a while, but it didn't lift my spirits. I was down and out and would have preferred to leave immediately, but that would have raised suspicion. I also had my daughter with me who was already concerned about my being so out of it, which I tried to play down."

"Roberto," Dr. de Angelis says calmly, putting his hand on Roberto's shoulder, "this doesn't sound good. It appears that you are unable to let go of your feelings for this lady, and that you are going into a full anxiety or panic mode when you see her with your friend. The anti-anxiety pills are not going to help you with that part. They merely allow your body to get rid of the fight or flight response once you are in an anxiety phase, but the underlying cause can't be cured with them. You may remember that I recommended that you might need help in form of therapy, if you can't stop your feelings for her on your own. Are you ready to come in and meet with our psychiatrist?"

"Well, Dottore, I wasn't finished yet. Listen to this. I think she also cares for me. I told her about my torment because of my feelings for her and she said she was very concerned and wants to help me. She said she would not tell Luca about our conversations because she doesn't want any tension between us. So we have a secret together and she is concerned, which means deep down she cares for me and would be with me if she hadn't started a relationship with him first. In addition, her private equity firm wants to acquire the company I work for, which is owned by Luca and his family. She is very interested in this highly profitable target, so I think she has an ulterior motive to be in a relationship with him hoping that she will win the bid that way."

"You don't know that for sure though or have you asked her and did she admit it?" Dr. de Angelis questions Roberto.

"I briefly touched the subject when I had dinner with Kataryna, that's her name, in Berlin a few weeks ago. Of course, she didn't admit it, but would you if you had an ulterior motive?"

"Roberto, for the time being she is with him regardless if there may be an ulterior motive or not, and you have to let go. Look what this is doing to you," Dr. de Angelis admonishes him.

Roberto runs his hands through his hair and shrugs his shoulders as if to say *yeah but I don't want to give up yet.*

Dr. de Angelis shakes his head. "I still think you should talk to our psychiatrist to see what he has to offer. It really can't hurt to just talk with a professional about this."

"There is more," Roberto starts out. "Luca's sister seduced me Friday night. She seems to want a relationship with me, but I am not sure that I can go through with this."

"Oh my God, this is getting really crazy now," Sergio, who has been listening silently so far, jumps in. "Are you saying you had sex with her or did she just try to seduce you and you averted it somehow?"

"She succeeded because I had a lot to drink that night. When I saw her sitting on the couch in a sexy position, I thought about Kataryna and that I would be all over her if she would be sitting there instead. So I got a bit aroused. I closed my eyes and when I opened them again she was practically half naked in front of me and started touching and undressing me. It went so fast I didn't really know what was happening to me. And now she is pursuing me. She wants to continue with what we started she said yesterday. I am afraid she may be in love with me."

"And how do you feel about her?" Dr. de Angelis asks.

"I am not sure," Roberto replies. "But if Kataryna were free this would not have happened."

"Kataryna is not free, so why not give it a try with this one? This may help you to get over Kataryna," Sergio suggests looking at his father for support.

"Only if you really like her and can imagine having a long-term relationship with her. Otherwise you may make someone else unhappy in the process," Dr. de Angelis explains.

"I will have to do some soul-searching," Roberto murmurs.

"Yes, do that. Also you should not be drinking that much alcohol with the anti- anxiety medication I prescribed. It could have a fatal effect."

Luca and Kataryna leave the Romano family's villa a few minutes after Carlotta and Roberto left. They take a scenic drive along the lake heading towards the Cernobbio area.

"This area is so beautiful and picturesque," Kataryna remarks looking around.

"Yes, it is. Some people take it for granted, though, and do not even notice the beauty anymore," Luca explains, "but I like to fully take in the serenity when I come up here. Sometimes I am sitting by the window in my villa, just looking at the lake and the surrounding area for a while without doing anything. It is very calming and reenergizes me after a hectic week at the office."

"I know what you mean," Kataryna says. "I do the same when I am in Hawaii, only that I am staring at an ocean there instead of a lake. I think you will love Hawaii."

"I am sure I will, especially with you next to me," he says.

Luca stops the car at a scenic point. "Look at this, Principessa," he says, as he leans over to take her into his arms. "I am surrounded by beauty, the lake in front of me and you next to me."

"Are you trying to seduce me in your car?"

He pulls her closer and kisses her passionately. "Do you want me to seduce you?"

"I think you better start driving before this gets out of control," she whispers giggling.

"This is just a little taste of what's to come as soon as we are home," he says kissing her neck and softly biting her earlobe.

"Please, say no more, otherwise we are going to have a delicate situation here in a moment."

She caresses his inner thigh and he starts moaning. "See, what I mean?" she asks.

"I sure do," he whispers, trying to stop her hand from going any further up. "I am in trouble already."

"Really?" she asks seductively, "let me see how much in trouble you are."

"Please don't go there," he almost begs her, "you know the effect you have on me."

"Well, sweetie, you started it," she replies, "and you know what they say? Don't start anything you can't finish."

Her hand moves up his thigh slowly and she can feel his excitement, which encourages her to continue her sexy assault. She applies more pressure as he starts groaning and breathing heavy, not being able to stop his inevitable orgasm under her persistent touch.

"I can't believe you did this to me." He breathes out holding her tightly.

"That will teach you to play with fire," she says laughing. "I told you to start driving, but instead you ignited the flame by kissing me so passionately and then breathing down my neck. So I had no choice but to extinguish the fire before you burn me up."

Kataryna is laughing out loud throwing up her arms over her head in delight over what she managed to accomplish. Luca is biting his lip smiling.

"You won again," he says, "but this day is not over yet. Get ready for a stormy evening, Principessa."

"Ooh, should I get worried?" she asks coquettishly pinching his thigh, still laughing.

"I promise an evening you won't forget," he replies, grinning mysteriously.

"Make sure you can keep your promises," she gives him a sexy smile. "You have raised a lot of expectations now. Otherwise, you may go down in history as the man who can't rise to the occasion."

"I accept the challenge, Principessa," he says softly, kissing her again deeply, letting his hand graze under her skirt caressing her and making it impossible for her to resist this intense feeling. Her fingers dig into his neck as she allows him to relieve her sexual tension.

They sit quietly for a moment recovering from the excitement and reveling in the beautiful scenery around them.

"I used to come to this scenic point just for the view," Luca starts talking again, "but now I have something else to remember it by."

"It's an experience I won't ever forget." She takes a photo of the view with her iPhone. "I think I will have this photo enlarged, framed and put up in my apartment, so this moment will be with me all the time."

Luca starts the car and takes Kataryna's hand as they drive off towards his villa.

"I called Mariya and told her that I would bring an overnight guest, but I didn't tell her who the guest is. She will be very excited when she sees it is you."

"I brought a little gift for her and Isabella," Kataryna tells him.

"How sweet of you." He kisses her hand he had been holding the whole time.

When they arrive at the villa, Luca parks the car and gets their luggage out of the trunk. He opens the front door as Mariya comes towards them excitedly.

"Signora," Mariya shouts out cheerily, "what a surprise. It is so nice to have you back here again."

Kataryna walks up to her and hugs her. "Nice to see you again, Mariya. I have been dreaming about your cooking."

Mariya looks down embarrassed. "Thank you, Signora. I made a nice dinner for you tonight. I hope you like it."

"I am sure I will. I like everything Italian."

Kataryna looks at Luca, who smiles at her broadly. "I hope that includes men.

Kataryna and Mariya laugh at Luca's statement.

"Of course, to be exact, one specific man."

Mariya takes Kataryna's carry-on. "Shall I take this to the same room you stayed in last time, Signora?"

"No, Mariya, grazie," Luca says quickly, putting his arm around Kataryna. "This will go with us to the master bedroom."

Mariya nods and smiles at them happily. Kataryna takes two small nicely wrapped boxes out of her bag and hands one to Mariya.

"This is for you Mariya, I hope you like it. Is Isabella here, too?"

"Yes, she is in the kitchen getting everything ready for your dinner."

"What time would you like to eat?" Luca asks Kataryna.

Kataryna looks at her watch. "It's almost 5 o'clock now. How about 7:30?"

"Your dinner will be ready at 7:30," Mariya promises as she heads towards the kitchen.

Luca and Kataryna arrive in the master bedroom suite. He walks up to her and embraces her.

"So Signora, what would you like to do for the next two hours before dinner? Would you like to take a nap?"

"Oh, please," she responds laughing, "you are so obvious. How about a relaxing bath first?"

Luca laughs out loud. "I know what you have in mind. You are going to trap me again into a torture situation and drive me insane with desire."

"I wouldn't call it torture, darling. I will bring you to the verge of ecstasy followed by a very satisfying conclusion. So why don't you get us something delicious to drink and I will let the water run meanwhile."

"Well, if you put it this way, bella, I will obey and get the drinks and look forward to another erotic adventure. I guess we will have to work up an appetite for our elaborate dinner later on. I am not going to the office tomorrow, so we can eat until midnight if we want to."

"Eat or play," Kataryna whispers into his ear. "Whatever we feel like."

Luca sighs deeply and smiles as he takes off to get the drinks. "I will be back in no time."

Kataryna turns on the water in the Jacuzzi tub, recalling what happened last time they were in this tub together. She is getting excited imagining how Luca will react when he sees what she has planned this time. She pours some bath oil into the streaming water and goes to the walk-in closet to get ready.

Luca returns to the bedroom suite with two drinks in Champagne glasses and fresh fruit. He puts the tray on the side table wondering if Kataryna is in the tub already. He looks for her in the bathroom. The tub is almost full. He turns off the water. The light is dimmed and erotic Italian music is playing, but Kataryna is not there. As he turns around she stands in front of him in a super sexy black satin push-up bra camisole and barely-there panties, with her hair pinned up and dangling earrings in her ears. She stares at him with smoldering glistening eyes, slowly walking up to him with a seductive swing in her hips and her above-the-knee black boots. Luca stares at her with wide eyes as a flash of electricity is running through his entire body.

"Oh my God," he manages to get over his lips, "what are you up to Principessa?"

Kataryna stands closely in front of him, undoing his shirt buttons and taking off his shirt. She kisses his neck and chest while taking off his pants. He takes off his shoes and steps out of the pants, still in awe of what is happening and highly aroused.

"Why don't you get into the tub for me," she commands him, whispering in his ear while caressing his thighs.

Luca gets into the tub wondering what she is going to do next. She leaves the bathroom to get the drinks and snacks and puts them on the edge of the tub. She takes a black satin scarf, puts it around his eyes and takes off her boots. Once in the water she kneels between his legs, feeding him a piece of pineapple. She pours some of the Aperol/Champagne drink on his neck and starts licking it off, running her tongue up to his ears and caressing his genital area at the same time. Luca screams out in ecstasy. He grabs her legs and tries to move but she has him pinned against the tub with her legs holding his apart. He can't escape her intense fondling. He starts panting and moaning and finally his hands find her skimpy panties and pull them down. He scoots down and kisses her thighs, his tongue moving all over her. She moans and breathes heavily attempting to pull away from him. Luca is on fire. He finds the strength to hold on to her and deepen her arousal. He tears the scarf off his eyes, ripping into her camisole to hold on to her as she tries to back away. He pulls her down to him and kisses her while removing her panties completely. The Aperol/ Champagne drink he poured over her chest runs into the bra cups. His tongue swirls around her breasts while he soaks up the remaining drink from her bra cups. Kataryna is panting, but manages to get back up on her knees struggling with him as he tries to pull her back down. He slings his legs in between hers holding them apart and running his mouth up and down her until she screams out in pleasure and climaxes. Turning her around he enters her from behind, groaning and clutching her tightly as he reaches his orgasm. They both fall back into the water exhausted, but deeply satisfied and more in love than ever.

"So, who do you think won this round?" Luca asks after they relaxed silently for a moment.

"It was pretty even. I did take you totally by surprise at first, but you put up an impressive fight and gave it right back to me." Kataryna admits.

"For a moment I lost all my senses," Luca says. "I felt like a heat-seeking missile going straight for its target. I didn't even recognize myself. You bring out sensations in me I have not experienced before. And that outfit almost knocked me on the floor when I turned around and saw you standing there."

"You definitely are stimulating the creative side of my brain, making me come up with things I have never done before. Not to talk about the ultimate orgasmic feelings I experience with you," Kataryna whispers.

"One thing is for sure. With you I will always have to be prepared for the unexpected. It is so exhilarating and makes me feel alive."

"Yes, we are a match made in heaven," Kataryna murmurs, "or as they say in financial terms-- a merger of equals."

"Well said, Principessa. That's exactly how I see it, too."

When they get out of the tub Luca takes a towel and gently dries off Kataryna. He touches her seductively briefly. She looks at him. "Really?"

"I couldn't resist," he says smiling, shrugging his shoulders. "You just bring it out in me."

They fall into bed happily. Luca picks up the phone to call Mariya.

"Mariya, we are going to eat around 8:30 instead of 7:30."

Kataryna looks at him. "OK, 8:30 sounds good. Gives us some time to recover and cool down."

"I don't know if I can ever cool down with you next to me," Luca says, "but let's give it a try."

"It will be a challenge for both us," Kataryna says, kissing his shoulder.

"Speaking about challenges. I have another one for you," he says in a more serious tone.

"What would that be?" Kataryna looks up at him, touching his face softly.

"I would like you to come up with a solution how we can be together more like this without having to travel long distance all the time."

"What would you say if I told you that I can meet that challenge?" she asks him flirtatiously.

Luca looks at her surprised. "Do tell. I can't wait to hear what you've come up with. This sounds promising."

"Gee," Kataryna says chuckling, "I am doing all the hard work today."

Luca pinches her playfully. "Please don't keep me in suspense any longer. Tell me."

She takes a deep breath and starts talking.

"When I told my partner Stephen about our relationship, he was very happy for us; but what I didn't know was that he had one more reason to be happy about that. You know that he is really excited about this acquisition deal and he told me then that he had been wondering if there might be more deals like this over here in Europe. So he had been thinking for some time to ask me if I would entertain the idea of moving to Europe for a while, but he didn't dare to ask me because he thought that might be too much of a sacrifice. When I told him about our relationship, he said he then had the heart to bring up the idea because he figured that we would want to be closer together. So he asked me and I told him I would consider it. He was ecstatic and suggested that we rent a small office space for me and an assistant in Milan if I wanted to move here for a while."

Kataryna smiles at Luca, waiting for his reaction. He pulls her tighter to him.

"So you have been holding this back for how long now? I am sitting here for weeks, racking my brain about how we can be closer together and you didn't tell me about this immediately," he says, tickling her. "I am beyond happy to hear this. Not in my wildest dreams did I think you would come up with something so perfect." He kisses her all over smiling happily at her.

"First of all my dear, I had to think about it a little bit and also check on what this would do to my personal tax situation, and then I wanted to wait for the right time to tell you. I think your birthday week is a damn good time to let you in on this little secret," she says giggling, tickling him back.

Luca picks up the phone and starts talking to someone excitedly in Italian. Kataryna wonders whom he is talking to and about what. *This is odd*, she thinks, *that he decides to make a phone call right after this revelation.*

When he hangs up the phone he turns to her.

"Now I have a surprise for you, Principessa. I just talked to my father. He wants me to give you his love, by the way. We have a vacant corner office in our building, which we just put on the market to rent out. I asked my father to take it off the market immediately because we will let you have that space."

"Oh my God Luca," Kataryna shouts out, "are you serious? Stephen and I haven't even discussed how much rent we are willing to pay."

"You can pay whatever you want to, my darling, I don't care and neither does my father; he just told me. It was just empty space we didn't need, but now we do need it. I am so happy that you are coming over here. I want to make it as easy as possible for you. I am in awe again how you met our challenge. Can this week get any better?" he asks.

"Well, it may. I understand that we will be submitting our letter of intent to acquire NatMedica in the next few days. Actually, our lawyers are working on it already."

"Wow, Principessa, this is amazing news. Please let me call my father real quick and tell him. Can you imagine this? Your firm will own NatMedica and take office space in our building, and you will live here with me in this villa. I must have done something right that the universe presents me with all these amazing gifts."

"Yeah, I thought so, too when Stephen suggested I move over here. This way I can also be closer to NatMedica."

Luca nods in agreement. "Amazing how all pieces are coming together."

He picks up the phone again. He first calls Mariya to tell her to get one of the best bottles of red wine from the wine cellar and then his father to let him know that Kataryna's firm is ready to submit a letter of intent. When he hangs up the phone he leans back into the pillows holding her closely to him.

"Well, you definitely won this round, Principessa. I really have to come up with something big now to make us even."

"I think we are both profiting from this outcome, so don't go overboard thinking you have to come up with something big. It is my

184 | Karynne Summars

pleasure to be able to come up with a solution. Don't forget I want this as much as you do."

"You are so sweet," he murmurs, kissing her. "Let's have dinner now and celebrate with an exceptional bottle of wine. I can't wait to see everyone's face when I tell them you are moving over here and take our office space."

"Just one question," Kataryna says, "how far is this office away from yours?"

"It is a corner office on the other side down the hallway. It has a private entrance area before you come to the actual office. I will show it to you tomorrow."

"OK, but can we be trusted to work that closely together?' she asks laughing.

"I see what you are getting at," he responds laughing. "As long as you don't show up in that black satin outfit you just had on we should be okay."

"Are you sure you won't be tempted to come to my office and have me for lunch?" Kataryna asks seductively.

"No, I'll respect your office, but I may call you and ask you to go home with me for lunch."

"Just lunch?"

"You know, our special kind of lunch. I have you and you have me."

"Yeah, and now I think it's time for dinner, otherwise we may not get out of this bed anymore tonight."

"You are absolutely right, Principessa. Let's have a nice long dinner followed by dessert."

They get dressed and head towards the kitchen where Mariya and Isabella are waiting to serve the menu they have prepared. Mariya shows Luca the special bottle of wine she got from the wine cellar.

"Excellent," he praises her. "We have several special occasions to drink to but the absolute best one is that Signora Kataryna will move in here in the near future."

Luca turns to Kataryna. "Do we have a time frame yet, when you will move over?"

"I haven't made any final plans for that yet. We can discuss it over the next days and see what works for me. I have a couple of loose ends to finish in New York."

Mariya and Isabella start cheering. "How wonderful Signor Romano. We can't wait to have you over here," they smile at Kataryna. "It is about time that a woman comes into this villa."

"Why don't you get two more glasses so you can have a glass of the excellent wine with us to celebrate this happy event," Luca addresses his two employees.

"Salute," he toasts, raising his glass.

"Salute and all the best," Mariya and Isabella say as they clink glasses with Luca and Kataryna.

Mariya's eyes tear up. She wipes them quickly.

"Hey, this is a happy occasion, Mariya, why are you crying?" Luca asks her putting his arm around her shoulders.

"I love you like a son and I am so happy for you," she responds, letting a tear roll down her face. "I know how much you missed Signora Kataryna over the last few weeks because you talked about her all the time and I prayed that she would come over here to be with you."

Kataryna is touched by Mariya's feelings and almost tears up, too.

"So, then we have you to thank for this coming together so soon," she says quickly, trying to put a little humor into the situation. "Well thank you for your prayers. They worked as you can see."

She walks over to Mariya and hugs her. "Now I would like to see a happy face."

"Oh, by the way, Isabella, I also have a little gift for you." She hands Isabella the box she brought with her.

"Thank you Signora," Isabella comes over to hug Kataryna. "You are so kind."

"You are welcome, Isabella. I like to make people happy," Kataryna says.

"And you are very good at that," Luca chimes in, putting his arms around her.

THIRTEEN

When Kataryna wakes up the next morning Luca has already gotten up. She gets ready and leaves the bedroom in search of him. Heading towards the kitchen and breakfast area she meets Mariya.

"Buongiorno Mariya," Kataryna greets her. "Have you seen Signor Romano?"

"Si Signora, he is in his office downstairs."

"How do I get there?"

Mariya shows her a set of steps leading to an area downstairs. Kataryna goes downstairs. She sees Luca sitting in his spectacular office with a view to Lake Como engaged in a phone conversation. His face lights up when she enters. He embraces her and ends his call.

"Buongiorno, Principessa, did you sleep well? I had to get up to make some phone calls because I am not going to the office today."

"Buongiorno, darling. What an amazing home office you have here."

"You can work out of here, too, any time. Sometimes it is better to work from home."

"I don't know if I would get any work done with this amazing view. This lake and the vegetation around it are like paradise."

Luca smiles at her happily. "I am so glad that you like it here. I want you to feel comfortable and not get homesick for New York once you are over here."

"No worries, with this view and you here, I won't get homesick. I love to be near water and it was always my intention one day to move to a place near water. Little did I know that it would be that soon and in addition come with a man like you. That makes it even more special."

Kataryna walks over to the large terrace door and takes in the beautiful scenery.

"How did I get that lucky?" she asks quietly.

Luca comes up behind her, putting his arms around her. "I ask myself that question every day since I met you. How about some breakfast? We have to leave around 11:30 a.m., to drive to Milano. I will show you your new office and then we have lunch with Carlotta and Enrico. He is so excited already to meet you. He has been practicing his English since Carlotta told him that we will have lunch together."

"Can't wait to meet him. Carlotta showed me a photo of him. He is very good-looking. Looks like he may be a heartbreaker one day."

"Please don't tell him that," Luca says, "he knows he is good-looking and the girls at school are after him already. Carlotta wants to make sure that he doesn't base his life on his good looks alone."

"That's smart of Carlotta. How is he doing in school?"

"He has good grades, but he also likes to play around and hang out with his buddies. Lately he has been talking about wanting to go to New York soon. I am sure he will bring that up today."

"Well, we better tell Carlotta later, that I am coming over here for a while. But occasionally I will have to go to New York for a week or so to look after my apartment and to meet with Stephen and the rest of the team, especially if we find another interesting European acquisition target. I believe Carlotta mentioned she wants to come over in March for Enrico's birthday. We can plan to be over there then."

After breakfast Luca and Kataryna take off to Milan. Kataryna looks out the window as they drive by Villa D'Este.

"This is where it all began," she murmurs, pointing to the majestic building.

Luca nods recalling that night. "I was so happy that you accepted my invitation to stay in my villa. I was pretty sure you would choose to stay at the hotel."

"I must have been in an adventurous mood that evening," Kataryna explains her decision. "But I felt pretty safe with you."

"And I was a complete gentleman," he says. "Although it was very difficult not to show my feelings for you. I was so excited and couldn't sleep for quite a while that night as I confessed already."

"Your patience paid off. I don't know how I would have reacted if you had started anything the first night, although I was pretty enchanted by you, too. But it was worth the wait, I think."

"No doubt about that. I would have kicked myself if I had scared you off by approaching you too soon. However, the next evening in Bellagio I got concerned when Roberto got so personal and flirtatious with you. I thought maybe I should have done something to let you know how I felt about you. It was a scary moment."

"That's why you got me out of there so fast," Kataryna laughs.

"Exactly. Even though we already had a couple of moments on the boat before we arrived in Bellagio, which were kind of telling me that we had a pretty strong connection."

"By the way, did Carlotta do anything yet about her feelings for Roberto?"

"No. She was disappointed that Roberto took off with his parents after my birthday party. I told her that wasn't the right night anyway and to be patient."

"Well, he took her back to Milano. Maybe on the way she got a little closer to what she wants to accomplish."

"Not with Verena in the car," Luca replies. "I thought Roberto was pretty quiet at my birthday party. He looked kind of tense at times. I heard him say he didn't sleep much the night before, but still he was so out of character. I am just relieved that he seems to have cooled off pursuing you. I guess the talk I had with him convinced him that he has to back off."

Kataryna is pretty uncomfortable with that statement and stays silent. She wants to change the subject immediately, but Luca senses something and probes further.

"Or do you think he hasn't given up on that idea yet?"

"No one really knows what goes on in other people's minds. However, even if he is still entertaining the idea, the more he sees us together the more it will become apparent to him that it wouldn't make any sense to pursue this."

"That's true," Luca admits.

"Let's see how things develop, especially after your firm has completed the acquisition and Stephen and you become his bosses."

"And hopefully something will develop soon between Carlotta and him," Kataryna suggests.

"We have arrived at your new Milano office, Principessa," Luca says excitedly as he parks the car in the garage. "Let's see how you like it."

When they get off the elevator at the top floor, Riccardo Romano happens to walk in.

"Ah, you are here already," Luca's father says, hugging Kataryna. "I am glad we didn't rent the office space out yet. This is ideal. Luca on one side of the building, you on the other and I am in the middle. Please come by my office before you leave for lunch."

Luca and Kataryna walk towards the space. As Luca had indicated it has a private entrance with a small foyer, which leads to the actual office. Luca opens the door to the space and they walk in.

"Wow," Kataryna marvels, "this is a beautiful office. I love the big windows, the view and the elegant furniture. It even has a couch. I think this will do nicely. Let me take a couple of photos so I can email them to Stephen."

She takes several photos with her iPhone and then sits behind the desk to see how it feels. When they leave she also takes a photo of the entrance area.

"I suppose I can put my firm's name on the door here?" she asks Luca.

"Yes, of course, we can have it done for you."

He kisses her on the cheek. "I am glad you like it. You looked very good behind that desk as if it was made for you. And the couch may come in handy, too."

"Don't get any ideas. You promised to respect my office," she says, grinning.

"Principessa, you have a naughty mind. I was talking about for you to take a break on the couch when you have worked very hard," Luca teases her.

"Yeah, right," she responds as they are heading towards Riccardo Romano's office.

Carlotta stands next to her father when they come in. She greets Kataryna with a hug.

"So great to see you. What have you been up to since yesterday? Did Luca show you some of our beautiful sights on the way back to his villa?"

Kataryna and Luca start laughing. "Yes, we explored some of the sights."

"What's so funny?" Carlotta asks, also laughing.

"Let's go have lunch," Luca says quickly. "Where is Enrico?"

"He is with Patrizia. Let's go and get him."

Kataryna kisses Riccardo good-bye as the three head out of his office.

"Thank you again for everything."

"It was my pleasure," Riccardo says. "I am so excited that you are taking the office here. By the way, our lawyers spoke today regarding the letter of intent and a possible closing date for the acquisition and they exchanged relevant information already."

"Wonderful," Kataryna responds, "I am glad that we are off to a good start."

As they are heading to Patrizia's office, Enrico comes down the hallway towards them.

"Oh my God, he is even more attractive in person than in the photo you showed me," Kataryna says to Carlotta and Luca.

Enrico walks right up to Kataryna and shakes her hand. "Hello Miss Kataryna," he starts, "it is a pleasure to meet you."

"Hello Enrico, I am also pleased to meet you," Kataryna hugs him.

Enrico looks at Luca. "Ciao Uncle Luca," he says casually, immediately turning back to Kataryna.

"My mother told me you live in New York. I really want to go there. When can I visit you?"

"Well, let's talk about it over lunch," Kataryna says. "Your English is very good."

Enrico smiles at her proudly. "Thank you. I spent last summer with my father in London when he had to work out of his company's office there for a while."

When they arrive at the restaurant, Enrico takes a seat next to Kataryna. They talk about Enrico's plans after he finishes school.

"I think I want to study in the United States," Enrico states, "but that's not until about two years from now. I would like to come to New York to visit before, of course.

"OK," Luca comes into the conversation, "I think it is time that we fill Carlotta and Enrico in what's going to happen soon."

Carlotta looks at them puzzled. "That sounds mysterious. What is going to happen soon?"

Luca flashes a smile. "Kataryna is going to move to Italy and run her business from here. She will be taking the vacant office we have in our building. We just looked at it and it seems to be a perfect fit for her. Needless to say, I am ecstatic."

"Wow Luca," Carlotta says, "that is a great idea."

"Actually, it was Kataryna's partner's idea. He wants to explore more European acquisition deals. Stephen deserves some kind of medal for that idea," he jokes.

"When are you moving over?" Carlotta looks at Kataryna.

"I haven't made a final decision. There are a few things I have to finish first in New York. I am thinking maybe at the end of January. I will be over here at that time anyway because we are going to attend Il Ballo del Doge in Venice in the beginning of February. So I hope it works out that way."

Enrico looks at them disappointed. "What about our trip to New York?"

"I still have to spend some time in New York occasionally," Kataryna answers. "So we can plan your trip after we return from Venice."

"I already told Enrico that I will take him to New York for his 17th birthday on March 25," Carlotta explains.

"Perfect, we can plan it around this time and have your birthday party in New York. My nieces Natasha and Sabrina will turn 16 in March. So we can celebrate all birthdays at one time." Kataryna suggests.

"Are they twins?" Enrico asks.

"Yes, they are identical twins. You can hardly tell them apart."

"Cool," Enrico says, "do you have a photo of them?"

Kataryna gets out her iPhone and searches her stored photos.

"Here you go," she hands Enrico the phone with the photo of the twins on display.

"They look hot," Enrico shouts out. "I can't wait to meet them."

"You might as well start communicating with them via email and Face Time or Skype," Kataryna recommends. "This way you already get to know each other a bit."

"That is a great idea," Carlotta says.

"I will introduce you to them via video call and then you can take over from there." Kataryna suggests.

"Sure, let's do that," Enrico says all excited. "My friends will be so jealous because they all want to go to New York."

"You want to take one of your friends along?" Carlotta asks her son. "It may be better if you are four instead of three."

"Maybe my cousin Stefano wants to come along," he suggests.

After they finish their lunch, Kataryna and Luca walk around in Milano for a while looking at some historic sites and doing some shopping. Kataryna gets a designer handbag for her sister and a couple of stylish outfits for her sister's twins for Christmas.

Carlotta can't wait to tell Roberto the news about her planned trip to New York. Once back in the office she picks up the phone to call him. His assistant answers the call and puts it through after Carlotta identified herself.

"Ciao Carlotta," Roberto greets her. "How are you?"

"Take me out to dinner and you can see for yourself," she replies flirtatiously.

"I don't know yet when I can do that," he says, "we are working on the closing of the NatMedica divestiture and I have to stay late over the next few days."

"Wrong answer," she says trying to appear witty, but deep down she is really disappointed about his nonchalant response.

"I really want to see you, Roberto," she insists a little more forceful.

"I'll come up with something," he tries to soothe her.

"I don't care if it is later in the evening. We can have a late dinner at my place."

"OK, maybe tomorrow night. I'll call you in the morning to confirm."

"Great. Oh, by the way, Enrico and I just had lunch with Luca and Kataryna. We were planning our trip to New York. Looks like we may do it for Enrico's birthday in March. Enrico can't wait to get over there."

"I guess you had a productive lunch," Roberto tells her.

"Yes, we did. The rest I'll tell you tomorrow night."

Carlotta is happy that she seemed to succeed to get Roberto back to her place. *Although,* she thinks, *he could be a little more excited about getting together.* When the divestiture is closed, she figures, he will be back to his old self, very outgoing and up for fun at a moment's notice.

Roberto hangs up the phone with a tightening of his chest coming on. He is not sure if he wants to have dinner at Carlotta's place. He thinks about Kataryna, knowing she is with Luca until tomorrow. Sadness comes over him imagining Luca and Kataryna together happy. He feels hopeless and helpless. Time to take another pill to avert a full anxiety attack, he decides.

Luca and Kataryna finish their sightseeing and shopping in Milan, and then drive back to his villa to spend their last evening together before she has to go back to New York on Tuesday. They have another relaxing dinner at the villa and then retire to the bedroom, making love and forgetting the world around them.

The next day Luca takes Kataryna to the airport where the family's corporate jet is waiting to take her back to New York. Luca boards the plane with her while the pilot is doing his usual pre-flight checks.

"If I didn't know that I will be with you again in a few weeks, I would be quite upset now," he murmurs.

"Me, too," Kataryna confesses, "but we had a wonderful time since Saturday and the memories of these unforgettable moments will be with me for the next week or so, and then it won't be long until we are together again."

They sit tightly embraced when the pilot enters the cabin and announces that he has completed his checks and is ready to take-off.

"Thank you," Luca tells him. "Just give us five minutes and I will be off the plane."

The pilot returns to the cockpit advising the co-pilot to let Air Traffic Control know that they want to take off in about 10 minutes.

Luca and Kataryna prepare to say good-bye. She walks with him to the exit where they embrace and share a final passionate kiss. Luca opens the cockpit door and tells the pilot something in Italian. The pilot nods and gives him a thumbs-up sign.

"What did you tell him?" Kataryna asks.
"I told him to make sure that you arrive safely in New York."

After Luca leaves the jet, Kataryna relaxes into the comfortable seat. *Great way to travel*, she thinks, sipping on the Champagne the flight attendant has brought her, as the jet starts taxiing towards the runway.

Kataryna arrives back at her New York apartment, takes a quick shower and falls into bed around 11:30 p.m. Her phone rings. She sees Luca's photo and his phone number coming up. Smiling happily she picks up the call.

"Hello my darling," she says, "you are up early."
"I didn't sleep well without you. As instructed, the pilot called me as soon as he had landed in New York. So I am up early."
"I am safely at home in my bed," she reports, "and I miss you."
"I miss you more," he replies. "Let's talk later on again. I'll let you get some sleep now."

"I will call you later. Stephen emailed me a few legal documents to read in preparation for the offering letter. I will work on these from home after I have gotten some sleep."

"OK, bella. Sleep well and dream of me."

Kataryna falls asleep after she heard Luca's soothing voice. She wakes up around 6 a.m., slightly jet lagged, but happy and looking forward to her call with Luca later on. After her usual morning ritual getting ready she sits down to have breakfast. She opens the documents Stephen and their lawyers had sent her for review. The first document is a legal opinion of their Italian and New York counsel regarding the target's statutes, which are attached. Some of the attachments are from the time the company was acquired by the Romano family holding company and the then existing rulings were adopted it appears. Kataryna looks at the legal opinions. The usual legal language. Blah, blah, blah. She fast-forwards to the conclusions. One of the conclusions is marked in bold and it catches her eye immediately. She reads it again word by word to make sure she understands it correctly. *No,* she thinks, *that can't be right* almost choking on the piece of bread she had in her mouth. Luca would have known that there is such a ruling, which predates the acquisition by the Romano family holding company. She dials Luca's cell phone number. His voice mail comes on. "Luca, it is 8 a.m., New York time. Please call me as soon as you get this message," she leaves on his voice mail and then continues to scroll through the documentation package.

A few minutes later her phone rings. She answers it on the first ring expecting to hear Luca's voice.

"Ciao Kataryna, how are you?" she hears Roberto saying.

Kataryna is startled by Roberto's voice and all kind of things run through her mind in a split second. Hoping he is not calling because of what she just discovered in the legal opinion, she greets him trying to sound relaxed.

"Hello Roberto. Other than a little jet lagged I am fine. How are you?"

"I am not well. I wanted to discuss something with you. I hope this is a good time to talk to you because I need your input on my personal situation."

Kataryna is relieved to hear that his call is not company-specific, although the personal situation is not really a good subject either, but at this moment she prefers to talk about his predicament.

"Go ahead," she responds. "I can talk for a few minutes. However, I am expecting a call from Luca, so when he calls I have to hang up."

"Let me ask you this first," Roberto starts. "Did Luca mention anything to you about his sister Carlotta being romantically interested in me?"

Kataryna is stunned by that question. *What a morning,* she thinks. She is still preoccupied by the legal opinion and now this question.

"Vaguely," she admits. "How did you hear about that?"

"Carlotta told me that she confided in Luca that I am her love interest."

"When did that happen?" she asks calmly even though she is floored.

"What I am telling you now is confidential and no one knows. You have to promise me that you won't say anything to Luca because I don't want to put Carlotta in a bad spot."

Kataryna's heart starts beating faster. *Oh, God,* she thinks, *what is coming next and can I make this promise?*

"I will use my best discretion," comes out of her mouth reluctantly.

"OK, I am going to trust you because I want you to know what happened and how. First of all, I need you to understand that my feelings for you have not changed and I don't expect that they ever will. The night before Luca's birthday Carlotta and I went out for dinner. In my mind it was two long-time family friends having a casual fun night out. I had to get out of the house because I was consumed by my feelings for you and tried to distract myself so I could have a fairly normal life, or so I thought. We had a couple of drinks at the bar first and then had dinner. We were drinking quite a bit and I tried to be good company. She started flirting with me, but I didn't take it seriously. I guess I made one or the other flirtatious comment, too, not knowing how she felt about me deep down inside. But nothing happened in the restaurant, no hugging or kissing or anything romantic, just a little banter here and there. Long story short, after we finished with dinner and left the restaurant, I asked her if she wanted to have a nightcap somewhere because I didn't want to go home yet. I guess I wanted to pacify myself because of these deep feelings I have for you and imagining you and Luca together drove me to the edge of insanity. Carlotta then invited me up to her apartment. She didn't want to go to another bar because she was getting quite tipsy already, she said. When we got to her place I continued drinking wine. She sat down on the couch in a rather seductive pose. When I looked at her sitting like this, I thought if it was you sitting there like this I would have been all over you. I closed my eyes to get away from that view and these thoughts. I guess my eyes were also getting a little heavy from all the alcohol I had that evening. When I opened my eyes again she was basically on top of me pushing her cleavage right into my face. I had no chance to escape it. She started touching me sexually, took off her underwear and seduced me. I gave in but all the time I imagined her hands and lips on me were yours. It was over pretty fast. I actually called out your name when I reached my peak but I don't think she even realized that. She either was too much into the sex or too drunk to realize what happened."

Kataryna is dazed by Roberto's account of events. "Oh my God, Roberto, I am speechless," she murmurs.

After a few moments she recovers and finds her balance again.

"How do you imagine your situation with Carlotta to play out?" she manages to ask. "She apparently has deep feelings for you."

"I think you already know that I have deep feelings for you, and not for Carlotta or have you forgotten that I proposed marriage to you?"

Kataryna is getting more uncomfortable with this conversation. Why doesn't he understand that she is in love with Luca and why does he seem to think that there is a chance for him and her to end up together?

"I am heavily medicated right now," he goes on. "As a matter of fact, I have to take this anti-anxiety medication every day. Yesterday Carlotta pressured me to see her again. She wants me to come to her place for dinner tonight."

"So since that night before Luca's birthday you haven't gotten together with her again?"

"No, she wanted to go out with me after Luca's birthday party but I was in no shape to do that. When I saw you walking in there as a surprise for Luca, I lost it and my emotions were all over the place. I still don't know how I made it through the evening seeing you two together, with him all over you. When I had the opportunity I took one of my pills to relieve the tension, anxiety and bewilderment I was feeling that night. Carlotta was not on my mind at all. I know she was disappointed when I left with my parents, but that didn't faze me. I just wanted to get far away from there, preferably with you of course."

"That doesn't sound good, Roberto," Kataryna asserts. "You have to forget about me. I think it is time for you to get professional help."

"Please don't lecture me Kataryna. This is difficult enough for me. Anyway, what is your advice regarding Carlotta? How do I get out of this dinner tonight?" Roberto asks.

"Why do you want to get out of this dinner? I think you and Carlotta could be good together."

"Because my heart is not in it. I am not interested anymore in dating around. I don't want her to get hurt or have to go through what I am going through right now. I am looking for a serious committed relationship. I found the ideal woman when I met you."

Kataryna takes a deep breath. "First of all, you should know by now that I am not available. I can't be that woman for you. It is not healthy to pursue this, Roberto. And secondly, don't you think it is too late to think about not wanting to hurt Carlotta?"

"I guess we are not going to solve this problem today. Incidentally Carlotta asked me if Verena and I would join her and Enrico on their trip to New York next year. So now you know what is going on in my life and what I have to deal with."

Kataryna's call waiting line rings. Luca is returning her call.

"I've got to go, Roberto, I have another call coming in. I wish you well and hope you will make the right choices going forward."

Kataryna hangs up with Roberto and takes Luca's call.

"Ciao Principessa. I was in a business meeting when you called. You got me worried when I listened to your voice mail. You sounded a little stressed. Are you alright?"

"I am alright," Kataryna is struggling to hold it together after her phone conversation with Roberto. "But you better sit down for this one," she warns Luca.

"You are scaring me, Principessa. What is going on?"

"I was reviewing the documents Stephen sent me in preparation for the offering letter. When I reviewed the legal opinions I couldn't believe what I read. I went over it three times to make sure I didn't misunderstand it. The opinion of our Italian legal counsel had all kinds of company organization documents attached going way back, which were adopted by your holding company when you acquired NatMedica. One of them states that if the company is offered for sale, the CEO of the company in place at that time has the right to acquire an equity share of up to 10 percent of the company, if he has been in the CEO position for at least five years and is in good standing. I was flabbergasted when I read this."

"There must be a mistake," Luca expresses, astonished. "I can't believe that our lawyers wouldn't have mentioned that before if that was really true. I will talk to our attorneys and have them review the company documents."

"If this turns out to be the case we would have a huge issue on our hands," Kataryna states. "Our approval for this deal is based on the fact that my firm would be the sole shareholder at the time of the acquisition. In addition, Roberto would be in a more powerful position if he would make use of his rights and come up with the funds, although we would own the majority shares."

"I will get back to you as soon as possible," Luca promises, "try not to worry too much meanwhile."

Kataryna hangs up the phone and holds her head. What a nightmare this is shaping up to be. She can't decide which one is worse, Roberto's account of events in his personal life or the legal opinions possibly giving him the right to acquire up to 10 percent of NatMedica. Obviously Stephen and the acquisition team haven't reviewed the documents yet; otherwise, she would have received a call from them already. She puts in a call to Stephen to alert him of the potential issue. He answers his phone with his usual sense of humor.

"Aha, Kataryna the Great is back from her love nest in Italy. Are you having withdrawal symptoms yet?"

"Very funny," she counters. "I guess you haven't looked at the documents yet you emailed me? You better sit down and listen to what I discovered in the legal opinion."

"No, I didn't get a chance to look at the docs yet," he responds. "What's wrong?"

"Look at page three of the Italian counsel legal opinion regarding the statutes. I just spoke to Luca and he is checking into this."

Stephen reads the conclusions of the legal opinion and whistles. "That's not good. What did Luca have to say about that?"

"He was very surprised and doesn't believe that this is really the case. He is checking into it but it may take a few days until we know for sure."

"Damn, and I thought we could get the offering letter out next week and move forward with a closing date."

"That's not gonna happen. If it is true we have to revisit our intentions to acquire this company unless Roberto agrees to forego his rights. If not, we would have to bring the new facts up to our acquisition committee before we can proceed."

"Okay, let's stay calm. It wouldn't be the end of the world. We would still be majority shareholders. As far as the approval goes, we have final say."

"Not so fast," Kataryna interrupts him. "Have you forgotten about the personal matter involving Roberto I told you about?"

"I thought that was resolved?" Stephen enquires.

"Not quite," Kataryna answers. "As a matter of fact things are getting more complicated in that area, but I don't want to go into more details right now. Let me think things through today and see what tomorrow brings."

"OK. See you tomorrow," Stephen replies.

At 7 p.m., Roberto half-heartedly leaves his apartment to have dinner with Carlotta at her place. He is anxious and sad at the same time. Sad because of his conversation with Kataryna earlier in the day who seemed to encourage him to have a relationship with Carlotta, and anxious because he doesn't know how he will react if Carlotta starts touching him in a sexual way.

"Ciao Carlotta," he greets her as he enters her apartment.

He hands her a bottle of red wine.

"I had a tough day at the office," he explains, "so I may not be the best company tonight."

Carlotta kisses him. "Come in and relax, I will make you feel better in no time. I am really getting concerned about you. This is not like you at all. A few weeks ago you were Mr. Entertainment and now you are dragging whenever I see you. I hope I don't have that kind of effect on you."

She takes his coat and jacket to hang them up and then walks up to him and hugs him.

"What is the matter with you and how can I help?" she asks, almost sad.

Roberto is touched by her concern and tries to lighten up to make her comfortable.

"I'll be okay as soon as I have a glass of wine," he says quickly, forcing a smile.

Carlotta hands him a glass and makes a toast.

"Here is to a hopefully beautiful evening. I am very happy that you could make it."

Roberto smiles at her and kisses her hand.

"Thank you for saying that. Where is Enrico?"

"He is at his father's house until tomorrow," she replies. "Truth be told I wanted to be alone with you until we figure out a way to make this public."

"Have you had any further conversations with Luca about me?" he asks.

"As promised, I didn't say anything to anybody about our night together but it was tough. Luca realized, of course, that I was disappointed when you didn't want to get together with me after his birthday party. So he tried to comfort me and said he didn't think that that was the right night for us to get closer and that I should be patient. I felt kind of bad then and wished I could have told him that we had already spent the night together."

"Thank you for keeping your promise. This is a delicate matter for me." Roberto explains.

"Why is it so delicate? We are not the first long-time friends to all of a sudden fall in love," she insists. "We'll just have to take the plunge and let everyone know. What are you so afraid of? Maybe our families will be happy for us."

"Slow down Carlotta," Roberto starts in a more serious tone. "I think first we should see if we are compatible or if this was a spur of the moment thing."

"For me it was not a spur of a moment thing. I am in love with you, Roberto," Carlotta says looking deep into his eyes, fighting tears. "But if you don't feel strongly about us, I guess I will have to live with that, but it won't be easy."

Roberto is terrified realizing that her feelings for him might be as strong as his for Kataryna.

"Let's drink to a nice evening," he says, raising his glass of wine.

He takes a big gulp. "How about some food now? I am starved. Something smells really good. Let's see what you have to eat for us."

He puts his arm around her shoulders as they walk to the kitchen. Carlotta is visibly relieved that he seems to be more approachable. Roberto gulps down more wine. He seems to get mellower with every glass. At one point he wonders what the combination of anti-anxiety medication and alcohol may do to him, but after the day he had he really doesn't care if he lives or dies. Carlotta gets another bottle of wine as they leave the dining table and sit down by the fireplace in the lounge area.

"Would you like some more wine?" she asks him, seating herself next to him, "or would you prefer an after-dinner drink?"

"What about you, what would you like to have?" Roberto asks her.

She gives him a big smile and moves closer to him. "Honestly, I'd rather have you," she whispers, kissing him. "But this time I would like you to undress me."

"Interesting offer," he says, toying with her. "How about an after-dinner drink first?"

Carlotta gets up to get an after-dinner drink for Roberto and puts on some soft music.

"Let's sit on the floor by the fireplace," she suggests, taking his hand and pulling him from the couch. He follows her swallowing the entire drink and pours himself another one. They sit embraced watching the fire, Roberto sipping on his third after-dinner drink.

Carlotta is wearing a sexy red dress with a zipper in the front. She takes the glass from him and puts his hand on the zipper of her dress.

"All you have to do is pull down this zipper and the whole dress opens up in the front," she guides him. "Look how easy I made it for you to undress me."

"Really?" he responds as the room around him starts spinning.

He pulls the zipper down. Carlotta sits in front of him naked. She starts kissing him, moving down his neck as she takes off his shirt and pants. He lets her undress him. He has no strength to resist anyhow. She kisses his stomach as she takes off his underwear to proceed to his groin and puts his hand between her legs.

"I want you so badly," she murmurs in his ear, getting more aroused.

She moves her body on top of him so he can enter her but Roberto doesn't move with her. She looks at him to entice him to move with her when she realizes that he has passed out. *Oh no,* she thinks, *this is not happening.* The alcohol must have knocked him out. She nudges him in an effort to wake him back up, but he still doesn't move. Carlotta is getting desperate but also worried that something more serious is happening here. She gets some ice water and tries talking to him while patting his cheeks. His face feels cool and clammy.

"Roberto, please wake up. You are scaring me," she pleads with him dabbing his face with a napkin and rubbing an ice cube over his mouth.

Roberto is trying to open his eyes but they won't obey him. He has a smile on his face because he is with Kataryna and they are in the process of making love. He grabs Carlotta and kisses her passionately as they continue to make love.

"I want you, too," he says holding her tightly and pushing into her. "From the first moment I saw you. Don't ever leave me."

Carlotta is elated hearing him say these words, although she doesn't quite understand what he means by "from the first moment I saw you." What moment is he referring to? But who cares, she couldn't be happier now that he admitted he wants her as much as she wants him.

After they climax, Roberto continues to caress and kiss her. Carlotta enjoys every moment of their intimacy.

He finally manages to open his eyes, squinting trying to make out where he and Kataryna are. The surroundings are not familiar to him and everything moves in slow motion. He looks at Kataryna in his arms with her head on his shoulder. He takes another look wiping his eyes. *Why does she have dark hair,* he thinks? God, everything is so blurry. Where are they and how did they get here? He touches her face and lifts it up to look into her beautiful blue eyes. His heart almost stops as he looks at Carlotta smiling at him. *What happened? Where is Kataryna and how did Carlotta get into the picture,* he asks himself? Before he can think about it any further he falls back into unconsciousness.

When Roberto wakes up Carlotta is standing over him smiling, handing him a cup of coffee.

"Here you go, sleepy head," she says, "you were out like a light last night. No more after-dinner drinks for you. I couldn't wake you to bring you into the bedroom, so you slept on the floor in front of the fireplace."

He can hardly move to take the cup. His arm is weak and his body feels like he has been hit by a ton of bricks. He has no recollection of how he got here. All he remembers is that he made love to Kataryna and he was totally at peace. But where is she? Carlotta sits down on the floor next to him.

"How are you feeling?" she asks, kissing him. "Would you like some breakfast?"

"Breakfast?" he asks, "what time is it?"

"It's a little after 9 a.m. I called my office to let them know that I won't be in."

"I have to get to the office," he says, trying to get up.

"I don't think you are in any condition to go anywhere," Carlotta advises him.

"Why don't you lie down in bed and I bring you something to eat."

"I don't know if I can get anything down."

On the second try he succeeds to stand up, but he is dizzy and shaky on his feet. He takes a sip of the coffee. Carlotta holds him up and helps him to the bedroom.

"Wow," she says, "I didn't realize that you had that much to drink."

"Is anybody else here?" he asks her.

Carlotta looks at him baffled. "No, who should be here? I am sure you recall that we had dinner here last night and after we made love you fell asleep instantly. Well, actually, you had passed out while we were engaging in foreplay. You woke up and as soon as we were done you were gone again. I figured you must have worked long hours this week and, together with the alcohol you had last night, it probably knocked you out cold."

"I feel like I was run over by a truck," he says, holding his head.

Carlotta sits down on the bed with him and hugs him. "I am so sorry you feel so bad. I hope you remember the nice evening we had." She kisses him softly on the mouth

"Can you bring me my phone please?" he asks. "I have to call my office."

Carlotta gets him the phone and then goes to the kitchen to make breakfast for them.

Roberto leans back into the pillows and closes his eyes. He begins to realize that making love to Kataryna last night was a dream, a figment of his imagination. He now knows that it was Carlotta instead and that the pills, in combination with the alcohol consumption, have played a trick on his mind. He promises himself to take it easy with the pills and alcohol or better yet not combine these two any more.

His assistant answers the phone on the second ring. He tells her that he won't be coming to the office today and then checks his emails on his phone. Nothing earth shattering, he decides, after scrolling down just glancing at each email. A lot of legal documents to review, but these will have to wait until he feels better again.

Carlotta brings a tray with breakfast to the bedroom and against all odds Roberto manages to get it down. He soon starts feeling a little better physically, but emotionally he knows he is a mess. He has to pull himself together though and put up a good front for Carlotta and the rest of the world.

"Now let's make some plans for the holidays," he hears Carlotta say. "What are we doing for New Year's Eve?"

A huge workload awaits Roberto when he comes to the office the next morning. He wasn't in any kind of shape or mood yesterday to look at all of his emails. His assistant brings him a cup of coffee and discusses a few phone calls with him, which came in yesterday when he was out. Once they are done with the briefing, Roberto focuses on his long list of emails. After glancing at several low-priority messages he starts reading the emails from the lawyers in connection with the divestiture of NatMedica. He opens the one, which says "Urgent" in the subject line and reviews the attachments, which are mostly legal opinions and related subjects. One of the attachments is an email from Kataryna's Italian counsel to NatMedica's counsel regarding certain rights for the purchase of equity shares by the existing CEO. He reads it again to make sure he understands it correctly. He can't believe what he is reading. His mind is still a little foggy from the events the night before yesterday. He calls the company lawyer to address the legal opinion and the fact that he would have the right to purchase up to 10 percent of NatMedica in case the present shareholders sell the company. The lawyer confirms that he does indeed have this right according to the statutes. Pleasantly surprised, Roberto hangs up the phone and smiles to himself. Good news for a change. These 10 percent will link him to Kataryna forever, if her firm acquires the remaining 90 percent.

FOURTEEN

On December 22, Luca boards the family's luxurious long-range corporate jet to fly to New York. He sits down on the spacious seating arrangements and reclines his seat. He closes his eyes imagining his arrival at Kataryna's apartment. He is so looking forward to being with her again and wonders what kind of erotic situations she may come up with. She always knows how to make it exciting. His thoughts are interrupted by the arrival of his sister Patrizia and her fiancé Francesco Barone who, as planned, are joining him for Christmas in New York.

"Ciao Luca," they greet him as they sit opposite him.

The company's flight attendant approaches them asking what they would like to drink.
"Signor Romano," she continues, "the captain tells me we are about ready for take-off. Would you please put your seat belts on? Please let me know what time you would like me to serve lunch."
"We will let you know when we are ready for lunch," Luca informs her.

Francesco puts his and Patrizia's seatbelts on and takes her hand.

Luca smiles at them. "You are such a cute couple. I can't wait for the big day when you are getting married."
"Neither can I," Francesco adds. Patrizia smiles at both of them.
"My two favorite men. I am so lucky to have both of you in my life."
"So, Luca," Patrizia starts a new conversation, "tell us a bit more about Kataryna moving to Milano. Obviously you are quite smitten with her."
"Smitten?" Luca repeats, "it's more than that. I am seriously in love with her. I can't wait to be with her again. The last couple of weeks have been total torture for me."
"And for her?" Francesco asks.

"I am not sure if this is as much of a torture for her as it is for me," Luca responds. "She says she misses me a lot and can't wait to see me, but I think she is handling it better than me. But that doesn't mean that she is not as involved in our relationship as I am. She just has the ability to stay more balanced about it, or so it seems. She is working a lot, too, which definitely takes her mind off it somewhat. As far as I am concerned, I am completely committed to this relationship and totally excited that she will move to Italy at the end of January."

"Bravo Luca, go for it," Patrizia cheers him on. "I can't wait for her to move to Italy. We didn't get much time to spend with her on your birthday. Francesco says he has a good feeling about her and he liked her immediately when you all met in Bellagio."

"Yes, I think she is a good match for Luca," Francesco adds. "In addition to being very attractive, as you have noticed, she is business savvy and has integrity. I can see how Luca fell for her immediately. You don't meet women like that every day."

Luca gives Francesco a dreamy smile.

"Look at him, cara," Francesco says to Patrizia, "he is in seventh heaven."

"I hope it all works out for you," Patrizia says to her brother touching his hand. "After what you have been through with your ex-wife Traviata, you deserve a good woman in your life."

"Yes, I do. Here is to Kataryna and her move to Italy," Luca says cheerfully, raising his glass of wine the flight attendant had served. "And you, Francesco, should prepare for Kataryna and Stephen to become the new shareholders of NatMedica."

After they have finished their exquisite lunch all three decide to take a nap. When they wake up it is about an hour and a half before landing in New York. Luca wakes up first and decides to take a refreshing shower and change into another outfit. Patrizia wakes up next and looks at her brother freshly showered, shaved and superbly dressed.

"You look great Luca," she whispers, trying not to wake Francesco. "Any woman would be lucky to have you in her life."

Luca hugs his sister. "Thank you for saying that. You just made my day."

"And you smell delicious, too," she adds giggling, breathing in his cologne. "Kataryna just won't have a chance when you walk in there."

The jet lands safely at Teterboro airport around 2 p.m. After the usual formalities they exit the airport and head towards New York City. Luca is getting excited and nervous at the same time. It won't be much longer before he gets to be with Kataryna. *Is she also counting the minutes*, he wonders? He calls her number to tell her they have arrived and are on their way into the city. Patrizia and Francesco have reservations at the luxurious Setai Hotel. Kataryna had invited them to stay at her apartment but Luca understandably wanted to be alone with her, which Patrizia and Francesco are totally okay with. They definitely did not want to disturb that love nest and actually wanted to have more privacy themselves on this trip.

"Hello darling," Kataryna answers her phone.

"Hi gatta selvatica," Luca greets her, "we just arrived and are on our way into the city."

"Great, I will expect you in about 50 minutes," she says. "Can't wait to see you."

"Neither can I."

Kataryna hangs up the phone. Her heart starts beating faster. *Wow, I've got to relax,* she thinks, *but I am sooo excited.* She has made preparations for dinner later on. For starters she will serve lobster salad. The main course will be wild salmon with a delicious homemade tartar sauce using Vegennaise instead of mayonnaise with fine herbs. As a side dish they will have rice pilaf and white asparagus sautéed in olive oil. She also made a cucumber salad just like her mother would always make with a fish dish. For dessert she bought a delicious chocolate tart from Café Sabarsky. They make the best European style cakes and tarts. The Champagne is chilling and will be served together with chocolate-covered strawberries as a welcome drink.

Kataryna looks over her wardrobe in her walk-in closet, contemplating what to wear. A sexy short purple knit dress with a low-scoop neckline catches her eye. *That will do,* she thinks. She quickly puts on matching underwear and a pair of pumps, no pantyhose, which would just be in the way, she giggles at that thought. She looks at herself in the mirror. Her long blond hair falls softly on her shoulders. *Voilà,* she says to herself, the princess is ready for her prince as she puts on her favorite Eau de Toilette.

After lighting the wood in the fireplace she stands by the window looking out over the Manhattan skyline and Central Park. She tries to imagine how she will react to Luca when he walks into her place. They haven't seen each other for a few weeks; well they saw each other via video calls, but that is not the same as having him right in front of her and being able to touch him. The mere thought of him gives her a tingly feeling as she recalls one of their seductive video calls. She quickly changes her train of thought in order not to get too excited before he arrives. She needs to keep busy with something to make that nervous feeling go away. A final makeup check seems like a good idea, so she heads to the master bathroom. Satisfied with the look she chose, she returns to the grand room.

Her iPod plays soft lounge music as the buzzer rings. *Showtime,* she thinks, as she walks to the door to answer the intercom. The doorman announces Mr. Luca Romano.

"Please send him up," she instructs him.

She walks out to stand in the hallway awaiting his arrival. When the elevator door opens, Luca steps out with a porter carrying his luggage. Kataryna takes a deep breath and smiles as Luca walks down the hallway towards her. The porter arrives first and puts the luggage in Kataryna's foyer. She hands him a tip and then takes Luca's hand and leads him into the apartment.

"Welcome to New York," she says, smiling seductively as she puts her arms around his neck.

He embraces her tightly. "You have no idea how much I missed you."

She kisses his cheek and then moves to his mouth. They engage in a long passionate kiss.

"I can imagine because I missed you the same. Let's have a welcome drink," she says breathless, leading him into the grand room.

"What a spectacular view of the city," he exclaims walking closer to the window.

"Wait till you see it at night," she says, moving towards the kitchen to get the Champagne and chocolate-covered strawberries. He follows her silently into the kitchen. Before she can open the refrigerator door he grabs her around the waist and pulls her close to him, kissing her up and down her neck. As she turns around he pins her back against the refrigerator door and kisses her passionately all over her cleavage. She slides down the refrigerator door to free and compose herself.

"Please," she sighs softly, "give me a chance. I am already way too excited."

He looks at her longingly, then smirks and opens the refrigerator door to take the Champagne out. Kataryna takes the strawberries and grabs the glasses, which are standing on the counter. They walk back to the grand room, both extremely excited. She places the glasses and strawberries on the coffee table and sits down on the couch with him. Both of them can hardly manage to stay cool. Luca opens the bottle and pours the Champagne into the glasses. He hands one of the glasses to Kataryna and raises his glass for a toast.

"Here is to us, trying to stay cool, at least for the next few minutes because I don't know how much longer I can keep this up."

"To staying cool," she says, clinking his glass.

He sits next to her on the couch one hand on one of her knees as both take a sip of Champagne. Kataryna takes one of the strawberries and puts it in his mouth. He eats it slowly with a seductive look on his face. The iPod plays "A Night to Remember," by Passenger 10, one of Kataryna's favorite songs. She takes a big sip of the Champagne, gets up and starts dancing to the rhythm of the music. She moves towards him and sits on his lap, straddling him and slowly moving up and down to the music.

"Ah," he moans, "here we go again with you in complete control over me."

Her already short dress moves higher up her thighs revealing her underwear. Luca tugs at her panties, which don't come down all the way since she is straddling him. He kisses her stomach and goes further down quickly as she softly caresses his hair and neck with her hands and lips. She opens his pants working herself into his underwear. He moans and kisses her softly between her legs as she starts panting and rubbing him harder and harder in turn. They both erupt into an orgasm as the pressure becomes too much for both of them to hold back.

"Oh, my God, we did this again," Kataryna murmurs as she slides down to lie on the couch with her head in Luca's lap, her eyes closed and her hands over her head, enjoying this tranquil moment.

"What is it with us rarely making it beyond this stage?" he asks quietly.

Kataryna opens her eyes and smiles at him.

"I guess we will have to work ourselves up to the big event again and try to exercise some self-control. All this sexual tension is building up when I think of you and then the minute I am around you and you touch me, I explode. I just can't be trusted with you so close to me as you can see."

"I couldn't have come up with a better explanation," he says, kissing her gently.

"But you know what they say," she goes on. "If you don't succeed the first time, try, try again."

"That is a piece of advice I will definitely take very seriously," Luca responds with a cute grin.

They remain still and tightly embraced for a while softly caressing each other, listening to the music playing and happy to be reunited.

"Nice music," Luca says pulling her off the couch and dancing with her slowly to the seductive music playing.

"Life is finally good," he whispers in her ear, kissing her softly down her neck.

"Almost too good to be true," Kataryna utters.

"What does that mean? Are you doubting my feelings for you?"

"No, of course not, but I am afraid when things are too good. I always think something bad is lurking around the corner and I so wish that nothing bad happens and we can continue to be happy together, but life is uncertain. You never know what may be in store for you.

Luca looks into her eyes. "That was very profound, Principessa, but why don't we just believe that the universe will be good to us."

She smiles at him sweetly. "Yes, let's do that. I am too happy now to have negative thoughts."

He kisses her gently and holds her tight, as they continue to slow dance into the late New York afternoon.

As evening arrives, Luca and Kataryna sit on the floor by the fireplace freshly showered and ready for dinner. Kataryna is wearing a gold-colored silk tank top style dress. Luca gets up and comes back with an elegantly wrapped gift and hands it to her.

"Thank you," she says smiling, "I wonder what is in there."

"Open it up and you will see."

She carefully removes the expertly done wrapping and opens the elegant box.

"Wow," she exclaims as she stares at the luxurious bowtie-shaped sapphire and diamond earrings. "It isn't even Christmas yet and I am getting such a precious gift already?"

"I thought they would go well with the royal blue suit you brought back from Italy. But more importantly, this is not a Christmas gift, Principessa," he responds, "that one you will get on Christmas Eve. It is just a token of my love. I am so happy that you came into my life and I want you to feel my love whenever you wear these."

She looks at him nodding. "I will certainly do that. I am also happy you came into my life. I didn't think I would be able to have these kind of feelings for anyone."

"I am so glad that you are willing to move to Milano because I want you-- mind, body and soul. I can't be without you much longer. Have you made a final decision yet when you will move over?"

"Well, that is for me to know and for you to find out, my Italian prince," she says, smiling seductively and blowing him a kiss.

"You are not getting off that easy. You have to give me a little bit more than that."

"Oh, you know how easy I can get off with you," she whispers in his ear. "As a matter of fact I am close to it right now."

Kataryna takes his hand and puts it on her thighs. He gets aroused immediately, realizing she is not wearing any underwear. She sits in front of him on her knees feeling his excitement and freeing him from his pants.

"You are so close to getting there," she tortures him while sitting on top of him moving her hips.

He pushes against her trying to enter her but climaxes before he succeeds. He grabs her thighs and puts her flat on the floor running his mouth all over her until she screams in delight.

"You are driving me crazy," he whispers, "this is unreal."

Kataryna starts laughing. "I guess we have so much built up tension and can't stop that from happening so fast, but it is such a pleasure to play with your deadly weapon so let's enjoy it and not worry about it."

"Deadly weapon," he laughs out loud, "what are you saying?"

"Well, you are killing me," she teases him.

"We got way off our original conversation," he says in a more serious tone.

"All roads lead to Rome," she responds, smiling broadly.

"Thank you for the excellent directions, Miss GPS," he responds laughing, "but I am not trying to go to Rome. I would, however, appreciate some guidance on how to enter the magic castle, Principessa."

"If I guide you will you follow me blindly?" she continues teasing him.

"I would follow you blindly to the end of the world, my love," he says staring deeply into her eyes.

"And I you. There is your answer."

"You just made my day and night," he says, kissing her softly.

"Your night I will make later," she whispers into his ear, softly sucking on his earlobe. "Let's have some dinner now so you will have the strength to make it through the night."

He closes his eyes and holds her tightly. She lies next to him grinning with deep satisfaction how well their first day together again went, reminding herself that they are going to be together like this for the next 10 days.

"I better get up now to get our dinner ready," she says, "otherwise, we may never get to eat tonight. I think we definitely need a little break from this excitement."

He smirks at her. "You've got a point there. But feel free to seduce me any time you wish."

Kataryna gets up slowly stepping over Luca one leg after the other.

"I thought we were going to take a break," he says, grabbing her legs with both of his hands.

"We are," she shrieks, running into the kitchen. He gets up to follow her.

"You better stay away from me and out of the kitchen if you want to eat. I won't be able to put this dinner together otherwise," she laughs.

Luca decides to cooperate. He leaves the kitchen and walks to the window to look at the Manhattan skyline. His iPhone rings. He picks up the phone and answers the call.

"Pronto."

Kataryna smiles as she hears him answer the phone and speak in Italian. She has no idea what he is saying, but it sounds so sexy.

"It's my mother," he whispers.

"Tell her I said hello," Kataryna says, walking back into the kitchen to get the rest of the food.

When she comes back in the room Luca has hung up the phone.

"My mother was concerned because neither of us has called her to tell her that we arrived safely. I completely forgot because you distracted me the moment I laid eyes on you. See, what you are doing to me?"

"Apparently, your sister was also too busy to call her mother," Kataryna says grinning as she takes her seat at the festively set dining table.

She holds out her hand. "Come sit down and eat. Would you like red or white wine?" she asks him.

"I'll have whatever you are having," he responds.

"Hmm, this salmon is delicious with that sauce together," he compliments her.

"Thank you," she says. "I was hoping you would like it. Wait till you see what we have for dessert."

He raises his eyebrows.

"No, I wasn't talking about sex. I got a super delicious chocolate cake from a restaurant here in New York. They make the best European cakes and tarts. I remember that you also liked chocolate when we had dessert at Villa D'Este."

"I am flattered that you remember," he says softly.

"I remember more than that," she flirts with him.

"So do I, because every moment with you is memorable."

"Let's change the subject," she says as she starts clearing the table, "this is getting way too dangerous again. I keep on finding myself at the corner of love and ecstasy with you."

"Si, Principessa, we shall stay off that for a while," he responds laughing, "we definitely can't be trusted with that subject."

While they are having the scrumptious Café Sabarsky cake, they are going over their vacation plans for after Christmas. The Romano corporate jet will be in New York because Paolo Montanari has chartered it again. They will fly to Maui, Hawaii, where they have rented a secluded luxury villa right on the beach in Wailea with spectacular ocean views. Luca has never been to Hawaii. He can't wait to experience this tropical island. They made plans to leave on December 26 and stay until January 1, spending New Year's Eve at a restaurant in one of the a luxury hotels. Kataryna is all excited to show him Maui's magnificent sights like Haleakala and other beautiful spots.

"I haven't been on a real vacation for a long time," Luca says, "and now I am actually taking one in Hawaii. The idea to experience this together with you makes it even more special."

"And special it will be," Kataryna responds, "you have no idea what the magic of Hawaii does to me. I hope you will be equally enchanted by this place."

"Thanks for the warning. I shall be prepared for the unexpected as usual with you."

"When are Patrizia and Francesco going back to Italy?" she starts a new conversation.

"With me on January 3. They are invited to a New Year's Eve party in Greenwich, Connecticut at one of Francesco's friend's house, who also has a vacation home in Italy. I think he is some hotshot trader at one of the major investment banks."

"That's great," Kataryna says, "Francesco is such a sweet guy. I really like him a lot and I can't wait to see your sister again tomorrow. I didn't get a chance to spend much time with her when I came over for your birthday. If she is anything like you, I know I'll love her."

"What about me?" he asks softly. "Do you love me, too?"

She looks into his eyes and gives him an intriguing grin. "You had to ask, didn't you? I guess you will have to wait a bit for that answer."

He smiles at her. "Well, we can always pick that subject up again in Hawaii."

"Good idea. Oh, look at the time. It is already 11 p.m. Time to get some rest. We have a long day tomorrow and you must be tired. For you it is actually 5 a.m., according to Italian time."

She clears the remaining glasses and plates from the table and brings them to the kitchen.

"Why don't you get ready for bed?" she suggests. "I will be right behind you.

"OK," he agrees, trying to suppress a yawn. "I am getting a little tired."

Kataryna puts the dishes and glasses in the dishwater, turns out the lights and gets ready for bed. When she walks into the bedroom Luca is in bed fast asleep. *Good night, Prince Charming*, she thinks, as she lies down next to him in her king-sized bed. She is exhausted from all the action during the day and the wine has also made her sleepy. She drifts off and soon is fast asleep, too.

FIFTEEN

Kataryna wakes up around 9 a.m., with Luca next to her still fast asleep. What a great feeling to have him here. She doesn't want to wake him yet because then they will get hot and heavy. There are still many things to prepare for the brunch she is hosting for Patrizia and Francesco. She gets dressed in a short leopard print dress with blue undertones. The diamond and sapphire earrings Luca gave her yesterday match the blue specks in her dress perfectly, as do the blue suede pumps she brought back from Italy.

Around 10 a.m. she peeks into the bedroom. Luca is still sleeping. She closes the bedroom door tightly so he won't be disturbed by any noise from the kitchen. The espresso machine is ready so Luca can drink his usual cup of coffee when he wakes up.

Kataryna has a cup of White Tea then gets out the eggs, crabmeat and avocado to start preparing everything for later. Patrizia and Francesco are due to arrive around 11:30 a.m. Kataryna's sister excused herself because she has a lot of preparations to do yet for the next day, Christmas Eve, when she will have all of them over for dinner. All is going according to plan.

Kataryna finishes her tea and puts the final touches on the brunch menu, carefully looking at everything so it will be perfect for the guests. She decides to also make a batch of Bloody Mary drinks in case someone prefers that to the Champagne. As she puts the horseradish into the tomato juice, she feels Luca's hands on her shoulders. He pulls her close to him with one hand while the other is moving underneath her dress.

"Wow, I wake up to find a wild animal in the kitchen," he whispers. "I want to tame this gatta selvatica."

She quickly frees herself from him. "Oh no, you are not taming anything right now. Your sister and her fiancé are due here shortly, so unfortunately there is no time for that kind of action."

She kisses him on his mouth. He looks at her with a smirk and sighs. "Why didn't you wake me?"

"I felt that you needed that sleep, and besides we will have the next 10 days together."

Luca stands in front of her in his underwear. She gives him an approving look.

"Would love, love, love to get into it with you, but I have important guests arriving here soon and I don't want to look disheveled. So, why don't you be a good boy and get dressed now and tonight we will see who tames who," she laughs.

He takes a step towards her gazing into her eyes. She steps back.

"Don't even think about attempting anything," she warns him, smiling. "Otherwise, this gatta selvatica is going to bring her claws out." She growls at him.

He takes another step forward and pins her against the counter, kissing her. As he releases her he lets his fingers touch one of her erogenous zones. She crosses her legs and puts her hand against his chest.

"You are flirting with disaster, my dear," she tells him seductively.

"OK, gatta selvatica, you win," he says, smiling, "but you will pay for it later."

"Looking forward to it," she cracks up laughing, as he leaves the kitchen to get dressed. "And don't come back into this kitchen again. It is off-limits for you this morning," she yells in his direction still laughing.

She hears a loud groan coming from him and has to laugh even more now. *What the heck is he getting into out there,* she thinks. A few minutes later he comes out of the bedroom area looking hot in a beige sweater and dark pants.

She looks at him, smiling approvingly, and kisses him on the cheek. "You look smoking hot, babe. You got it going on," she whispers.

Luca looks at her kind of flushed and grabs her around the waist.

"Thank you. So do you."

"Jeez," Kataryna breathes out, "you can cut this sexual tension with a knife."

"If you had awakened me earlier, we could have taken care of that little problem."

"It wouldn't have made that much of a difference," she murmurs. "You know it doesn't take me long to get charged up again when you are around me."

"I have a feeling we are going to have a night with fireworks after coming home from dinner with my sister and Francesco."

"In that case," she says in a sexy voice, "you better get that fire extinguisher ready."

They both laugh out loud as the buzzer comes on. Kataryna frees herself from Luca's hold after she lightly strokes his inner thigh and smiles at him coquettishly. He lets out a deep groan and slaps her lightly on her behind.

"You are so in trouble, Principessa."

"I know, but I like to be in trouble with you," Kataryna says laughing, quickly walking to the intercom to answer the buzzer.

"Please send them up," she tells the concierge who called up to announce her guests.

Luca joins her as she opens the door to welcome Patrizia and Francesco into her home.

Kataryna embraces Patrizia. "I have been so looking forward to see you again."

"Me, too," Patrizia says, "we didn't get to spend much time on Luca's birthday because he just wouldn't let go of you."

Kataryna turns to Francesco and embraces him.

"Francesco, it's so good to see you again, too. How have you been?"

Francesco hugs her and greets her with a kiss on each cheek.

"I am well, Kataryna, great to see you. You look amazing."

Luca watches the whole welcoming scene smiling.

"Hello, you two lovebirds. What have you been up to since yesterday?" He looks at his sister.

Francesco grins. "Probably the same you two have been up to."

All four break out into laughter.

"Brilliant assumption," Luca says, still laughing.

"Well, that calls for a toast," Kataryna exclaims.

Luca pours the Champagne and hands each of them a glass.

"Here is to family and love."

"Famiglia e amore," Francesco repeats in Italian.

Patrizia and Francesco walk over to the large window admiring the spectacular view of the city. Luca joins Kataryna in the kitchen.

"I know you ordered me not to come into this kitchen today," he jokes, "but I have only good intentions to help you serve the brunch."

"How kind of you. Okay then, you can help me carry these," Kataryna points to some of the dishes on the counter next to her. He walks up to her and softly touches her in a sensitive spot before taking the dishes. She starts squeaking out loud and steps to the side to escape him.

He grins at her victoriously. "Revenge is sweet, Principessa."

Patrizia, who heard the loud squeak, comes running into the kitchen. "Is everything alright?" she asks concerned.

"I am fine, no worries," Kataryna quickly replies slightly flushed and embarrassed.

Luca looks at her laughing and hugging her. Patrizia gives her brother and Kataryna a questioning look and then starts laughing, too. Assuming that something intimate occurred here she backs out of the kitchen somewhat embarrassed.

"I am sorry."

Luca stops his sister. "As long as you are here already you might as well help us carry some of these dishes."

Francesco is in the grand room admiring the tasteful furnishings and taking a closer look at some photos of friends and family displayed on a console table. He picks up the photos one after another and wonders who the persons in them are. There is one photo of a nice-looking couple, which must be Kataryna's parents. He seems to see some resemblance between Kataryna and the couple. Right next to this photo is one of a younger couple. Looks like this could be Kataryna's sister and her husband, and the two pretty girls who are identical twins must be their children. *Nice family,* he thinks. He never had a brother or sister and often wondered what it would have been like growing up with a sibling. He moves on to the next photo, a stunning dark-haired kind of exotic-looking woman. Next to that one is a photo of another family, which looks like they could be German.

"Brunch is being served," he hears Kataryna saying as she walks up to him.

"I was just looking at your photos," Francesco says, "you have to tell us later on who all these people in the photos are."

"Sure," she says, "but now it is time to eat."

She leads him to the table. Soft music plays in the background as the four are enjoying their brunch and each other's company.

"So what would you like to do this afternoon?" Kataryna asks Patrizia and Francesco.

"I know you are still staying in New York until the 3rd of January so you will do a lot of sightseeing then. Why don't we just walk around a little bit on Fifth and Madison Avenue and look at the great window and Christmas decorations," she suggests to them.

"That sounds good," Patrizia says. "We can look at some stores. I have to get some gifts for my parents, my sister and a few friends of mine."

"Yes," Francesco adds, "we better take care of that because we are going to stay with one of my friends in Greenwich from December 30 until January 1, while you two are basking in the sun in Hawaii."

"I am looking forward to that," Luca says, putting his arms around Kataryna.

She nods. "So do I. Can't wait to get out of the cold."

"Thank you for arranging the meeting with your partner Stephen while I am in New York," Francesco says. "Unfortunately he won't meet Roberto in person, but I understand they have communicated quite a bit via video conference in the last few weeks to prepare for the closing."

Luca looks at Kataryna. She frowns. Francesco looks at them puzzled.

"What was that look about? Is there something I should know?" he asks cautiously, anticipating a comment from Luca.

"I don't want to go further into it right now, but Roberto has been acting kind of strange recently. I didn't really want to mention it because I thought that this would straighten itself out, but at this point I am not sure what the future will bring. In addition, we are still looking into the 10 percent equity share right for the CEO."

Francesco takes in a deep breath. "Now that I think of it, Roberto has not been himself lately. When I told him that Patrizia and I are joining you on the trip to New York for Christmas, he was very quiet and looked kind of stressed. I was wondering about his reaction because it wasn't like him. And lately he looked kind of sick and worked from home frequently. Do you know what's going on with him?"

"Not really and I don't want to dig deeper into this situation for the time being. I want to enjoy my vacation with Kataryna, and then come January we will look at the situation more closely. Maybe by that time things will have gone back to normal. If not, we have some important decisions to make. Needless to say, I am thrilled for various reasons that Kataryna and Stephen will acquire NatMedica, one of them being a personal one."

"What if things don't go back to normal?" Francesco enquires. "Mamma mia, this could be a deal breaker on many levels," he adds in a concerned tone.

"Relax," Luca responds, "if things turn out really bad, we may have to relieve Roberto of his duties and put you in the CEO position."

Francesco looks at him shocked. "You mean before the closing? Wow, this is not how I wanted to rise up into this position," he murmurs.

Kataryna shakes her head. "I am afraid that won't be possible if in fact he has the right to purchase the 10 percent equity. If you would try to remove him as CEO he would not be considered to be in good standing and couldn't acquire the equity share, which I am sure, would turn into a tough legal battle."

"Let's wait and see what the lawyers say about his right and now let's change the subject," Luca insists sternly. "I don't want to have this conversation in front of Patrizia and, anyway, we are here to have fun."

"Hey guys, how about going out shopping now?" Patrizia proposes excitedly when she returns from the powder room.

"Great idea," Kataryna agrees. "Let's walk off this food a bit to make room for dinner later on. I made a reservation at an excellent restaurant."

"Yeah, I need some fresh air," Luca says. "Patrizia, you can help me find a suitable Christmas gift for our parents."

As usual during the winter holidays the department store windows on Fifth Avenue have spectacular decorations. Patrizia is totally excited. She can't decide which one she likes best.

"They are all so awesome and unusual," she exclaims, as she takes a photo of each one of the decorated windows. "I am going to send these to Carlotta." She attaches them to an email to her sister and copies her mother, too. A few minutes later Carlotta writes back: I am so jealous. Wish I could be there with you.

After some serious shopping, Luca and Kataryna return to the apartment to get ready for their dinner out. They meet up again with Francesco and Patrizia in the trendy restaurant downtown.

"Great choice of restaurant, Kataryna," Francesco compliments her. "But it's not surprising because I could see already when I met you the first time that you have excellent taste."

"Thank you Francesco," Kataryna says. "I guess you knew that by the man I chose to hang out with," she laughs and looks at Luca.

"That was so sweet," Patrizia says to Kataryna touching her arm. "Yes, my brother is a fine specimen, but so are you. I was hoping he would come up with a good one next time around."

Luca appears slightly embarrassed. "How about you guys focus on something else than me? This wine for instance. It is very good and so is the food here."

"Let's focus on Francesco now," Patrizia says. "Here is to the love of my life." She raises her glass and the others follow.

"Good idea," Kataryna calls out. "I'd like to hear a little bit more about Francesco."

"Well, business wise you already know everything from my bio and our meeting in Bellagio. And you know that Patrizia and I are getting married in June 2013. By the way, I expect you to be there. What else can I tell you?" Francesco asks Kataryna.

"Do you come from a big family?" Kataryna goes on.

"No, it's just me. My mother miscarried several times, so I don't have any brothers or sisters. That's why I love the Romano family gatherings so much. It's never boring. They always have something going on. The latest is you and Luca, of course, and look, now we are all sitting here together and it already feels like a family gathering."

"Wait until tomorrow at my sister's home," Kataryna says. "You will like her and her husband, too, as well as Natasha and Sabrina, their identical twins. They are a handful, but beautiful girls. They are 15 years old going on 20, very outgoing and curious about life. The girls are looking so much forward to meeting you all. They even started learning some Italian words and phrases just to impress you."

"How nice," Francesco responds. "Do they speak German, too?"

"You bet, fluently. Aleksandra made sure that they kept up with it. She speaks mostly German to them."

"Great, then I can surprise them with some German."

"You speak German?" Kataryna asks visibly surprised.

"Yes, my mother is actually German. My father lived in Germany for several years when he attended a residency in a German hospital. That's when they met and fell in love. So to honor my mother, I took up German and we sometimes speak in German at home. But I don't speak it as well as her, of course."

"But well enough so we can speak in German, if we don't want the others to hear what we are saying?" Kataryna asks jokingly.

"Wait a minute," Luca comes into the conversation laughing, "I don't think I like what I am hearing here."

"Neither do I," Patrizia says, shaking her finger at Kataryna.

"Just kidding," Kataryna quickly offers, "but don't forget when you guys go off in Italian, I don't know what you are talking about either."

"Luca can teach you some Italian," Patrizia offers, "so you are in the loop at our family gatherings."

"Yeah, sure, let's see if we can accomplish that," Kataryna responds, "but all joking aside, I will take an Italian language course before I come over."

After they are finished with dinner, Luca and Kataryna take Francesco and Patrizia back to their fancy hotel where they all have a nightcap.

"See you tomorrow at 5 p.m., at my sister's place. I wrote down the address for you." Kataryna hands them a note with Aleksandra's address and phone number as they are leaving the hotel bar.

"We are so looking forward to tomorrow," Francesco says.

"You didn't mention that Francesco was half German," Kataryna says to Luca, as they are getting back into their car service to take them home.

"I have been too preoccupied with us getting to know each other better than remembering to tell you about Francesco's ancestry," Luca explains. "Honestly, it didn't cross my mind. And then we immediately had the Roberto drama, so you can imagine where my priorities were."

"Sure, it's not a big deal, just an interesting tidbit. Your sister marrying a man who is half German and you in a relationship with a German."

"That's true. It didn't even occur to me until a few minutes ago."

The car service drops them off at Kataryna's apartment building around midnight.

"I am a little tired," Kataryna says as they enter the apartment.

"Me, too," Luca says. "We were very active today and then all the food and wine."

"So shall we have a mellow night then?" Kataryna asks him smiling.

"Carpe noctum," Luca responds, smiling back at her.

"That is a pretty ambiguous statement, my dear," Kataryna comes back with grinning. "Can you be more specific?"

"Let's just go to bed and see what the night has to offer."

Kataryna starts laughing out loud as she heads towards the bathroom to get ready for bed. When she gets to her bedroom, Luca is asleep with a cute smile on his face.

"Carpe noctum, huh?" she says amused, looking at Luca asleep. That'll be a good subject for tomorrow's breakfast. She turns out the light, gets into bed and closes her eyes. Before she can drift off Luca jumps on top of her.

"Carpe noctum," he laughs out loud. "Gotcha, you thought I was asleep."

Kataryna shrieks. "Wow, you scared me half to death. That was pretty devious. You are going to pay for this."

"This time I had the element of surprise on my side," he says still laughing. "Usually you surprise me with your seductive games and outfits, which almost bring my heart to a stop. So we are kind of even now."

"Nice try, Signore," she responds. "I didn't know you are that competitive."

His arousal is digging right into Kataryna now.

"And now on top of it you are coming at me with your deadly weapon. I guess you are determined to kill me tonight," she says jokingly hardly being able to contain herself.

"I am going to kill you with love," he whispers in her ear.

"You think?" she asks coquettishly. "What if I don't let you? What are you going to do now with all that pent-up energy and your engorged body part?"

"You wouldn't," he says, not sure if she is kidding.

He kisses her neck and ear and starts caressing her.

"I am not feeling a thing," she lies casually, but deep down she is getting all hot under his touch.

"Liar," he softly whispers in her ear, "your body tells me something else. It really, really wants me."

"But I won't let my body have you." She softly bites his neck.

"I am going to fight you for your body."

"No, no, no," she cries out, throwing her head around, "you won't win this one. I am shutting my body down."

Luca positions himself right between her legs and starts kissing her breasts. The soft pressure of his arousal hits her right in the G-spot and she climaxes, relaxing her legs and giving him a chance to thrust into her. He starts moving and groaning and reaches his orgasm instantly.

"Ooh, Principessa, that was so exciting," he murmurs. "I think we seized the night."

"Seems to be a never-ending story with us," Kataryna admits. "And you are catching up with me."

"I am proud of my small victory tonight, but I know you are way ahead of me in that department and the tables will be turned soon again. I am sure you are going to assault me with all your weapons when I least expect it."

"Yes, darling, you can count on that. Good night. Let's sleep in tomorrow."

SIXTEEN

Christmas Eve has finally arrived and Aleksandra has made all preparations for the Christmas Eve dinner with Kataryna, Luca, Patrizia and Francesco. She is making the traditional German Christmas goose, red cabbage, potatoes, dumplings and root vegetables. She also made a Christmas Stollen, but not the typical one with raisins. Cranberries replaced the raisins and she also added some other interesting ingredients. Aleksandra came up with this recipe because Kataryna doesn't like raisins and it has been an immediate hit.

Aleksandra is a fabulous cook and has a very successful catering business. She has built a large and loyal client base over the years, which her husband Brian Edwards was able to contribute to because of his executive vice president position in a major public relations firm. Brian has access to well-known affluent corporate executives and the occasional celebrity, who are always on the lookout for excellent caterers for their elaborate parties. Once they tried out Aleksandra's catering, these clients were hooked on her extraordinary delicious and healthy food preparations and presentations. Their guests were raving about the selections, too. Many of the corporate executives also have the food for their corporate jets catered by Aleksandra, which prompted her to hire additional staff on a permanent basis. Business could not be better and Aleksandra is in her element.

At 4 p.m., Aleksandra puts the final touches to her dishes and table setting. Her sister and the other guests are due to arrive at 5 p.m. Aleksandra can't wait to meet Luca, the man her sister fell in love with and is talking about constantly. She met Luca via a video call Kataryna had arranged and can understand why her sister is so excited about him. Apart from his good looks, he has an exceptionally engaging personality.

The twins Natasha and Sabrina are still in their rooms trying to figure out what to wear. Aleksandra goes to their rooms to check on them and help them decide.

"What have you two come up with?" she asks as she enters Natasha's room.

"We can't decide," they both answer almost simultaneously."

"Well," Aleksandra says, "you got the whole closet full of clothes. I am sure you'll find something suitable."

They go over a couple of options and make their final choices. Aleksandra looks at her girls and smiles. *They are so beautiful*, she thinks, *and soon they will start dating.* Oh boy, she will have to prepare for some turbulent times when their hormones start raging. She thinks back to the time when she was 15 years old. Times have changed. *I was not as grown up yet at 15 and I didn't have such a harmonious childhood like Natasha and Sabrina have,* she recalls.

Kataryna, Luca, Patrizia and Francesco arrive at 5 p.m., sharp and the Edwards family welcomes them into their home. The twins run towards Kataryna who receives them with open arms.

"Aunt Kataryna," they yell joyfully hugging her, "we missed you."

Kataryna embraces them and then introduces her family to Luca, his sister and Francesco.

"We are so delighted to finally meet you in person," Aleksandra says to Luca as she kisses him hello.

"So am I," Luca responds. "Thank you for having us over for Christmas Eve dinner. There is nothing better than spending Christmas with family."

Luca brought two bottles of exquisite Champagne and gives them to Brian. The twins are staring at the three Italians. After a few shy moments they come out with a couple of Italian phrases they learned, especially for this occasion starting with Buon Natale, which means Merry Christmas in Italian.

"Frohe Weihnachten," Francesco wishes them in German.

"You speak German?" Sabrina asks Francesco astonished.

"Yes, I do. My mother is German," he responds, "just like yours."

"Cool." Natasha and Sabrina are giggling and the ice is broken.

Aleksandra starts serving welcome drinks and appetizers while Brian puts the gifts the guests brought under the Christmas tree. Festive German Christmas music is playing in the background.

"Here is to a beautiful and merry Christmas and many more to come in the future," Aleksandra toasts. "We are so happy that you are here."

"It is our pleasure," Luca says. "Unfortunately, our sister Carlotta couldn't come with us to New York because of prior arrangements with her son's friend and family but she would have loved to be here and so would her son Enrico."

"Too bad they couldn't make it. I am sure Enrico, Natasha and Sabrina would have had a good time together," Kataryna says looking at the twins. "But we have discussed that Carlotta and Enrico will come to New York for Enrico's 17th birthday in March."

"Our birthday is also in March," the twins exclaim excitedly. "We will be 16."

"I know," Kataryna responds, "we will celebrate all three birthdays together."

Kataryna gets out her iPhone. "Here is a photo of Enrico." She shows it to the twins. They tear the phone out of her hand.

"Let's see. Cool-looking guy," Natasha says, "our girlfriends will be jealous."

"I already suggested to Enrico that you three should start communicating via video calls and emails so you get to know each other a bit before he comes over," Kataryna informs them.

"Great idea, Aunt Kataryna," Sabrina responds. "We can start with an email tomorrow and then arrange a video call. Does he speak English?"

"Yes, he does," Luca tells them. "He spent some time in London last summer. So he is fairly fluent."

"Good," Natasha says, "because we wouldn't get very far with our little Italian."

"Please have a seat at the table, we are ready to start our Christmas dinner," Aleksandra says, as her husband is carving the goose.

"Let's toast the cook," Francesco says before they start eating, raising his glass. "We heard that you are an excellent cook. By the way, I also like to cook and I think I am pretty good at it. Maybe you and I can collaborate one day and come up with a great menu for our families."

"It would be a great pleasure to collaborate with you," Aleksandra replies. "Let's come up with a game plan, either here in New York or maybe in Italy."

"You would love Luca's kitchen," Kataryna says to her sister, "so I think Italy would be a good place to do that. Luca would just have to give Mariya the day off so she lets us take over the kitchen."

"Well," Francesco says laughing, "we still need someone to clean up after us. I doubt that Luca, Kataryna or Patrizia would want to clean up our mess."

"I like the way you think, Francesco," Aleksandra proclaims. "I think we will get along just fine."

"Luca and I love to eat, so you two can knock yourselves out," Kataryna adds. "The more capable cooks we have among us, the better for us."

"So, I understand you are staying in the New York area until the beginning of January?" Aleksandra asks Francesco and Patrizia.

"Yes, we are. We should get together again before we leave. How about we have a nice dinner out one evening, our treat of course?" Francesco suggests to Aleksandra and Brian. "We will be staying at Kataryna's apartment while they are in Hawaii and we will also spend some time with a long-time friend of mine who lives in Connecticut."

"Great," Brian replies, "let's come up with a suitable date. Aleksandra and I will make some restaurant suggestions and you will have the final say."

After they finish dessert the twins get antsy. "When are we going to open the presents?"

"I guess we better get to that quickly before you die of curiosity," their father teases them.

Kataryna gets up to get the presents from under the tree and hands two gifts to each of the girls.

"Merry Christmas, this is from me. Hope you like it."

They open the first box and get excited seeing the Apple logo on the inside package.

"OMG, a mini-iPad," they yell excitedly and immediately focus their attention on the second larger box, tearing off the gift-wrap. Inside they find a stylish outfit, which Kataryna bought for each in Milan.

"Wow, Aunt Kataryna, these outfits are super cool and no one over here will have these. We can't wait to wear them."

Luca hands each of them a gift, which his sister selected for the girls, a pair of beautiful Murano glass earrings. From Francesco and Patrizia they each get a cool Italian leather handbag.

Kataryna opens her gift from Luca containing a diamond and sapphire necklace matching the bowtie earrings he had already given her the day he arrived.

Her face lights up. "I will thank you properly later."

He smiles. "I am sure you will come up with something extraordinary."

It is Kataryna's turn to give her gift to Luca. She hands him a rather large package with a canvas painting of her and him together. "This is a fabulous gift, Principessa," he says totally taken by it. "A canvas painting of our two photos merged, what a great idea. I know just the place to hang it. How do you come up with these things?"

"I guess being in love brings out my creative side," she says kissing him. "Buon Natale, Frohe Weihnachten and Merry Christmas."

Aleksandra opens her gift from Kataryna. "Wow," she exclaims, "what a beautiful handbag. Thank you so much."

"Yeah, right out of Milano. When I saw it I knew it was you," Kataryna tells her.

Luca presents his gift to Aleksandra, a spectacular multi-colored Murano glass bowl, which happens to fit perfectly into her home's décor. Francesco and Patrizia's gift for Aleksandra is a beautiful designer scarf and matching Italian leather gloves. Patrizia and Francesco's gift from Kataryna are two opera tickets for the Met.

As the beautiful evening comes to an end, Kataryna reminds the twins of the video call she has arranged in the morning with Enrico.

"Thank you for the beautiful dinner, Aleksandra," Luca says. "I am looking forward to spending more time with all of you."

"We are so happy that you spent Christmas Eve with us," Aleksandra says to Luca, Patrizia and Francesco. "It actually feels like we have known each other for a long time."

"I feel the same way," Francesco responds, "and don't forget Aleksandra, you and I will cook together for the gang in the not too distant future."

"You bet," Aleksandra replies, hugging him and Patrizia. "I can't wait. I really love you guys."

"And we love you," Francesco says, "I felt right at home here. I especially liked the German Christmas songs you played. My mother likes to put these on, too, each Christmas. It is so festive. We will call you to arrange for dinner out in the next few days."

Luca and Kataryna arrive back at Kataryna's apartment around midnight.

"What a beautiful Christmas Eve dinner," Luca says, "we all fit together very well, don't you think?"

"Yes, we bonded well, "she replies, "but I never had a doubt that we wouldn't. My sister is a very gracious and loving person."

"By the way, Principessa, I have another little gift for you," Luca says handing her a medium-sized box he got out of his luggage.

"What? Are you serious?" she yells out. "You are spoiling me."

"Well, this one I am going to enjoy as much as you hopefully will," he whispers

"Oh really? I can't wait to see what is in here."

She rips the package open and stares at the contents, a sexy midnight blue satin camisole and matching panties.

"What a stunning color," she utters, "goes perfectly with the diamond and sapphire necklace and earrings you already gave me. Yeah, I can see now why you will like it; there is not much material. In fact, it's quite skimpy. Let me try it on to see if it fits."

Kataryna goes to the bedroom to change into the sexy outfit, accessorizing it with the matching earrings and necklace.

"Have a look at your creation, Signore. Fresh from Milano I suspect," she says swaggering towards Luca, pivoting like a runway model.

Luca stares at her coming at him. "Just like I imagined it would look on you. That blue really brings out the color of your eyes."

"Yeah, right," she murmurs seductively, "as if you are focusing on my eyes when I am wearing this thing. Well, enjoy the view, my dear. I have a feeling I won't be wearing this much longer if I let you have your way."

"Principessa, you look so gorgeous. I don't want to take it off you yet. I want to savor the moment."

"And then who says that I will let you take it off me anyway," she teases him.

"Are you challenging me?" he asks taking a step towards her.

Kataryna takes a step back. "Are you stalking me?"

"Do I have to chase you around the apartment or will you be a good girl for me tonight?" he sighs.

"I opt for not being a good girl tonight."

He grins. "So you are going to make me work for it?"

"Sure, a little bit of hard labor hasn't hurt anyone yet."

Luca runs his hands through his hair contemplating what to do or say next.

"Hard labor? What do you have in mind?"

"Well, let's start out with something easy. How about you getting something nice to drink for us?"

Luca bows. "Si Signora, che cosa vuoi bere?"

"What? Fragst Du mich was ich trinken moechte?" she hurls at him in German.

"Nice move, Principessa, I should have expected that," he says laughing. "I believe you are trying to outsmart me."

She nods. "You guessed it. The hunter becomes the hunted."

"Wow, how did you manage to turn that one around again?"

"A little reverse psychology, darling and you fell right into the trap," she laughs out loud. "And by the way, where is my drink? I assign you one easy task and you are already slacking off? It's going to get more difficult from here on. So get with the program, Prince Charming."

"You are on a roll now. God help me," he says, getting a bottle of wine and two glasses.

He pours the wine and hands her a glass. Kataryna takes a seat on her couch. Luca sits next to her after pouring a glass of wine for himself. She gets up and sits opposite him in a lotus position.

"You don't want me to sit next to you?" he asks frowning.

"No, why don't you stay where you are. If you sit next to me you may get the urge to overpower me."

"Yeah, of course, we can't have that," he says jokingly, "that would mean that I win the game."

"Exactly. You catch on quickly."

They stare at each other smiling mischievously drinking their wine slowly and listening to the music Kataryna had turned on.

"You look like you are on the prowl," Luca murmurs.

"Let's say that I am ready to assign you a follow-up task."

"OK, what would you like me to do for you, Principessa?"

"I would like a nice relaxing massage."

Luca starts laughing. "Sure, I can do that. That's almost too easy."

"Not so fast," she quickly interrupts him. "Here are the rules. You cannot touch me in any sensitive spots or you are disqualified immediately."

"Define sensitive spots," he responds.

"I have to spell this out for you? Really?" she tantalizes him. "I think you should know my sensitive spots by now."

After thinking for a moment Luca responds.

"OK. Here is another question for you though. Can you trust me not to touch these spots?"

"I will give you a chance to prove that you are trustworthy and follow the rules."

"I believe you just beat me again," he sighs, "but I'll accept the challenge."

Kataryna gets up, walks over to him and kisses him softly. "I will get the bed ready for my massage."

Luca sits quietly for a moment finishing his wine and psyching himself up for the challenge he will have to face. He is excited already and realizes how tough this is going to be for him, but he has a plan.

Kataryna is on her bed, which she prepared with soft bath towels under and next to her for the massage. She is face down still in the sexy midnight blue outfit when Luca enters the bedroom and takes off his clothes. She smiles at him seductively and hands him the Arnica massage oil.

"Good Luck," she whispers, seeing that he is already in a state of arousal.

"What about your top?" he asks, "isn't this going to get oily?"

"No, you have to take it off, of course."

"So I am allowed to undress you?" he asks softly.

"Yes."

"OK, then lift up your arms for me please."

Kataryna sits up and lifts her arms. Luca kneels behind her and removes first the necklace and then the top slowly. He closes his eyes as the wicked massage game begins and then takes the Arnica oil and rubs it over Kataryna's shoulders and back. He breathes in the aroma of the oil. Oh, it smells so good. The aroma will stay with him forever as will the memories of this exhilarating moment. The idea that he can't touch her certain zones increases his excitement, which he expected as the forbidden fruit syndrome kicks in and makes him want it even more. He takes more of the oil and rubs it down her arms. Kataryna is lying on the bed face down as Luca moves down to her thighs and legs applying the oil and massaging it lightly into her skin.

Except for some erotic music in the background everything is quiet. He feels his breathing become deeper as the song "Touch Me" by Denise Guttenbach comes on. He massages her in slow circular motions. She is still wearing the skimpy panties, which he takes off carefully in order not to touch any sensitive spots. After massaging her back and the back of her legs, he asks her to turn around. He puts one of the towels over her when she turns on her back, and then starts massaging the front of her legs and thighs. His arousal is becoming painful. He comes dangerously close to the forbidden areas, but manages to not touch them.

Kataryna enjoys the relaxing massage, but also gets more and more excited. She tries to hide it by moving around a bit trying to ease the tension.

Luca looks at her. "Everything okay?" he asks her sweetly, grinning.

She nods yes and closes her eyes again. She is about two seconds away from grabbing him and giving in to him. He must be in agony, too, she figures, but he is holding up pretty well. One of them is going on the attack any moment. They both individually sense it, but who will surrender first? Luca moves the towel and it falls between her legs. The motion right there puts her over the edge. Luca is also at the brink of a climax. He can't take it anymore and neither can she. They both grasp each other, giving up control and seizing the moment to passionately relieve each other's sexual tension.

After some quiet moments in a tight embrace and totally relaxed, they talk about how powerful this experience was.

"The purpose of this task was that I wanted to prove to you that the largest sexual organ is actually the brain," Kataryna tells him.

"You proved your point, Principessa, this was so effective. I wonder if we can ever top this."

"Oh ye of little faith," she responds, kissing him, "I am certain we will come up with something in Maui."

Carlotta and Enrico arrive at the Romano villa in Bellagio early afternoon on Christmas Eve.

"Mamma, when are we going to have that video call with the girls in New York?" Enrico asks.

"Tomorrow at 4:30 p.m.," Carlotta replies. "Uncle Luca and his girlfriend are going away the day after tomorrow and she wants to introduce you to the girls before they leave. Your father will pick you up at 5 p.m., tomorrow. You are going to have dinner at your cousin's house and stay there overnight."

"And what are you going to do tomorrow night?" he asks his mother.

"I will stay here. We are having Roberto and his family over for Christmas Day dinner."

Enrico's phone pings, alerting him that a text message has arrived. He reads it and types a message back to his cousin Stefano. He looks at his mother and smiles.

"You look like the cat that swallowed the canary," she says. "What is going on?"

Enrico breaks into laughter. "I told Stefano about the twins in New York and he is so curious what they look like. He also wants to go to New York now."

"Oh dear," Carlotta says, "I can see this is going to be a big thing."

"Yeah, and he hasn't even seen a photo of them yet. Can you imagine what he is going to say when he sees how hot they look?"

"OK, hotshot, let's get ready for dinner now," she responds. "I guess I have to get used to my son growing up fast."

Carlotta looks at her son wondering what the future will bring for him. She has realized some time ago that he has an edge and it scares her a little. Somehow he reminds her of Roberto as a 17 year old. She always hoped that Enrico would grow up to be like Luca. That's why she chose her brother as his godfather. Luca is a great mentor and spent a lot of time with Enrico after her divorce. Hopefully, he will still have some time for Enrico going forward now that he is in a relationship with Kataryna. Actually both would be a good influence on her son, she decides, personally and professionally.

Valentina and Riccardo Romano are already sitting at the dining table when Carlotta and Enrico walk in.

"This will be an unusually quiet Christmas Eve dinner with almost everyone in New York," Riccardo states, "but we will make the best of it and next year I am hoping that we will have everyone over here again."

After dinner the family exchanges gifts and they discuss arranging a welcome party for Kataryna when she moves to Italy.

"I can't tell you how happy I am for Luca," Valentina says, "but I am a little worried about you Carlotta. I hope you will meet a suitable man soon and also be happy."

"Mamma, this is nothing that one can just make happen. But I can assure you that I am willing and ready to do something about it."

"What are your plans for New Year's Eve?" Carlotta's father asks.

"I have a couple of invitations. I haven't decided yet which one to accept."

Carlotta starts yawning. "I think I am ready to go to bed. Tomorrow is another day."

"I am also getting tired," her mother admits. "Let's call it a night. Buon Natale."

Enrico is up early the next morning, all excited about the upcoming video call. He looks at his clothes to decide what to wear. His cousin Stefano and him had been text messaging until late at night, mostly about the New York girls and Enrico's trip to New York in March. They were coming up with all kinds of scenarios.

"Breakfast is served," Valentina Romano tells her daughter and her grandson.

The new iPhone, Enrico got for Christmas, starts ringing. He looks at the caller ID and starts cracking up.

"Seriously?" he says out loud, accepting the call. "What do you want already that early in the morning?" he asks the caller.

"I just wanted to wish you a Merry Christmas," Stefano responds laughing.

"Sure. I got to hang up, we are having breakfast now," he explains. "I'll see you later, remember my dad and I are coming over to your house for dinner. We can talk then."

At 3 p.m., Roberto, his parents and Verena arrive at the Romano villa.

Riccardo Romano sets up his large screen video conference monitor for the call with New York in his home office.

"We are ready to go," he says, "how about you Enrico?"

"I will be right there grandpa," he responds.

"Ooh, this is so exciting," Carlotta says, "I can't wait to meet the twins."

"What is all the excitement about and who are the twins?" Roberto inquires.

"We are setting up a video call with New York. Kataryna is going to introduce her nieces, who are twins, to Enrico, so they can get to know each other before we go to New York in March," Carlotta answers him.

"When is that going to happen?"

"In a few minutes. Let's all go to my father's office so we can be ready when they call in."

The idea of seeing Kataryna with Luca in New York doesn't sit well with Roberto. He can already feel his chest tightening up.

"You go ahead," he says, "I may peek in later."

"I want to meet the twins, too," Verena says heading towards the home office.

Valentina Romano hands Roberto and his parents a glass of Champagne.

"I am so happy that you are joining us today. It is really quiet here without Luca, Patrizia and Francesco," she states.

"Buon Natale. Thank you for inviting us all." Roberto raises his glass.

The video system sounds an alert that a call is coming in. Riccardo pushes the accept button. Kataryna, sitting in the middle between Natasha and Sabrina, comes on. Behind her Luca and Aleksandra start waving at the Romano family.

"Hello everyone," Kataryna greets them. "May I introduce you to my nieces Natasha and Sabrina." She points to them. The girls wave hello to everyone.

"Behind me is their mother, my sister Aleksandra, and the man next to her I don't think I have to introduce," she giggles.

Carlotta starts talking first. "Hello Aleksandra, it's great to meet you. We understand you are a fabulous cook. We can't have enough of those in the family."

"Hi Carlotta, great to meet you, too. I had the pleasure of cooking for your brother, your sister and Francesco yesterday."

"As promised Enrico, here are the twins." Kataryna starts a new conversation. "Maybe you guys can talk a little and get to know each other. Meanwhile, Patrizia and Francesco should arrive here. They are getting packed because they are moving in here tomorrow when Luca and I are leaving for Hawaii. We all will have an extended Christmas Day brunch over here after the video call."

"Hi Natasha and Sabrina," Enrico greets them with a cool hand gesture, "who is who?"

"I am Natasha," the twin with the blue top says. "And I am Sabrina," the other one adds.

"You can easily tell us apart because I am the good-looking one," Natasha injects quickly making everyone laugh.

"Yeah, you are the good-looking one, when I am not around," Sabrina counters making a cute face at her sister.

"Whoa," Kataryna says laughing, getting up from her seat. "I am getting out of the firing line and moving into a more friendly territory."

She stands next to Luca and hugs him. He puts his arms around her. "I will protect you, Principessa."

Enrico is amused by the competitive banter on the other side of the ocean. He comes into the conversation again. "So what do you two like to do?"

"We like to go to the movies and hang out with friends. In the summer we play tennis and go swimming."

"How about you?"

"Pretty much the same. I also play soccer occasionally and I am learning to play golf, but that takes so much time so I am not really good at it yet."

"Cool," the twins respond. "Are you on Facebook?"

"I am on several social media sites. We can connect that way, too, if you want, but I am not spending a whole lot of time on that."

"We'll send you an email later on so we can stay in touch until you come to New York."

"Sounds good. I am looking forward to New York. Have you two been to Italy yet?"

"Yes, but we hardly remember anything. Our parents took a trip with us through a couple of European cities when we were about 11. One of the cities we went to was Rome, but that was so long ago. We have never been to Milan."

"I am sure you will visit your aunt once she is over here. I can show you around in Milano then."

"Yes, of course, we are planning on visiting her in Italy. That's so cool that she is moving over there for a while. But we will miss her over here."

"You are so sweet," Kataryna jumps in, "but don't worry, we will see each other a lot."

As she looks back onto the screen she is surprised to see Verena standing in the back.

"Hello Verena, how are you doing?" she greets her. "Are you staying with your grandparents for Christmas?"

"Yes, my dad and I came up yesterday. We are having dinner here tonight and tomorrow we will go back to Milano."

Kataryna realizes that Roberto is also at the Romano's villa. *Good,* she thinks, *he is spending Christmas with Carlotta and is probably purposely staying away from this video call. That could be a positive sign.*

Kataryna's intercom buzzer comes on. Luca goes to answer it. "Patrizia and Francesco have arrived," he yells into the room. He waits at the door to greet them once they come up with the elevator. Kataryna is still busy with her nieces and Enrico, when she spots Roberto coming into the room standing next to his daughter behind Enrico.

"Hello Roberto, Merry Christmas," she says in a somber tone seeing his strained face.

"Merry Christmas," he replies, giving her a kind of sad smile. "Good to see you. These lovely young ladies must be your nieces."

"Yes, they are Natasha and Sabrina. And the lovely lady next to me is my sister Aleksandra, their mother."

Aleksandra and the twins wave hello to Roberto, who stands there staring at Kataryna.

Patrizia and Francesco, who just entered the apartment, walk up to the monitor.

"Buon Natale. We are having a great time here with Kataryna and her family. Carlotta and Enrico, you will love it here when you come over in March."

Verena looks at her father pouting. "I want to go, too. Maybe I can join Carlotta and Enrico in March."

"Why don't you," her father responds casually.

"Why don't we all go? Roberto, you should come along, too," Carlotta suggests.

Kataryna watches the situation unfolding with suspense. What is he going to do now?

"Thank you for thinking of me, Carlotta but Verena is old enough to go alone."

Carlotta smiles at him. "Yes, she is, but I would like some company. The kids surely don't want to hang around us all the time."

"No, we don't," Enrico immediately jumps in.

"You should join us, papà," Verena says, "the more the merrier. We already planned going together. Why wouldn't you want to come? I think you need some time off anyway. You have been way too stressed lately and are not yourself sometimes. It would do you good to get away occasionally."

"I guess you are overruled, Roberto," Kataryna says laughing. "A change of scenery can't hurt. It may also be necessary and beneficial for business reasons once we get this deal closed."

Roberto smiles at Kataryna running his hands through his hair. *Wow, did she just try to convince me to come to New York? Could it be a sign that she is seeking my company?*

"If you think so Kataryna, I will have to take it under consideration," he responds grinning.

"Thank you Kataryna," Carlotta says, clapping her hands, "you seem to have some influence on Roberto."

Luca, who had been absent getting drinks for everyone, enters the video scene again.

"So what did I miss?" He puts his arms around Kataryna when he spots Roberto.

"Ciao Roberto. Buon Natale," he greets him. "I am glad you are at my parents' house. They complained that it is much too quiet there without us. So I guess you all will have a nice Christmas Day dinner. How are things at the office?"

"Nothing new to report from the office," Roberto answers casually. "The lawyers are producing a lot of paperwork, so I expect to have that on my desk after Christmas and so will you."

"Yeah, my father is handling that while I am away," Luca replies. "I don't want to be disturbed with that on my first vacation with Kataryna. She will have my full attention. We have better things to do in Hawaii than reading emails and legal documentation," he smirks, as if to say, you know what I mean. "If something really important comes up my father will contact me, of course."

Luca's father who has been sitting quietly through the video session nods, "it's you and me for the next few weeks, Roberto. We will handle everything and let Luca and Kataryna enjoy paradise."

Roberto feels a pressure in his chest coming on. *Yeah, sure they will be in paradise while I am in hell,* he thinks. He manages to nod at Riccardo Romano indicating that he understood that they would be working on this together until the beginning of January when Luca returns to Italy.

"OK, let's wrap it up," Kataryna says, "the kids know each other now and can be in touch on their own from here on. Merry Christmas to you all and stay well."

She makes a point of looking at Roberto when she says that. He acknowledges her eye contact with him. An electrifying sensation runs through his body as he gazes directly into her eyes. He wants to jump through the screen and take her far away with him.

Kataryna ends the video call and then hugs Patrizia and Francesco to say hello.

"That was great," Enrico says when the call ends. "The girls are really cool. I am looking forward to spending time with them in March."

"I am so excited about our trip," Carlotta says tugging at Roberto, who seems to be absent-minded and doesn't react.

Carlotta nudges him in his side. "Hey, where have you been?"

Lost for a truthful answer he comes out with, "I am having an out-of-body experience."

Carlotta laughs. "Really? Sounds intriguing. Why don't you take me along on that journey."

The others are laughing now, too. Verena looks at her father sideways. She is not convinced that this was as funny for him as for the others around them. She senses that something is off again with him and vows to get to the bottom of this.

Valentina asks the guests to take their seats at the dinner table. Roberto excuses himself indicating that he is headed for the restroom. Once he closes the door he bangs his head against the wall and then takes out the pills, which will relieve his tension soon. He stares into the mirror. *Where do I go from here,* he asks himself? Something's got to give. He closes his eyes and relives Kataryna in the video call asking him to come to New York with the others. He wants to focus on that positive thought rather than imagining her and Luca in paradise.

With the help of the pills, Roberto makes it through dinner and even manages to crack a joke or two occasionally. He learns that Kataryna will be moving to Milan for a while and renting office space in the Romano building. *Well,* he thinks, *the hits just keep on coming. It's about time that I came up with a plan.* He can't wait to be alone again and reflect on his future and talk to Sergio tomorrow to vent.

"Thank you for the lovely dinner," Roberto's father says, patting Riccardo on the shoulder and kissing Valentina on the cheek.

"I'll be in touch regarding the paperwork if there is anything we need to discuss," Roberto says to Riccardo, as they are heading to the front door.

He turns to Carlotta and kisses her on the cheek. "Have a good night, I'll call you in the next few days."

"I hope you do," she whispers in his ear, "so we can talk about New Year's Eve."

"OK, " he utters as he turns away to exit the villa.

Roberto and Verena get into his car. He rubs his eyes and exhales. They drive quietly for a while. He turns to Verena when they stop at a traffic light. She hasn't said a word since they left the Romano villa.

"Are you crying?" he asks her. "What's wrong?"

"You are asking me what's wrong?" she sobs. "What's wrong with you? Are you terminally ill?"

"What makes you think that?" Roberto asks concerned. "No, I am not terminally ill."

"Then please tell me what is going on. I watched you tonight. I know you are not okay. Can we have a drink somewhere and talk?"

Roberto drives to the next bar. "Let's have a drink. I will tell you what's going on."

They sit at a secluded table and order their drinks with the waiter attending to them.

"First, you have to promise me that you will not talk to anyone about this, not even your mother. This has to stay between us. There are only two other people who know this, well actually three, if you count the person who this is about. Sergio knows and his father."

She looks at him puzzled. "Dr. de Angelis? So you are sick?"

"No, Verena not in that sense. Please promise me that you will not tell anyone. I think I should be able to trust my daughter."

"I promise, papà. I will not tell anyone. I love you and want to be here for you in whatever way I can."

Roberto is touched by his daughter's concern for him. He is glad that he can talk to her about his pain because he needs a close ally in addition to Sergio.

"I love you, too," he starts, "and I am happy that we are so close despite my divorce from your mother. Here is what's going on. I am in love with a woman who I think may love me, too, but she can't allow herself to have these feelings because she is in another relationship." He pauses and takes a sip of his drink.

"When and how did you meet her?" Verena asks astonished, but relieved that he is not ill.

Roberto thinks before he answers her. "About a month ago at a business meeting."

"OK, and then what happened?"

"I had dinner with her one evening and told her that I am in love with her. That's when she explained that she is in a relationship, a fairly new one, and that won't allow her to have these kind of feelings for me."

"What's so special about her that you can't move on and forget her? As far as I know almost every woman you meet is after you, which is understandable with your great looks, position and standing in the business world."

Roberto has to chuckle for a moment. "Thank you for thinking I am so good-looking."

"Actually, papà, you are super hot looking. Even some of my girlfriends have told me how attractive they think you are. So why are you so stuck on this woman who can't return your love?"

"I don't know how to explain it other than she is everything I always wanted and more."

"Wow, that is a pretty strong statement. She must be very attractive. You said you met her at a business meeting. What kind of business is she in?"

"She is in finance and yes, she is very attractive but that's not all. Since I met her I haven't been the same. I can't eat, I can't sleep and I am highly agitated. This is where Dr. de Angelis comes in. I am on anti-anxiety medication to be able to relax. I had several anxiety attacks, but I didn't know what it was. I thought I was having a heart attack. It is a terrible tight feeling in my chest, which is not only scary but also quite painful. Dr. de Angelis said that anxiety attacks, if not treated, could turn into a real illness."

"Oh my God, papà. That's horrible. Is this medication supposed to help you get over her?"

"No, it won't be able to do that. It can only relieve the anxiety symptoms. The rest I would have to take care of by moving on, but I can't get over her. That's why I have been drinking quite a bit of alcohol lately to numb the pain, to be able to sleep and to be free for a little while from this torment."

"You have to try to move on, if she is not willing to leave her existing relationship."

"Well, this is what drives me so crazy. Her relationship with this other man started only a few hours after I met her first. Had I not let her leave with that man, I could be the man she would be in a relationship with now. I just can't get over that my life is in shambles because of a missed opportunity. I am looking for a way to turn this around before she gets deeper into this relationship. You know what they say-- all is fair in love and war."

"Sure papà, go for it, you have to do what you have to do to achieve your happiness. Let me know how I can help."

"Thank you for your support. That's very sweet of you, but I don't think there is anything you can do."

"I have an idea. Maybe we can hire a private detective who can check out what is going on with this relationship."

"That won't be necessary. I know exactly what is going on in that relationship."

"Well, I would really love to meet the woman who has dominated your thoughts and turned your world upside down."

"You have met her already, Verena."

Verena looks at her father puzzled, and then it hits her. "Is it Kataryna Taylor, Luca's girlfriend?"

He nods silently and sadness comes over him. "Yes, Kataryna is the object of my passion."

"That changes everything, papà. Let's go through this in more detail. Maybe I can give you my perspective as a woman then."

"If I could only get her away from Luca long enough for her to admit that she has feelings for me, too. But I know that will be next to impossible. He is around her all the time and once she moves to Italy and lives with him, I may never have a chance to get her away from him. You heard that she will even rent space in the Romano office building."

"When is that going to happen?"

"I am not sure. I think sometime around February. She is coming over for the Carnevale in Venezia and wants to make the move to Italy at the same time."

"How about you and I go to New York after Luca is back here?" Verena suggests.

"That would be difficult to pull off," Roberto counters. "How would I justify going away in the middle of the closing of the divestiture? In addition, if I would show up unannounced in New York, it might scare her. She would call Luca and all hell would break loose. No, I have to come up with something better."

"Yeah, you are right," Verena admits. "Are you going to the Carnevale in Venezia, too?"

"Yes, I got tickets for Il Ballo del Doge. I will probably go with Carlotta. While we are on the subject, there is something else you should know."

Verena looks at her father with wide eyes. "What else?"

"Carlotta is in love with me. She seduced me the other night and wants to have a deeper relationship."

"No way," Verena shouts out, "why did you let her seduce you when you are in love with Kataryna? She is Luca's sister."

"It's a long story. Suffice to say that I was under the influence of a lot of alcohol that night because I wanted to numb myself. She totally overpowered me. It went so fast. I didn't even realize what was happening until it was over."

"What are you going to do about it going forward?"

"I told her that I don't want to go public with this. Meanwhile, I have to figure something out."

"I suppose you know that if you succeed to get Kataryna away from Luca and at the same time break Carlotta's heart, it would be the end of your friendship with the Romano family."

"Yes, I am acutely aware of that but my love for Kataryna is stronger than preserving my friendship with the Romano family."

"Needless to say, you could no longer stay in the CEO position at NatMedica either. The question is would the Romano family still go forward with the sale of the company to Kataryna?"

"Probably not, unless we kept our relationship a secret until after the closing, in which case I would stay on as CEO, as well, and Kataryna and her partner would become my boss."

"Looks like you have a plan," Verena says, smiling deviously. "By the way, I would love to have her as my stepmother. She is really something special. I need a mentor like her so I can get my act together professionally."

Roberto looks approvingly at his daughter. "I am glad we had this talk. I feel so much better now that I have you as my confidante."

SEVENTEEN

Kataryna and Aleksandra start preparing the Christmas Day brunch in the kitchen while Luca, Patrizia and Francesco are talking to the twins in the living room.

"Have you heard anything from the lawyer yet regarding the search for our brother?" Aleksandra whispers.

"No, nothing yet. I am going to send him an email in the next few days to see if he has anything encouraging to report."

"I have to say there is a lot of excitement in our family all of a sudden brought on by your relationship with Luca. He is such a great guy and because of that my daughters are making new friends in Italy, too. Not to forget your acquisition deal. And who knows, maybe we will find our brother soon."

"I know. Although there is a little bit of a cloud hanging over this," Kataryna reveals.

"What cloud could there possibly be?" Aleksandra enquires. "You are on a roll here, sis."

Kataryna tells her sister briefly about Roberto and his infatuation with her.

"Are you talking about the Roberto who was in the video call earlier?"

"Yes, that's him. I feel so terrible about him having such a hard time letting go of this idea with me. I don't want him to suffer like that. I wish he would snap out of it."

"Well, he is a good-looking and intriguing man. I could also see you with him if Luca didn't exist, of course. I am sure he will get over it soon. He is probably too proud to just give up like that."

"From your mouth to God's ears," Kataryna responds. "I am concerned about his anxiety attacks. He is on anti-anxiety medication because of me. There is much more to the story but I can't get into details now. Just one more tidbit; Luca's sister Carlotta is in love with him."

"Oh, my goodness," Aleksandra calls out, "could this get any more complicated?"

"Hi," Luca comes into the kitchen smiling. "What's going on in here? Do you ladies need some help?"

"No, thank you. We are ready to serve the food," Aleksandra replies as the intercom buzzes.

"And just in time for your husband to arrive," Kataryna laughs.

"Yeah, somehow that man has a sixth sense when it comes to food being served."

"In that case he is fortunate that you are his wife," Luca comments.

As Brian enters the apartment the twins are running towards him. "Daddy, we had a video call with Italy. We met Enrico and his mother. It was so much fun."

"Good, I am glad you two had fun," their father responds as he heads towards the others to say hello.

After the lavish brunch everyone is sitting around the fireplace enjoying the beautiful Christmas Day. It is late afternoon and dusk is setting in.

"It is getting late. Are you packed yet?" Aleksandra looks at her sister.

"Yeah, pretty much, and then there are always the famous shops at Wailea," Kataryna says. "You know I never leave Hawaii without some serious shopping. Remember last time we were in Maui together, I spent a fortune on the fabulous and unique jewelry they have over there?"

"Oh, yes," Aleksandra recalls cheerily, "how can I forget the bird of paradise necklace and earrings you bought over there."

Kataryna shows Patrizia and Francesco around the apartment again so they can feel at home while she and Luca are in Hawaii.

"Thank you so much for letting us stay in your fabulous apartment," Francesco expresses his appreciation. "We will enjoy the spectacular view of the city."

Aleksandra comes up with an idea for Patrizia and Francesco.

"How about we have lunch at the restaurant by the ice-skating rink at Rockefeller Plaza tomorrow? You can see the Christmas tree close up and Natasha and Sabrina can do some ice-skating before lunch."

"Hey Patrizia, do you want to join the girls ice-skating?" Francesco asks his fiancé.

Patrizia chuckles. "I wouldn't dare. I haven't been on ice-skates for a long time and I want to enjoy New York without broken bones, but I would love to go to the restaurant and watch the girls skate."

"Great, then let's do that. Why don't you come to our place after breakfast with your luggage and we will go to Rockefeller Plaza from here? After lunch, we'll take you to Kataryna's place. Brian can join us for lunch, too. He works in one of the buildings around Rockefeller Plaza."

"Perfect. I am looking very much forward to that," Patrizia says. "We can make some videos of the girls ice-skating and of us with the beautiful Christmas tree and then send the video to Carlotta and Enrico."

Once everyone is gone, Kataryna and Luca sit by the fireplace with a drink and relax. Luca smiles to himself.

"What are you smiling about?" Kataryna asks him.

"I am just so happy I can't stop smiling," he responds, pulling her closer to him.

"If this is a dream I don't ever want to wake up," Kataryna whispers, kissing him.

"Neither do I, and tomorrow we will be in paradise."

"Yes, we will, in every way."

After a 13-hour flight the Romano corporate jet lands safely at Kahului, Maui airport around 4 p.m., Hawaiian time. Luca and Kataryna had changed into light clothing before landing. The temperature is 78 Fahrenheit and a light trade wind is blowing as they are leaving the airport in their Mercedes SL Roadster rental car. The air is filled with the beautiful scents of plumerias, gardenias and tuberoses. Kataryna breathes in the heavenly scent and the warm air. She immediately feels the calming effect the Hawaiian Islands always have on her. The beauty of the scenery stuns Luca as they drive into the Wailea area heading to the luxury villa on the beach they rented.

"Wow, Principessa, this really is paradise," Luca exclaims excitedly. "What a beautiful place, the scent of the flowers and you next to me. We must have done something right that we are given this amazing life."

"Yes, I keep on asking myself why I deserve all this."

"That's easy, because you are an angel."

"I wouldn't go that far," Kataryna says quietly, enjoying the view of the ocean.

"You are my angel," he says, "you came into my life when I needed you most."

They enter the driveway of the stunning beachfront villa where the rental agent, who hands them the key to the villa, meets them. The place is tastefully furnished with contemporary pieces and has everything anyone can want. The view is spectacular and opens up to the beach, with a marvelous swimming pool and hot tub right in front of it. Adjacent to the pool is an outdoor in-ground fireplace.

"This is going to be an amazing week," Luca marvels, taking in the view of the magnificent Pacific Ocean.

"Yes. Get ready for the magic of Hawaii. It will be an unforgettable experience," Kataryna promises. "Let's have an early dinner and get some rest. We will start with something easy tomorrow. First, we will have a nice long breakfast on the terrace and then drive around looking at some sights. In the afternoon I suggest we lie in the sun a bit and enjoy our fabulous secluded pool. Then we definitely have to stop by the fabulous Na Hoku jewelry store. I would like to get a gift for your mother, Carlotta and Patrizia and have a look at some of their exquisite pieces for myself. I cannot leave Maui without stopping by there. And after dinner, well, the sky is the limit."

"Excellent," Luca replies smiling, "you got it all figured out. I will let you guide me through paradise."

Kataryna wakes up refreshed the next morning and excited about her plan for the evening. She gets their breakfast ready and serves it on the terrace. *Oh what a view*, she sighs. *I could get lost in that ocean.*

A few minutes later Luca steps out on the terrace.

"Wow, what a view," he exclaims. "Just the right wake-up call."

"Isn't it? I was just thinking the same thing looking at the ocean in front of us."

"I was actually talking about you in that swim suit," he whispers in her ear, "but the ocean is nice, too."

"Gee, we haven't even had breakfast yet and you are starting already with the sexy stuff. However, my darling, you will have to wait until tonight for that."

"Really? Why?" he asks smiling broadly. "I don't know if I can wait that long."

"Because I have something super special planned and I want you really excited for that. You will be glad we waited."

"Sounds extremely interesting. I can't wait for the evening to come."

Kataryna smiles at him impishly and puts a piece of papaya in his mouth. "Let's eat, Prince Charming, before we get any ideas."

After breakfast and a swim in the pool, which of course doesn't end without some kissing and touching, the two take off to do some sightseeing. First they drive down the coast towards Makena, which again presents spectacular views of the Pacific Ocean and breathtaking villas along the beach. Luca takes a series of photos of the views and of Kataryna in front of the ocean with his iPhone and emails them to his family. Leaving Makena, they continue their drive through the town of Kihei and then swing over to the other side of the island to visit Lahaina and the Whaler's Village in Kaanapali, where they decide to have a casual lunch in one of the restaurants on the beach. After lunch they do some shopping in the Whaler's Village stores. On the way back to Wailea, they stop at the amazing scenic points to take more photos.

"You are right, Principessa, Hawaii is a magical place," Luca admits as they head home to get changed for their evening out.

"I was sure you would like it, but you haven't even seen that much yet. There is so much more to visit in the next few days. I suggest that we get our sightseeing out of the way and the last two days or so we relax by the pool and do whatever," Kataryna says.

"The pool sounds good but the 'doing whatever' has me even more intrigued," Luca declares.

Kataryna grins broadly. "You are really turning on the heat today, my dear. Are you hoping to get attacked in the car again like at Lake Como?"

"Oh no, don't even think about it. We are in a convertible."

"Okay then, take it down a notch, otherwise I will turn into a mountain lion and eat you alive."

"I will not say another word," Luca says laughing. "It is just so relaxing to be on vacation and have nothing to worry about, other than having as much fun as possible with you. So I am a little giddy. It is really intoxicating. I feel like I am on some kind of get-happy drug, but it is a natural high."

"I am always on a natural high when I am in Hawaii," Kataryna responds, "so I know exactly how you feel."

After returning to their beachfront villa, they relax by the pool and then get ready to go out for dinner. Kataryna goes to one of the bedrooms to check if her delivery had arrived. Yes, wonderful, everything is there like she ordered. She goes back to the master bedroom to get dressed in her short turquoise dress and matching shoes. It is a beautiful dress with a low-cut neckline and slits on each side revealing a lot of leg. Luca emerges from the bathroom freshly showered.

"Wow, I am glad I am coming home with you tonight," he sighs, looking at her in that dress.

"First of all you are going out to dinner with me tonight," Kataryna counters, "and then we will see what happens next. Don't get too focused on taking this dress off me tonight. I may have other plans."

"The suspense is killing me," he whispers in her ear, running his lips down her neck.

"Just hope and pray that the excitement later on is not killing you," she whispers, stepping away from him to avoid getting further excited by him.

Luca shows up dressed in dark blue silk pants and a tan-colored shirt, looking fabulous against his skin and dark hair. Kataryna nods approvingly. "You clean up pretty nice," she jokes, "and you smell good, too."

She breathes in his cologne. "Let's leave quickly. This is getting way too tempting."

The valet attendant at Gannon's greets them with "Aloha and welcome," and then drives off to park the Mercedes. An amazing view awaits them as they are seated on the terrace overlooking the Pacific Ocean.

"This is breathtaking, Principessa," Luca murmurs.

"Are you talking about me or the ocean?" Kataryna kids him.

He smiles and kisses her on the cheek. "Both, of course."

The waiter brings their food selections, which are delicious and together with the amazing view make this an enchanting evening for the two. One of the friendly staff takes a photo of them, which comes out perfect against the backdrop of the ocean and the beautiful sunset. Luca emails the photo to his sisters with a short message: Greetings from Paradise. I couldn't be happier!

Carlotta emails him back instantly: You two look fabulous and that sunset, wow.

"So you want to get a drink somewhere else or go back to the villa?" Kataryna asks Luca as they are getting into the car.

He leans over to her. "I think we need some alone time now. I can't wait for the exciting evening you promised me to start."

"As you wish, darling, the villa it is," Kataryna murmurs, mentally preparing for the big surprise she has in store for Luca. She starts to crack up imagining his reaction when she delivers the surprise.

"What is going on with you?" Her infectious laughter makes him laugh, too. "You must really have something big up your sleeve."

They laugh for the rest of the short drive to their villa. Once inside, Kataryna asks Luca to make a refreshing drink for them and bring it to the terrace by the pool. She disappears into one of the guest bedrooms, changes into her special outfit and exits from there to the terrace, where she lights the outdoors fireplace by the pool and turns on her iPod to the song "Paradiso" by Ross Couch.

Luca arrives on the terrace with their drinks and stops in his tracks as he sees Kataryna in a super sexy Hawaiian hula outfit, with just several layers of flower leis covering her breasts, and a very short skirt ripped in the style of a hula skirt. A flower lei decorates her hair. She starts dancing seductively with improvised hula dance moves in front of the fire.

"Hello. I am Princess Kailani. I will be entertaining you tonight. Come and sit down here to watch the show and bring me my drink," she tells him in a sexy voice batting her eyelashes.

She sways her hips to the music and the sexy skirt moves sideways revealing her thighs and buttocks while the flame from the fireplace flickers in front of her. Luca takes a sip of his drink watching her seductive hula dance. He is so mesmerized by her with emotions ranging from love to lust. She dances over to him to get her drink and takes a sip while continuing her enticing Hawaiian dance.

"You are so quiet my prince," she whispers, "are you not pleased with my fire dance performance?"

"You rendered me speechless," he murmurs. "I don't want to spoil this beautiful sight and moment with idle chatter. Please don't stop dancing."

"Would you like to dance with your Princess?" she dares him, extending her hand to him.

Luca gets up slowly embracing her. Kataryna takes off his shirt while kissing his neck and chest softly. He feels the coolness of the leis against his skin, an unusual and erotic sensation. The flowers in her hair smell heavenly. Luca can't decide which of the sensations he should focus on as she starts removing his pants and he steps out of them.

"So what would you like Princess Kailani to do to you?" she whispers in his ear as she maneuvers him towards the hot tub in front of the fireplace.

"If you do anymore I am going to go insane with desire," he breathes into her ear.

"I don't want this to end yet," she coaxes him, "so try to hold out a little longer."

He takes a deep breath. "The key word is little here."

Kataryna takes his hand and they step into the hot tub. Luca sits down holding her tightly against his chest, kissing the top of her head. She wraps her legs around him and starts moving in rhythm to the erotic music playing.

"Can we take off your underwear because I am going to die here any moment?" he murmurs in her ear.

"We could," she replies sweetly, "if I was wearing any."

Luca grabs her and pulls her closer just in time to enter her and make them both erupt like a Hawaiian volcano seconds later.

After quiet moments of caressing, Luca makes a request. "I would like another date with Princess Kailani before we leave Hawaii," he whispers, "she really got to me. Actually I want to take her home with me."

"I'll be sure to tell her," Kataryna promises. "As far as I know she will definitely go home with you."

"Good morning, my beautiful Princess Kailani," Luca greets Kataryna as they wake up together with the flower leis between them, still smelling heavenly. Luca picks up one of the leis and inhales the scent of the flowers.

"That aroma brings back unforgettable memories of last night."

She kisses him. "It sure does, my handsome prince. Didn't I tell you that the Hawaiian experience is magical?"

"Yeah, but I had no idea how magical it would be. So tonight it will be my turn to create a magical night," Luca promises. "I just hope I can blow you away like you did me last night."

"I have faith that you will," Kataryna assures him. "But now we have to rise and shine because we have a date with Haleakala National Park, another Hawaiian phenomenon, which will amaze you. Up there you are actually standing above the clouds and looking down at them. It is such an unusual sight. I can't wait for you to see this. We can say we were on Cloud Nine."

"I am on Cloud Nine every day I spend with you," he responds.

Up in Haleakala National Park Luca takes photos of the clouds beneath them. He asks one of the other tourists to take a photo of them together and then prepares an email to his entire family attaching their photo with a message: Kataryna and Luca on Cloud Nine. A Must-See!

When they return to the villa late afternoon they relax by the pool again and go over the plans for the next few days. Luca reads a couple of emails his sisters sent him earlier. Everyone is in awe of the beautiful photos he has been emailing.

For their evening out Kataryna is going to wear her Hawaiian-print black with pink flowers dress, which has an intriguing low cut crisscross neckline. Another stunner Luca tells her.

"So, where are you taking me for our magical evening?" she asks him curiously.

"You will know as soon as we get there," he teases her. "This is my evening to surprise you."

They pull into the driveway of one of Wailea's luxury hotels. The valet attendant rushes to the car and opens the doors for them with the typical "Aloha" greeting. They take the elevator to the hotel's top floor.

"I am impressed," Kataryna marvels when they enter the restaurant, "this is truly magical. I have never been to this restaurant before."

"See, I can also come up with surprises," Luca states proudly.

"How did you know this restaurant?"

"I asked a family friend who has been here recently. He highly recommended it."

"Well, for your efforts you definitely deserve another heavenly night," she giggles.

"Let's see what this night brings," he says fidgeting.

Kataryna looks at him. *He is so cute, getting a little nervous to make sure I like the evening he planned,* she thinks as the hostess seats them at their table.

"The best seat in the house," she giggles, winking at Luca. "My name is Lokelani. Please let me know if there is anything I can do to make your evening perfect," she offers.

"Thank you Lokelani," Luca responds grinning, "we are fine for now."

"I think Lokelani was flirting with you," Kataryna tells Luca. "I can't blame her."

Luca shakes his head smiling. "You have a vivid imagination. Lokelani was the person on the phone I made the arrangements with and I was very specific what I wanted. By the way, there is only one woman I want to be flirting with and I am looking at her."

He raises his glass of Champagne. "Here is to another magical evening. Hopefully also one we won't forget for the rest of our lives."

While having their appetizers they are chitchatting. During the fabulous main course they even talk a little bit of business regarding NatMedica. The waiter brings the dessert menu and a bottle of Dom Perignon Champagne.

"Gee, darling," Kataryna says, "are we having more expensive Champagne?"

"Why not? We deserve it and it is a special night."

"If you say so," Kataryna raises the glass, "thank you for the wonderful evening. You really know how to make me feel special."

He smiles nervously. "The evening is not over yet. Anyway, we were talking about merger stuff earlier. I wanted to propose another possible merger."

"What else do you have to offer?" Kataryna asks astonished when the waiter appears at their table with a beautifully arranged tray with orchids, candles and a small box. Kataryna looks at the tray wondering why only their table gets this beautiful arrangement. She looks back at Luca.

"How about a merger of you and me," he says taking her hand and placing the small box from the tray in it.

Kataryna opens the box, which holds a stunning diamond engagement ring. The inside lining of the box is engraved with her name and the words "Will you marry me?" in Italian, German and English. She is speechless and stares at the ring for a few moments and then at Luca.

"I am not a big fan of marriage generally," she says smiling.

Luca stares at her in shock. He didn't expect that kind of a response after all the loving moments they had shared together. He sits there motionless, not knowing what to do or say next. *Did she just turn down my marriage proposal*, is going through his mind? He is hurt inside.

Kataryna gets up and walks over to him whispering in his ear, "but I will make an exception in your case because I love you madly."

Luca gets up relieved but still shaken, takes the ring and puts it on her finger.

"I love you madly, too. You almost had my entire world collapse," he whispers, "please don't ever scare me like this again." He clutches his chest and lets out a deep sigh.

"I am sorry, darling," she says almost in tears, putting her arms around him, realizing how shocked he must have been for a few moments.

"I didn't mean to scare you like that. I just wanted to make a statement how much you mean to me that I will take that step with you. Seriously, you are very good at making me do things I normally would not do and especially not that fast. So that should tell you how special and important you are to me."

"It does now," he responds.

"That ring is absolutely spectacular. I couldn't have picked a better one myself."

Luca smiles happily. "You only deserve the best."

"And with you that is exactly what I am getting," she declares.

"Here's to us," he raises his glass, "and a happy and long life together."

"Not to mention an exciting life," she adds, clinking his glass. "You know, variety is the spice of life."

"Well, in that case our life will be very spicy because you know how to come up with variety, Princess Kailani."

"That's right. I can be quite creative when it comes to you. So, stay tuned for more of that."

"I can't wait to experience what else you come up with."

"Well, for tonight you can make love to your new fiancé on the beach in front of our villa, and then we can watch the stars in the Maui sky."

"Sounds like a fantastic proposition," he says. "On that note I am ready to leave if you are."

"Sure, we can get started on our adventure on the elevator down."

Luca smirks at her. "Please, don't put me into that kind of position in a public place. I would probably die of embarrassment if there are other people in there with us."

Kataryna laughs out loud imagining Luca in an excited state in the elevator. "I will take it under advisement."

"I don't know if I can trust you to play nice in the elevator."

"Wow, Luca, we just got engaged and you don't trust me already. That is a contradiction if ever I have seen one," she continues laughing.

"That's right, because you are a little instigator, which I love in you, but not at my expense in public," he jokes.

"I will be on my best behavior," Kataryna promises with a wicked grin.

"Good girl, but let's limit that to the elevator and then consummate our engagement on our secluded beach," Luca suggests.

On the way out Lokelani, the hostess, hands Luca a CD.

"What did she give you?" Kataryna asks curiously as they are approaching the elevator.

"I had asked Lokelani to have a photographer make a video and take some still photos of our engagement night. So our evening is on this CD now and we can watch our own engagement ceremony whenever we want to. That is why she was winking at me when we arrived to let me know that everything was in place."

"Wow, Luca Romano, you really outdid yourself tonight. What a fabulous idea. I will cherish that CD forever."

"So will I. Except for that one moment where it appeared that you would not accept my proposal and I was in a state of shock for a couple of minutes. I wonder how that comes out on the CD."

Kataryna giggles. "Oh my God, you are right. I hope it doesn't look too bad. Now I could kick myself for doing that to you."

"Don't kick yourself, Principessa. Actually, it had a much bigger impact when you came over and whispered--but in your case I will make an exception because I love you madly--in my ear. The way you came over to me and said that made a huge impression on me and got me excited at the same time. It was much more effective than a simple 'yes' would have been."

"That is exactly the point I was trying to make in that moment. So are you still excited?"

"That question will be answered when we are back at the villa," he murmurs holding her tightly. "Now I have a question for you. Do you still love me madly?"

"Hmm. How madly I will show you when we are back at the villa."

Lying in each other arms on the beach after the consummation of their engagement they watch the stars, which light up the sky. Kataryna has just the right song for that moment on her iPhone, which she puts on.

"How is that you always have the right song for every occasion?" Luca asks.

Kataryna looks at him charmed. "I guess I am creative and multi-talented."

"Yes, I can vouch for that, my love. You are very creative," Luca agrees, "so what's the plan for tomorrow?"

"Depends on when tomorrow," she says coquettishly, "day or night?"

"Let's start with the day. Do we have any excursions planned?"

"I have two suggestions. Either we go whale watching here in Maui or take a helicopter flight over to the Big Island looking at Mt. Kilauea, one of the volcanoes."

"Hmm, both sound great," Luca thinks out loud. "Let's do the whale watching tomorrow and then the day after the volcano tour."

"Good choice," Kataryna praises him, playing with his hair. "In the evening we will have a private chef come over and cook for us here in the villa and enjoy this fabulous place."

"I love the way you think," he compliments her, "just one request."

"Name it," she says.

"Can we invite Princess Kailani for after-dinner drinks?"

Kataryna starts cracking up. "Wow, the Princess really got to you. Should I be jealous?"

"Never." He kisses her.

"I have something interesting to tell you tomorrow when we have our private dinner here," Kataryna reveals.

"Is this the beginning of some erotic game you are putting on for tomorrow?" Luca grins.

"No, absolutely not. I am serious, there is something I am working on that I want you to know about."

"Another deal?" he inquires.

"No, it's something personal, but a bit on the dramatic side. Well, let's go to sleep now. We have to get up really early tomorrow for the whale watching tour."

After breakfast the two take off for their tour. Luca is amazed by the humpback whales and takes plenty of photos again. Kataryna is happy that Luca is having such a good time. When they get back to their villa late afternoon, they take a swim in the ocean.

At 6 p.m., the private chef arrives and starts preparing their seafood dinner. Kataryna chose to wear a sexy gold-colored bikini with a short see-through cover up over it, but revealing enough for Luca to make a comment how he can't wait until later when the cover up comes off.

She put her hair in a side swept ponytail and pinned an orchid on one side of her hair. Luca touches her face and smiles at her admiringly.

"You look so beautiful, Princess," he says, hugging her. "I love that orchid in your hair. I feel like I am in some kind of fairy tale world."

"It's an edible flower," she whispers in his ear, "you can eat it out of my hair later on."

"That's an offer I can't refuse," he whispers back, "but I am not going to stop there."

"Oh, oh, danger zone," she giggles and frees herself from his embrace. "Keep it cool, darling. We've got a chef in the kitchen. We can't give in to any urges now."

"Oh really?" Luca challenges her. "Then how come you can show up in such an enticing bikini and, to top it all off, tempt me to eat the flower out of your hair?"

"I said later on, meaning for dessert or later," she corrects him sweetly.

"Thank you for clarifying that, Princess. I will try to distract myself until later if you promise not to make any further insinuating remarks. But one even only slightly seductive statement out of your sexy mouth or suggestive body movement and the deal is off. The chef will get a good show and live to tell about it."

Kataryna is laughing so hard she can hardly contain herself and Luca joins her not being able to hold back laughing either.

"You are so much fun," she says, staying away a safe distance from him.

"Yeah, and I love you, too," he reponds still laughing.

At 7:30 p.m., the chef and a helper appear on the terrace with some appetizers, and place them on the table where Kataryna and Luca have taken their seats.

"Please let me know when you would like me to serve the main course," the chef says as he approaches them.

"In about 30 minutes," Luca instructs him, and Kataryna agrees.

They are both impressed with the appetizers. Luca pours the wine and makes a toast, "to us."

"Salute," Kataryna toasts in Italian fashion.

"You mentioned last night that you wanted to tell me something a bit dramatic," he starts a new conversation. "Is this a good time?"

"Yes, I was just going to go into that."

Kataryna tells Luca about her lost brother who was adopted as a baby and whom she never knew because her parents had told her and

Aleksandra that the baby had died. Luca is astounded. He didn't expect anything like that.

"And your lawyer hasn't been able to find a trace yet?" he wonders.

"No, and I haven't spoken to him in a couple of weeks. I will send him an email tomorrow. I am really serious about finding my brother."

"Yes, I can understand that, but let's be careful. How old is he now?"

"He should be around 32 years old."

"I hope he is in a good place and had a good upbringing."

"According to my father a well-off couple adopted him, but he never knew the name of the couple. Apparently they wanted to stay anonymous."

"There must be some official record somewhere," Luca states.

"The lawyer said he will get another attorney on board specializing in these type of cases, but he cautioned me to be patient because this was so long ago."

"And your father just came out with this when you were in Berlin in November?"

"Yes, and we had some emotional moments over this."

"Did he say why, after all this time, he decided to tell you now?"

"He indicated he wanted to get it off his chest just in case something happens to him."

"We will do everything possible to find your brother," Luca assures her.

Kataryna hugs him. "Thank you for supporting me in this. You are a keeper."

The chef approaches them on the terrace to serve their shrimp and lobster dinner. Kataryna takes a bite of her food and looks at the beautiful scenery, as another one of these famous Hawaiian sunsets appears on the horizon.

"We are so lucky to have all this," Kataryna gestures to the magnificent view in front of them.

"This and each other," Luca finishes her sentence. "By the way, we haven't discussed yet when and how to announce our engagement to our families and friends. I was thinking that we announce it officially after the closing of the acquisition deal. What would you say if we had a Valentine's Day party at the Lake Como villa and then make the announcement as a surprise?"

Kataryna likes the idea. "You are good. That sounds like a nice plan. However, that means that we would have a very busy week. We are in Venice from February 7th to the 9th and on the 11th or 12th we scheduled the closing of the NatMedica acquisition. Then on the 14th of February our surprise engagement party. That is a major line-up of events."

"That's OK, thereafter we'll have a relaxing weekend to recover from all that," Luca suggests. "By relaxing I mean just you and me at the villa doing whatever we want to do or doing nothing at all."

Kataryna smirks. "Does the 'nothing at all' include no sex either?"

"Ha-ha," Luca laughs, "of course not. In my mind sex is a relaxing activity."

"Just asking," she clarifies, taking off her cover- up and heading for the pool, swaying her hips in a mock hula dance move. "Would you like to join me in the pool?"

Luca gets up and follows her. "I thought you'd never ask."

"Princess Kailani awaits to feed you dessert."

She elegantly gestures to the orchid in her hair and places another one in her bikini top.

"You can't stand on one leg alone," she giggles as Luca nods approvingly.

"Are there any more orchids hidden somewhere in your swimsuit?" he inquires in a sexy voice.

"Seek and you shall find," she entices him to look for more of the tropical flowers.

The next day Luca and Kataryna take their trip to the Big Island where they board a helicopter for the Mt. Kilauea volcano sightseeing. Another first for Luca watching the crater from the air, which he says is breathtaking. On the way back they pass tropical areas with beautiful waterfalls and land safely again in Hilo. They decide to have an early dinner and then rest up for the next day, which is New Year's Eve.

After a relaxing day and a light lunch at the beach, Kataryna and Luca return to the villa late afternoon and sit by the pool before getting ready for the evening activities. At noontime they had called Luca's family in Italy, where it was midnight, to wish them a Happy New Year. Kataryna called Aleksandra and her family at 6 p.m., as New York City greeted 2013 and Luca called his sister Patrizia right after the call to

Aleksandra. All were in a happy mood, but said they missed Luca and Kataryna. They vowed that they would all ring in the 2013/2014 New Year together.

Kataryna is dressed to kill for their New Year's Eve gala. Her cobalt blue, satin evening gown is artfully embellished, with embroidery, and a beautiful sweeping train perfectly complementing the diamond and sapphire earrings and necklace Luca gave her. Kataryna had the dress custom-designed especially for her by her good friend, emerging fashion designer Chabella. Chabella designed the dress style inspired by the colors and the jewelry Kataryna had shown her. The engagement ring rounds up the perfect look. As usual, the dress shows off all of Kataryna's assets. It is tightly fitted with a low-cut neckline and showing off her tanned legs, looking gorgeous with the high heels she is wearing.

"Wow," Luca says, staring at her proudly, "you'll need a license for that kind of dress. How am I going to make it through the evening? I am getting weak already."

"I suppose we will have our own fireworks once the clock strikes midnight in Maui," Kataryna predicts.

"So help me God," Luca says, laughing taking her in his arms. "Shall we embark on our first New Year's Eve adventure together?"

"Yes, we better go now because I am getting kind of weak myself. You look so great in that elegant black suit, it just turns me on," she whispers in his ear followed by a light kiss on his neck. "All you have to do now is whisper something in Italian into my ear and I am going to surrender right this minute."

"Oh, no, you temptress you had to say that to put more fuel into the fire, didn't you?"

"It was so inviting I couldn't help myself. Honestly, I have no control over what I do when you are near me. I just have to go with what comes naturally."

Luca smiles playfully. "If I would go with what comes naturally now we would be late for our reservation."

"Why don't we table that thought for later and build up the anticipation," she suggests, leading him out the front door.

"Could you be any more eloquent expressing that thought?" Luca compliments her.

As expected, the dining room in one of Wailea's top restaurants is festively decorated, and the live entertainment has started as Luca and Kataryna arrive. They have one of the best tables. Kataryna had made sure of that when she made the reservation months ago. At that time she didn't even know yet that she would spend New Year's Eve with Luca here, but she had been sure that she wanted to be in Hawaii to ring in the

New Year with someone. Luca has ordered a bottle of Roederer Crystal Champagne and Beluga caviar in preparation for the midnight toast. When the entertainers announce the countdown to the New Year the waiter opens the Champagne and pours it into their glasses just in time for the "Happy New Year" and the fireworks over the Pacific Ocean welcoming 2013.

After the New Year's toast they stand tightly embraced on the terrace of the restaurant watching the spectacular fireworks.

"Let me start the New Year by telling you how much I love you," Luca says pulling her closer.

"I love you back and didn't I predict that we would have our own fireworks at midnight," she whispers, "but I was actually thinking of a different kind of fireworks when I said that earlier."

"If we were alone I would make that kind of firework happen right now," Luca whispers, kissing her, "but we will do that later and start the New Year properly our way."

Around 2 a.m., they arrive back at their villa. After changing into more comfortable clothes they take a walk along their secluded beach, enjoying the beautiful early morning hours of January 1 at the Pacific Ocean. Kataryna put on a beach cover-up without anything underneath.

"The New Year starts with my two favorite things, you and a body of water around me," Kataryna proclaims. "I never thought I could be this happy, but it is all falling into place all of a sudden."

"I am also completely taken by this extreme happiness. This better not be a dream."

"It is all very real," she whispers as they lie down on their lounge chair. "Let me prove to you that you are not dreaming."

She takes his hand, putting it under her cover-up and starts caressing his inner thighs with her lips. Luca spins into ecstasy as she slowly continues her way up.

"Now let me show you that you are not dreaming either," he whispers, kissing her navel and moving south.

"I have a beautiful and relaxing day planned for us later on," she says as they are laying in each other's arms winding down from the excitement a couple of minutes ago.

Kataryna wakes up around 10:30 a.m., rested and extremely happy. She looks at the man she loves next to her still sleeping. She gets out of bed to get ready and prepare a nice New Year's day Champagne brunch for them. This is their last day in beautiful Maui and she has planned something special for them.

At 11:30 a.m., Kataryna comes back to the bedroom in a sexy red "Princess Kailani" outfit, this time with maile leave leis around her neck and red flowers in her hair, to wake Luca with a cup of coffee and some tropical fruits.

She softly kisses his cheek and whispers, "Good morning, my love" in his ear, straddling him. Luca wakes up immediately and sees his Princess Kailani sitting on top of him handing him a cup of Kona coffee. He takes a sip of the coffee.

"I never had a more beautiful wake-up call," he murmurs, "you are a true vision Princess Kailani."

He kisses her neck and cleavage inhaling the intoxicating scent of the flowers in her hair, bringing them both dangerously close to arousal again.

"As much as I want to, we can't proceed with that now," she declares in a low voice, "because we will have company not too long from now and I prepared a nice Champagne brunch for us already."

She feeds him a piece of pineapple and papaya and has the same.

"Company?" he asks, "I'd rather spend some time alone with you, especially after that kind of wake-up call."

"The company will only stay an hour or so after which we will be alone and even more ready for the inevitable."

Luca sits up and looks at her puzzled. Kataryna runs her hand through his hair and kisses him lightly on his lips.

"I have ordered a couple's massage from the spa at one of the hotels. They will give us a side-by-side massage out on the terrace after which we will be so relaxed and the rest I leave up to your imagination and strength."

"You are blowing me away again with something so unique and beautiful." He plants kisses all over her face and mouth.

"Must be the power of love," she murmurs, embracing him. "Does that make you want to get up now?"

"How can I resist that charming plan," he says getting up to take a shower.

Kataryna takes their brunch to the terrace meanwhile so they can eat as soon as he gets there. While she is waiting for Luca to join her she sends an email to her German lawyer.

From: Kataryna Taylor
  To: Norbert Bergmann
Subject: My Brother

Hello Mr. Bergmann,

Have there been any new developments in the search for my brother? I haven't heard from you in a while and was wondering what steps you have taken. Please contact me at your earliest co convenience.

Thank you in advance and Happy New Year.

Best regards,
Kataryna Taylor

Luca arrives on the terrace freshly showered as she presses the send button.

"What are you doing, Princess?" he asks. "You are not working, are you?"

"No. I just contacted my lawyer in Berlin to see if he has any update for me on the search for my brother."

"Good," Luca responds, digging into the food in front of him. "Just making sure that you are keeping our agreement not to look at work emails while we are in Hawaii."

"I am fully in compliance with that agreement," Kataryna vows smiling, raising her hand in an "I swear" fashion.

Luca raises his glass of Champagne. "Here is to us not working."

They finish their brunch and head down to the beach to take a walk, anticipating the couple's massage. An hour later the spa staff arrive at their villa and set up the massage tables on the terrace. New Age music plays in the background, as Kataryna and Luca get comfortable on the massage tables.

"I see we have a male and a female massage therapist," Kataryna remarks, "which one do you want to do your Lomi Lomi massage?"

Luca looks at her grinning. "Do you really think I am going to let the male do this kind of massage to you? You are getting the female, Principessa."

"I guess that settles that," Kataryna responds amused, "but make sure that you pay attention to what the therapist is doing so you can give me that kind of massage in the future."

Luca has to laugh. "That's pretty ambitious, but I will do my best to pick up a few pointers."

After an hour and a half the massage therapists finish up their deeply relaxing and therapeutic Hawaiian Lomi Lomi massages.

"That was truly amazing. Thank you for introducing me to this type of massage," Luca says, as they are resting on their lounge chair by the pool just covered with bath towels, "but truth be told I liked the massage you gave me the morning after we spent the first night together in my villa even better."

"Well, my darling, that was a very special and private massage. If you are really good I might do it again one day."

"You have no idea how good I can be," he responds laughing.

"I am so relaxed now and a bit tired," Kataryna says, hardly able to keep her eyes open.

"Me, too," Luca admits.

Putting Kataryna's head on his shoulders and his arms around her they drift off into a deep sleep. Around 4:30 p.m., they wake up energized, aroused and ready for the hot tub to embark on an afternoon of love before their flight back to New York that evening.

At 9 p.m., Luca and Kataryna board the Romano family jet, which arrived in Maui the night before. Kataryna asks the flight attendant to store the flower leis she bought to take back to New York in the refrigerator. While Luca is talking to the pilots in Italian, Kataryna closes her eyes and tries to relive the beautiful time they had here in Maui. She checks her phone while Luca is still chatting in the cockpit and sees an email from her lawyer in Berlin, which must have crossed with the one she sent him. She opens it anxiously.

From: Norbert Bergmann
   To: Kataryna Taylor
Subject: Your Brother
Dear Ms. Taylor,
I apologize for not being in touch earlier, but I am still waiting
for a response from one of my contacts in your personal matter.
I can safely say now that we are on a hot trail. I may have
important relevant information for you soon.
Best regards and Happy New Year,
Norbert Bergmann

Maui Air Traffic Control has cleared their flight for departure, Luca announces as he joins Kataryna getting comfortable in the spacious seats.

"You are in deep thought, Princess," he observes. "What's on your mind?"

"I got an email from my German lawyer. He is on a hot trail regarding my brother, he wrote, but he wants to be 100 percent sure before he will disclose more. I am so excited. This year seems to be starting with a bang on many levels."

"Yeah, you can say that again. But thank God it's all good stuff. Wow, can you believe it? We got engaged, you are moving to Italy, closing the acquisition deal, and on top of it you may soon get to meet the brother you didn't know you had until recently."

"Yes, that is pretty amazing." Kataryna puts her head on Luca' shoulder. He puts his arms around her as the jet takes off into the Maui skies.

"By the way, my love, may I remind you that you are still wearing your engagement ring? If we really want to keep this a secret until February 14, you have to take it off before we get back to your apartment. If Patrizia sees it the cat will be out of the bag, and knowing my little sister this piece of news would be all over Italy the minute we land there the day after tomorrow. She can't keep anything in."

"OK, darling, please remind me again when we have landed. For now I want to keep it on my finger. It makes me feel closer to you if that is even possible."

"Nicely said, Principessa, I feel the same way. I am kind of torn about waiting until February 14."

"Me, too, but let's wait. It will be so nice for everyone experiencing our engagement ceremony when you put this ring on my finger. I can't wait to see their faces when we pull that one off."

"As usual, you are right. It will be worth it and it is only about six weeks from now. Meanwhile, you and I know that we are engaged heading for the best merger I have ever been involved in."

Kataryna smiles at him. "You are so cute. I am really glad that fate brought us together."

"Yes, that company has been very good to me. First, it is extremely profitable, and then it brought us together because I have to divest it."

After a 13-hour flight the jet lands safely in New York. The two have been sleeping on the plane and are rested when they arrive at

Kataryna's apartment on January 2. An entire welcoming committee awaits them when they open the door. Francesco and Aleksandra prepared a delicious welcome dinner for them.

"Wow, what a great surprise," Kataryna yells out, hugging her sister and the twins.

"We hope you are not too tired for this," Patrizia says, "but we figured we had to do something for dinner, so Francesco and Aleksandra decided to cook for us."

"We are happy to see you all," Luca jumps in, "this way we can spend a cozy farewell dinner together."

Kataryna hands the twins the swimwear she bought for them in Hawaii and then gets out the beautiful flower leis and puts them around the others' necks. The aroma of the fresh flower leis fills the room. She glances at Luca, who gives her a mischievous smile when she puts one of the leis around her own neck.

"Listen to this," Kataryna starts telling the others. "Luca fell in love with another woman in Hawaii and asked her to come home with him."

They all look at her puzzled. Luca gets out his phone to show them the photos of Kataryna's "Princess Kailani" dress up.

"Here she is," he says, "now wouldn't you want to take that heavenly creature home with you?"

"Wow, Kataryna, that is so beautiful," Patrizia compliments her. "I can see you two had a really good time in Maui."

"Yes, we did," Luca responds elated. "You have got to go there. It is an amazing experience, especially when you have your own Princess Kailani doing a fire dance for you."

"OK guys, let's eat before you go overboard with that conversation." Aleksandra orders them to the dining table.

"Just reminiscing," Luca murmurs as Kataryna gives him a certain look recalling that night

After Aleksandra and her family leave, Luca, Kataryna, Patrizia and Francesco sit by the fireplace with an after-dinner drink, sharing their vacation experiences and then retire to their bedrooms.

"I can't believe I have to leave you here tomorrow," Luca says with a sad face.

Kataryna sighs. "Yes, it will be tough not to have you around, but there is a light at the end of the tunnel. In about four weeks I will be with you again in Italy."

She heads towards the bedroom door.

"Where are you going?" he asks.

"Why don't you get into bed. I think I need some more dessert." She returns to the bedroom with a bowl and presents it to him. "How about a whipped cream massage?"

In the morning of January 3 the two couples have a relaxing brunch.

"Did you order car service for us?" Luca asks his sister.

"You don't need any car service. I will drive you to the airport," Kataryna insists.

They get into Kataryna's Mercedes CLS and arrive at the airport at 3 p.m., to board the Romano jet. Kataryna parks the CLS next to the jet and joins them on board until the pilots have finished their preflight check.

"I miss you already," Kataryna tells him. "I wish I could stay on and fly away with you."

"Why don't you," he challenges her. "That would really make my day."

One of the pilots comes into the cabin. "We will be ready for take-off in about 10 minutes. We have to close the doors and start rolling."

Kataryna hugs Patrizia and Francesco and then turns to Luca, who kisses her all over her face and neck, which makes her giggle. He escorts her to the door.

"I love you. I had the best time of my life," Luca whispers.

"So did I," Kataryna responds. "I still love you madly. I can't wait to be with you again at the end of the month. Call me as soon as you are home."

She watches the flight attendant close the door behind her. A momentary sadness comes over her, but she quickly remembers that this separation is only for a short time.

As the jet starts rolling down the runway she speeds up her Mercedes CLS to drive along with it until it lifts up into the sky. She throws Luca, who has been watching her driving along with the jet, a farewell kiss.

Shortly after midnight Kataryna's phone alerts her to a text message. She smiles as she reads it.

"Are you awake?"

She dials Luca's number.

"Ciao, Principessa, I am home but miss you terribly. How are you doing?"

"Other than missing you I am well. I fell asleep around 10 p.m. and just woke up in time to see your text. I guess my body clock is set for all things involving you."

"I am glad you are awake so I can at least hear your voice. Hopefully my day in the office will distract me from you for a while, but when I get home tonight it will be very lonely without you. Please let me know as soon as possible when exactly you want to move over, so I can send you the jet."

"That is so sweet. Thank you. I am shooting for January 31."

"Good, I will put it in the calendar. By the way, that was a pretty daring stunt earlier speeding down the runway in your CLS."

"Yeah, I know. I don't do these kinds of stunts usually, but somehow I got inspired. I think the CLS and your jet make a nice couple."

EIGHTEEN

At the end of January, Kataryna arrives in Milan and occupies her new office in the Romano building. Everything was set up as Luca promised. She smiles proudly as she sees her firm's name on the door. *We are moving up in the world*, she thinks, *we have an office in Milano now.*

The first two days she acclimates herself in her new office environment. On day three the first order of the day is a meeting with Roberto to discuss his 10 percent equity share acquisition, if he chooses to make use of his rights. Roberto and his lawyer meet with Kataryna and her Italian counsel in her office.

"Ms. Taylor," Roberto's lawyer starts the negotiation, "you asked to meet with us regarding the 10 percent equity share my client has the right to acquire."

"Yes. Until recently my firm was not aware that such a clause exists. Our offer to acquire NatMedica was based on our firm becoming sole shareholder."

Kataryna directs her attention to Roberto. "It was our intention to give a certain amount of shares in the future to the CEO and CFO as a bonus, based on performance covenants to be achieved."

Roberto stares deep into Kataryna's eyes. His emotions are all over the place. He doesn't want to give her a hard time, but on the other hand he also doesn't want to forego his rights and give up his leverage. He wonders how he could use the equity shares right to his advantage regarding his personal interest in Kataryna.

"Can we discuss this further, Roberto?" Kataryna asks him in a friendly tone.

"Remember that I had already expressed an interest to acquire an equity share in the company during our first meeting in Bellagio," he replies. "It just so happens that I now actually have the right to do so. Why would I want to give up that right now?"

"If you acquire the 10 percent equity share you will have to pay a lot of money out of pocket for it. However, if you wait and the company achieves the results we would agree on, you can actually get an equity share without having to pay for it with your own money. Isn't that a far more attractive option?" Kataryna proposes.

"Not necessarily," Roberto's lawyer submits. "There is no guarantee that the results will be achieved and as such no guarantee that my client would be able to obtain an equity share then and at what percentage."

"Is this your final decision, Roberto?" Kataryna addresses him warmly.

Roberto looks down in deep thought.

"Let me sleep over it," he responds, looking at his lawyer. "I am not prepared to make a final decision at this very moment."

He feels awkward and would rather be on Kataryna's side than opposing her. This is truly a conflict of interest for him. He wants the love of this woman rather than shares in her company, but if he has to buy the shares just to be close to her he may have to pull that trigger.

Kataryna senses that he is either uncomfortable or not sure what he wants to do. She wonders if he could come up with the funds for the shares he is entitled to. She is aware that him and his family are wealthy, so the answer is probably *yes,* unless the lawyer is bluffing to get a better deal for Roberto down the road. They end the meeting with Roberto stating that he will be in touch soon regarding his decision. Roberto and his lawyer get up to leave.

"When do you think you may have an answer for me?" Kataryna asks him.

Roberto shrugs his shoulders. "Soon."

When the two lawyers step out of the office to talk among themselves, Roberto walks up to Kataryna to kiss her good-bye.

"I think we still have some other unfinished business," he says quietly. "I'll be in touch soon."

Kataryna chooses to ignore that statement. As far as she is concerned there is no unfinished business between them.

Kataryna's lawyer steps back into her office after Roberto and his attorney have departed.

"I suggest that you and Roberto get together alone to discuss this matter," he recommends. "It appears to me that you can accomplish more that way. Roberto seems to be more cooperative when you two negotiate. To that end, I think another meeting with lawyers present would be detrimental, especially since his attorney wants to play hardball in order to impress his client. As soon as I realized that I decided not to say anything else because I didn't want to cause a standoff and kill your chances."

"I believe you may have a point there," Kataryna agrees. "I had the same feeling."

"And here is another fact to consider. With Italians or any type of Latin culture, it is best to keep it amicable rather than confrontational," Kataryna's lawyer states. "The way you approached Roberto, you defused the situation his lawyer tried to create. I was impressed. Why don't you give Roberto a call and meet him on neutral ground."

"Thank you for your excellent advice," Kataryna says.

"You pay me well for my advice," he laughs. "But seriously, try the soft approach and you may get what you want."

"I will strike while the iron is hot," she says, smiling mischievously, extending her hand to him. "I will keep you posted."

Kataryna returns to her desk and starts to plan her meeting with Roberto. A half hour later she picks up the phone to call him.

"Pronto," she hears him answer his phone.

"Ciao Roberto," Kataryna starts, "I think we should meet without lawyers to discuss the equity share issue. Would you be free for dinner tonight by any chance?"

"That's the best offer I had in a long time," he responds cheerfully. "Do you have a place in mind?"

"I was hoping you could suggest something. I am too new here and Luca is out of town on business. I don't want to bother him with trivial stuff."

"No worries, I know a perfect place where we can talk undisturbed."

"OK. Give me the address and I will meet you there."

"How about if I pick you up?"

"Sure. Thank you. I will be at the office, so pick me up from here around 7:30 p.m., please."

Kataryna hangs up the phone. *I may turn this around yet*, she thinks. *Stephen and Luca will be proud of me.* At 7:30 p.m., her cell phone rings. Kataryna accepts the call.

"Your chauffeur is here, Signora," Roberto advises her laughing.

Kataryna steps out of her office and takes the elevator down. Roberto is waiting for her, leaning against his car. He sees her exiting the building and opens the door for her.

"Excellent service," she praises him, getting into the car.

"I was pleasantly surprised to hear from you," he says, as he starts driving. "How have you been?"

"Pretty good, but the move was a little strenuous. I am still trying to catch up with my work in New York, in addition to working on closing this acquisition. I think I have to go back to New York for a couple of weeks after the Carnevale in Venezia. I just couldn't get everything done in time."

"Yes, bella," he says, "it doesn't make any sense to rush into anything. Haste makes waste."

"This is a beautiful restaurant, Roberto. I am glad I let you choose the venue," Kataryna exclaims when they arrive.

"The owner is a friend of our family," he explains. "I told him that we need a more private table, so we can talk without other people listening in."

"Roberto," the man rushing towards them, greets him. "Buonasera."

The two men continue a short conversation in Italian. Kataryna smiles and extends her hand as Roberto introduces her to the owner.

"Signora," he kisses Kataryna's hand. "It is a pleasure to meet you and have you dining in our restaurant. I have reserved a beautiful table for you two and I moved some other tables around so you have some privacy."

"Thank you so much. That is very kind of you," Kataryna shows her appreciation for the warm welcome and service.

"Grazie, Gianni," Roberto says.

Gianni leads them to their table, which is behind a beautiful arrangement of plants and next to a fireplace.

"Your favorite wine is already on the table, but let me know if you would prefer something else," Gianni says.

Roberto looks at Kataryna. "What would you like to drink?"

"The wine is good," Kataryna says. "You can never go wrong with Italian red wine."

Roberto gives her a warm smile. "I am so happy to see you. As always you look gorgeous."

"It looks like you are in good spirits again," Kataryna remarks approvingly. "I am happy to see that."

"Of course I am in good spirits. You called me and asked me to have dinner with you. Let's drink to that." He raises his glass.

"Yes, but you know that we are here to discuss the equity share issue and not personal matters."

"Before we get to that I want to talk about our personal situation. Let me get straight to the point. I just can't get over you. I want you in my life. Sooner rather than later."

Kataryna sighs. "Are we back to that again?"

"No, we are not back to that again," he makes his point softly and takes her hand, "we never left that."

Kataryna gazes into the fire. She has no idea what to say next knowing this is a tenuous situation. She realizes that Roberto is still fragile when it comes to her.

"Roberto, please let's not go there. You know that I am in a committed relationship with Luca. It is stronger than ever and I don't want you to have a panic attack." Kataryna strokes his arm softly to soothe the impact of the statement she just made.

"We need to talk about it because it is therapeutic for me. So please just give me this time and be honest about what I am going to ask you. Can you do that for me, please?" he begs her.

"How is this therapeutic when your emotions are running high because of your feelings for me?"

"My anxiety attacks are a result of your relationship with Luca, not because of you or my feelings for you. I embrace my feelings for you. My impression of you is that you are a compassionate person. I need your empathy now. You may never have experienced unrequited love, so you can't possibly know what I am going through. Just take my word for it that it is pure hell. For the sake of my healing process, please tell me, if I had been in Luca's place and met you first and spent two days with you like he did, would we be in an intimate relationship right now?"

Kataryna grasps her chest and breathes in deeply trying to avoid having to answer his question.

"Why does this make you so uncomfortable?" he asks, taking her hand in his. "Please look at me and answer the question honestly, so I can get some peace of mind."

Kataryna looks him straight in the eyes. She chokes up, barely able to speak and fighting tears.

"Maybe," she whispers her voice cracking.

Roberto closes his eyes and exhales, kissing her hand and holding it against his face.

"But you won't leave Luca?" he probes after some quiet moments.

"No, of course not," she responds quickly.

"Why not? Because you feel sorry for him or because of the acquisition?"

"Because I love him," she responds with a tear coming down her face now.

Roberto embraces and comforts her. She lets him hold her for a while. *They need this moment for closure,* she thinks.

A young woman sitting at the bar with a view of their table watches them in suspense while sipping her Prosecco. She looks at her iPhone, opens the photos she took of them and emails them to her father.

From: Verena Silvestri
   To: Roberto Silvestri

Subject: Sacred Moments

7 Attachments

Sent from my iPhone

Kataryna composes herself and faces Roberto. "Now that you have your answer and we resolved this issue, can we move on to the equity share option, please? What are your thoughts on this?"

Roberto gazes at her. "Resolved? I wouldn't call it resolved. We just established that you and I could be together if I had met you first."

"Slight correction," Kataryna comes back with softly. "I said maybe. It is still a hypothetical in my book."

"Why?"

"I immediately realized that Luca and I had a strong connection when we met for dinner the first night I was in Milan. I hadn't felt like this in a long time."

"Yeah, but if I had been the one to have dinner with you the first night you were in Milan, you may have had those feelings for me," Roberto challenges her.

"Roberto, what-if-scenarios are not going to change the facts at hand. You have to move on. If you won't seek professional help from a psychiatrist, I can suggest a book for you, which you can work with in the privacy of your home. It might help you to cut your emotional ties from me."

"A book?" Roberto inquires perplexed, "how is a book going to help me get over you?"

"Well, it is a special book and you have to have an open mind. I learned about it in a seminar the author gave in New York. I was skeptical at first, but I can attest that the methods suggested in this book can be helpful."

"If anyone can make me read this book, it would be you, so go on please," Roberto says.

"The book is called 'Cutting The Ties That Bind', by Phyllis Krystal. It is based on a visualization method and describes certain techniques, which can be used by people, who want to free themselves from attachment. However, you must be willing to do the exercises for some time. Therefore, this is not an immediate problem-solver but rather over time."

"Just for you I will take a look at it. Even if only to have another connection with you," he says with a heavy heart. "Although I can tell you right here and now that I don't want to cut any ties with you."

Kataryna is pleased to hear that he is willing to look at the methods in the book. She is perceptive enough, though, to understand that it is not only going to be an uphill battle for him, but also a long and winding road.

"Let's take it one step at a time," she says patting his arm. "I believe there are two exercises in the book, which may be the best ones for what we are trying to accomplish."

"We?" he asks smiling. "So are you going to do the exercises with me to cut your ties from Luca?"

"No, we are going to cut your emotional ties to me to be able to coexist as friends and business partners, which brings me back to the equity share issue. If you give up your rights to the 10 percent now and in a year or so meet the results we set, you will end up with shares without having to pay for them from existing cash. Isn't that a much better way to get equity than having to dish out cash now?"

"I have an even better idea," Roberto says laughing. "I give up my rights to the equity shares if you marry me. I even sign a prenuptial agreement that I can never get hold of this company."

"That is not negotiable, Roberto," Kataryna says in a more serious voice. "Let's get real now."

"I had to give it another try," he says, shrugging his shoulders. "I need some more time to think about it. Let's revisit this in about two weeks from now.

"Two weeks?" Kataryna shouts out surprised. "I was hoping to have the closing of the acquisition completed in two weeks."

"Really? Isn't that a bit ambitious, especially since we are all going to be in Venice for the 'Il Ballo del Doge' on the 9th of February?"

"No, it would work. We are going to Venice on the 7th of February and attend a few events and leave for Milan on the 10th. We could schedule the closing for February 11 or 12."

"I don't know if I would be ready on the 11th or 12th if I decide to acquire the 10 percent share," he replies.

"Well, that doesn't have any impact on my firm's acquisition of the 90 percent," Kataryna says. "I can go ahead on that date. You and the Romano Holding Company would have to deal with the remaining 10 percent acquisition whenever you are ready. Meanwhile, the Romano family will remain a 10 percent shareholder. Although I believe you also have a deadline by which you have to decide, otherwise your option is forfeited. Luca and I are determined to close this by February 13 at the latest. We have already drafted a press release with a February 14 date."

"What's so important about completing this by that date? Why couldn't it be February 15, for instance, or the week after?"

"Well, we have our mind set on that date. My sister is coming over from New York and I want to spend some time with her. And my partner Stephen wants to take his wife to Italy for Valentine's Day. So he would be here for the closing that week."

"I see. Hmm, let me think about it."

"Please do and as soon as possible because I need to know how much money we will have to transfer on the closing date. If you insist on taking over the 10 percent, the funds transfer I need to make would be substantially less and I don't want that amount sitting around idle in the bank."

"OK, I will get back to you soon," he says feeling somewhat pressured.

After they finish their dinner Roberto takes Kataryna home. His chest starts tightening up as he parks in front of Luca's building.

"I have a task for you for tonight," she says turning to him. "Please go online and get the book."

"I don't know if I am going to be well enough to do anything tonight," he responds. "As a matter of fact, I can feel my chest tightening up already having to leave you here."

He gets out the vial with pills and takes one. Kataryna looks at him sadly. She wants to hug him and comfort him, but her instincts tell her that would probably backfire and set the wrong tone. He may fall totally apart if she does that and then what? She just touches his hand softly.

"Roberto, please get the book or see a therapist. Please don't get dependent on these pills. As the CEO of NatMedica, I need you to be well, and as my friend I want you to be happy and emotionally stable around me."

Roberto shakes his head. "I have no idea how to do this. I think death would be easier than what I have to deal with."

Kataryna is in shock to hear him make this kind of statement. She had heard this before from another man whom she had left because she didn't see any future with him. She recalls how difficult that was for her, and how she feared everyday that he might do something rash when he was depressed about their break-up.

"Look Roberto," she starts, "don't do anything stupid. I need you to get well. Luca thinks you are over this. He would probably not react well if he knew what is going on with you. I am still hoping that we can work this out. And don't forget Carlotta. She also has no idea what demons you are dealing with. Can you imagine what would happen if she finds out that you are in love with her brother's girlfriend? I can tell you it would be a family drama of epic proportions. Good night, Roberto. Be well. I am officially worried about you."

"Thank you for your concern and guidance," he says quietly, kissing her on the cheek and holding her tightly for a moment.

"I don't want to leave you here," he whispers. "Can you come to my place for a while? We can download the book you suggested and you can show me how this works."

"No, Roberto, you should know that this is not a good idea."

Kataryna exits the car with emotions ranging from sadness to anxiety going through her. She definitely hadn't expected such an emotionally stirring evening. Hopefully some meditative exercises will calm her down and let her sleep. As she walks into the bedroom to get ready for bed her cell phone rings. Luca's photo pops up. She quickly answers it.

"Ciao Principessa. I had a pretty grueling day dealing with lawyers and other stubborn individuals. I just got back from dinner and I am pretty beat. I can't wait to be back home tomorrow. I actually wanted to drive back tonight, but everything took longer than expected and I am too tired to drive."

"I am glad you are smart enough to make that decision," Kataryna says. "The last thing I need is you in a car accident because you are falling asleep at the wheel."

"No, we can't have that," Luca says quietly. "After all we still have an engagement party to attend on February 14."

"Yes, we do and I can't wait. As a matter of fact, I was just getting ready for bed and when I put my jewelry away looked at my engagement ring again. It is so stunning and I want to wear it soon."

"And you will, come February 14. Mariya has arranged everything with the caterers. With your family and friends I am figuring we will have about 70 guests."

"And no one knows the real occasion."

"The invitation says it is a welcome party to Italy for you."

"Clever, this way no one will have to come up with a gift," she says.

"Yeah, it will be a huge surprise. I can't wait to see everyone's face. So, how was your day? Did you meet with Roberto and the lawyers?"

"Yes, I did. But it didn't go well in that forum. My lawyer recommended that I meet with Roberto without attorneys on neutral ground. He said that it was too confrontational with the lawyers present and that Roberto appeared to be more agreeable when I talked to him."

"When are you going to meet with him?"

"I did already tonight. I wanted to get it behind me and make sure we can keep our closing timeline intact."

"Great. How did it go?"

"He said he wanted to think about it a little more and indicated he would make a decision in about two weeks."

"Two weeks? That's not acceptable; we want to close the latest on Feb. 13, right?"

"Preferable even before, on Feb. 11 or 12," Kataryna reminds him. "I told him that I would appreciate if he could let me know a.s.a.p. so I know what kind of funds I will need to transfer on the closing date."

"Good. How did he react to that?"

"He asked why we are so set on that date. He thought that it was a bit ambitious because we will be in Venice until Feb. 10. I told him that we are ready to move forward and if push comes to shove I would go ahead and acquire the 90 percent by that date. I will check in with him tomorrow to see what direction this is going."

"Well, I can also call him and try to help it along or have my father talk to him."

"No, Luca, I don't think we want to have too many people involved. Too many cooks spoil the soup, as they say."

"OK Principessa, I will let you deal with it. How did he seem otherwise? Was he outgoing and happy or distant and withdrawn?"

"Neutral. Neither overly happy nor distant, why?"

"Carlotta mentioned the other day that he appears worried or something like that at times. Did you pick up on anything?"

"I don't know him as well as you two do, so I can't say for sure. He appeared stressed though. What time will you be in Milan tomorrow?"

"I figure around 11a.m. I will come straight to the office to deal with all the issues, which came up in today's meetings."

"OK, darling, see you tomorrow. Drive carefully. Love you.

"Love you, too."

Kataryna hangs up the phone and lies down on the bed. *What a day,* she thinks but the call with Luca made her feel better again. Her thoughts go to Roberto wondering how he is feeling now. Thinking of checking up on him she reaches for her phone. No, bad idea, she decides, he is probably sleeping and her voice would only shake him up again. She puts the phone down and closes her eyes. Her phone pings announcing an email. She opens it. An email message from Roberto appears:

From: Roberto Silvestri
   To: Kataryna Taylor
Subject: HOURGLASS

Downloaded the book. Please call me.
R.

Kataryna is thrilled to read that he downloaded the book, which could be the first step to his recovery. Somewhat relieved she dials his number. He picks up instantly.

"Thank you for calling me back right away."

"So what do you think about the exercises in the book?" she asks him.

"I only looked at the two you had mentioned earlier. I can see myself doing the Hourglass exercise."

"Better than nothing," Kataryna replies. "When are you starting with that?"

"Well, it says that you can do the exercises with a partner. I think I need some coaching for me to take this seriously. Are you willing to do this with me?"

"I would like you to try to do it on your own because I am the person you are supposed to cut the ties from emotionally."

"I'll give it a try tonight," he responds.

"Remember to do some deep breathing first to relax yourself. This is not something that works overnight. So don't expect any quick results. It may take a while until you see some changes."

"OK, let me talk to the universe," he says laughing as they end the call.

Kataryna feels her anxiety subside. He is okay and he even laughed. Thank God. She falls asleep the minute she puts her head on the pillow.

Trying to get an early start to work on the final closing details for the NatMedica acquisition and some of the U.S. deals she still is involved in, Kataryna arrives at her office at 8 a.m. the next morning. She goes through her emails and responds to the ones from Stephen in New York, so he will have these when he gets up in about five hours. At 9 a.m., her office phone rings.

"Buongiorno Kataryna," she hears Roberto's voice, "I thought I'd call my favorite therapist and report on my experience with the exercise last night."

"It is way too early to call this an experience, Roberto, you just started yesterday. I told you this is not a quick fix."

"As soon as I start asking the universe to bring me whatever I need, I see your face," he explains, "maybe this is some kind of a sign."

"No, it isn't," Kataryna responds impatiently. "You are not doing it correctly. I told you not to wish for or think of anything specific when you do this visualization."

"In that case, I guess it would be better if you agreed to partner up with me and help me do it correctly," Roberto tries to convince her.

"No, Roberto, I won't do that. I am really out of my comfort zone here. I can't go on like this much longer without telling Luca if I don't see any improvement in you. Now let's change the subject. Did you think about the equity shares any further or are you at least leaning in a certain direction?"

"No, not yet. As I said I need some time to think it through."

"You do that. I've got to go now," Kataryna states. "I have a lot on my plate. Call me when you have decided. You are running out of time soon."

Roberto hangs up the phone. He didn't like what Kataryna told him. Did she say she wants to tell Luca about him still pursuing her? He is trying to recall her exact words. That wouldn't be good because Luca would lay down the law and possibly try to force him out of his position. He comes to the conclusion that his patience would also be over if Luca were to confront him again because of Kataryna and that could get pretty ugly. He stares out of the window into nothing for a few moments to digest the call with Kataryna, and then looks at his emails on his phone. Coming across the photos of him and Kataryna in the restaurant last night, which Verena took and sent to him, he smirks. "Game on Luca."

N I N E T E E N

"I am so excited about going to Venice and the fabulous events we will be attending there," Kataryna says to Luca as they are packing their suitcases. "I can't wait to see my costume. I hope they did it exactly the way I ordered it. But I did bring my own custom-made wig and headdress for this costume. I didn't want to leave it to chance that they wouldn't get it right. The wig was fitted right to my head. They cut it while I had it on."

"Let's see what it looks like," Luca says excited.

"Oh no, you will see it all together when I have the costume on and I also have to wear a special eye makeup with it."

"OK, Principessa, but don't forget you will also be wearing a mask."

"I know, but the makeup has to be just right underneath the mask so I can get into that character for the night."

"Gee, Principessa, you got me intrigued. I can't wait to encounter that character."

"I'll give you a little hint," she teases him, "you are going to have to drop the Principessa for that night and replace it with Queen."

Luca makes a pensive face. "All I can think of with that hint is my Queen of Hearts. I doubt you will show up as Queen Elizabeth."

Kataryna starts laughing like crazy at that thought. "You are right my dear, it will be a much more iconic and seductive Queen you will encounter."

After attending various events in Venice, the night of the costume ball has arrived. Kataryna starts getting ready by meticulously applying her eye makeup, which she had practiced with a makeup artist in New York. She puts on deep red lipstick and her custom-tailored black wig. Looking at herself in the mirror she is satisfied with the results. *Hello Cleopatra, Queen of the Nile,* she says to her mirror image.

The dress to fit the character is made in various deep jewel tones mixed with mesh inserts on both sides, in all the right places, which give the appearance of being open in these areas. *Very clever,* she thinks. Last she puts on the elaborate headdress and mask. Perfect. She couldn't be more pleased with the outcome. This is going to be one of the most fun nights of her life. She exits the bathroom and slowly prances towards Luca, who is standing with his back to her getting dressed. He turns around and stares into the eyes of the iconic Cleopatra in front of him.

"Whoa, Cleopatra. I didn't expect that," he murmurs visibly stunned. "This is amazing and so perfect for you. You look so mysterious with that wig and that makeup. I almost didn't recognize you, but that's the idea for tonight."

"I am glad you like it. You will have to live with that look the whole night."

"I will enjoy every moment of it. If I had known that I would have come as Caesar or Mark Antony."

"Caesar was assassinated and Mark Antony committed suicide because he was falsely informed that Cleopatra had died. I am glad you didn't show up as either one of them."

"On second thought, so am I," Luca agrees.

"And upon these news, Cleopatra killed herself, too with the bite of a cobra. Or so they say."

"Too much drama. Tonight we are going to rewrite history and have Cleopatra stay alive and take on another lover, me, with whom she will live happily ever after at a villa by Lake Como." Luca suggests.

Highly entertained by Luca's rewriting of history, Kataryna decides to introduce another scenario.

"Do you think that the Queen of the Nile will make you forget Princess Kailani?"

"No. Princess Kailani is a very sweet and enchanting character. I will never forget her. Cleopatra is more like a femme fatale. Tonight I think I may be in for the most enigmatic experience of my life. I have a feeling it will be an electrifying night."

"I can guarantee that," she grins seductively. "Do you understand now why you will have to drop the Principessa tonight?"

"Yes, Regina," he bows to her.

"Regina? How did you know that?" She looks surprised.

"Regina means Queen in Italian. What do mean by how did you know that?"

"Actually, Regina is a popular female first name in Germany. My mother told me once that Regina was one of the choices for my first name before they settled on Kataryna."

"Wow, this is almost a little spooky."

"I would call it destiny. Apparently the universe wants me to be Regina."

As they are getting ready to leave, the phone rings. Luca picks up the call.

"Ciao Carlotta, we are leaving for the Palazzo in the next few minutes. Let me send you a photo of us so you can find us later on."

He takes a photo of him and Kataryna with his cellphone and sends it to Carlotta. She confirms that she received it. Kataryna can hear her yell out, "Wow, you two look amazing."

Carlotta sends Luca a photo of herself in costume, too. "I don't know what Roberto is wearing. He will pick me up in about 10 minutes. See you later."

The Palazzo is elegantly decorated with the themes of Romance on the ground floor as well as Passion and Eros on the other two floors. Kataryna is thrilled. She has never been to an adult event so fairytale like. And wow, all these elaborate costumes. Some are even a bit scary looking but exciting at the same time. She wonders who these people are behind the masks. When she had read up on the event it said that many celebrities attend this Grande Ball because they can remain incognito behind their masks. This is so spectacular and surreal. Magic is in the air. She really feels like a Queen tonight and Luca is her King, not only tonight--but also for life. They enjoy the lavish food, the Champagne and everything else this place has to offer.

Kataryna carries a scepter. She playfully hits Luca on his behind with it and then continues to move it up and down his thighs, giving him a seductive look.

"I am the Queen of the Nile and you shall please me tonight," she commands him. "You will do whatever I want and you will grant me access to your body without resistance. But you can't touch me without my permission because I am the ruler and you are my slave."

"Go for it, Cleopatra, my body is yours. You can keep it forever."

He embraces her tightly and kisses her down her neck. His hands are all over her and he becomes very aroused by this game, imagining how they will make love later on. He is sure she will come up with an even more seductive game once they are alone in their suite, but he can hardly contain himself right now.

"You better stop this, you beautiful seductress, unless you are ready to leave right now or I am going to have a huge problem any moment," he whispers in her ear.

He pulls her close to him so she can feel his excitement, which in turn arouses her. He is ready to have her right here and now.

"We can leave in a little while," she whispers. This was so much fun. I just have to use the ladies' room before we leave."

"Hopefully not to cool down too much. I want you hot and bothered, Cleopatra" he whispers.

"Oh no, I really have to use the ladies' room," Kataryna giggles, "and there is no cooling down when I am with you. You have me in a constant state of arousal."

"And you me," he says.

As she trying to spin out of his arms, she sways to the side a bit. Luca grabs her to make sure she doesn't fall.

"Oh, oh, I had too much of that exquisite Champagne," she says. "I am a little dizzy."

"OK, Your Majesty, why don't we visit the restroom now so we can go to our sex chamber where you can have your way with me."

"I can't wait to lie down on the bed. You can undress me slowly and make sure I am having an even more amazing night."

"I will do my absolute best to amaze you," he moans into her ear.

"I know you will and you are the only one who can," she says softly, kissing him.

He puts his arm around her shoulders and guides her to the restrooms.

"I wonder where Carlotta and Roberto are," Luca says. "We didn't run into them the whole night."

"Maybe they got sidetracked and left early, you know what I mean," Kataryna suggests. "I don't think we are the only ones having a magic night. Let's call Carlotta once we are outside. It's too noisy in here."

Carlotta and Roberto have been moving from floor to floor looking for Luca and Kataryna. There are so many people. Carlotta shows Roberto the photo Luca sent her earlier.

"This is what they look like in their costumes. Let me know when you see them."

Roberto has already spotted them, but didn't reveal it to Carlotta. He watches Luca and Kataryna from the sideline almost going insane with jealousy and desire for Kataryna. She looks so mysterious and enticing in that Cleopatra inspired costume. He wants to be in Luca's place and enjoy this wicked erotic game with her. It is painful to watch Kataryna being so affectionate with Luca. His groin is hurting. He needs a relief from this torture. He is prepared to do anything to possess this woman, whichever way he can get her. It's time to put his plan into action. He excuses himself from Carlotta, leaving her to visit the men's room.

Luca escorts Kataryna to the ladies' room and then heads into the men's room. Roberto follows him. They are alone in there but probably not for long. It's now or never. Roberto gets out a syringe and steps behind Luca who is washing his hands not realizing what is about to happen. He quickly injects the fluid content into Luca's neck and holds him as he sinks to the floor unconscious. After dragging him into one of the stalls he removes Luca's costume and exchanges it for his. Taking another look at Luca unconscious on the floor he then quickly leaves the men's room walking towards Kataryna who is sitting in a chair near the restrooms waiting for Luca with their capes. He embraces and kisses her on her mouth not disturbing his or her mask. Her mouth smiles at him. She puts her arms around him tightly.

"I am glad you are back. It was lonely without you and I am still dizzy," she whispers in his ear.

"Let's go," he says in a low voice, taking her hand, leading her to the exit.

When they arrive at the hotel suite he starts kissing her passionately.

"Oh, my Italian prince," she says giggling. "I am a little tipsy so you can have your way with me tonight."

After taking off her mask she starts dancing around him seductively caressing his thighs and starting to undress him. He picks her up and puts her on the bed and then sits down next to her.

"How about a little game, Cleopatra?" he whispers in her ear.

She smiles sweetly still with her eyes closed. Even his voice sounds a little strange, she thinks, oh my, how much did I drink? But it is so exciting, making love to a masked stranger. She recalls the theme of the ball--"Amore"- "it's all about love" and in a few days they will be officially engaged.

He takes two silk scarves out of his pocket and ties each of her hands to the headboard.

"Uh, I see you are stepping it up tonight, Prince Charming. This is getting interesting. I think I like this side of you. I only wish I was more alert right now. It would make this experience even more intense."

Roberto kisses her face and her breasts, moving down to her stomach. His hands go under her long dress as he strokes her legs and parts them to kneel in between them. He slowly takes off his remaining clothes watching her as she lies there with eyes closed, smiling, enjoying the game he is playing with her. He kisses her legs moving up to her thighs.

"Did you ask the Queen for permission to do that?" she teases him putting her foot against his chest gently.

He takes off his mask and tugs at her panties with his mouth, prompting her to move her legs to prolong the game.

"Not so fast, Signore," she giggles as she tries to pull away from him.

"I am ready for you and have been for a long time," he moans, kissing her thighs and grabbing her buttocks.

"So am I," she moans.

She opens her eyes and looks down at him under her dress. *He is in rare form tonight,* she thinks, *he won't even come up for air.* She pushes her hips towards him moving the dress upward as he lifts his head staring into her eyes.

"I knew we were made for each other," he breathes into her ear, putting himself on top of her.

"Oh my God, Roberto, no, no, please," she screams out loud in total shock, "get off me and untie me immediately."

Her heart is racing in fear. She feels paralyzed by his body on top of her and her arms tied to the headboard.

He sits up shaking his head. "Just let me make love to you. I know you love me, too."

"Roberto," she says calmly, "you don't want to do this against my will. This is rape. I love Luca and only want to be with him. Please untie me and we will talk about it. I will help you to get over this."

"I don't want to get over you. Please allow me to love you," he responds as if he didn't hear her plea. "I will make you completely happy. I won't hurt you, I just want to love you forever."

"No, no, no," she screams louder now, tearing at the silk restraints trying to free her hands. "I don't want you to do anything to me. If you really love me, let me go, please," she begs.

"Please calm down," he groans, trying to put his hand over her mouth. "You are only getting me more excited and I may climax before I can please you."

Kataryna lets out a loud scream, calling for help and moving violently in an attempt to get free. He touches her face to calm her. She bites his hand making him scream out in pain. He throws himself on her and parts her legs with his hands, staring at her with blazing eyes. She starts moving her legs wildly, trying to get him off her, but his strength is overpowering her. He holds on to her legs keeping them apart.

"Be still," he says softly, kissing her thighs "I need to get these panties off you so we can make love."

"You are insane," she yells. "I don't want you."

"How can you say that? You kissed and embraced me and told me that I can have my way with you tonight," he says. "I have been waiting for this since the day I met you. You have captured all my senses. I can't be without you any longer."

Kataryna is getting more desperate fearing that she can't stop him much longer and the inevitable is about to occur.

"Because I thought you were Luca. Whatever I said earlier was only meant for him. Don't you understand that?" she screams at him. "If you had come up to me as yourself I would have never allowed you to touch or kiss me. Where is Luca? What did you do to him?" she asks frantically almost in tears.

"He is fine; just a little sleepy now," he answers softly, touching her face.

"You drugged him and took his costume to mislead me," she cries out. "This is not love. Let me go, Roberto. You will go to jail if you continue."

"I am in jail already without you in my life."

His hand moves towards her panties. She screams loudly trying to kick him with her legs.

"Don't touch me. I don't want you and I don't love you."

"Why not?" he asks coolly. "Every woman I meet wants me. Why can't you love me? I don't look that much different from Luca."

"This is not about looks, Roberto. People don't fall in love with looks alone but with the entire person. Please don't go any further. As you said you could have any woman you meet. There are wonderful women out there for you. And what about Carlotta? Where is she? Have you thought about how she will feel when she finds out what you are doing to me? If you continue this you are going to hurt several people."

"I don't want these women. I want you," he whispers caressing her face softly. "And you just said you are ready for me, too. Why are you giving me mixed signals?"

"I was ready for Luca, not for you, Roberto. You were disguised in Luca's costume. Your mind is playing tricks with you. Please untie me and I will make sure that you get medical help."

"Medical help? I am not sick. I am in love. Only you can help me. So please give yourself to me. Stop fighting me. Just free yourself from Luca and you will understand why we are meant to be together. Please give me a chance."

Kataryna realizes that he doesn't seem to fully understand what he is about to do and the consequences he would face. She needs to take this in another direction in a last-ditch attempt to get him to untie her.

She breathes in deeply to relax and calm herself.

"OK, Roberto," she says, forcing a smile, "why don't you untie me first so I can touch you. I don't like to make love being tied up. I want to be in control over you. I promise you will love what I have in mind."

He smiles at her as his face comes closer to hers. He starts kissing her passionately. She plays along hoping to get free this way. His lips move down kissing her neck and cleavage. Kataryna is squirming as his hands move up and down her body.

"Roberto," she whispers, "please untie me. I want to touch you."

She moves one of her legs between his grazing his genital area as he kneels in front of her. He starts groaning and puts himself on top of her, removing the scarf from her right hand. Kataryna's hand and arm are numb from the restraint and her attempts to free herself. As he tries to untie her left hand he climaxes into an orgasm, collapsing onto the bed moaning.

Disaster averted, she thinks relieved, when the suite door bursts open and two security guards rush into the room pulling Roberto off the bed and away from Kataryna.

"Are you alright, Signora?" one of the guards asks her. "What happened here? A hotel guest heard you screaming for help and alerted the front desk. Who is this man? Did he hurt you?"

"No, he didn't hurt me," she explains. "He is out of his mind. He needs medical help. But I need your help finding my fiancé. He may have been drugged and is probably unconscious in the men's room at the Palazzo. Can you please check into it and find out where he is?"

"We will make a few calls and get back to you as soon as possible," the security guard assures her. "Meanwhile you are safe now.

But who is this man here?" he points to Roberto, who has been restrained by the other security guard after he put his clothes on.

"He is a friend and business partner of ours. I believe he is on some kind of controlled substance probably in combination with alcohol and totally lost his sense of reality."

"How would you know that?" the security staff asks her.

"He told me weeks ago that he had been put on anti-anxiety medication and that he had several episodes of hallucinations involving me."

"Should we call a doctor to check you?" the security guard asks.

"No, that is not necessary," Kataryna says. "I am fine, just a bit shaken. All I need is to find my fiancé and make sure he is okay. Where are you taking him?" she points at Roberto.

"The police will be here in a moment and take him to the station."

A few moments later two policemen arrive on the scene and put Roberto in hand cuffs. He goes with them silently appearing dazed.

"What happened here? Who is this man? Did he try to rape you?" one of the policemen asks Kataryna.

"He is a family friend. He somehow managed to get hold of my fiancé's costume. So I thought he was Luca. We engaged in some erotic banter and touching. I had a lot of Champagne tonight at the ball and was not alert enough to be able to detect that he wasn't Luca, my fiancé. At one point he asked for my permission to make love to me, which I didn't give of course. I coaxed him into untying me, which he was in the process of doing when the hotel security staff burst into the suite. I believe he is temporarily out of his mind because he is on some kind of controlled substance. I suggest you try to contact his doctor in Milan who prescribed the medication for him. More importantly, though, I need you to find my fiancé and make sure he gets medical attention because it appears he may have been drugged."

After the police leave, Kataryna calls housekeeping to have the sheets changed, then gets out of her costume and takes a shower. *What an ordeal*, she thinks. What was Roberto thinking? How can such a successful, smart and attractive man act like this and what is going to happen to him now? She almost feels sorry for him realizing the uphill battle he will be facing. *Where is Carlotta*, she wonders? She is probably looking for Roberto all over the place. I have to find her and tell her what happened. She will be devastated, but it is time to face the music.

Kataryna recalls her interactions with Roberto in the last few weeks. She was so sure that he would see the light and move on and now this. The thought of telling Carlotta what happened and destroy her world scares her. And what is Luca going to say when he finds out that Roberto never gave up pursuing her and that she kept it from him? She starts crying thinking about the pain Carlotta and Luca will have to go through.

The hotel telephone rings. She picks up the phone.

"Signora, this is the Head of Hotel Security," the male voice says, "we have been told that an unconscious man who was found in the men's room at the Palazzo was brought to the hospital. Are you ready to take down the address?"

"Yes, please go ahead," Kataryna responds taking the pen and paper on the nightstand. "Can I get some kind of car service or taxi to take me there?"

"Yes, of course, I will have a car waiting for you. When will you be ready to leave?"

"Please give me about 10 minutes. One more question. I need to contact Signora Carlotta Romano. Can you help me locate her? She is the sister of my fiancé."

"Certainly, Signora, let me check."

While Kataryna is waiting anxiously for the information, she sees her message light blinking. Checking her cell phone, which she had not taken to the ball she sees five missed calls. She listens to her voice mails, which include messages from a desperate Carlotta trying to reach her. The Hotel Security comes back on the line.

"Signora, we tried to call the room of Signora Romano but she did not answer. We also sent one of our staff members up to her room, but she did not answer the door either. We left a message for her and asked her to call your room as soon as she gets our message. Is there anything else we can do for you?"

"No, thank you. Just have the car ready for me in about 10 minutes, please."

Kataryna calls Carlotta's cell phone. Her heart is racing as she hears it ring.

"Kataryna," she hears Carlotta almost screaming into the phone. "Where are you?"

"Carlotta," Kataryna tries to stay as calm as possible. I am in my suite. Where are you?"

"I am in the hotel lobby. I lost Roberto somehow and couldn't find you two either when I looked for all of you at the Palazzo. There was so much commotion all of a sudden. I heard they found an unconscious man in one of the men's rooms, so the ambulance came and it got crazy because everybody was gathering around and I couldn't get out. When I had the chance I went all over to look for Roberto. I called his cell phone but couldn't reach him either. So I came back to the hotel a little while ago. I don't know what to do."

"Carlotta, I will come down to the lobby and explain what happened. Are you still in your costume?"

"No, when I came back to the hotel I changed clothes. Why are you asking?"

"Stay where you are. I will be right down."

Kataryna rushes down to the lobby. Carlotta runs towards her as she exits the elevator.

"What is going on Kataryna? I called Roberto's, Luca's and your cell phone. No one answered their phone."

Kataryna hugs Carlotta who is close to tears. "I have a car waiting outside to take us to the hospital. I will explain everything on the way."

"Why are we going to the hospital? Did something happen to Roberto? Where is Luca, is he not coming with us?"

Kataryna guides Carlotta to the car waiting outside. Once they are inside Kataryna takes Carlotta's hand and starts talking.

"I don't even know where to begin, Carlotta," she says. "Luca is in the hospital. He is the unconscious man they picked up with the ambulance from the Palazzo."

Carlotta shrieks. "Oh my God, what happened to my brother? Did he have a heart attack?"

"No, he didn't," Kataryna pauses for a moment and holds her head. "I hate to have to be the one to tell you this but Roberto drugged him and left him unconscious in the men's room. I hope and pray that Luca is all right."

"What?" Carlotta yells out, "you are not making any sense. Why would he do that?"

"He drugged Luca and then exchanged costumes with him, so I would think he was Luca when he came out of the men's room."

"Why did he want you to think he was Luca?" Carlotta asks, clearly in distress.

"He wanted to convince me to make love to him because he has been pursuing me since we met for the first time during the business meeting in Bellagio in November. He did not want to accept that I am in a relationship with Luca, although I told him various times that I love Luca and that he should move on and find his happiness elsewhere."

Carlotta stares at Kataryna with wide eyes, tears rolling down her face.

"I can't believe that my brother would not have told me about this after I confided in him and told him that I was in love with Roberto. I know he wasn't thrilled about it at first when I divulged my romantic interest in him, so that would have been a perfect reason for Luca to discourage me from pursuing a relationship with Roberto."

"Unfortunately it is more complicated and involved than that," Kataryna continues in anguish. "Luca didn't know to what extent this had escalated because I didn't tell him. I wanted to protect his and Roberto's friendship and professional relationship, and I thought I could handle it on my own. Please allow me to explain everything in more detail later on so you will understand why I thought this was the best way to handle it."

"I am at a complete loss, Kataryna," Carlotta sobs, "I have no idea what to think at this point. But at the moment the well being of my brother is my only concern. The rest I will deal with later."

The car pulls into the hospital driveway. Kataryna and Carlotta rush inside. Carlotta speaks to the administrative staff trying to locate Luca. The front desk clerk makes a phone call and a few minutes later a doctor approaches them. He has a conversation with Carlotta in Italian. Kataryna is anxious to find out what he has to say about Luca's condition, especially since she believes she heard him say that Luca was in intensive care. The doctor gestures them to follow him.

"What did the doctor say?" Kataryna asks, frightened to get bad news.

"Luca is in intensive care and has not woken up since he was admitted. They have drawn blood to get various lab tests done and they did a brain scan in order to determine why he is unconscious. The scan didn't show anything. The doctor is waiting for the blood work to come back from the lab, which will hopefully reveal more."

"Did you tell him that Luca was drugged?" Kataryna asks.

"Yes, I did. He is going to tell the lab to run additional specific toxicology tests."

"Can we see Luca?"

"Yes, the doctor is escorting us to his room now."

Kataryna is in distress. Her mind is racing. Luca has not woken up yet. That is not good. This incident occurred hours ago. What the hell did Roberto give him?

Carlotta interrupts her thoughts. "Where is Roberto now and what happened when you got to the hotel suite with him?" she wants to know.

"Roberto is in police custody. I think the doctor should call over there to see if he can find out what he used to drug Luca. It might speed up the diagnosis."

The doctor opens the door to Luca's room and lets the two women in. Luca is lying in the hospital bed unconscious with oxygen tubes running though his nose, a drip of some kind of fluid in one of his arms and a heart/blood pressure monitor cuff attached to the other arm. When they see him like this, Kataryna and Carlotta both cry out. "Oh my God, please be okay."

Kataryna runs to Luca's bed and takes his hand in both of hers. Carlotta goes to the other side of the bed and takes his other hand. Both are sobbing with tears running down their faces. Carlotta starts talking to Luca in Italian. Kataryna looks at her silently feeling sorry for Carlotta's anguish that she might have been able to avoid, if she had told Luca about Roberto's continued infatuation with her. *What was I thinking*, she wonders? Luca will be so disappointed if he ever wakes up. The thought of Luca not ever waking up again shakes her to her core and she starts crying uncontrollably. The love of her life is in a coma because of her actions or rather non-actions in this case. This was supposed to be such a beautiful and eventful week with the closing of the acquisition in two days and then their surprise engagement party on Valentine's Day. None of this will take place if Luca doesn't wake up. Even if he wakes up, will he be well? How will he react when he finds out he ended up being drugged by his friend and business partner because his fiancé kept a secret from him? Will he ever trust her again or could this even be the end of their relationship?

The doctor re-enters the intensive care room with a patient chart in his hand. He looks at the two women crying and holding Luca's hands.

"We got the lab tests back," he reports in broken English. "They show that he was given an anesthetic agent and some other substance we could not identify. It appears that these two substances were mixed and injected into him. He was very lucky because the injection was done in the neck and barely missed his carotid artery." He points to a bruise in Luca's neck to show them the injection site. "If the syringe had gone in there he would have died. We are trying to flush out whatever is in his system with the drip you see here in his arm. Since we don't recognize the second substance we don't know what antidote to administer. We may try a remedy we usually give on overdoses, but there is no guarantee that it will work. In any event you two should go back to your hotel. There is nothing you can do here and we can't have you stay in ICU that long. In addition, you also need some rest so you have the energy to deal with this."

"I don't want to leave him alone here," Kataryna reacts. "Please let me stay. I know that he would want me with him if he could speak."

"I am not leaving either," Carlotta jumps in. "This is my brother. If anyone stays it will be me."

The doctor shakes his head. "No, I am sorry. You both have to leave now. If there are any developments in the next few hours we will call you. It is 3 a.m., now you need some rest. You can come back after 9 a.m."

Carlotta and Kataryna reluctantly leave the hospital to go back to their hotel. The hospital staff had called a cab for them, which is waiting outside. They both fall exhausted into the seat and close their eyes.

"OK Kataryna, start talking about Roberto pursuing you. I need to hear the whole truth," Carlotta demands.

"Why don't we get some rest first and meet for breakfast in my suite before we go back to the hospital. We need privacy and time for that conversation."

"I don't know if I can sleep now," Carlotta murmurs. "I may have lost a brother and someone I am in love with all in the same night."

"I am in no better position, but we have to try to get some rest to regain our strength. Why don't you come to my suite around 9 a.m.? I will order room service for us," Kataryna turns to hug Carlotta who appears numb and distraught.

Exhausted and worried Kataryna falls into bed. The events of the night appear in front of her again. What if Luca doesn't wake up? She can't bear that thought and starts crying again. As total exhaustion overcomes her she finally falls asleep.

"Good morning Carlotta," Kataryna greets her as she opens the door to let her in.

"There is nothing good about this morning," Carlotta responds. "I called my parents and told them what happened. They are in shock and on their way to Venice. We are going to take Luca to a clinic in Milano with the assistance of our family doctor."

Kataryna nods. "Good, hopefully they did find out from Roberto what he used to anesthetize Luca. This is so surreal, I still can't believe what happened."

"Why don't you tell me what happened. I have been thinking about this the whole night."

The two manage to eat some of the breakfast. Kataryna describes how Roberto followed her to Berlin and that she had told him then that she was in an intimate relationship with Luca; and that Luca had a man-to-man talk with him, too, asking him to respect that.

"Obviously he didn't," Carlotta contends. "What did he do next?"

"At first he didn't do anything, so we thought that Luca's conversation with him had convinced him to give up on this idea. Then one day he called me in New York and told me that after his meeting with Luca he had chest pains. He went to see a doctor who ordered all kinds of tests and then told him that he was physically okay. The doctor prescribed anti-anxiety medication to relieve the tightness in his chest, which apparently helped."

"Did he tell you when these symptoms would appear?" Carlotta questions her.

"He said whenever he heard anything about how happy Luca and I were or what we were doing, etc. And then, of course, there was Luca's birthday party where I showed up as a surprise. He said he lost it when he saw how much in love Luca and I were and that he had to medicate himself immediately."

Carlotta smirks. "Now it all makes sense. His strange moods, not being himself and a few other situations I experienced with him."

"I am sure he started to over medicate himself at one point and then couldn't stop it anymore," Kataryna suggests. "I am so sorry that you have to go through this Carlotta. During more recent conversations with Roberto, I encouraged him to seek professional help and focus on his relationship with you."

"What did he say about that?"

"As to my suggestion to get professional help, he said he wasn't crazy, just in love."

"And as to focusing on his relationship with me?" Carlotta asks gingerly.

Kataryna takes a deep breath before answering. "He said the last thing he wanted to do is hurt you. He was afraid that you might be as much in love with him as he claimed he was with me; and if he couldn't get over me or, in his twisted thinking, would succeed with me, you might end up on anti-anxiety medication like he was."

"I still don't understand why you did not tell Luca how infatuated Roberto was with you," Carlotta states, now in a more accusatory tone.

"I thought I could help him get over me and save their friendship in the process. At one point Roberto had made a somewhat suicidal remark, and I thought if Luca had known he would have read him the riot act and push him over the edge. I did not want to be responsible for Roberto doing anything to hurt himself."

"How did you think you could help him?" Carlotta probes further.

"I suggested that he get professional help. When he refused to go that route, I recommended a visualization method, which is supposed to cut emotional ties from people. I asked him to work with that if he doesn't want to see a psychiatrist. I actually had dinner with him last Monday, but not for personal reasons. This was in connection with trying to get him to give up his rights to the 10 percent equity shares of NatMedica so my firm could acquire the entire company. My lawyer had suggested that I meet alone with him, so I arranged a dinner meeting. However, during the dinner he turned the conversation into his "not being able to get over me" situation. Honestly Carlotta, it was heart wrenching and reminded me of a prior situation in my life. I urged him to download the book, which teaches these methods."

"After what I went through, maybe I should also take a look at this method," Carlotta wonders.

"It can't hurt, Carlotta. I have used it many times when I faced difficult situations or crossroads. I would be happy to go through it with you."

"I wonder what Roberto is going through right now," Carlotta says. "I guess they will have to detox him."

"I think we better get going now to see how Luca is doing," Kataryna responds, "it is already 9:30 a.m. When will your parents get here?"

"They said they wanted to leave Bellagio at 8 a.m. I expect them to arrive here around noon."

Kataryna and Carlotta arrive at the hospital, both anxious about what they will be told regarding Luca's condition. They meet with a specialist who reports that all of Luca's neurological tests came back normal and that an anesthesiologist has been reviewing Luca's lab tests to see if he can come up with any remedy to wake him up. A staff nurse escorts them to Luca's room and hands Carlotta a cell phone they found on Luca when he was admitted.

Kataryna goes straight to Luca. She kisses him and starts talking to him, hoping he can hear her.

"Please wake up Luca. I am so scared. If you can hear me, please fight and come back to us."

"Oh my God," Carlotta screams out hysterically. "This is not Luca's phone. It's Roberto's and what is this?"

She stares at the phone screen in disbelief. Kataryna turns around wondering what Carlotta is getting so agitated about. Carlotta struts over to her and hands her the phone.

"So you have been involved with Roberto or how do you explain this?"

Puzzled, Kataryna grabs the phone. "What?" she screams out in shock. "I have no idea what this is all about."

She is overwhelmed and utterly confused by the photos on Roberto's cell phone. One of them shows Roberto with his arm around her shoulders holding her close. Another one shows Roberto kissing her hand, and a few other photos display similar ambiguous situations. Kataryna stares at the photos and then it comes to her. These were taken by someone when Roberto and she had dinner last Monday to discuss the equity share issues, and he started talking about how he couldn't get over her and was trying to rehash what if she had spent time with him before Luca. *How do you explain these photos and that they do not tell what really occurred? Who took these photos and why are they on Roberto's phone?* All this is going through Kataryna's mind in split seconds as she attempts to make sense of it.

Carlotta storms out of the room. Kataryna follows her.

"Carlotta, please let me explain. This is not what you think. I swear I never had any romantic involvement with Roberto. I don't know who took these photos and why Roberto has them on his phone. This is the evening I told you about, when Roberto and I had dinner to discuss his equity share right, and he started talking about how distraught he was over me. It got quite emotional. I felt so sorry for him and tears came down my face. That is when he put his arm around me to comfort me. That is also true for the other photos. All are in the same context."

Carlotta starts crying. "I don't know what to believe anymore. I need some time to digest this and find the truth."

Kataryna steps towards her and grabs her by the shoulders. "Carlotta, please look at me."

Carlotta looks up wiping the tears off her face.

Kataryna takes a deep breath and exhales. "I have never loved any man like I love your brother, and I will fight for this relationship every way I can. I am not the kind of woman who engages in affairs or cheats. All I tried to do is help Roberto find his way again and preserve his friendship with your family. I thought that his infatuation with me was short-lived and would blow over. But I guess the old saying--no good deed goes unpunished--rings true once again."

Carlotta frees herself from Kataryna. "I need to be alone now."

"All I am asking is that you give me the benefit of the doubt, Carlotta. Please don't rush to judgment. Remember that the hotel security personnel intercepted Roberto's intentions with me because other guests heard me scream for help. If Roberto and I had been romantically involved, why would I have screamed for help?"

Kataryna feels her life spinning out of control as she returns to Luca's room and takes his hand again. Tears stream down her face. *This is not happening*, she thinks.

Around noon Luca's parents and their doctor arrive at the Venice hospital. The doctor examines Luca's chart and monitor, which show his vital signs within normal range. The private ambulance service staff proceeds to prepare Luca for the transport back to Milan.

"Where are you taking him?" Kataryna asks concerned.

"To a private clinic in Milan. I believe the medical director is Dr. de Angelis," the nurse, who came with the ambulance, informs her.

"Can you please give me the address?"

"You can go with us if you wish."

"Thank you. I will."

"I am also going with you," Luca's mother states. She puts her arms around Kataryna.

"I am sorry for what you had to go through. You can tell me everything on the way to Milano."

Carlotta looks at her mother and Kataryna. She feels weak and nauseated and can hardly stand up straight. Her father holds her up.

"Riccardo," Luca's mother addresses her husband, "you and Carlotta can drive Luca's car back to Milano. We can all meet again at the clinic."

As soon as Luca has been positioned in the ambulance, the family doctor, Kataryna and Valentina Romano get in too. Kataryna sits next to Luca and holds his hand. After they had been driving for a while Kataryna tells Valentina what happened the night before at the Palazzo and at the hotel suite. Valentina is shocked.

"I can't believe that Roberto would go to such lengths," she states. "He must have completely lost his mind."

"I think he may have taken too much of this anti-anxiety medication, and together with his infatuation with me, it must have put him over the edge. He will need to get professional help now," Kataryna explains.

After a three-hour drive, the private ambulance arrives at the de Angelis clinic in Milan. Luca is set up in a private room. His doctor is speaking to a specialist at the clinic. Dr. de Angelis meets with Valentina and Kataryna to update them on what they intend to do for Luca. He advises them that Roberto has also been transferred to the clinic from Venice, and that he is located in a locked part of the clinic for detox treatments and psychological counseling.

"Do you know what he used to inject my son with?" Valentina Romano asks.

"Yes, Signora Romano. He told us what he used and the good news is that one of the substances is a natural tranquilizer but it is a newly developed product, which is not on the market yet. We are reaching out to the manufacturer to learn more about it. We should get something from them shortly, so we can see what the active ingredients are."

"So is it just a matter of time until Luca wakes up again?" Kataryna questions him.

Dr. de Angelis looks at Kataryna, realizing that she is the woman Roberto is so infatuated with.

"In my opinion, yes, but the sooner the better. We will continue to flush and hydrate him. I will get back to you as soon as I have more information."

Kataryna allows herself a sigh of relief, even though she can't completely relax yet. This is not an exact science and who knows what still can go wrong. When Carlotta and her father arrive at the clinic, Valentina tells them what Dr. de Angelis had explained to them. An hour later Dr. de Angelis meets with the family again.

"We have the product description and active ingredients now. The product on its own should not be harmful, but we don't know how much was used and what effect it has in combination with the anesthetic and alcoholic beverages your son had that night."

"Are you sure that is all he gave him?" Riccardo Romano asks.

"I personally spoke to Roberto after he got here earlier. He is my patient and also a good friend of our family. I trust that he would tell me if he gave anything else to your son. I will be back in an hour or so with any update on your son's condition."

"Carlotta, I am going to prepare a press release announcing that Roberto stepped down as CEO of NatMedica and that Francesco has been promoted to CEO," Riccardo Romano tells her.

Carlotta nods silently. He then turns to Kataryna.

"The closing for your acquisition of the 90 percent shares is scheduled for the day after tomorrow. Are we still going forward with that?"

"I believe so, but I will have to contact my partner in New York to advise him what happened and report the change in the management."

"For the time being Francesco will have to take over the responsibilities of the CEO and CFO until we fill the vacant CFO position. I called to let him know that the press release is going out tomorrow. Patrizia and Francesco are on their way over here."

Just as Riccardo finished his sentence they walk in. Patrizia rushes to Luca's bed and kisses him on the cheek. Francesco walks up to Kataryna after talking to Riccardo. She lets go of Luca's hand for a moment to greet him.

"Congratulations on the CEO promotion, Francesco."

"Thank you, Kataryna. Unfortunately, I can't be as happy about this promotion as I would be under normal circumstances."

"Of course not, but we have to make the best out of it."

"Are you still going forward with the acquisition?" Francesco enquires.

"I am waiting for an answer from Stephen. I sent him an email earlier."

Riccardo joins Francesco and Kataryna. "The lawyers just emailed me advising that everything is set for the closing the day after tomorrow."

He puts his arm around Kataryna. "I think we should get something to eat now. You haven't eaten since breakfast."

"I am not leaving here," Kataryna insists. "I want to be here when Luca wakes up."

Valentina comes over to them. "Patrizia can get something to eat for all of us so we won't have to leave."

At 7:30 p.m., Kataryna's cell phone alerts her that she has a new message. Stephen sent her an email that the acquisition is a go and that he will meet her for the signing of the documents the day after tomorrow. She informs Riccardo and Francesco that the closing of the acquisition will take place as planned.

Kataryna is exhausted. She had little sleep the night before and an emotionally charged day. She sits down in one of the comfortable armchairs and dozes off.

In addition to her heart being shattered, Carlotta is also physically drained. How ironic that Roberto is in the same building just in the locked section of the clinic. She feels a wave of nausea coming on. Her father sends her and his wife home to rest.

Riccardo and Kataryna stay with Luca in the clinic. He tells her stories from Luca's childhood and how Luca and Roberto were like brothers when they were growing up.

Kataryna jumps up. "I think Luca just moved his hand," she exclaims excitedly.

She softly kisses Luca's cheeks and continues to talk to him. He moves his head and slowly opens his eyes.

Kataryna smiles at him. "Hi, how are you?"

He looks at her, then at his father. His eyes are still heavy but he manages to keep them open.

He looks around the room. "Where are we?" he finally manages to speak.

"We are in a clinic in Milan," Kataryna says, looking at his heart rate and blood pressure monitor, which still show normal values.

"Why? What happened?" He looks at his left arm, discovering the drip and a cuff around his finger.

He takes a deep breath trying to sit up. Kataryna arranges the pillows for him and hands him a glass of water.

"How are you feeling?" she asks.

"A little groggy. My entire body feels kind of heavy and lethargic. Did I have a heart attack?"

"No, darling," she starts tearing up. "What is the last thing you remember?"

"I can't remember anything at the moment. Let me think."

He pauses and closes his eyes for a moment.

"Ah, I know," he says, "we were at the ball in Venice and were getting ready to leave. But I can't remember how we got back to the hotel or anything else thereafter."

"You were drugged in the men's room before we left and you have been unconscious since last night."

"What? How did I get drugged?" He looks at his father.

"It's a long story. We will tell you tomorrow when you are more alert."

Riccardo responds dialing his wife's cell phone number. "Ciao Valentina. Luca just woke up." He hands Luca the cell phone.

"Ciao mamma. I think I am fine just a little shaky and hungry and I have no idea what happened."

Kataryna calls the nurse and asks her to get the doctor on call and some food for Luca.

"Why don't you go home, Riccardo," Kataryna says. "I will stay with Luca."

"I will go to Carlotta's to get some sleep, but you make sure that you also get some rest."

"After I feed Luca, I will lie down on these two armchairs," she says.

"No, you won't," Luca protests, "you will lie down in this bed with me."

"Even better," she says, kissing him on his lips.

"And then you will tell me what happened to me."

Kataryna feels a touch of anxiety coming on. He is not going to be happy when she discloses the entire episode and she has to confess what went on behind his back. He will probably be quite upset. The nurse enters with a tray of food as Riccardo leaves the room to head to Carlotta's place. Kataryna picks up the fork and starts feeding Luca.

"I think I like this," he says smiling wearily. "I just wish I had more energy to thank you properly."

"You sure are back. I am so relieved."

Exhaustion finally catches up with Kataryna. She gets into the hospital bed with Luca, puts her head on his shoulder and closes her eyes.

"OK, Principessa," she hears Luca say, "please tell me how and why I ended up drugged."

"I don't want to go into details right now. I am so exhausted. For now, I will just tell you that you were drugged because someone wanted something you have."

"I didn't have much money on me. So what could they possibly have wanted? Oh, my expensive watch?" he guesses.

"No, we got your watch. It was given to Carlotta by the hospital staff."

"Then what? Tell me already," he urges her.

"Me."

"What? Someone wanted you? Is that what you are saying?"

"Yes."

"Oh, my God. Did you get hurt? What happened to you?"

"OK. Here it goes. This is going to be tough. Roberto drugged you in the men's room. He then took your costume and picked me up where I was waiting for you and took me to our hotel suite."

Luca stares at her in disbelief. "What did he do to you?" His tone is serious.

"Well, I had no idea that it was him instead of you in that costume. If you recall, I was a little dizzy from too much Champagne that night. So I wasn't that alert either and initially I behaved as I would with you."

"Please don't tell me that he had full access to your body," Luca probes horrified.

"No, not full but partial. He had tied my hands to the bed with silk scarves, which came with your costume."

"He tied you to the bed? This is a nightmare."

"Because I was so dizzy I had my eyes closed the whole time. He had taken off his clothes and pinned me on the bed. When I opened my eyes and he lifted his head to look at me, I saw that it was Roberto instead of you and I started screaming and fighting to get my hands free."

"What did he do then?"

"He tried to convince me to make love to him, but I tricked him and averted it."

"How did you do that?"

"When I realized that he was not in full command of his senses and wouldn't listen to me telling him that I love you only and that I have no feelings for him, I knew I had to come up with a plan fast. I asked him to untie me so I could participate. He must have believed me because he untied my right hand and when he leaned over to go for the left hand my leg grazed his genital area. He collapsed on the bed and ejaculated. A few seconds later the security personnel of the hotel stormed through the door because some hotel guest had reported that they had heard me scream."

Luca is holding his head. The heart rate/blood pressure monitor starts beeping. A nurse runs into the room to check on Luca. He tells her he is fine, but due to the high values on the monitor she calls the doctor.

"We should have waited with these details," Kataryna says quietly. "I knew this would upset you. Please calm down. Nothing happened."

"Nothing happened?" Luca screams out, "at a minimum he touched you inappropriately. Just imagining that is unbearable."

"I chose to move on," Kataryna explains calmly. "The bigger of a deal we make of it, the more difficult it will be to forget it. This man is sick. He lost all rational thinking."

"I don't know if I can be that indifferent about it."

"For me the most important part is that I know how much I love you and that we are moving forward with our relationship. I am not letting anything cloud this feeling. In the end it is a matter of trust."

"I trust you but I can't erase the image of him touching you in that way from my mind that easily."

"I understand because you just found out. I was also struggling with it right after it happened, but fast-forward 24 hours later I am over it."

"What happened after the security staff came to the suite?"

"He got arrested by the local police. They asked me a couple of questions to see if he hurt me. Since he was on a controlled substance they let him go to the clinic to detox. Actually he is here in this clinic, but in the locked area. Dr. de Angelis is his doctor who prescribed the anti-anxiety medication he had been on for some time."

Although Luca's blood pressure and heart rate had come down again, he is still stirred up.

"It's going to take a while for me to get over this," he murmurs before they finally fall asleep.

Luca and Kataryna are still sleeping and cuddled up in each other's arms when Carlotta and her parents arrive at the clinic the next morning. They both wake up as the family gathers around them. A few minutes later Dr. de Angelis arrives to check on Luca.

"I don't see any reason to keep you here. You are free to go home if you wish," the doctor informs Luca, handing him the discharge papers. Carlotta hands her brother the change of clothes she brought for him.

"Let's get out of here," Luca says, taking Kataryna's hand.

Riccardo Romano drives them to Luca's Milan apartment.

"You two have been through a lot. Why don't you take it easy for a few days," he recommends.

"We have the closing scheduled for tomorrow," Kataryna says. "Other than that I am not planning to get too much involved in anything."

"It shouldn't take too long," Riccardo responds. "So, Luca, how are we going to handle the remaining 10 percent we still own? Now that Roberto is out as CEO, he doesn't have those rights to the shares anymore."

"Kataryna and I will discuss the 10 percent issue when we are back to normal. Right now I am rather preoccupied with what happened in Venice."

"I still can't believe it. It is heartbreaking that such an intelligent man messed up his life like that. But when it comes to psychological conditions aggravated by chemical imbalances in the brain one never knows how people react," Riccardo states. "Hopefully his treatment will be successful."

"I feel so betrayed by him," Luca murmurs. "He could have killed me, although I don't think that was his intention. But the thought gives me chills."

Carlotta, who has been listening silently, is feeling a wave of nausea coming on again. *If they only knew that I also went through a trauma yesterday,* she thinks. *At this point, no one needs to know that I had an intimate relationship with Roberto. It's bad enough that Luca and Kataryna know that I was in love with him.* She wonders how her brother felt after finding out what Roberto tried to do to Kataryna? Hopefully Kataryna has been truthful when she explained that Roberto did not get to consummate his sexual advances with her. She recalls the compromising photos on Roberto's cell phone. Kataryna's explanation sounds plausible, but should she show the photos to her brother and let him decide?

After Luca's parents have left for Bellagio, Kataryna reveals more details about Roberto's infatuation with her.

"While this doesn't change anything at this point, I want you to know that Roberto had contacted me a couple of more times after you and I had told him about our relationship. I didn't tell you then because, first of all, I wanted to prevent a blow-up between you and him; and secondly, I thought I could handle it on my own. I tried to help him to get over me and move on. Other than the Venice incident, of course, I think the most dramatic interaction I had with him was when he came to Berlin under the pretense of a business meeting, which you knew about. But what I didn't tell you was that as soon as I got to the restaurant he turned it into a private conversation, declaring his love for me. He then proceeded to propose marriage."

Luca is burying his face in his hands, shaking his head in disbelief. Carlotta is also in shock. She hadn't heard that before. Roberto proposed marriage to a woman he hardly knew. Wow, that is huge.

"At that moment he didn't know yet that Luca and I had started an intimate relationship," Kataryna adds. "I told him later on, though."

"Is there more?" Luca wants to know.

Kataryna addresses the photos on Roberto's cell phone, which Carlotta found. She explains the circumstances again.

"While they look as if something romantic was going on, I assure you that this was in connection with his plea for me to reconsider a relationship with him. It was an emotionally charged moment. When I started to tear up, he put his arm around me to comfort me. Nothing else happened. I told him to get professional help. Later on he made a suicidal remark and I became very concerned about him."

"I think a blow-up between him and me at an early stage of his obsession with you would have been much better than what happened a few days ago," Luca offers after some moments of silence.

Tears are running down Kataryna's face. "Of course, I know that now. I totally underestimated the situation."

Carlotta sits next to Kataryna and takes her hand. "Thank you for being completely open with us. I think this incident in Venice will bond us three forever."

The closing of the NatMedica acquisition the next day is uneventful. Stephen and Kataryna's private equity firm is now the 90 percent shareholder with 10 percent still in the Romano family hands. Carlotta submits the press release she had prepared to announce the change of ownership. After the usual closing luncheon, Kataryna, Stephen, Luca and Francesco reconvene to go over current company business and to discuss the search for a new Chief Financial Officer, so Francesco will be able to completely focus on his CEO responsibilities as soon as possible.

"We are looking forward to seeing you all the day after tomorrow at our party welcoming Kataryna to Italy," Luca says as they adjourn the business meeting. "We will have a lot to celebrate that night."

TWENTY

Valentine's Day, February 14, 2013

The villa is expertly decorated with red roses and rose petals, as well as candles in all sizes ranging from large floor candles at the entrance doors to small tea lights on tables giving each room a warm and romantic glow. Soft Italian music is playing in the background coming through the surround system.

Baci Perugina, small chocolates with a hazelnut inside are on the dessert table in true Italian tradition for this day. Each of the chocolates contains a loving lyrical quote in four different languages. The caterers, together with Luca's staff members Mariya and Isabella, are busy in the kitchen preparing the lavish food and getting ready to serve the Champagne as soon as the guests arrive.

Kataryna, once again, had asked her friend Chabella to design a special dress for this occasion. The sleek, feminine red dress is dashing, with a modern, asymmetrical hem and an elegant plunging neckline. Her sexy high-heeled red shoes match the dress exactly. She put red lipstick on her lips and is wearing her diamond earrings. Luca chose a designer tuxedo type suit in black with a white shirt and a red tie.

"Principessa, you look spectacular and very alluring in that red dress, but I am going to have to change one thing," Luca whispers in her ear.
"Really? And what would that be?" she asks with a naughty grin, expecting a sexually suggestive remark from him.
"Not what you might be thinking. We will keep that for later."

He opens a drawer and hands her a beautifully wrapped gift box.
"Happy Valentine's Day."
Kataryna carefully unwraps the box and opens it. "These are beautiful and they go perfectly with this dress. Thank you so much."

She kisses him and then takes off her diamond earrings to replace them with the stunning ruby and diamond drop earrings Luca just gave her for Valentine's Day. They walk hand in hand towards the grand room. Kataryna looks at the elegantly decorated foyer and grand room.

"Very romantic," she marvels. "What a great set-up for our huge surprise tonight."

Luca greets the photographer he hired to make a video of the evening and take still photos just like in Hawaii. He gives him instructions in Italian and asks him to take a couple of photos of him and Kataryna by the fireplace before the guests arrive.

Aleksandra, Brian and the twins as well as Kataryna's and Aleksandra's father and his girlfriend, who are staying in the guest accommodation area of the villa, arrive in the grand room and are amazed by the elaborate and beautiful decorations.

"So, honey," Brian says to his wife, "now you can never say that I didn't take you to a romantic place on Valentine's Day."

"Ha-ha-ha," Aleksandra imitates a weak laugh, "we wouldn't be in this beautiful and romantic place if it wasn't for my sister and her boyfriend, who happens to own this place. Next year you better come up with something on your own, my dear."

"Of course," he responds laughing, "I will ask the Italians for assistance then. They seem to be experts in setting up a romantic scene."

Luca's parents, Patrizia, Francesco, Carlotta and Enrico are the next to arrive and join them. Kataryna introduces her family to the Romano family and to Francesco, who starts speaking in German to Kataryna's father and his girlfriend. Soon all the other guests arrive and the party is in full swing with Champagne flowing freely and lavish hors d'oeuvres being served by the catering staff. Luca lets everyone get settled and then asks the guests to gather around him and Kataryna. He starts with some introductory words thanking them for accepting his invitation, and then leads into the occasion for this party.

"You all have received the invitation, which said that this is a welcome-to-Italy party for Kataryna. As you know today is also Valentine's Day. That is one reason for the romantic decorations here tonight, but the real reason is that Kataryna and I would like to announce our engagement."

He takes the engagement ring out of his pocket, faces Kataryna and puts the ring on her finger.

"I know you accepted my proposal already when I asked you in Hawaii, but I am going to ask you again in front of all these witnesses: Will you marry me?"

"Yes, I will," Kataryna responds, "there is nothing I would rather do."

Luca raises his glass of Champagne. "Let's all drink to the happiest day of my life."

The guests are pleasantly surprised and shout congratulations in Italian, German and English.

"What a lovely surprise. Words can't describe how happy I am for both of you," Luca's mother says.

Carlotta has tears coming down her face as she congratulates her brother and Kataryna who almost tears up too, thinking of what Carlotta must be going through right this moment.

Carlotta hugs Kataryna tightly.

"I will count on you to help me through my situation."

Kataryna nods and puts her arms around Carlotta. "I will do anything in my power to help you through this."

"I am very happy about this engagement. I had hoped that you would become my daughter in-law the first time I met you at our house for Luca's birthday party," Riccardo Romano pronounces.

"I am equally enchanted by you and your entire family," Kataryna tells him, "I am so looking forward to the family get-togethers on Sundays at your villa in Bellagio."

"Now it's my turn," Aleksandra cuts in. "Congratulations, I am very happy for you, but at the same time a little sad because you will be so far away from us."

"Yeah, but closer to me," Kataryna's father chimes in happily, clinking his glass of Champagne with his daughters and Luca.

"Welcome to the family," he looks at Luca, "and thank you for bringing my daughter closer to me. New York is just too far away."

Francesco and Patrizia are next in line to deliver their congratulations.

"Wow, Kataryna," Francesco declares joyfully, "you are now my boss and will be my sister in-law once you two get married. Unreal. I couldn't be in a better situation."

"Yeah, isn't that great? Honestly Francesco, I felt a deeper connection between us the first time we met. We seem to be kindred spirits," Kataryna admits hugging him.

"The feeling is totally mutual. I also feel very close to Aleksandra. We all are going to be one big happy family."

Patrizia embraces Kataryna. "You two got engaged in Hawaii already and didn't tell us when you came back to New York?" she jokingly scolds her.

"Luca said that if we tell you, the news would be all over Italy the next day. So we had to keep it a secret at that time. But isn't it a nice surprise?"

"Of course it is. I wish you two all the best. I think you make a great couple."

Enrico comes up to Kataryna and Luca. "Congratulations Uncle Luca and Kataryna. Should I call you Aunt Kataryna now?"

"You can call me whatever you want to, Enrico," she says. "Did you say hello to Natasha and Sabrina yet?"

"I was just going to go over to them, but then Uncle Luca started his speech and my mother held me back to pay attention."

Kataryna takes him over to the twins. "Hi there, young ladies, say hello to Enrico. I believe you guys already met via video."

She walks back to join Luca who is in conversation with Francesco's parents.

"These are exciting and eventful times for the Romano family," Dr. Vincente Barone says, "you two got engaged and Francesco and Patrizia are getting married in June. And you, Kataryna, own NatMedica now. In a way the company stays in the Romano family. I don't think anyone could have predicted such a perfect outcome. I am so glad it turned out this way because I know now that Francesco is in good hands with you."

"I guess one has to trust the universe to make things happen the way they should be happening. But to be exact, my firm owns 90 percent of NatMedica; the remaining 10 percent are still in the Romano family hands at this time. I have a 50 percent partner in the firm, so I personally own only 45 percent."

Luca grins. "Yeah, but together with the 10 percent my family still holds, once we are married, the Romano family will hold the majority shares."

Kataryna's partner Stephen walks up to them to express his congratulations. "Nicely done, Kataryna."

"Are you referring to my engagement or the majority shares?" she kids him.

"Both," he responds. "But maybe Luca will still sell us the remaining 10 percent."

Luca raises his eyebrows. "Do we really have to talk business on my engagement night?"

"Sorry, that was not my intention," Stephen responds apologetically. "There will be a time for that in the future."

Luca pats him on the back. "No problem, Stephen. I am sure we will be able to work something out. I actually may have an idea how to handle this."

Stephen grins. "Look who is talking business now."

Enrico, Natasha and Sabrina have gotten more acquainted meanwhile discussing Enrico's trip to New York in March and their birthday parties.

"Maybe my cousin Stefano will also join us," Enrico says. "He really wants to go to New York badly."

"That would be great," Natasha responds, "does he speak English?"

"Not as much as I do, but he can make light conversation. I will tell him to brush up on his English so he won't be lost."

"It's only about a month away," Sabrina jumps in, "so he better get going with that."

"So, are you getting to know each other a little better?" Carlotta joins them. *These girls are beautiful*, she thinks. "How about you and your parents come to Milano tomorrow for some shopping, sightseeing and dinner at our place?"

"Sounds great," the twins answer.

Carlotta heads towards their parents to finalize the plan.

"Your mother is so beautiful," Natasha tells Enrico.

"Yes, I know she is and just between us, she is also pretty cool. I lucked out with that one. How about your mother?"

"We are also very lucky with both our mother and father," Sabrina responds.

"And you have a cool aunt, too," Enrico declares, "I am excited that she will be married to my uncle. He is my godfather and has been an important person in my life since my parents got divorced. He took me under his wing when my father was out of the country working in London for a while. In the warm months my mother and I spend a lot of time at his villa," Enrico informs them, "hopefully your aunt doesn't mind."

"I am sure she won't," Sabrina jumps in. "I hope we can also spend some time here during our summer vacation."

"As you can see, there is plenty of room for all of us here," Enrico replies.

Around 1 a.m., the last guests leave the villa. Kataryna and Luca enter the master bedroom, which is filled with warm candlelight. A crackling fire is burning in the fireplace. Luca leads Kataryna into the bathroom. The sunken Jacuzzi tub is filled with water already and has rose petals floating on top. Kataryna's favorite Italian lounge music is playing in the background. Chilled Champagne is sitting on a side table by the tub with Baci Perugina chocolates next to it.

She smiles at Luca seductively. "Nice touch with the rose petals in the water, darling."

"This is the place we spent our first night in," he whispers, holding her close. "I thought this might be the perfect occasion to continue this tradition. So whenever you are ready, my love, let's embark on a romantic night in the water. I also haven't forgotten another thing you told me the first time you came to this villa."

"What else did I say?" she asks softly leaning in to him.

"You said you like fire and water. That's why the fireplace is on, too. So which of these elements would you like to have as a background for our engagement night first?"

"Tough choice, both sound intriguing. I am going to let you decide for us," she whispers, kissing him on the cheek.

"Why don't we get warmed up in front of the fireplace," he suggests, "and then continue in the water, just like our first time together."

"Salute," she toasts, taking the Champagne glasses and handing one of them to Luca, "excellent idea."

He hands her one of the Baci Perugina chocolates. "Let's see what kind of a message you have in there."

Kataryna unwraps the chocolate and reads the message inside:
You will have my eternal love.
"I gladly accept it and give you mine in return," she whispers.

Luca slowly opens the zipper of her dress revealing her sexy red underwear. She opens his shirt buttons and plants light kisses down his chest until the shirt is off completely. His pants are flying off next as they get more and more excited and engulfed in their sensual foreplay. The fire is roaring and so is their arousal until they reach their peak and relax in each other's arms.

"That was amazing," Luca marvels, "you think we can top that in the water?"

"We can do anything we put our mind to. We have proven that many times."

The warm water feels divine as they enter the tub and sit down opposite each other just like the first time. Rose petals float all over them, smelling so sweet. Kataryna puts some of them on her chest for decoration.

"Remember the rules, darling," she whispers sweetly, "no touching."

He grins. "Are you trying to turn this tub into a torture chamber for me?"

"No, into a pleasure chamber, I hope."

She starts swaying her hips and maneuvers his legs in between hers staring into his eyes meeting his intense gaze.

He sighs. "I can foresee a volcano eruption shortly."

"Don't you dare," she warns him seductively, "you have to extinguish my fire first."

"Extinguish? I haven't even started to fuel your fire yet," he murmurs, giving her his typical enigmatic smile.

He takes her hand and pulls her close to him. An intense familiar sensation comes over her. She starts falling all over him, letting him first fuel and then extinguish her fire. When they finally retreat to their comfortable bed, Luca holds her close and she cuddles into him.

"I love you more than anything else," he says, "the only thing you have to do now to make everything even more perfect is to come up with a wedding date for us."

"I love you madly, darling. Let's look at the 2014 calendar tomorrow."

Luca groans. "2014? No way, Principessa, 2013 is our year."

Kataryna wakes up in the morning with rose petals all over her and Luca next to her sleeping. She gets up to prepare for breakfast with their families and then wakes up Luca. Mariya and Isabella have set up the table and are ready to serve the food.

"Good morning," Aleksandra greets her sister, "how was your night?"

"As usual very romantic and exciting," Kataryna reports happily. "But I have a huge challenge ahead of me. Luca wants me to come up with a wedding date in 2013."

"Whoa," Aleksandra exclaims, "we got to get busy then. He sure is in a hurry."

"You can say that again, but I really love him and if it makes him happy, I will make it happen."

"I assume you will get married in Italy?"

"I will let you know soon so you can plan your trip. I suppose it will be Italy because his family is here."

Aleksandra agrees that Italy sounds great. "Maybe you can do it in Portofino or Capri? I would love to go there and that would be an excellent excuse."

Luca comes up behind them. "What would be an excellent excuse?"

"Aleksandra would like to go to Portofino or Capri, so she hopes we will have our wedding there."

"Well, Aleksandra, you will get your wish in June already because Patrizia and Francesco are getting married in Portofino."

He embraces Kataryna and kisses her shoulder. "And you, my love, please come up with a date for us so we can decide on the location. I will give you about two hours," he laughs.

"How generous," Kataryna jokes, "I thought I only had one hour. How about September?"

"Perfect, September it is. So now let's see what we can get in September 2013. We need a space for about 300 people. I will have our company event planner make some calls and present it to you for approval."

"Three hundred?" Kataryna shouts out.

"At least 300," Luca corrects her. "I would invite the whole world for this one if I could."

The rest of the family members are trickling into the kitchen looking forward to a relaxing brunch.

"Who wants to go to Milano after brunch?" Carlotta asks.

Aleksandra, Brian and the twins opt for going to Milano to do some shopping and sightseeing and then have dinner at Carlotta's place. Francesco and Patrizia, who want to swing by their office briefly, are also headed for Milano. Luca, Kataryna, her father and his girlfriend, decide to take a tour of Lake Como on Luca's fancy boat and then have dinner at Luca's parents' villa in Bellagio. When the boat docks in Bellagio, Luca's father picks up the guests and brings them to his villa.

Luca's phone rings while they are having welcome drinks. He looks at the number displayed, but doesn't recognize it. Kataryna watches him on the phone for a while with the caller speaking in Italian. His tone is quite serious. She wonders whom he might be talking to and what kind of problem he is tackling. When he finally gets off the phone, he takes a deep breath and sighs. Kataryna walks up to him. He pulls her aside so they are alone in his father's study.

"Believe it or not, I just got a phone call from Roberto's psychiatrist at the clinic."

"Really? What did he want?" Kataryna asks anxiously.

"Roberto wants to see us and officially apologize for what he did. The psychiatrist believes that it would be good for Roberto and for us if we would meet with them in the next few days. He said it would bring closure to Roberto and probably to us, too. In addition, he wants to see how Roberto reacts when he sees us together."

"How do you feel about that?"

"I told him that I don't want you exposed to this and that I would meet with them alone, but he insists that you should be part of this session."

"I will take it under consideration," Kataryna responds.

"When I think about what he tried to do to you, I tend to want to decline this request."

Kataryna puts her arms around him and kisses him.

"Let's think about it and decide later."

"He has disrupted our lives enough."

"Sure, but please consider that he is sick. If we can help him to get better we should do it. It might give him and us some peace of mind and closure."

Luca kisses her softly. "As usual you may have a point, but I am very uncomfortable with this idea."

"If you don't want to do it we won't," Kataryna promises, "but wouldn't you like to get some closure, too? It can't be easy for you after so many years of friendship with him. You two were really close until I showed up in your lives. So in a way, I feel a bit guilty and as such should be part of the solution."

"Oh, no, don't even go there. You are not at fault. You even tried to help him to get well before he completely lost it in Venice."

Luca's father steps into his study joining Luca and Kataryna. "Is everything all right here?" he asks.

Luca tells him about the phone call he just received.

"I know it is a difficult situation for you, Luca," his father says, "but I think you should do it. I spoke to Roberto's parents the day before yesterday. They are devastated and embarrassed that their son was able to do something so irrational."

After dinner the four take Luca's boat back to his villa and arrive there just as Aleksandra and her husband return from Milan.

"Did you have a nice day?" Aleksandra asks her father.

He nods and tells her about the beautiful sights along the lake and the fantastic dinner they had at Luca's parents' villa.

"We had an exciting day in Milan," Aleksandra reports, "the girls did some shopping, of course, but we also looked at some sights."

"Where are the twins?" Kataryna asks her sister.

"They are at Carlotta's staying overnight there. Enrico wants them to meet his cousin tomorrow and hang out."

"Very nice. I am glad they hit it off with Enrico right away. But I am not surprised, he is so charming and a very good-looking guy. I am sure they will take a lot of photos with him and show them off in school when they are back," Kataryna states giggling.

"Yeah," Aleksandra responds, "he is a very good-looking boy. I am almost afraid of that."

"Are you afraid that another one of your family members will end up with an Italian in Italy?" Luca chuckles.

"I am just afraid he could be a heartbreaker down the road," Aleksandra explains, "what if one or even both of my daughters fall in love with him? You know they are at that age now."

"OK, Aleksandra, just relax," Kataryna says, putting her arm around her sister's shoulders, "after all, they are thousands of miles apart."

"Sure, I guess I am just a little over-protective when it comes to the girls."

The next morning Kataryna's father and his girlfriend are leaving to go back to Berlin. Aleksandra and Brian go to Milan to pick up the twins since they are going back to New York the next day. They return to the villa late afternoon.

"That was a short trip," Aleksandra says, "but the girls have to go back to school, otherwise we would have stayed longer."

"We'll be in New York next month anyway with Carlotta and Enrico to celebrate his and the twins birthdays," Kataryna reminds her sister.

"How about a nice farewell dinner?" Luca asks, "Mariya has prepared something special for us. I am going to get a couple of nice bottles of wine from the wine cellar."

"Sounds good," Kataryna responds, "I am looking forward to a relaxing family evening with great food and wine."

"Me, too," Aleksandra adds, "we are kind of exhausted from running around in Milan the whole day. Carlotta wanted to join us, but then she didn't feel well and had to lie down. So Enrico went with us and he wanted to impress the girls with all kinds of activities."

"Carlotta has been through a lot in the last few days. I am not surprised that she wasn't feeling energetic enough to go out with all of you," Kataryna explains.

"Well, you have been through quite a nightmare, too," Aleksandra adds.

"That's true but, thank God, that is over and I had a very happy event right after that ordeal. Contrary to Carlotta, who lost the man she was so in love with in such a dramatic way. I am surprised how well she is holding up under these circumstances."

Luca and Brian return from the wine cellar with a couple bottles of excellent wine. The two couples and the twins sit down for their farewell dinner. Luca raises his glass to make a toast.

"Let's drink to a happy and healthy reunion in March. Thank you for making the long trip over, although you didn't even know that it would be our engagement party. I am looking forward to spending a lot of time with all of you in the future."

"I wouldn't mind spending my summer vacation here," Natasha jumps in.

"You and me both," her sister Sabrina adds.

"Is it this place or Enrico that has you so excited to come here for your summer vacation?" Aleksandra asks them point-blank.

"Mom!" they protest. "How embarrassing."

Luca smiles at Aleksandra who rolls her eyes. "They are welcome to stay with us any time."

Kataryna's phone rings. She answers the call. "Ah, it's Francesco, our new CEO," she laughs. "Ciao Francesco, you want to impress me with late working hours?"

"I was actually calling to say good-bye to Aleksandra and her family."

Kataryna hands the phone to her sister who talks with Francesco for a while.

Monday afternoon Kataryna and Luca decide to meet with Roberto and his psychiatrist. Both of them are a little apprehensive about facing Roberto for the first time after the Venice incident. Roberto's psychiatrist Dr. Giordano meets with them alone first.

"Thank you for agreeing to come in. This might be uncomfortable, but I believe it could be beneficial for both sides. If you are ready I will get Roberto now."

The doctor leaves the room. Luca takes Kataryna's hand.

"If at any time you are too uncomfortable to continue, we will leave," he tells her determined.

"I think I will be able to handle it," she responds quietly. "He is probably more uncomfortable than we are."

The psychiatrist enters the room with Roberto who looks frail and tense. He walks up to them and extends his hand to say hello. They shake hands and sit down.

"As I explained, Roberto asked for the opportunity to talk to you both to apologize for his actions and the distress he has caused. He has been through a detox program since February 10. We expect the entire treatment to take about three months after which we will evaluate his situation again."

The doctor looks at Roberto. "Whenever you are ready, please go ahead."

Roberto glances at Luca and takes a deep breath.

"Luca, I truly regret my actions and I hope you can forgive me for drugging you that night in Venice. My emotions, in addition to the combination of medication and alcohol, got the better of me. I have no idea how I was able to do what I did. Kataryna," he looks at her visibly strained, "words cannot express how sorry and ashamed I am for putting you through this situation. My feelings for you completely blinded me and I was out of control because of the medication I had been taking for some time. In addition, I mixed the controlled substance with a trial natural product, which was supposed to treat my depression. Dr. de Angelis, who had prescribed the anti-anxiety medication, had no idea that I had taken too much and that I had added the natural anti-depressant product; and on top of that, I drank alcoholic beverages, which he had advised me not to do. I only have a vague recollection what exactly occurred that night. Thank you for allowing me to address this in person with you. I hope you can find it in your hearts to forgive me one day."

Kataryna nods silently. She tears up and quickly wipes her eyes.

Luca puts his arm around her. "Are you okay or do you want to leave?"

"I am okay," she assures him.

Luca looks at Roberto. "I really don't know what to say. I am still in shock wondering how this could have escalated in such a way. I just wish you had gotten professional help before it got out of control. I will need some time to get over this."

"I understand. I did not expect that you would come in here and just forgive me. Thank you for letting me express my apologies in person."

Kataryna is still struggling with her emotions. She feels sorry for him and realizes that he has a long road of recovery ahead of him. She feels Luca's tenseness. The psychiatrist who has been watching the interaction among the three cuts in.

"Is there anything else you would like to say, Roberto?"

"Yes," he looks at Luca again. "How is Carlotta? I need to see her and apologize to her, too."

"That would be up to her," Luca responds coolly. "I really don't know what she is feeling. She has not been open to discuss it with anyone. She may need some professional help, too. I am not even sure yet if we are going to tell her that we met with you. I don't want to open any wounds."

"If she decides on getting professional help, I would be happy to have a consultation with her," Dr. Giordano offers.

"Thank you," Luca responds, "we will take it under consideration, but I am not going to approach her with this until she is willing to open up to us."

Luca gets up, taking Kataryna's hand. "I think we should leave now."

He turns to Roberto. "I wish you a successful recovery."

The two prepare to leave the clinic. Neither one of them says anything until they are out in the open.

"I am glad this is over," Luca exhales, opening the car door for Kataryna. "He is out of our lives now. We just have to take care of Carlotta to make sure she recovers from this ordeal."

"Let's be compassionate about what he is going through," Kataryna admonishes him, "after all, he is sick and has a tough road ahead of him."

"It is really sad," Luca admits, "he was like a brother to me, but it could have been worse. He could have killed us both. I have heard about crimes of passion many times."

TWENTY-ONE

Carlotta is staring at herself in the mirror. She doesn't like what she sees and on top of it, she is feeling dizzy. Roberto has really done a number on her. She recalls their times together. Bittersweet. How could she have missed all the signs? He was such a different person lately. She thought that his long working hours and maybe the uncertainty of what the new shareholders would do were to blame for his uncharacteristic mood swings. Instead, it was another woman, her brother's fiancé; he was infatuated with. Life can be cruel. Luca's happiness is Roberto's demise.

Carlotta examines her own feelings for Roberto. She is not over him. These kind of feelings don't just go away like that, but she also knows they have no future. Even if he wanted to resume their relationship and she would forgive and trust him, her family would never accept him and let him come that close to Kataryna. It would be like letting an alcoholic hold a bottle of wine. A constant reminder of what he can't have. No, there has to be a clean break and she will just have to deal with that.

She returns to her office from the ladies' room, trying to get some work done to distract herself from her personal situation. Her phone rings. She doesn't recognize the number appearing on the screen.

"Pronto," she answers the phone.

"Signora Romano?" a male voice asks.

"Yes, this is Signora Romano speaking."

"This is Dr. Giordano. I am Roberto Silvestri's psychiatrist at the de Angelis clinic. Do you have a few moments to talk?"

Carlotta swallows hard. "Sure, what can I do for you?" *So much for distracting herself from Roberto.*

"Signora, in the course of his treatment here, Roberto elaborated on his relationship with you. Needless to say, he is going through a rigorous detox program, and now that his mind is somewhat clear again, expressed a strong desire to speak with you in person to tell you how sad he is that he inflicted this emotional pain on you. Would you be able to handle that or would this be an imposition?"

"At this point I am not sure how I would react. I would like to think about it. I haven't been feeling well since the incident in question. I need to get my strength back first and then decide if I can go through this."

"I understand. Please take your time and let me know if I can be of any assistance to you regarding your own emotional well being. I sincerely apologize if my call has triggered any emotional stress for you, but my patient urged me to contact you."

"No problem. I'll be in touch when I am feeling better. Ciao."

Carlotta buries her head in her hands as a wave of nausea sends her back to the ladies' room. *Wow, this is ridiculous*, she thinks. *I can't keep any food down either.*

Kataryna enters the ladies' room as Carlotta exits.

"Ciao Carlotta," she greets her, "are you okay?"

Carlotta leans against the wall, her face flushed and clammy.

"No, not really. I think I have to lie down."

"Let me take you home," Kataryna says, taking her by the hand and leading her towards her office. "Please sit down on the couch. I will get your things and take you home."

Kataryna hands Carlotta a glass of water and proceeds to get her handbag and coat. She stops by Luca's office to let him know she will be taking Carlotta home. Luca is pleasantly surprised when he sees her coming into his office. He gets up to embrace her.

"Principessa, what a nice surprise. You never come to my office. Does that mean you can't wait until we get home?"

She smiles and kisses him on the cheek. "I wish, but that's not why I am here. I just wanted to let you know that Carlotta is not feeling well. I will take her home. Can you pick me up from her place later on?"

"Yes, of course. What's the matter with Carlotta?"

"I am not sure, but I think she needs to rest and maybe also talk to someone. I am hoping to find out what's going on with her. I think the recent events in Venice have taken quite a toll on her, which is understandable."

"Okay, thank you for taking care of her."

Kataryna returns to her office with Carlotta's coat and bag. Carlotta is lying on the couch holding her head and crying. Kataryna hurries over to her and hugs her.

"I am so sorry you have to go through this. I hope you don't hate me. Can you even look at me without thinking about Roberto and his obsession with me?"

"I am not holding it against you. It is not your fault, but at the same time it is so painful. I don't want to take any pills because I am afraid I would overdose and end up like him, but maybe I can get a mild tranquilizer to take the edge off."

"Shall we call your doctor and go see him?" Kataryna suggests.

"Yes, let's do that. I don't know if I can go on without anything."

"Let's go to the doctor first and then we'll go home and I'll show you some of the visualization exercises, which have always helped me in difficult situations," Kataryna suggests.

Carlotta calls the family doctor to make the appointment. After a general physical exam, Carlotta has blood drawn, which is sent off to the lab, as well as some other tests done before the doctor wants to give her a prescription for anything. While they are waiting for the tests to come back, Carlotta tells Kataryna about the call she received from Roberto's psychiatrist.

"What did you tell him?"

"That I have to get my strength back first and then I will think about it. I don't know if I can face him. It may be too painful. I still have strong feelings for him. I am thinking about seeing a therapist to help me through this."

After about 45 minutes the doctor appears with the test results.

"Looks like you are in good shape, Carlotta. We didn't find anything to cause concern, but I can't give you any of the typical medication to help you relax or go to sleep," he says.

"Why not? Carlotta asks dumbfounded.

"Because you are pregnant."

Kataryna and Carlotta stare in horror at the doctor.

"Are you sure?"

"Absolutely, but we can run the test again."

Kataryna puts her arms around Carlotta. They both start crying after the doctor excuses himself to see another patient. After they compose themselves they head home to Carlotta's apartment. Kataryna prepares a special herbal tea, made from Valerian Root, they purchased in the pharmacy, to calm their nerves. Both are still in shock from the news when Luca arrives to pick up Kataryna.

"Shall we go out for dinner?" he asks them, "or do we eat in?"

"I can't eat anything," Carlotta says quietly, "why don't you two go ahead and go out."

"We are not leaving you here like this," Kataryna responds, "you have to eat something, too."

Carlotta shakes her head. "I really can't get anything down."

"What's the matter with you? Are you really sick or is it emotional stuff?" Luca probes.

She looks at her brother with tears in her eyes. "I was just told I am pregnant."

Luca is floored. "NO," he yells out. "I guess we don't have to ask who the father is, although I was not aware that your relationship with him had advanced to that phase."

"I didn't tell anyone," Carlotta utters. "Our first time together was the night before your birthday party. He had requested to not make this public yet."

Luca is visibly shaken. "I am speechless, Carlotta. Didn't that tell you that something was wrong?"

"No, not really. To be honest, he didn't initiate the sex. I did, and we had been drinking a lot that night."

"And when did you see him again?" Luca enquires.

"About a week later I had him over for dinner because I wanted to move this forward. He was in a strange mood when he first arrived, but after a couple of glasses of wine he relaxed and we had a nice evening. I served after-dinner drinks by the fireplace and he downed two in a row. To make a long story short, I initiated the sex again and he actually passed out for a few minutes. We eventually finished having intercourse after which he fell into a deep sleep, and I couldn't get him awake anymore until the next morning. When he woke up he was in bad shape and acted strangely, asking if there was anybody else there."

Kataryna is listening in suspense to Carlotta's account of events. That must have been the dinner, Roberto had told her in their telephone conversation, he tried to avoid going to. She recalls that she had encouraged him to have dinner with Carlotta. She regrets having pushed him towards Carlotta then.

"That is the morning when we made plans to spend some time during the holidays," Carlotta continues. "So we spent Christmas Day with our parents and he invited me to a New Year's Eve party at his friends' house. I also persuaded him to take me to the Carnevale in Venice. The rest is history."

Luca looks at Carlotta and then at Kataryna. "This is kind of ironic. I am looking at two very important women in my life here, who in one way or another were emotionally influenced by him. One, who was so in love with him that she didn't realize that something was off, and the other because of her compassion for him and wanting to preserve my friendship with him. I hope you two have learned your lesson from this experience."

The three just sit there silently for a while, looking at each other when Enrico comes home. He looks at his mother, his uncle and Kataryna.

"You three look as if you have seen a ghost. It's just me. What's up?"

"Ciao Enrico," Luca greets him, "we are just debating what to do for dinner. Did you eat yet?"

"Nothing substantial. I could go for something good," Enrico responds.

"Let's order some food in then," Luca suggests, picking up the phone to make the call.

When Enrico leaves to go to his room, Luca instructs his sister and fiancé that they will keep this amongst themselves for now.

"Do you have any idea how far along you might be?" Kataryna asks.

"My guess would be that I conceived on January 1. We went out for New Year's Eve and I stayed overnight at his place. So, about seven weeks."

"I guess you will start to show not too long from now," Kataryna states.

"I will have a lot of soul searching to do in the next few weeks," Carlotta responds. She turns to her brother. "In a twist of irony, I received a phone call today from Roberto's psychiatrist. Apparently Roberto asked if I would agree to see him so he can apologize to me and explain himself. I told him not at this time and that I want to think about it. But that was before I knew I am pregnant."

"We went to see him on Monday," Luca tells her. "He looked kind of frail, but that is to be expected with what he is going through."

Carlotta looks at her brother wide-eyed. "You did? What did he say?"

Kataryna takes a deep breath. "He told us he was sorry for what he did to us and tried to explain how it escalated to what happened in Venice. He also said that he would like to see you in person to tell you how sorry he is."

Carlotta is holding her head. "In a way I would like to go see him, but I am so afraid that I will fall apart when I am in front of him especially now that I am pregnant with his child. The situation was painful enough without the pregnancy."

"Don't rush into anything. Think it through carefully," Luca recommends.

Enrico enters the living room area as the doorbell rings and the food Luca ordered arrives. They all sit down to eat and soon the conversation revolves around Enrico. Carlotta wonders how and what to tell her son when the time comes.

A few days after Luca and Kataryna's visit, Dr. Giordano sets up a therapy session with Roberto.

"Let's discuss the recent visit of Luca and Kataryna," the doctor says, "how did you feel about it? Did it give you some piece of mind?"

"I am grateful that they accommodated me, so I could share my feelings with them. However, seeing Kataryna brought back some anxiety and I didn't sleep well that night."

"Can you be more specific, please? What exactly happened when you saw her?"

"The first few minutes I felt embarrassed over how I betrayed her by posing as Luca in Venice and attempting to make love to her. She has been so compassionate the whole time and tried to help me get over her. Then moments later I felt so deeply for her again and the embarrassment turned into sadness."

"How did you feel about Luca?"

"I felt bad for what I did to him and sad that we will probably never be close again."

"Have you accepted their relationship now?"

"I know that they love each other and are engaged now. While it hurts, I have come to terms with that and will move on. But I know that the kind of love I am feeling for her will always be there, I just can't act on it."

"Are there any ill feelings towards Luca?"

"No. I wish him well. It is not his fault that we fell in love with the same woman."

"Good. We are making progress then. Is there anything on your mind you wish to discuss with me today?"

"Yes. Did you call Carlotta Romano yet?"

"I did, but she is not ready to see you. She wants to think about it to see if she can handle it."

"I don't blame her. I guess I wouldn't want to see me either if I was in her place. I just hope I didn't hurt her too bad. She is a beautiful and wonderful woman, but she just caught me at the wrong time. Actually when we grew up together I had a huge crush on her. But I never did anything about it because she was too young at that time."

"Well, Roberto, give it some time. You need to heal. Let's talk again tomorrow."

Luca and Kataryna arrive at their Milano apartment shortly after 11 p.m.

"I assume Carlotta is going to have the baby?" Kataryna asks Luca, as they are getting ready for bed.

"Of course she will have the baby. We are Catholic and we value life, especially when it is a child conceived in love. However, I am not sure if she should tell Roberto that he is the father."

"Why would you want to keep that from him?" Kataryna is surprised at Luca's statement.

"I don't want him that close to our family. I don't trust him around you."

"That would be up to Carlotta. We don't have a say in that and I don't want to be the reason a child doesn't get to know his biological father," Kataryna cautions him. "That kind of reminds me of my brother somewhere out there. He also doesn't know his biological family, although this is a totally different story."

"Maybe he will find out soon. Have you heard anything from your lawyer?"

"No. I will give it another week and then contact him again. I think we had enough excitement for this week."

"Yeah. Thank God tomorrow is Friday. I think we should take Carlotta and Enrico with us to the villa for the weekend, " Luca suggests.

"Definitely. She needs moral support now."

Luca's face turns serious. "I got a phone call from the police today. They were asking if we want to press charges against Roberto. Where do you stand with that?"

"Oh, no, let's not do that." Kataryna is horrified at that thought. "He has enough to deal with. He wasn't in his right mind when he did that to us and he is the father of your sister's child."

"You are very forgiving, my dear," Luca remarks firmly.

"Are you seriously considering pressing charges?" she asks.

Luca shrugs his shoulders. "I am not sure. I have to think about it some more."

As expected Carlotta is having a rough night. Thank God, Enrico is asleep already so she won't have to explain her nausea. She goes to bed hoping that the dizziness will subside soon so she can get some sleep. At midnight she is still awake. When she closes her eyes she sees Roberto and wonders when she should tell him about the pregnancy. How will he react? After tossing and turning for another hour contemplating this and that, she finally falls asleep.

Friday morning the Romano family gathers for a board meeting in Milan. Carlotta greets her mother and father who came in from Bellagio.

"Carlotta," her mother says concerned, "you don't look well. Are you feeling okay?"

"I have seen better days," Carlotta answers, glancing at Luca.

Luca cuts in immediately in an attempt to avoid any further prying. "We are taking Carlotta and Enrico with us to the villa this weekend. I think she needs some tender loving care and Mariya's excellent cooking. We will come up to Bellagio on Sunday for lunch for a family gathering if you are around."

"Good idea," Valentina Romano cheers.

"I don't know if I can keep any food down," slips out of Carlotta's mouth. She immediately realizes what she just said.

"Why?" her mother asks with interest.

"I think I have some kind of bug," she quickly turns her statement around.

"We'll see how you will feel on Sunday," Luca suggests.

He immediately moves on to the business points they set the meeting for to make sure Carlotta's secret is safe for a while. Close to the end of their agenda, Carlotta feels a bout of nausea coming on. She excuses herself to visit the ladies' room.

"I am concerned about Carlotta," Valentina Romano tells her family, "she doesn't look good."

Patrizia follows her sister to the ladies' room. She enters just as Carlotta has recovered from vomiting, but senses something is off.

"You poor thing. You probably have the stomach flu, which is going around," she comforts her sister. "Let me know if I can get you something. You should go home after the meeting and get some rest. Mamma is worried about you."

"I am okay but I will go home soon and lie down."

Carlotta's parents take her home after the meeting to spend some time with her. Her mother prepares a chicken soup for lunch. Surprisingly Carlotta feels much better all of a sudden. After her parents leave, Carlotta picks up the phone.

"Ciao Dr. Giordano, this is Carlotta Romano. I would like to make an appointment to see you."

"Ciao, Signora Romano. I am pleased to hear that. Are you prepared to have Roberto join us for this session or do you wish to see me alone?"

"Please have Roberto join the session. I am ready to talk to him. Can we do it next week, Tuesday?"

"Certainly. How about at 3 p.m., next Tuesday?"

"I will see you then."

Friday afternoon Luca and Kataryna pick up Carlotta and Enrico for their weekend at the Lake Como villa. Kataryna notices that Carlotta is looking much better today. The drive to Lake Como is uneventful. Enrico tells Kataryna about his email communications with Natasha and Sabrina in New York.

"I am going to arrange a video call tomorrow evening for all of us with my sister and the twins," Kataryna states.

"If you ladies don't mind," Luca says, "Enrico and I are going to hit a couple of golf balls tomorrow if the weather is cooperating."

"We don't mind," Kataryna responds, "Carlotta and I will relax at home and have a wellness and beauty day. We will take a beautifying mud bath in your fabulous master bathroom bathtub."

Luca grins mischievously and takes Kataryna's hand.

"If that bath tub could talk it would have some interesting stories to tell."

Kataryna grimaces. "Those stories would also make a fascinating movie."

When they arrive at the villa, Carlotta and Enrico get settled in their rooms. Luca and Kataryna head to the master bedroom to change into comfortable clothes before dinner.

"So, you want to make a fascinating movie?" Luca coaxes her as he watches her get undressed in the huge walk-in closet. He slowly walks into the closet and closes the door, taking off his clothes. Kataryna starts laughing.

"What did you have in mind?" she teases him in her sexy black underwear taking a step back.

"I was thinking about a christening ceremony in this closet," he murmurs as his excitement increases.

"You naughty boy. I wonder what the pope would say to that kind of christening."

"Well, he just announced his retirement, so he probably has not much to say anymore," Luca counters playfully, grabbing her and pulling her close to him.

"I see you have an answer for everything, don't you?"

They stand in the closet holding each other, being unable to stop laughing. A moment later Luca's lips and hands are all over her and she submits to his sweet sensual assault.

"That was a fascinating surprise," she whispers, as they are relaxing on the closet floor.

"I am slowly catching up with you," he smiles, "usually you have the element of surprise in your corner."

"You sure are, you sexy man. Did you plan this or was it a spur of the moment thing?"

"It wasn't planned, but a seed was planted when we talked about the bathtub in the car. Immediately the image of us in that tub came to my mind and you know what that does to me."

"Yes, I do. Congratulations, darling, this christening ceremony image is something, which will stay with me forever. I will never look at this closet the same way again."

"Since we just christened it, we should give it a name. How about the Den of Passion?"

After they are showered and dressed, they head to the kitchen to check on their dinner.

"Although this was a satisfying experience, somehow I am still stirred up," Kataryna whispers as they walk down the hallway.

"Me, too," he sighs, "we may just have to turn in early. So why don't you start yawning in about an hour."

Mariya and Carlotta are in the kitchen collaborating on some of the food choices when Luca and Kataryna arrive.

"There you are, you two. What took you so long?" Carlotta asks in an upbeat tone.

"Something urgent involving the pope, we had to deal with, came up," Luca responds casually, grinning broadly.

Kataryna looks at him and breaks into laughter unable to contain herself. Luca also loses it. They stand, embracing, in front of Carlotta, laughing uncontrollably. Kataryna buries her face in Luca's chest trying to simmer down.

"Well, it definitely isn't boring here," Carlotta says, also laughing. "I have no idea how the pope would tie into this, but I can imagine what might have caused your delayed appearance here."

They take Carlotta in the middle and hug her. "I am going to let Kataryna explain to you later how she brought the pope into this situation," Luca tells his sister.

"I can't wait to hear this one," Carlotta chuckles.

Enrico enters the kitchen texting on his cell phone. "What can't you wait for, mamma?"

"For you to show up here. I am starving."

The four have a relaxing family dinner occasionally interrupted by Enrico's cell phone pings as he receives text messages from his friends, which prompts Carlotta to ask him to shut off the phone for a while. He reluctantly does so and survives the dinner without the constant pings. After dessert he retreats to his room where he turns his phone back on and discovers an email from Natasha and Sabrina. He writes back that Kataryna has planned a video call tomorrow night with everyone.

Luca, Kataryna and Carlotta settle into the living room area sitting by the fireplace with an after-dinner drink. Carlotta sticks to mineral water for obvious reasons.

"I decided to meet with Roberto and his therapist on Tuesday," Carlotta informs them.

"Are you sure that's a good idea?" Luca challenges her.

"Yes, Luca. I have got to do it. There is no point in avoiding the inevitable. My pregnancy is going to show soon. Before I show, I need to know how Roberto will react to that piece of news. Thereafter, I can tell our parents and Enrico. I won't be able to keep this a secret much longer."

"As far as Roberto is concerned, it doesn't matter how he will react. We will make sure that the child has a loving environment. I assume that you are not considering a future relationship with him if he should suggest that because of the child. Maybe you shouldn't even tell him that you are pregnant with his child."

"Oh, no, Luca. I want this child to know his father and I am pretty sure that Roberto wants to be involved in the child's life. You better get used to the idea that I will be tied to him for the rest of my life. And for Enrico's sake, I want to have an amicable relationship with Roberto."

Kataryna listens to them silently trying to imagine what she would do if she were in Carlotta's place. She can't even fathom the entire situation. Flashbacks of Roberto's face appear in front of her eyes and how he looked at her when he had her pinned down on the bed in Venice with her hands restrained by the silk scarves. Although the situation was dire, she wasn't afraid of him then. But what would have happened had he succeeded in penetrating her? Thank God she was clever enough to avert that scenario. She shakes her head to come back to reality and then starts yawning. Luca looks at her smiling wickedly and also fakes a yawn.

"Sleepy time," Kataryna announces laughing.

Once they are in their bedroom, Luca and Kataryna become wide awake and get lost in each other.

Saturday goes by fast. Luca and Enrico leave for the golf range after breakfast. Kataryna and Carlotta go through their beauty and wellness ritual and relax on the bed in the master bedroom afterwards. They enjoy their girl talk, sipping tea and getting to know each other better. Kataryna shows Carlotta some of the visualization exercises, which she vows to do.

Carlotta hugs Kataryna. "I love you like a sister," she says, "I am so glad you will be my sister-in-law."

Kataryna takes Carlotta's hand. "I love you, too, Carlotta. We will have good times together and help you with the baby. If you want to take a vacation or need some rest, we will babysit."

"Are you and Luca planning to have any children?"

"We haven't discussed it so far. Right now Luca is my priority. The rest I will leave up to the universe. If it is meant to be it will happen. Although, I will turn 40 next year so by then we should decide if we want to do that."

Sunday morning has arrived. Kataryna loves Sundays. She was born on a Sunday. Sunday children are said to be vivacious, creative and determined, she once read. She knows she has those attributes, otherwise she would not be as successful professionally, and she is definitely creative when it comes to her love life with Luca. However, the kind of creativity she has displayed with Luca is very special. No one before him could entice her to want to be this creative or keep her interested to excel each time. There is a first time for everything, is one of her favorite proverbial expressions, which fits perfectly with this situation.

She looks at the clock. It is 8 a.m. They had made plans to have breakfast around 10 a.m., and leave for Bellagio at noon. She tries to go back to sleep but doesn't succeed. *I guess I wake up Luca then*, she decides. She starts kissing him softly, first on the cheek and then going on to his ear and neck. He opens his eyes and kisses her arm, which is wrapped around him.

"Buongiorno, Signore," she greets him seductively. "Would you like to get married for 20 minutes?"

Luca cracks up laughing. "What? Actually I would like to get married for a lifetime, but I see where you are going with this right now, so the answer is yes."

She puts one of her legs over his and then lies on top of him. He gently grabs her buttocks and they start moving, very slowly and sensually.

"Ti amo follemente," she whispers in his ear, running her hands through his hair.

"I also love you madly, Principessa, but you have to go in for the kill soon; otherwise, I will have an out-of-your-body experience of a certain kind again," he moans into her ear.

With one skilled movement Kataryna slides up, pushes him into her and starts moving until they reach the point of no return.

"Your declaration of love in Italian put me over the top," Luca tells her, kissing her forehead. "That was so touching."

"As you can see I am making an effort to learn Italian. Now you know how I feel when you whisper something Italian in my ear. It is quite stimulating."

"Thank you for the hint. It has been placed in my memory bank forever."

Mariya starts serving breakfast when Luca and Kataryna arrive in the breakfast room. Carlotta is standing by the terrace doors drinking an herbal tea.

"Buongiorno, Carlotta. How are you feeling?" Kataryna asks, hugging her.

"Surprisingly well," Carlotta answers, "no morning sickness so far."

"Good. That means we can go to Bellagio today and have lunch with mamma and papà," Luca jumps in as he kisses his sister on the cheek.

At noontime the four take a trip up the lake to Bellagio. Enrico hangs out with the captain who shows him various functions of the boat. When they arrive at the dock in Bellagio, Riccardo Romano picks them up. After the usual extensive family lunch they all relax in the living room.

"Have you three recovered from the Venice incident yet?" Luca's father asks after Enrico left the room.

"Depends on what you mean by recovered. Kataryna and I are moving along fine. We met with Roberto and his psychiatrist last Monday. He apologized to us and appeared remorseful," Luca explains, looking at Kataryna for her reaction.

She nods in agreement. "It will probably take a while until I can erase that from my memory completely. At times I have some flashbacks and I start thinking: what if Luca hadn't woken up again? These moments are kind of disturbing for me." She immediately moves closer to Luca to hold on to him.

"How are you doing, Carlotta? I guess you were not as much affected as Luca and Kataryna," her father continues.

"Unfortunately, I am more affected than you know," Carlotta responds, "but I don't want to get into that today. Besides Enrico could come back any moment."

Carlotta's mother looks at her, surprised about the statement she just made, although she already had a feeling that there is something going on with Carlotta.

"I am going to meet with Roberto and his psychiatrist on Tuesday," Carlotta adds.

"It's good that you are extending an olive branch. His parents are so distressed over this and his daughter is devastated," her father adds.

"We can talk more after I have seen him on Tuesday," Carlotta closes the subject.

"It is getting late. We should get going," Luca recommends.

The four are back at Luca's villa at 8 p.m. After a light evening snack, they all turn in to prepare for a new week at work.

❖ ❖

Tuesday morning Carlotta wakes up slightly nauseated. Is it morning sickness or nervousness about her meeting with Roberto and his psychiatrist later on, she is asking herself? Enrico is already in the kitchen eating breakfast while texting.

"Buongiorno," Carlotta kisses her son on the cheek. "What are you doing after school today?"

"I am meeting Stefano. We want to go see a movie."

"Just you two?" Carlotta asks.

"I don't know yet who else may come along. Why?"

"Just asking to see who you hang out with these days. Is there a special girl you like?"

"There are a couple cool girls we hang out with."

"I see. So nothing exclusive?"

"What are you trying to find out, mamma?"

"I think it's time that we had a more serious conversation about girlfriends, etc., soon."

"OK, what about you, mamma? Are you seeing anyone?"

"Not at the moment. But I need to talk to you about something. I would like to have dinner with you and talk."

"Sure. Are we going out or eating in?"

"We will eat in. We need a more private setting for that conversation."

"OK. I've got to leave for school now," Enrico ends the conversation, kissing his mother as he runs out the door.

Carlotta has a light breakfast and then gets dressed to go to work. She has to leave the office around 2 p.m., today since her meeting with Roberto and his doctor starts at 3 p.m. She looks at her body in the mirror. She gained a few pounds, but doesn't show a real baby bump yet. Nevertheless, it is time to let Enrico know what is going on, but first she will have to face Roberto this afternoon and inform him of her pregnancy.

The morning passes pretty fast. Around noon Luca comes to her office.

"Can we talk about your visit this afternoon?"

"What do you want to talk about?"

"Do you intend to tell Roberto about the pregnancy today?"

"Yes, of course. He needs to know and I want to see if he would want a relationship with his child, so I can prepare myself accordingly."

"Let's assume that he does want a relationship with his son or daughter. How do you imagine this to work?"

"I haven't given it much thought yet. I guess it will work the same way like with Enrico's father. He will get certain visitation rights, etc."

"What about birthdays and holidays?"

"Where are you going with this, Luca?"

"Basically, I want to know if Roberto would attend family gatherings when his son or daughter has a birthday, and what you envision when we get together for Easter, Christmas, etc."

"I don't know yet. We will have to wait and see how that develops."

"I am not sure if I can handle that after what happened in Venice. The probability of him coming so close to Kataryna worries me."

"I knew you would have a problem with him ever getting too close to her again, but I can't change the fact that he is the father of this child. So we have to see how this plays out."

Shortly before 3 p.m., Carlotta arrives at the de Angelis clinic where she proceeds to Dr. Giordano's office.

"Signora Romano," the doctor greets her. "Thank you for coming in today. Is there anything you wish to discuss before Roberto joins us? How are you holding up after what happened?"

"I am taking it one day at a time," Carlotta answers. "To be honest, it is not easy."

"I understand, but how do you feel about Roberto?"

"I haven't really worked that out yet. All I know is that I am deeply hurt and disappointed. I have no idea how I will react when I see him."

Dr. Giordano nods and picks up the phone. "Would you please bring Roberto Silvestri to the therapy suite."

He gets up and motions Carlotta to follow him. "We will be going to the locked wing of the clinic now where Roberto has to stay for the time being."

The doctor takes out his electronic card key and swipes it, opening the door to the locked off area. They get seated in the therapy suite. Carlotta's heart starts beating faster. She is getting pretty nervous now, not knowing what kind of emotions will overcome her once Roberto appears in front of her. A few moments later, Roberto enters the room, flanked by two men in lab coats who leave after the doctor gives them a signal. Carlotta just stands there staring at him, unable to move. He looks even more attractive to her than before, if that is possible. Her knees are getting weak as he walks up to her to greet her.

"Ciao Carlotta," he says quietly, "thank you so much for coming to see me. I know I have no right to even ask that of you."

She nods, fighting tears as the image of him and Kataryna in Venice flashes in front of her.

"I guess we all need some closure," she manages to get out, her lips quivering.

He takes a deep breath and exhales. "Yes, we do."

Dr. Giordano observes Carlotta's reaction and body language. He is pretty sure that she still has deep feelings for Roberto.

"My idea is that you two express your honest feelings to each other, even if they are negative at this point, like maybe in your case Signora Romano. I will do my best to work with you towards a common goal of achieving neutral feelings and getting closure this way. This will allow you to move on with your life. To that end, why don't you start, Roberto?"

Roberto closes his eyes and holds his head. When he opens his eyes he looks straight at Carlotta and starts speaking.

"Carlotta, there are no words that could express how low I feel right now. A few minutes ago I wasn't even sure if I could go through with facing you today. Not that it is an excuse for what happened. I was so messed up in my head because of my infatuation with Kataryna that I took all these pills to relieve my anxiety attacks and reality totally escaped me."

Carlotta looks at him. "I know that I seduced you the first night you came back to my apartment, but why didn't you stop me?" she asks quietly.

"We both had a lot to drink that night and it went so fast that I really didn't have a chance to stop you. You were determined, Carlotta. Thereafter, I didn't have the heart to turn you away because you had told me that you were seriously in love with me. I couldn't have told you the reason why I wouldn't be able to see you in that way. I was so afraid you would end up taking pills like me, if I had rejected you."

"Well, you are not the only one who made a mistake in this situation. Kataryna feels guilty that she never told Luca that you still had these feelings for her. She didn't say anything out of compassion for you. I guess all three of us have to accept a piece of this burden."

"Thank you for saying that, Carlotta. You are very kind, but that's the person you are and always have been."

He is starting to tear up wiping his eyes. "As a matter of fact, when we were growing up together I had a huge crush on you. Whenever I came over to hang out with Luca, I was hoping you would be around so I could see you. I never did anything about it. I was afraid that our families would get upset because I was already 22 and you were only 17. Once I dropped a hint with Luca. He said I shouldn't get any ideas because you are too young to date a man of my age. I had a very tough time then. I went out with a few women, but I didn't have the same feelings for them as I had for you. When I was 23 my then-girlfriend got pregnant and I married her. But I never had the feelings for her like I had for you. I think because of that I wasn't the best husband. As you know, that marriage didn't last."

Carlotta shakes her head, tears streaming down her face. "I can't believe what I am hearing," she sobs.

Dr. Giordano, who has been listening silently the whole time, cuts in.

"I am very pleased with how this session is going. Please let me know if you want to stop for today. We should set up another session if you both think it would help you."

"I don't want to stop yet," Carlotta says. "Let me ask you this, Roberto. How do you feel about Kataryna now?"

"I have accepted the fact that Kataryna and Luca are getting married and I wish them well."

"Do you think you could be around her without anguish, knowing that she will be Luca's wife?"

"I am a different person now and expect that this would never be an issue again. But the healing from the entire episode will take some time."

He looks at his psychiatrist. "What do you think, Dottore?"

"You are showing promising progress, Roberto."

Carlotta takes a deep breath. "There is something else I would like to convey today."

She pauses for a moment. Both men look at her, interested to hear what she has to say.

"I am pregnant with your child, Roberto."

Dr. Giordano looks at Roberto first, then at Carlotta.

"Well, that changes the entire scenario. Here is a question for both of you. How do you feel about that?"

"Obviously, I am not as happy about it as I would be in a normal situation," Carlotta responds. "I was shocked when I found out. But at least, as far as I am concerned, it is a child that was conceived in love, so regardless of what the current circumstances are, I will love that child. Other than my brother and his fiancé, no one knows that I am pregnant. That is another tough situation I will have to deal with soon."

"I am also in a state of shock because of the circumstances," Roberto responds, "but at the same time I am elated that I will have another child. I couldn't imagine a better mother for my child than you Carlotta. God works in mysterious ways."

"You two will have a lot to work out," the psychiatrist states.

"When is the child due?" Roberto asks.

"According to my calculation sometime in September, which is kind of ironic because that's when Luca and Kataryna will get married."

"Will you keep me updated on the developments?" he inquires.

"Yes. I will send you an ultrasound photo and let you know what sex the child will be as soon as I find out."

"Needless to say, I will make the appropriate financial arrangements for the child," Roberto promises.

"Why don't we set up another session after you had the ultrasound exam? It may be best if you two start getting used to raising a child together," the doctor recommends.

"I will let you know," Carlotta says almost business like getting up to leave.

"I hope to see you soon," Roberto says, stepping towards her.

She lets him hug her briefly. "Be well," she utters, leaving the room.

Dr. Giordano follows her. "Thank you again for your visit, Signora Romano. Let me know if you need anything. I hope you will come back soon. I believe that this is therapeutic for both of you because you have a lot to work out."

"My next step is to let my son and parents know that I am pregnant with his child. That is not going to be easy. They don't even know that I had an intimate relationship with him."

"I understand. Do you still have feelings for him?"

"Of course I do, especially now that I am pregnant. When he came into the room today my initial reaction was to run towards him and take him in my arms, but then reality set in and I caught myself again."

She extends her hand to him to say good-bye. "I will be in touch, Dr. Giordano."

When Carlotta gets home Enrico is waiting for her in his room, busy on his laptop.

"Ciao Enrico," she hugs and kisses him. "I picked up dinner for us from your favorite restaurant. We can eat soon and then have our talk."

"Did I do something wrong, mamma?" Enrico asks.

"No, why do you think that you did something wrong?"

"Because you sound so serious and set a special time for us to talk. We are still going to New York next month, right?"

"Yes, of course. That is your birthday present. Why don't we have our talk first and then eat."

They get comfortable in the living room sitting next to each other. Carlotta puts her arms around her son.

"I wanted to tell you that I had a romantic relationship with Roberto."

"Oh, that's cool, mamma. I like Roberto. Are you getting married?"

"No, but I am pregnant with Roberto's child."

"Then why aren't you two getting married?"

"Let's just say that isn't in the cards right now."

Enrico shrugs his shoulders. "OK, if you say so."

"Your grandparents don't know yet. Please don't say anything until I have told them. I just wanted to let you know first."

The two sit down for a nice dinner. Enrico took the news well, but how will her sister and her parents react?

TWENTY-TWO

Kataryna gets to her office Tuesday morning. She was hoping for a light day at work, but judging by the emails she's already received, it doesn't seem to be shaping up that way. Her assistant brings her the usual morning tea. Going through the emails one by one, she prioritizes the immediately important ones and starts responding.

At 11 a.m., Francesco calls her to discuss some resumés he received from headhunters for the chief financial officer position. Another task for her to tackle later on today, review the CVs and email the ones being considered to Stephen for discussion. *Could this day get any busier,* she wonders? Carlotta comes to her mind. She wonders how she is feeling about her visit with Roberto this afternoon, where she will divulge that she is pregnant with his child. Kataryna is sure that the evening might also bring some excitement on a personal level after Carlotta tells her son. The last two weeks have really been one thing after another. *It is time for some peace and quiet*, she thinks as she reverts back to her emails.

At 12:30 p.m., Luca comes to her office.

"Would you like to have lunch with me?"

"That would be lovely. I need a little distraction, but it can't be a long one. I have a ton of work on my desk."

"I'll have you back here in an hour and a half," he responds smiling.

"Good. Maybe I can run some of the CVs for the CFO position at NatMedica by you?"

"I'll take a look at them and give you my opinion."

They get seated in a restaurant not far from their office. The waiter comes by to take their order. Kataryna hands Luca the CVs she printed out, which she wants him to review. While he is looking at the CVs, Kataryna checks her emails. As she scrolls down the long list of emails, she spots one from her attorney in Berlin. She opens it, getting excited to hopefully get some news about her brother.

From: Norbert Bergmann
  To: Kataryna Taylor
Subject: Confidential

Dear Ms. Taylor,

We were finally able to obtain a copy of the birth certificate and subsequent adoption records for your brother. Attached please find the necessary documentation, which reveals the identity of the adoptive parents. If you would like our office to investigate the current location of the adoptive parents, please advise. We are looking forward to hearing from you how you would like to proceed.

Best regards,
Norbert Bergmann

Kataryna's heart is racing as she opens the attachments. First the birth certificate. It shows that a male child was born to Greta and Klaus Wolf on May 31, 1980 in Berlin. Next she opens the adoption papers, which are also dated as of May 31, 1980. She reads through the legal language and finally reaches the section with the names of the adoptive parents. She stares at the name trying to make the print larger to make sure she read it correctly.

"Oh my God," she yells out as the waiter arrives with their food.

"Did I bring the wrong food?" the waiter asks worried.

Luca looks at her surprised. He signals the waiter to put the plates down.

"What's the matter, Principessa?"

Kataryna is shaking her head. "You are not going to believe this."

"Tell me," Luca says concerned, taking her hand.

"I got an email from my German lawyer with copies of the birth certificate and adoption records for my brother."

"That's great. Now we are one step closer."

"Yes it is, but here have a look what it says."

She hands him her iPhone. Luca reads the adoption document, which identifies the adoptive parents as Dr. Vincente and Mrs. Sylvia Barone. He is stunned and takes a closer look at the document.

"That can't be. They never mentioned any adoption."

"Well, when is Francesco's birthday?" Kataryna asks.

Luca thinks for a moment. "I am not sure of the exact date but I recall that it is in May because that was considered when they planned their wedding."

"Francesco is my brother. I am so excited. It really is a small world. I have to call Aleksandra."

Luca calms her down. "Please let's make sure first. I hope you know that you can't just barge in there and tell him what you found out. If he was never told that he is adopted, it would be a huge shock."

"What do you suggest?"

"First, let me find out from Patrizia when his exact birthdate is. If it is the same, then I would suggest that I speak with Vincente Barone and let him know what we learned. He should have the opportunity to talk to Francesco first and explain it to him, if he is not his biological son."

"We should speak to him together," she says determined.

"I recommend you let me do it. You are too emotional about this. We have to approach this the right way."

"OK, darling. I will let you talk to Dr. Barone. Gee, what a day. Between our business and personal lives we sure have a lot going on right now."

"You can say that again. In about an hour Carlotta will face Roberto and tell him he is the father of the child she is carrying. I saw her before we went to lunch. She will call us later to report how it went."

They finish their lunch and leave the restaurant. Kataryna is overjoyed that Francesco may be her brother. She can't wait to call her sister.

"Remember Principessa, not a word to anyone other than your sister for now," Luca tells her as they part to get back to their offices. She just nods and smiles.

Kataryna dials her sister's number. "Aleksandra," she shouts into the phone when her sister picks up.

"Hey sis," Aleksandra says, "how is life in Italy?"

"Good. I have some incredibly exciting news. Our lawyer in Berlin sent me the paperwork, which reveals the adoptive parents of our brother."

"No way! That is fantastic! What is our next step?"

"Please sit down. You are not going to believe what I found out," Kataryna responds excitedly.

"I am sitting."

"Francesco Barone is our brother."

"Are you sure? That would be too good to be true," Aleksandra is stunned.

"Luca will confirm Francesco's date of birth. The paperwork is pretty clear. However, there may be a snag. According to Luca the Barones have never mentioned that their son is adopted and Francesco has never indicated either that he may be. He may not know that Dr. and Sylvia Barone are not his biological parents."

"Really? How do we go about telling him?"

"Luca offered to meet with Dr. Barone in private to tell him what we found out, and that Francesco has to be informed that he is adopted because we are his biological family."

"Wow, that is going to be one difficult conversation for them if he really was never told. When is Luca meeting with Dr. Barone?"

"Immediately if not sooner. Meanwhile, please don't tell the girls, otherwise, they may blurt it out when they speak to Enrico and then it goes viral. I promised Luca that we would keep it between us for now. I will let you know as soon as he has spoken with Dr. Barone. I am so excited. I can hardly contain myself. Francesco is not just the CEO of the company I partially own, but also my brother. How cool is that? It just hit me; he will be Luca's brother-in-law twice. Once from my side and once from his sister's side when they get married in June."

"OK, keep me posted. I think I need a drink now and reflect on this news. Can I tell Brian at least?"

"I guess that would be okay if he can keep his mouth shut until further notice."

Kataryna can hardly focus on her tasks anymore. She is trying to imagine what Francesco will say when he finds out. Will he be as excited as her and Aleksandra?

At 4 p.m., Luca comes to see her.

"I spoke to Patrizia. Francesco's date of birth is May 31, 1980, and he was born in Berlin, Germany."

"Thank you, darling," she kisses him on the cheek. "When are you going to meet with Dr. Barone?"

"I will call him at home tonight and set something up."

Luca and Kataryna arrive at their Milan apartment around 7 p.m. They have a light dinner. Kataryna can't stop talking about Francesco. At 8 p.m., Luca picks up the phone to call Dr. Barone.

"Ciao Vincente. How is everything?" Kataryna hears him say.

"I need to see you on a personal matter. Can we meet for dinner in the next few days?" Luca continues.

"Tomorrow would be perfect. Shall we say at 8 p.m.?"

Luca hangs up the phone and hugs Kataryna. "I will meet him for dinner tomorrow evening. Happy?"

"Yes, thank you. I am glad you are handling this."

She puts her head on his shoulder. They sit quietly for a while when the phone rings. Carlotta is calling to let them know how her visit with Roberto went. Luca puts the speakerphone on so Kataryna can listen in.

"Before I go into details," Carlotta starts, "let me ask you a question, Luca. When you were hanging out with Roberto around the age of 19, did he ever mention that he had a crush on me?"

"Gee, that is a long time ago. I don't recall what exactly he said, but he made a remark once that led me to believe he was interested in you. Why?"

"He told me today that he had a huge crush on me when we were around that age, but that you discouraged him because I was only 17 then. So he ended up marrying someone he didn't have these strong feelings for because she got pregnant. Anyway, my visit with him was pretty emotional. After I told him I was pregnant, he said he would make financial arrangements for the child and would like to be involved in the child's life and upbringing."

"How do you feel about that?" Luca asks.

"I am okay with that. We will have to work out the details though."

"Just be careful, Carlotta."

"He is very sorry for what he did to all of us. The doctor said he is making good progress. Time will tell. I also told Enrico tonight that I am pregnant with Roberto's child, but I did not go into any other details. He doesn't need to be burdened with the whole story; otherwise, he may develop ill feelings towards the child and Roberto. I will tell our parents and Patrizia in the next few days."

"OK. Let us know if you need anything. We are always here for you," Luca states.

"Thank you. By the way, the baby should be due at the beginning of September. I hope I can attend your wedding."

"We are planning to have the wedding mid to end of September."

"OK. We will see how it works out. Have a good night."

"Thanks, you too. See you tomorrow."

Luca and Kataryna look at each other. "Another eventful week for us," he says. "Let's see what happens tomorrow."

❖ ❖

Wednesday night Luca and Vincente Barone meet for dinner in Milan. Luca has reserved a more private table for them in order to have the delicate conversation.

"Luca, good to see you. How are you and Kataryna?" Vincente Barone greets him, taking his seat at the table.

"We are fine. Just a lot of things going on in our lives right now."

"Of course. You got engaged, planning a wedding. On top of that you closed the NatMedica divestiture and had to deal with a change in management at the company. Not that I am complaining. I am proud and happy for my son's rise to the CEO position, but the circumstances were quite a surprise."

"Absolutely, that came out of the left field," Luca admits.

"So, I am curious why you wanted to see me tonight."

Luca takes a deep breath. "This is another situation none of us could have imagined in our wildest dreams. It involves Francesco."

Vincente gives Luca a perplexed look. "Francesco?"

Luca hands the adoption document to Vincente. "We need to talk about this."

Vincente's face turns pale as he reads the document. "How did you get this?"

"Before I answer that question, let me ask you if Francesco knows that he was adopted."

Vincente shakes his head; obviously taken aback by what is unfolding in front of him.

"No, he doesn't and I don't have any intention of telling him. We adopted him right after he was born. The mother never saw the baby. The papers were drawn up a week before the birth so that we could take him right away. I briefly met his mother when she was in the hospital delivering the baby, but she didn't know that we were the adoptive parents. I had a residency at that hospital so it was not unusual that I went to see her together with the attending physician. She was a very beautiful and kind lady. She was sad that she had to give up the baby because of certain circumstances in her life. The attending physician had assured her, though, that her son would go to a very good family and would have a good life. He also told her that the adopting couple was so grateful because the wife was unable to have children. She said that she would be able to live with her decision knowing that she is doing something good for the couple and that the child would have a good life."

"That is a very touching story. However, I am afraid you will have to tell Francesco that he is adopted sooner rather than later."

"Why? How are you involved in this?"

"Kataryna is his biological sister. Her father, whom you met at our engagement party, told her in November last year that she had a brother who had been given up for adoption. She was determined to find her brother and hired a lawyer in Berlin to help her identify the adoptive parents. The lawyer sent her this paperwork yesterday."

"Is there anything we can do to avoid having to tell him?"

"No, Vincente, there is no way around it. Kataryna and her sister want him to know that they are his siblings. I am sure their father also wants to get to know his son. Their mother passed away a few years ago."

"You have to give me some time to think this through. My wife will be devastated and I have no idea how Francesco will react."

"I feel for you, but Kataryna is determined and I fully support her. In addition, Francesco has the right to know that he has a biological family. When the two sisters and Francesco first met there was an immediate deeper connection between them, but until yesterday we had no idea why."

"I will have to see when would be a good time to have this conversation with my wife. She hasn't been feeling well lately and I don't want to add this now on top of it."

"As long as you understand that if you are not moving forward with this in a timely fashion, Kataryna will do it for you. I believe it would be better for all parties if you had that conversation with Francesco and explain why you never told him before."

"Sure, Luca. I will do my best to speed this up."

When Luca arrives back home in his Milan apartment around 11 p.m., Kataryna, who has been waiting anxiously, meets him in the living room. "How did it go?"

He puts his arms around her. "He was shocked when I presented the adoption paper, but all is well. He seemed cooperative. We just have to give him some time. His wife is not feeling well, so he doesn't want to burden her with that now."

"OK. I can live with that. We will give them this time."

Luca is pleased to hear that she is willing to be patient, but he senses that deep down she is anxious to start her brother-sister relationship with Francesco. He wants to distract her for a while.

"How about you meet me in the bedroom in a few minutes so I can take your mind off this at least for tonight?"

She smiles at him approvingly. "What would I do without you? And tomorrow, darling, we will invite Francesco and Patrizia to Lake Como for the weekend."

Carlotta takes the day off from work to prepare dinner for tonight's discussion with her parents and her sister Patrizia. They were curious what Carlotta needs to discuss with them, but she didn't give them any hint. Carlotta tries to calm her nerves. No more alcohol for her, so she has the usual herbal tea to calm down. When the doorbell rings her anxiety returns.

"Hello everyone," she greets them, giggling timidly when they enter the apartment.
"Hello Carlotta," her mother hugs her. "Is Luca joining us, too?"
"No, mamma, that won't be necessary. You will understand in a moment. Enrico is staying overnight at his cousin's house, so he won't be here either for this."

The three look at each other puzzled. She offers them an aperitif and serves herself a tomato juice. After some light conversation and finishing the appetizers, Carlotta becomes serious.

"Mamma, papà, Patrizia, I have something important to tell you which in a way affects us all, but it's not easy after what we have experienced in Venice. I hope I make it through this without getting too emotional."
"That sounds pretty serious, Carlotta," her father says.
"It is, papà. Let me start from the beginning. The night before Luca's birthday I started an intimate relationship with Roberto."
Carlotta's parents and Patrizia look stunned. "Oh, Carlotta, we are so sorry. That makes the whole situation even worse for you." Her mother sits next to her putting her arms around her.

"Thank you, but I have myself to blame because I forced it in this direction. I was so in love with him that I didn't fully grasp that he was not himself and emotionally not available for a relationship with me. I want to spare you the details, but we did have several intimate encounters and I just found out that I am pregnant with his child."

"No!" Patrizia shrieks, "are you sure?"

"Yes, I am. Luca and Kataryna already know. That is why Luca is not here tonight. I have also told Enrico that I am pregnant with Roberto's child. He took it very well. He even asked if Roberto and I are getting married. Needless to say, he doesn't know the other details."

"Under different circumstances I might have been happy about a relationship between you and him," Carlotta's father states solemnly.

"I went to see him at the clinic together with his psychiatrist who said that Roberto is making good progress with his treatment. I told him about the pregnancy. He said he would make financial arrangements for the child and would like to be involved in the child's life. So we will have to come up with an arrangement."

"Do you still have feelings for him?" her mother asks.

"After the incident in Venice, I thought I didn't, but when I saw him and he apologized for what he had done and then told me that he had a huge crush on me when we were younger, my feelings for him rekindled. Anyway, he will be locked up there for a while. That may give me the distance I need to get over him. On the other hand, our child will be a constant reminder and will tie us forever."

"That's so sad," Patrizia comments. "How did Luca react?"

"He was as floored as you are. He actually wanted me to entertain the idea of not telling Roberto that he is the father."

"I am sure he wouldn't have said it if he had thought it through. He was just worried about Kataryna, I believe," Carlotta's father offers as a probable explanation.

"Believe it or not, Kataryna was with me when I found out that I am pregnant. She has been more than supportive and did not agree with Luca on that point."

"Good and very generous of her after what she has been through in Venice. Are you going to visit Roberto again in the clinic?"

"Yes, after I have an ultrasound, I promised I would let him know the gender and bring him a photo. I am about two months along. We will know in a month or so."

"When are you and Enrico going to New York?" Patrizia asks.

"In about two weeks. Kataryna needs to be over there for business then and Luca is also coming. We will have a birthday party for Enrico and Kataryna's nieces over there. Enrico and I will be staying for two weeks. Kataryna and Luca are going back after a week."

"So you will be back for Easter?" Patrizia figures.

"Yes, we will all spend Easter together in Bellagio. The week after Easter I will schedule the ultrasound."

"Maybe I will visit Roberto in the clinic meanwhile, together with his parents," Carlotta's father says. "After all, he is the father of my future grandchild. That calls for a family meeting."

Carlotta smiles at her father. "Good idea. Now that this is off my chest, why don't we have dinner?"

Luca and Kataryna arrive at the Lake Como villa Friday night looking forward to a relaxing weekend after the eventful week. Mariya has prepared one of her signature dishes for the two. When they retire to the lounge area with an after-dinner drink by the fireplace, Luca decides to discuss the plan for the weekend with Kataryna.

"We better talk about our weekend guests, Principessa," he starts. "Are you going to stay cool, calm and collected when Francesco and Patrizia arrive here tomorrow morning?"

"What do you mean?" she asks.

"Will you be able to sit opposite your brother, who has no idea that he is your brother, and behave as usual?"

"I promised that I will not say anything until Vincente has spoken to him. But I know what I know, so I am going to see him in a different light from now on. That's why it is important that he is told as soon as possible."

"I understand and so does Vincente, but until then you will hold back, right?"

"If I had a choice I would tell him tomorrow, but I won't. However, tomorrow is the second of March. I want this to be done before we leave on our trip to New York on March 15."

"That might be an ambitious timeline." Luca murmurs.

"You have to have a defined goal for everything. Actually my immediate goal is to get you in that bathtub now." Kataryna looks at him provocatively.

"Now you are talking, Principessa. That is a goal I can definitely meet."

Kataryna jumps out of bed as soon as she wakes up Saturday morning. Luca is shaking his head laughing.

"Come back to bed," he says, "it will be at least another two hours until they get here."

"I can't sleep anymore," she responds excitedly.

"Who said anything about sleeping?" he laughs, grabbing her by her waist and pulling her back into bed. "I want to take advantage of all that energy you seem to have this morning, although we had a pretty active night."

"Well, Signor Romano, you have a one-track mind."

"I have a two-track mind, you and me."

He whirls her around and kisses her all over. "How about a massage?" he whispers.

"Are you giving or do you want to receive?" she asks.

"I will attempt to give you the famous Hawaiian Lomi Lomi massage."

Kataryna laughs out loud. "OK then, massage away. I just have the feeling this is going to be a very short Lomi Lomi massage."

Luca sighs as he puts her legs around him and lies on top of her. "Oh Principessa, this is what I would call a spoiler alert."

"I call it a self-fulfilling prophecy because you are already way past the massage stage, darling and there is no way back now."

Mariya starts serving the sumptuous brunch she prepared, when Patrizia and Francesco arrive. Kataryna hugs Francesco extra tight this morning when she welcomes them.

"I am so happy that you are joining us for the weekend," she exclaims.

"It is always a good day when your boss is so happy to see you," Francesco says laughing, kissing her on the cheek.

Kataryna gives him a long look, beaming with happiness. Luca watches her cautiously and springs into action.

"Hey, what about me?" he challenges her, putting his arms around her.

"I don't think you can complain, my dear. You got plenty of attention in the last 12 hours."

The four start laughing after Kataryna dropped that obvious hint of what they have been up to.

"Actually we almost had to cancel our weekend with you," Francesco explains, "my mother is sick and took a turn for the worse last night."

"What is the matter with her?" Luca asks. "Did she see a doctor yet?"

"After she felt so sick last night, my father called Dr. de Angelis. He will see her on Monday. They are going to check her out from head to toe at the clinic."

"Let's hope it's nothing serious," Kataryna says. "Please give her our best wishes for a speedy recovery."

"Thank you Kataryna. I will do that. Obviously, we all want to know what's wrong with her. After all, I am in her gene pool, so if it is something really bad I want to know sooner rather than later." Francesco tells them.

Luca looks at Kataryna to watch her reaction to that statement. She gazes at him and swallows hard before she responds.

"I wouldn't worry about that," she tries to reassure Francesco, putting her hand on his arm. "You may not even have her genes."

Luca is getting nervous. He swiftly takes this conversation in another direction.

"How is the search for the new CFO going?" he interjects.

"I think we are close to coming up with a short list," Francesco responds, looking at Kataryna for confirmation.

Kataryna nods. "I agree. There are three impressive candidates, two men and one woman. We should talk to the headhunter next week to let him know which ones we want to invite for an interview. Stephen will attend the interviews via video conference."

Patrizia, who has been pretty quiet the whole time, decides to put her five cents in.

"What does the female look like? I may not be too crazy about the idea of Francesco working with an attractive female CFO."

Kataryna looks at her, grinning broadly.

"Do you think Luca would prefer that I hire an attractive male CFO?"

"All things being equal, I would prefer the female," Luca opposes his sister.

"Sure, you do." Kataryna teases him. "That was a no-brainer."

She shrugs her shoulders at Patrizia. "I guess we will have to see who makes the cut when we meet with them. Not to mention that Stephen has a word or two to say about it. So brace yourself Patrizia. Having said that, I don't think you will have anything to worry about with Francesco, regardless of how attractive the female CFO may be."

"Thank you Kataryna," Francesco says smiling. "I am glad I have you on my side."

"More than you know," she responds, prompting another intense stare from Luca cautioning her not to overdo it with the innuendoes.

The four have a relaxing weekend at the Lake Como villa and Kataryna manages to not make any further ambiguous remarks, which could raise eyebrows.

"Thank you for the lovely weekend. That was a lot of fun," Patrizia and Francesco say, as they get ready to leave Sunday evening.

"We should do this more often," Kataryna responds. "As a matter of fact, the next time we will include Carlotta. She needs all the support she can get now."

"Thank you, Kataryna. You are a great addition to our family," Patrizia says, hugging her tightly.

"You sure are. If I would have had a sister I would have wanted her to be like you," Francesco says.

Kataryna just smiles at him sweetly thinking--*your wish will come true soon.*

Karynne Summars, the author of the erotic romance/suspense and family drama novel entitled "Desperate Pursuit in Venice", was born and raised in Berlin, Germany. She currently lives in New York and Marbella, Spain. When not writing or promoting her book, she likes to travel, spend time with family and friends, read, watch movies and listen to relaxing music on her favorite Internet station Chilltrax. The sequel to "Desperate Pursuit in Venice" is scheduled to be published towards the end of 2013.

Contact and Social Media

Official Website: www.KarynneSummars.com
Facebook:www.facebook.com/pages/Desperate-Pursuit-in-Venice/580572938620559
Twitter: @karynnesummars
Email: karynnesummars@karynnesummars.com

Member
World Literary Cafe
Indie Writer's Network
Goodreads